IN THE
WARSAW
GHETTO

Glenn Haybittle

Published by Cheyne Walk 2019

Published by Cheyne Walk

www.cheynewalk.co

ISBN- 978-1-9999682-0-5 (paperback)
978-1-9999682-1-2 (ebook)

'Every man's death is a standing in for every other. And since death comes to all there is no way to abate the fear of it except to love that man who stands for us. We are not waiting for his history to be written. He passed here long ago. That man who is all men and who stands in the dock for us until our own time comes and we must stand for him. Do you love him, that man? Will you honour the path he has taken? Will you listen to his tale?'

— Cormac McCarthy, Cities of the Plain

Book One

1

The world seems strange and quiet. On the far side of the river, just above eye level, a red kite writhes a moment on its string and then flails. Ala, shielding her eyes from the reflected sun glitter, feels a current of empathy with the kite's struggle to unfurl and soar. Her uncle, sitting beside her, is also mesmerised by the kite. Perhaps he too feels an intimate connection with its failure to catch the wind.

Ala digs her bare toes into the warm sand. Eager for the ripple of sensual life to make play in her body again. Tonight, she thinks, sand will fall from my clothes when I undress, sand will crunch beneath my bare feet when I walk over to my bed.

"Why did you never marry?" she asks her uncle.

"Are you really interested or just being polite?"

"Mother says I don't know how to be polite."

"She's hard on you, isn't she?"

"She's jealous. That's all. She'd like to be eighteen again."

"I can't imagine my brother ever makes her feel she's eighteen," he says.

"Dad is set in his ways."

"Family trait, I'm afraid."

"So why didn't you marry?"

"You think I'd be a good catch?"

"Stop fishing for compliments and answer my question."

"Relationships might bring out the best in one, but they also bring out the worst. I'm not sure I want to subject anyone to the worst in me. Neither do I want to experience it myself. My insufficiencies, my immaturities, my insecurities. Alone, I avoid the worst of myself."

"And perhaps the best of yourself."

"Yes, that's the monotonous reproach I hear in the dark. But despite all my perceived failings, I still feel special. I sometimes wonder if there is anyone who doesn't secretly feel special. I hope you feel special. Because you are. Very special."

Ala smiles and digs her toes into the warm sand again.

"I suspect," her uncle continues after lighting a cigarette, "nothing has more power to alienate one from the wellsprings of all one's creative vitality than being trapped in a loveless marriage. Probably they are the people who no longer feel special, the unhappily married."

"Like my mother and father."

"I wouldn't say that. Your mother and father allow each other certain necessary freedoms. They've become good at turning a blind eye."

Ala, her long black hair fastened into a bun, intermittently performs stretching exercises. She is aware, a little, of showing off. She wants to impress her uncle. Always has done for as long as she can remember. His opinion of her is important. She demands of him an unfailing keen observance. "The formality which exists between my mum and dad never ceases to baffle me," she says, doing centre splits with her toes pointed. "They behave together like awkward acquaintances who haven't yet found anything they have in common."

"Your father resists any emotion with momentum in it. He's like a parked car. He was like that as a young boy too. Sometimes I think he's still waiting for his true life to arrive. That said, he doesn't like change. He doesn't like its violence."

"We dancers are trained to be wary of change," says Ala. She always feels a wobble of vulnerability when she refers to herself as a dancer, as if she is passing across a forged document. A dancer is what she hopes to become, not yet what she is. "We have to censor our appetites every day. We're highly sensitive to every single thing we take into our body, how it affects our balance. We have to ensure we can awaken every muscle at a moment's notice. And to achieve this we have to repeat the exact same regimes every day. Every deviation is dangerous. I've been trained to be an ethereal being. Or an ethereal being with muscles. Ethereal beings don't eat sausages or drink alcohol." Neither do they have pubic hair or menstruate, she thinks, but these are intimacies she cannot share with her uncle. She hasn't even told her mother that she misses periods regularly or that she was instructed to shave her pubic hair the first week she joined the corps of the Ballet Polonaise.

"Sacrifice is perhaps the hardest discipline of all to learn in life," says Max. "It's often to belittle yourself to the agency of something greater. You have to believe in that something greater. I'm not sure I do. You're lucky."

"I feel lucky, even though I don't like the competiveness of dance. Often what you gain is at someone else's expense."

"All life is like that."

"I suppose it is. You're right about the sacrifice. There's no room in my life to do anything but dance, recover from the aches and stresses of dancing and prepare my body for more dancing. I feel closeted, like a child. You know how we hate our world to be invaded by anything foreign as children? Always suspicious of unknown tastes, unknown people, unknown clothes even."

"I rather liked everything foreign when I was a child. It was the familiar I was less keen on. Except when it came to clothes. I remember this pair of itchy trousers I had to wear every time we visited my grandparents. How I loathed those trousers. And I loathed my father for making me wear them."

"Is that why you no longer speak to your father, because he made you wear itchy trousers?"

"I think you've come up with the perfect explanation," he

says scratching the back of his head, one of his characteristic gestures. "My father was just like that itchy pair of trousers."

"You see that tree over there, the one all alone and bent out of shape by the wind? That's you."

Max laughs. "I think you're right. I seem to have made it my mission in life to repel all human intimacy. Divine intimacy too, come to think of it."

"Why did you convert to Catholicism then?"

"To annoy my father, to get rid of those itchy trousers? Maybe I just was fed up with being disliked for something that had no bearing on who I am."

"Do you believe that? That being Jewish has no bearing on who you are?"

Max watches a flight of birds, returning to nests. "No. I don't believe that at all," he says.

"Wasn't there ever someone you wanted to marry?"

"I imagine being married must increase the number of secrets you keep a hundredfold. All the discords and falsities and petty guilty irritations you feel but cannot voice without performing a cruelty which will damage the self-esteem of both parties. I don't want to experience those petty irritations let alone pass them on."

"No one can live without being the cause of pain," she says, stretching out her long legs and flexing her toes. "But stop evading the question."

"Okay," he says, running the flat of his hand back and forth over his thick black hair, "there was a girl. Sabina Milajkowski. I spent a lot of time with her, when I was at university, but she always seemed to be behind glass. Physically elusive. No matter how much intimacy we created with talk she remained as if behind glass. She said she found me physically unattractive. I was quite vain about my looks in those days. I thought it was a defect in her makeup that she couldn't see me as I saw myself. One day, when we were sitting by the river, not far from here, she told me she didn't find me physically attractive. I stripped off in front of her and threw myself in the river in mock protest. I pretended I was drowning. She just laughed. You're not coming in to save me? I said. No, she said. Her smile always made it easy to forgive anything she did or said. I've never known someone so apparently self-possessed and entitled and yet so short of confidence as her. In the end I reasoned it was this lack of confidence that prevented her from seeing things as they were."

"That she was really in love with you?"

"Exactly," he says, allowing a handful of sand to spill through his fingers. "I've since learned she probably had a kind of second sight. I wasn't made for marriage. She saw that before I myself did. Probably I gave her no choice but to turn me down. Perhaps that was even what I wanted deep down where I didn't know myself."

"Tell me something else about her."

"She's hard on you, isn't she?"

Ala watches the concertina reflections of trees in the water. Then a bird that swoops down and wets its breast in the lake and the glistening drops that fall from its feathers as it soars back into the higher air. "She's jealous," she says. "That's all. She'd like to be eighteen again."

"I've never in my life seen anyone look so beautiful in green. She sometimes wore these green socks."

"You were in love with her socks?"

"It always felt like she was showing something very intimate about herself when she wore those socks. Her legs would be tanned and she'd be wearing a thin printed dress. And it was such a stunning shade of green. Sort of lime green."

"It all sounds a bit superficial to me," says Ala with a teasing smile. "Anyone can wear green socks."

"But sometimes someone will wear something that allows you a glimpse of their secret self. The essence becomes distinct for a moment."

Ala wonders if there's anything in her wardrobe that makes her essence distinct. She wonders what her essence is. Perhaps, she thinks, it's something only other people can detect.

"Anyway, Sabina Milajkowski married someone else. A successful businessman and a Catholic to boot. I only met him once. He was one of those men who pantomimes himself as relentlessly busy as if his time is a gift he's offering you."

"Do you ever see her?"

"I haven't seen her for years. She moved to Lublin."

"Do you think she still thinks about you?"

He allows a tiny spider to crawl up onto the back of his hand and watches it as if it were threading out a message there. "It's very important to me I believe that," he says.

"You're not like other adults."

He laughs. "That's a kind way of saying I haven't grown up much."

"Well, I like that. It makes you easier to talk to. Most men your age have a formula they run through. It's like they're blotting a letter already written. They get embarrassed if you say anything they think is indiscreet. I like the way you share yourself. It's like you always have an innocence of purpose. Was my father more like you before he married? Before he began cowering under the tyranny of my mother? When I think of Dad I see someone who wants to be somewhere else. He's always the first to want to leave anywhere we go, whether it's the theatre, a restaurant or a visit to relatives. He always wants to go home and yet I never feel he's happy at home."

Max lets the spider return to the earth. "My brother was always very secretive. When we were boys he often invented ailments so as to return to his hiding places. My father had a boat, a simple flat-bottomed boat like a punt. And he liked to take it down the river after dinner. Your father always had an excuse ready so it was me who accompanied our father on the boat. He never stopped talking. Your grandfather, I mean. He'd tell me what he expected me to achieve in life. He wanted me to become a historian of the Jews. Because that's what he wanted to be. He left your father in peace for some reason. It was me who he sought to fashion into a likeness of himself."

"I remember you used to carry me on your shoulders. Dad never did."

"It was the first thing you demanded every time I saw you. And the faster I ran the more you enjoyed it."

"Do you know what mother once said about you?"

"I'm not sure I want to know. I know I promised not to talk about Hitler or Stalin, but between them they've greatly reduced my sense of my living space. A barb from your mother might leave me without a leg to stand on."

"She said there's one fact that tells you everything you need to know about your character."

"And what might that fact be?"

"That you love Italian art, but that you've never found the initiative to go to Italy."

"She's got a point. At least though I still have Italy to look forward to. Sometimes I think that's all happiness is, having something to look forward to."

"There are so many things to look forward to in life. There must be other things you look forward to besides visiting Italy."

"But there's nothing I look forward to so much. Except, of course, seeing you dance again. Any chance of that happening soon?"

Ala springs to her feet and performs an arabesque followed by a *grande jeté*.

"Bravo," he says. He then makes a fluid sequence of movements with his hands.

"What was that you did?"

"Sign language. The man I work for is deaf. I learned finger-spelling so everything I said wouldn't be written down on paper which was how we initially communicated."

"It's like you're making your hands dance. I love it. Will you teach me?"

"What would you like to say?"

Ala picks a blade of grass. "How about, make the blood speak through the muscle. It's one of Madame's catchphrases."

He signs out the sentence for her. She copies it. He corrects her errors.

"Madame would love this. She's always looking for new expressive gestures. She's tired of the boundaries of classical ballet. She makes us do all kinds of strange things. The other day we had to choose a partner and sit back to back with him and communicate silently with our shoulders. I'll show you."

Ala sits down with her back pressed against her uncle's back. "Sit up straighter," she commands him. She rocks her shoulder blades against his back.

"Can you guess what I'm saying?"

"I haven't a clue. Are you flirting with me?"

Ala laughs. Then jumps to her feet.

The presence of the planes is first sensed as a vibration that makes itself felt at the back of the neck. Soon black specks form a sinister grid over the horizon.

"Are they ours?"

"I don't know. Let's hope so."

2

Max looks down at the white oleanders on the balcony beneath his apartment in Nowolipki Street. To his eyes the pollen-heavy flowers have acquired an otherworldly brilliance in this new apocalyptic world. He takes a deep breath, hoping to catch some whisper of their scent, but he only smells the acrid smoke rising from the blackened shells of buildings further down the street.

Indecision has been his constant companion since the war began. The Biblical exodus on the streets horrified him. He wanted no part of it. Entire families, constrained to make a fateful choice over dining room tables, fleeing the city in cars, carts and on foot with their prized belongings. The sight of people herding together for security only accentuated his longstanding sense of himself as an outcast. He has blamed this sense of alienation on his Jewishness in the past. Converting to Catholicism changed nothing down in the depths of his being.

There is no electricity or water in his apartment. He sits down in his favourite armchair and again ponders what he ought to do. He has to admit he is an able-bodied man. And as all able-bodied men have been ordered to leave Warsaw and congregate on the far side of the Vistula he knows this is what he should be doing. But he has no desire to leave his home. Earlier he went to see his brother, Samuel, who used the excuse of his poorly healed broken femur to stay at home. Henryk, Samuel's son, Ala's brother, had already left. He could not find his friend Edek.

Soon the siren begins wailing again and the maddening escalating shriek of the Stukas returns. More bombs fall. Max wonders what is happening where his parents live. He occasionally sees his mother when she visits Warsaw but hasn't seen his father for seventeen years. He's the first to admit how ridiculous the feud has become. Yet he cannot bring himself to end it. He gets up and walks to the window. Earlier a blue truck with a loudspeaker attached to its roof drove past his building. A scratchy voice announced that the number of German planes shot down today far exceeded those of the Polish air force. And yet German bombers continue to fly over Warsaw unmolested.

Max sits back down in his armchair. There are several paintings on the walls. His favourite a seaside landscape by Roman Kramsztyk depicting a lonely empty boat. He finds himself remembering the night boat trips with his father. The boat easing through the black current. The moonlight silvering the whispering reeds and the leaves overhead. The air pungent with resin and algae and wet earth. The whisper of the willow leaves trailing in the water. His father standing with the oar, as if he owned and orchestrated the entire night. The lamp beside him, attracting winged insects. The further they travelled from town the narrower and more overgrown became the banks, the more stars appeared overhead. His father never stopped talking. As if were he to ever stay silent he would melt like icicles on eaves. He sought to infect Max with his love for Hasidic folk tales, pivotal moments in Jewish history, Kabbalistic mysticism, Hebrew scripture. Max has never since known anyone so passionately and blindly engrossed in articulating his thoughts. As if words were magic spells, capable of revealing and animating every hidden secret in life. Max believed that he paid little or no attention. But he has since discovered that he has assimilated much of what his father spoke about. His father demanded admiration rather than affection. Affection made him uneasy. It's affection Max now feels for his father. For a moment he gets a draught of his father's smell which has a medicinal tang to it.

It was the pornographic photograph that sundered their relationship. The photograph surfaced at school. It depicted a naked fat man in a deckchair with a girl kneeling between his legs. She had the tip of the man's giant erection in her mouth. This photograph bewildered Max in more ways than one. Firstly, he couldn't believe the size of the man's organ. It bore virtually no resemblance to his own erection which, at that time, he had taken to studying in detail. Secondly, he had never heard of a woman putting a penis in her mouth. It had never occurred to him as an idea.

At school Max was self-conscious about his circumcised penis. And also about its diminutive size compared to almost all the other boys. The photograph branded itself in his mind's eye. However, he never expected to see it again and so was mortified when his father produced it later that night.

"Your mother found this in your pocket."

He showed Max the photograph. For the first time in his life he experienced the visceral meaning of the word shame. That both his mother and father identified him with this obscene image was like a poison coursing through his veins to the heart of him. Max wanted to protest his innocence. He had no idea how it got into his pocket. He learned the next day it was a prank on the part of his classmates who were delighted by the outcome. His father showed Max the photograph and then almost immediately set fire to it. It stank out the room as there was some balled fluff in the ashtray where it curled up and burned down to ashes. But that photograph never went away. The feeling he had committed a deplorable crime and incurred the deep disappointment of his mother and father brought down a black curtain on all the carefree happiness available to him, stole from him all the enchantment and reassurance of his home. His childhood, he was made to feel, was over forever. He knew shame whenever constrained to meet his mother's or his father's eyes. Memories of shame have greater reserves of power to haunt than even memories of love. It was the second time in his life that he discovered how curiosity could come to seem a crime. The first was the insistent guilt he felt after he and a friend as five year old boys had forced a girl to show them her private part.

3

Ala's body is accustomed to moving through space, to shaping and making space speak. In the hot suffocating scrum down in the cellar, she has no space. She can barely move. And the volume of noise her body and mind have to withstand is without any precedent. It is noise as torture. Every new detonation seems to loosen the teeth in her gums, jar her bones in their joints and resound down into the core of her being with a fragmenting crescendo. At times she struggles to believe the noise isn't a physical beating she is undergoing. A visceral bludgeoning which pares her down to a primal urge to scream. She discovers there is a wild beast deep down in her being, awakening for the first time. Devouring everything that makes her who she is. Leaving her with nothing but the impulse to scream and keep screaming.

Brick dust and plaster shower down in a shroud when the blasts are nearby. There is grit between her teeth, under her armpits, between her breasts. Dust tickles the hairs on her arms, at the back of her neck. Her heart thuds in her ears together with a relentless maddening high-pitched ringing. Now and again, when there is a lull in explosions, the smell of smoke is overlaid by the whiff of greasy socks and stockings, a belch of fried onions, the escaping gas of a digestive system, the festering odour of mildew. Ala sits with her mother. She misses her father, her brother, her uncle. All three are somewhere out there in the inferno. An unknown man is pressed against her. Anxiety leaks out of him like a pungent bodily secretion. Yesterday he told everyone the zoo had been bombed and lions and tigers were prowling through Warsaw's streets. She thinks often of her dog, Luna, the whippet, alone and terrified up in the apartment on the third floor.

The elation felt at the news that England and France have declared war on Germany has as if melted into slush.

4

The maid lets Max in. He is still disorientated by the devastation outside. His memory set the task of recalling the appearance of buildings no longer standing. New vistas have sprung up everywhere. He had to skirt deep and wide craters in the road. He walked past a crowd carving up a mutilated horse. He could see into the bathrooms and bedrooms of apartments missing their outer wall. The loneliness of the ruined buildings made him feel more alone in the world, a feeling he sometimes likes, but not now.

Mr Kaminski is sitting at his desk, studying an illuminated manuscript. He's about seventy years old, unmarried and something of a dandy in his dress. He looks frail, diminished inside his clothes. He removes the monocle when Max enters and caresses his arctic white hair.

Max fingersigns to the art dealer who has employed him for ten years. "The dome of St. John's Cathedral has gone."

"Yes, I heard. The Philharmonic building is dust too." Mr Kaminski's sign language doesn't have its customary flourishes today.

"I almost envy you your deafness. The noise has been brutal. It's driving me insane."

"I can feel the vibrations."

Of course he can, thinks Max, ashamed of his stupidity. And maybe all the destruction is even more frightening if you can't hear it. Because he can't hear the world Max has often imagined Mr Kaminski must see it with more intensity, more clarity. His eyes widened to stricken attention as happens when we stand before works of art or a calamitous accident. No wonder then Mr Kaminski has chosen to surround himself with beautiful visual images. He sees them with a heightened appreciation. And they must make deafness matter less.

"You look tired," Max fingersigns.

"Not feeling so good today."

Their relationship has always been formal. Max knows little about Mr Kaminski's inner life. He has been deaf ever since Max has known him. In the early days of their relationship lip reading had proved both comical and frustrating. Therefore, a pad was deployed and Max had to write down much of what he wanted to say. Mr Kaminski was delighted the first time Max attempted to communicate with sign language which he spent much of his free time mastering. Max himself enjoys conversing with his hands. Often it seems to him his most admirable achievement. But it's an achievement he has kept secret, until the other day when he shared it with Ala.

"Listen Max, you have been a loyal friend to me for ten years. As a gift of my appreciation I would like you to have the portrait Modigliani did of me. As you know I have no family to speak of. I would like you to be the custodian of my young self. I know you will look after it. I have always said you remind me of Modigliani. Of course, you aren't wild like him, but physically there are similarities. Take it off the wall now, please."

Max is embarrassed. He loves the painting. Whenever he stands before it he feels the world is sharing a secret with him. But he doesn't feel he is worthy of possessing it. It's a surprise to him to be confronted with this crater in his self-esteem.

"I can't accept," he says.

"Of course you can. I also have a job for you. I'm not well enough to perform it myself. There are two paintings and a sculpture I want you to buy for me. A Picasso, a Schiele and a sculpture by Giacometti. Works the Nazis have outlawed as degenerate art. The seller is a rather shady German. Things as they stand he is presently keeping his head low. We've agreed on a price. Twenty thousand dollars which amounts to about sixty thousand zlotys, give or take the odd thousand. Here's the money and here's the address you're to go to. Tomorrow at eleven in the morning."

5

The sirens have stopped wailing. The air has stopped screaming. There are no more earthquakes. When she and her mother venture out into the street Ala asks herself if she shouldn't be more frightened, more shocked. Perhaps, she thinks, she is taking the lead from her mother who appears to be taking this momentous moment of history in her stride. It's like everyone else she sees on the streets has overnight stopped looking at themselves in mirrors. As if appearance has ceased to matter. As if everyone has abandoned all thought of decorum. Her mother, on the other hand, is, as always, impeccably made up, groomed and dressed.

Now it is Ala's eyes which have to withstand the unprecedented. Life has overnight ceased to be continuous. She keeps staring as if by force of will she might return all the devastation to its former reassuring order. This part of Warsaw has always been an extension of home for her, part of her shape, a responsive intimate part of her identity. So much she was attached to, so much that lent her footholding weight is now obliterated. It's as if one of the mirrors by which she recognises herself has ceased to reflect her. The teetering balancing act of unsupported walls makes her feel unsteady on her own legs. Buildings taken for granted are no longer standing. There are voids where previously history stood. Feathers like snowflakes rise up into the smoke infested air as if she is inside a macabre snow globe.

Within five minutes she has seen three dead bodies. Flies crawling over the bloated decomposing flesh. A young woman lies with her arms outstretched. Her filmed-over eyes staring up at a sky she no longer sees.

Ala and her mother have to jump over fallen trees. Shards of glass crunch beneath Ala's inappropriate summer shoes. There are craters in the roads, filled with water and objects that overnight have become useless. Tramlines ripped out of the cobbles. Lampposts grotesquely twisted out of shape by the heat. A stink of sewage and, now and again, escaping gas. She sees into the exposed privacy of strangers' homes. A gaping second-storey bathroom with only one buckled remaining brick wall, a blue bathrobe still hanging from a hook. The violence is no longer in her eardrums. It is eerily quiet. It's in her eyes now.

She sees a young boy wandering about in torn and filthy pyjamas. His face a white mask with smudges of red pigment.

"Shouldn't we make sure he's all right?" she says, tugging at her mother's arm.

"Someone qualified will take care of him," her mother says, barely affording the little boy a glance.

Ala stops in her tracks and frowns at her mother. The anguish on the little boy's face has become a physical ache in her being. Her mother continues to walk away. Nothing in her purposeful stride to suggest this isn't just another ordinary day. Two women take the little boy in hand. Ala feels cheated, as if she has failed another audition. This seems to be the purpose of her mother. To keep her off life's stage. She follows several yards behind, hating the stiff proud poise of her mother's red-hatted head.

She follows her mother to the family jewellery store. The pavement is smeared with pulverised brick and mortar dust but the store is undamaged. Her mother inserts the key and crouches down to lift the iron grill a fraction and then crawls through the small space with an ease that Ala can't help admiring. It's not often she sees her mother perform tasks demanding of bodily agility. When Ala ducks down inside the shop it is the first unaltered sight she has seen for some time and it makes her feel a bit safer. Her mother is in the backroom filling her handbag with the store's most valuable pieces.

"Ala, you mustn't think I'm without feeling," she calls out, her husky voice accommodating a softer note.

"I don't," she replies automatically. But she does feel that. It's one of her mother's habits to leave a room and then shout from another room when intimate feeling is discussed.

"For the time being it has to be family first. We've heard how the Germans have treated Jews in Germany and Austria. And they deliberately targeted the Jewish district with their bombs on Yom Kippur. We need to expect the worst now. And first priority is to make sure all our assets are safely in our own hands."

6

Mr Kaminski's building is no longer there. Max stands before the hillock of smoking debris where it used to be, where, only two days ago, it stood. He talks with a woman and finds out Mr Kaminski was inside the building when the bomb struck. They found his severed hand with the tell-tale signet ring. Max wonders now if his employer had some kind of premonition of his impending death and that was why he gifted him the Modigliani painting which has been saved as a result and by which Max knows he wanted to be remembered by the world.

The man Max went to buy the works of art from had fled his apartment. The concierge told Max he went into hiding when it was discovered he was German. He still feels a twinge of disappointment that he never got to see the Picasso, the Schiele and the Giacometti. He was surprised later that evening to discover the transfusion of exotic excitement fed into him by the feel of the wads of soft crisp banknotes in his hand, as if he was about to embark on an adventure. And he thought with how much more clarity and confidence all these banknotes might enable him to see into the future if they belonged to him. Now they do belong to him, bundled inside a brown paper bag in the knapsack hanging from his shoulder. He already knows he is going to keep the money. Despite the sludge of guilt that sucks at his thoughts. The only person who knows he has the money is the mysterious German who has vanished from the face of the earth. But he feels no thrill of thanksgiving at finding himself suddenly financially secure because Mr Kaminski was his friend and he grieves that the two of them will never again strike up understanding like fire from sticks by sculpting out words in the air with their hands.

7

Ala and Lily are sitting on the wooden boards in front of a wall of mirrors. Both are filmed in sweat. Ala's calves are aching. They compare their misshapen feet, stripped of another pair of ruined toe shoes. Then they discuss which male dancer has the most beautiful behind.

"Stefan wins for me," says Ala, who, like Lily, has never kissed a boy.

"For me too. Why are behinds so attractive? They shouldn't be when you think what they're for."

Ala watches herself mock grimace in the mirror.

"Do you think Madame is beautiful?"

Ala looks over at her teacher. As usual her long black hair is bound into a glistening knot pinned at the back of her head. She has a pursed wide mouth and high chiselled cheekbones. It's only when she smiles that radiance blazes through the forbidding severity of her features. Ala tells Lily this. "It's just a shame she doesn't smile very often," she adds.

Ala is still upset about the torrent of abuse she received from her teacher earlier. She wanted to explain why she was so distracted, but Madame's icy presence forbids all personal intercourse. When Madame shouts at her – she shouts at every member of the class frequently – it's like she inflicts on Ala a physical injury. It has occurred to Ala that both the two female mentors in her life are relentlessly critical of her, her mother and Madame. She rarely receives a word of praise from either of them. The difference is, she wants to learn everything Madame knows. She does everything Madame tells her. Her mother, on the other hand, is often a barometer for what she wants to avoid.

Ala danced clumsily today because her body carried the weight of what she witnessed on her way to the class. Two German soldiers ordered a passing Polish teenager to punch a bearded and robed elderly Jew in the face. The boy, no older than fourteen, was reluctant. A crowd gathered around the scene. Ala looked closely at the old Jewish man, standing with his hands clasped behind his stooped back as if carrying the weight of the world's sorrow. His face was kind, his body frail. Sympathy for him welled up in her, as if he was an intimately loved member of her own family. Eventually, one of the German soldiers pointed his rifle at the boy and cocked the trigger. The boy wet himself and everyone laughed when the broadening stain on his crotch was pointed out. Then the boy threw a half-hearted punch at the kind old Jew. He was pushed out of the way by a Polish thug who knocked the old Jew to the ground with a full-blooded punch to the face. Although some people in the crowd appeared uncomfortable, others cheered. Ala reprimanded herself afterwards for not intervening. Even though she knew there was nothing she could have done to prevent the humiliation of the kind elderly Jew. She loathed how helpless she had been made to feel, how reduced in scale.

The task Madame has now set the class is to bend down and gather something up – first with longing, then with fear, next with amusement and finally with anger. More and more often Madame is introducing disciplines of theatre and mime into her dance classes. Madame rarely speaks of her years with Diaghilev and the *Ballets Russes* except to say that without the Russian revolution she would be ignorant of much she now knows. She has mentioned Nijinsky and Balanchine. And that she became stifled by the dictates of classical ballet. That she wants to fuse theatre and dance, incorporate stylised everyday gestures into the vocabulary of dance. She has set herself the goal of extending the boundaries of classical ballet. Ala sees this as an opportunity to use some of the sign language her uncle has taught her. She has memorised ten or so sentences, none of which are appropriate, but no one will know that. And she wants to impress Madame. She lives to impress Madame.

When it's Ala's turn, she steps out onto the boards and finger-signs her favourite of the gestures Max taught her.

"Ala, what are you doing?"

Everyone laughs, as though Madame has given them licence.

Ala, slumping, thinks this is one of those days when it's her turn to be a magnet for the world's every discharge of poisonous energy.

"It's sign language deaf people use to communicate."

"And what were you saying to your imaginary deaf companion?"

There is more subdued sniggering.

"I understand there is sadness in beautiful things."

"And how much of this language have you learned?"

"Not much."

"Show me something else."

Ala can see she has Madame's interest.

8

Max is listening to Schubert's *Piano Trio No 2 in E flat major* on the gramophone when the hammering on his front door crashes him out of his wistful mood. His heart is racing with both alarm and indignation when he goes to see who it is. Two German soldiers in grey-green uniforms, forage caps and lacquered boots stand facing him.

"You have ten minutes to leave your apartment. Pack what you need."

"Why?"

"No questions."

The two Germans follow him into his apartment. The Germans intimidate him. He doesn't like to acknowledge this. The shock of the smartness and authority of their uniforms, the vigour and haughty self-confidence with which they carry themselves. They are like men who never succumb to doubt. Max has never liked such men. One of the soldiers follows him into his bedroom. Watching everything he does, pretending he's indifferent to the intimidating power he wields.

Max stuffs some clothes into a knapsack. He asks himself which of his possessions it would cause him most heartache to lose. But he can't think clearly. The only thing he can think of is the money he has hidden underneath the floorboards.

"Not married?" says the German.

"No."

"Maybe you are lucky there. Or maybe not."

Max smiles politely and then dislikes himself for seeking to ingratiate himself to the German soldier.

Max walks over to the Modigliani portrait which is now hanging on his bedroom wall.

"No furniture," says the German.

Max opens the drawer of his bedside table. The button he tore from Sabina's dress is there, beside the pale brown passport he has never used. He and Sabina had been inseparable throughout their time together at university. She rarely showed any interest in other males and when she did it was usually to playfully provoke him. Everyone thought they were boyfriend and girlfriend. But they never once kissed. He tried once, clumsily, and she shoved him off. Told him she didn't think of him like that. He has never been sure how she did think of him. It's remained the most frustrating mystery of his life. He remembers she always somehow imparted more confidentiality when she looked away than when she looked him in the eyes. A memory of her often now stops him in his tracks, absents him from the task occupying his hands. It has been a constant effort for him to keep his mind intact against the erosions of loneliness. When he thinks of her he is overcome by shyness, a shyness he has shed in most other areas of his life. On the night he tried to kiss her he had afterwards torn a button from his shirt and placed it in her hand. This shirt, minus the button, is still hanging in his wardrobe. He told her to keep it as a memento of a beautiful evening. Then he had torn the button from her dress. She was angry at first. It always made her uncomfortable when he put his hands on her. But they laughed about it as he walked her home. He wonders now if she still has his button. He thinks of that button as an emblem of the power she has over him. He has never since granted anyone so much power to hurt him. There are moments when he thinks he could have done more to ensure Sabina did not disappear from his life. And then he wonders if it is possible to avoid what happens to us. He suspects it isn't. As if there is a kind of encrypted thread running through us that is responsive to outside magnetic prompts. A thread that is aligned to the source of all life's code. As if the inception of everything begins outside of time but unfurls its narrative within it. Then he usually laughs at himself. For not being able to express himself better and for acknowledging the possibility of his father's god and blaming Him for his own failures of nerve.

He takes the button out of the drawer. To hold an object that belonged to someone you have loved and lost alters for a moment the weight of your hand and then the weight of your entire body.

"What is this?"

"Nothing."

"Show me."

As Max suspected the German enjoys the power he wields, despite his show of indifference.

"Sentimental value," says Max feeling further diminished in stature. He pockets the button. He wonders if keeping it makes it more likely he will see its owner again.

Outside, Max feels light on his feet. Homeless, he has to fight down a precipitation of panic rising from oceanic depths within.

Mr Rundstein is standing outside with his wife, two young sons and teenage daughter. They live in the apartment beneath Max's.

"They told me they need this building and the building next door as a barracks," says Mr Rundstein.

"Did they say for how long?"

"They wouldn't say. I'm surprised they've evicted the Catholics as well." He nods over at the Sawicki family who are now leaving the building.

Though he has converted to Catholicism and it happens he feels a fraud whenever called upon to feel solidarity on religious grounds, Max makes no secret of being Jewish to other Jews. He's not so candid with Catholics. Only because he sees no reason to give anyone an easy reason to dislike him. He has come to believe we become a composite of what people think of us, how they treat us. The prejudice he met as a Jew affected negatively his self-esteem. The easy solution was to pretend, racially and religiously, to be no different from the person he was talking to.

"What are you going to do?"

"I don't know. We're thinking of maybe going over to the Russian zone. We have relatives there. They say the Russians treat the Jews well."

German propaganda has been spreading stories of Jews welcoming the Russian army into Polish towns with open arms. Many Poles as a result now view Jews as traitors and communists.

"I've got no idea what I'm going to do," says Max, fingering the button in his pocket, as if it is the only ballast that now weights him to the earth.

9

In the Saxony Gardens Ala lets Luna loose and runs with her across the lawns. She pretends she wants to capture her. Luna deftly shimmies past her outstretched arms. Two German gendarmes take a shine to her whippet and ask Ala questions about her. They are both middle-aged men. One of the Germans kneels down and strokes Luna's head while the other asks her what she thinks of German soldiers. When she mentions she is a Jewess they become embarrassed. First of all, they think she is joking. Then they abruptly curtail the encounter and walk away.

The ruins of buildings no longer standing play tricks with her memory, make it seem less reliable. She tells Luna how dependent identity is on memory. She often saves her most philosophical ideas for her dog. "You, like me, are the sum of everything you remember. The problem is, memories perhaps are no less subject to change than the world of surfaces which might mean we never quite know who we are."

Near home she meets Mr and Mrs Zimmerman, the elderly couple who live next door. They have always been kind to her, ever since she was little. They invite her in for tea. They want to talk about the situation. They want to know what she as a young person thinks. Ala tells them about the German soldiers she met in the park.

The front door bell rings. Mrs Zimmerman exchanges a surprised look with her husband, then gets up to answer it. Ala hears a gruff commanding male voice, followed by some polite resistance from Mrs Zimmerman. Then two males enter the drawing room. The charge of aggression they bring with them makes Luna sit up. She lets out a tentative protest bark. The younger of the two men, wearing a flat cap pulled low over his forehead and trousers belted high on his waist, has a black eye and is holding a gun. Ala can tell he is wary of her dog.

"Mr Zimmerman," says the older square-faced man. He is wearing a long leather coat and has a large mole on his stubbled chin. "You have been fined 3000 zlotys for failing to bow to an officer of the German Reich." He speaks in Polish but with an exaggerated German accent. "I have been entrusted to collect the fine. Refusal to pay will lead to the immediate arrest of you and your wife."

Mr Zimmerman is very polite. He refutes the charge. The man in the leather coat begins shouting at him. He tells Mr Zimmerman that if he has any love for his wife he will pay the fine and stop impeding the course of justice.

"You're nothing but a pair of common criminals," says Ala. She flushes at her impudence.

"You want to call the police? Be my guest." The man in the leather coat grins. He cackles through bared teeth because everyone knows anyone can now rob Jews with impunity. "What's a pretty thing like you doing with these old cronies anyway?"

Ala frowns at him.

He turns to his companion. "Keep an eye on them while I take a look around for subversive materials."

Ala sees the teenager is enjoying the fear of the elderly couple. That he is itching to shout at them, perhaps even hit them. To demonstrate and feel more keenly his power. She catches his eye, determined to show him she is not intimidated. He stands with his mouth half open, holding the gun in one hand, jingling coins in his trouser pocket with the other hand.

When the older man returns to the drawing room Ala notices jewellery spilling out of the bulging pockets of his leather coat. Mrs Zimmerman notices too. She bows her head.

"I'm going to shoot your dog," says the boy with the black eye. He closes one eye as he aims the trigger.

"Don't you dare." Ala jumps up and covers Luna with her body. The boy pulls the trigger. There's a hollow click, a small spark and a childish pop.

"Ha ha! Cap gun," he says.

"Right, it's the Silbermans next," says his companion.

The Silbermans are Ala's parents. As soon as the two men are out of the door she telephones home. Her father answers.

"Two men are about to rob you. Don't answer the door. They're common criminals."

There's a mirror above the telephone and in the glass she sees not a blossoming young woman as she likes to see herself but a pale shaken little girl still in need of the love and support of a mother and a father.

Mrs Zimmerman is silently crying when Ala returns to the drawing room.

10

"I've never known anyone talk less than you do," Max says, keeping a careful eye on the German guards. "How do you do it? Stay silent so much of the time. It's like Dad talked you into muteness."

His brother smiles, without showing his teeth. He never shows his teeth. He wears dentures as a result of the skiing accident that also left him with a broken femur which has never properly healed and requires him to wear a built-up shoe on his left foot. One of the German guards singles Samuel out for this disability and taunts him every day. Max has come to understand how much withering embarrassment the ugly shoe causes his brother. As if it tells you all you need to know about him. Max and his brother are part of an obligatory Jewish work detail. Their task to remove rubble from the bombed buildings and preserve all the bricks that might be used again.

"Fat lot of good converting to Catholicism has done you."

"I know. You've got to hand it to German bureaucracy. Talk about leaving no stone unturned. They weeded me out."

"I never understood why you did that. Why you wanted to hurt our father so much."

"It was a practical decision at the end of the day."

"No, it was a hurtful cowardly decision. What were you doing? Putting him and his paternal love to the test."

"He drove me mad. I couldn't hear myself think with him talking so incessantly in my ear. Do you remember the fear we lived in as children whenever we had committed what we thought of as play but what he deemed a grave transgression? To tell the truth, I didn't expect the feud to go on so long. Sometimes you begin something believing it will soon be over but discover it carries on under its own steam. Perhaps there's some mysterious untouchable law that dictates the length of everything."

"You only have to get on a train to put an end to this ridiculous situation."

"Not so easy for a Jew these days."

"You at least recognise you're still a Jew then?"

Max smiles. His father always has the same face when Max recalls him. He is as if caught unawares. We remember people principally by only one of their many faces. Or so Max thinks. As if every face has a quintessential expression, a crystallised gesture, which is eloquent of the overriding feeling inspired in us by the person. He finds it is the same when he thinks of Sabina. She too has only one face. She is smiling but there is more loneliness than mirth in her smile. Max wonders what face of his she remembers. And realises nowadays he prefers the moments of life when he is not called upon to have any face.

"Here comes your daughter." Max lets go of the wheelbarrow and fingersigns to Ala. "Germany is a nation of trumped up pig farmers," he signs. A phrase he has taught her.

Ala signs back with difficulty as Luna is tugging at the leash. It's perhaps a childish game but it allows both him and Ala a smirk at the expense of the Germans. It's the first time he has taught anyone anything. An initiation into adulthood at thirty-nine years of age. The incongruous and essentially useless nature of the knowledge he is passing on sometimes strikes him as a derisive indictment of his entire life.

Max observes how stiffly his brother greets his daughter. He knows Samuel never shows emotion but sometimes he wonders if he has any communion with his feelings at all. Sometimes, to speak eloquently, you must remain silent. Max knows this. But often to remain silent is a crime. He picks up the handles of the wheelbarrow again when he sees a German guard, the one with blue ice in his eyes, look his way. He has wondered if any of these German guards are now living in his apartment. Since losing his home he often has the sensation his bodyweight has diminished to that of a child.

11

January 1940: Ala looks at the young men clambering amongst the rubble. All stripped down to shirtsleeves, despite the wintry cold. She is looking for someone who attracts her. More and more often this is becoming the case. That her eyes seek out the promise of beauty in this bleak new world. Both she and Lily are virgins. Both claim to be impatient to know what they are missing, despite secret misgivings and mysterious inherited scruples. One day, before the Germans arrived, they stuffed rose petals inside their bra and knickers and went out on the streets glowing with the secret knowledge of what lay concealed beneath their underclothes, especially when any good-looking boy looked at them. She catches sight of a good-looking boy now and for a moment the soft red petals are as if restored to the secret parts of her skin. He is wearing a black turtleneck jersey and his dark unruly hair falls over his eyes. He has thick long eyelashes like a girl. He looks like the photograph of Kafka she once fell in love with. She discovers later from her brother his name is Marcel. That his father was a factory worker and his mother worked in a school canteen before the Germans arrived. That his younger sister was killed by a bomb. She left the underground shelter to feed her cat.

February 1940: Ala's mother has pasted a notice on the inside of the front door. DON'T FORGET YOUR ARMBAND!!!

Often, Ala purposefully doesn't wear the armband. In part, to annoy her mother. But mostly as an act of defiance. Lily doesn't wear hers either and they get on the Aryan part of the tram.

If there are any Germans, they say something disdainful about the *untermenschen.* It's how the Germans refer to Jews. But *untermenschen* has become their code word for the Germans. Then they have coffee in a café where they don't serve Jews. They always steal spoons and ashtrays from these cafés. This is another act of resistance. It's children of the Hitler Youth in brown uniforms the colour of diarrhoea who go around selling the notices. *Für Juden Eintritt Verboten.* It isn't yet law not to serve Jews, so these establishments are acting of their own volition at present.

Often nowadays, especially when she leaves the house without her armband, Ala is compelled to ask herself how Jewish she looks. Though always vividly and critically aware of her appearance, subjecting it to obsessive scrutiny in mirrors, this is a question she has never asked before. She knows she doesn't look as Jewish as many of the people in the poor districts. But it's like there's a hairline crack in the mirror when she looks at herself now. She seems altered. It's neither a good thing or a bad thing. She's not trying to disassociate herself from her brethren. Her mother thinks it's vanity and self-importance that compels pious Jews to draw attention to themselves. She says Catholics make do with a tiny cross which is often hidden and Jews should resort to a similar kind of discretion if they have to insist on wearing their faith. She says all the garb and facial hair they sport is no less provocative than were she to walk the streets in her underwear. She seems to believe all prejudice should be of an aesthetic rather than a racial nature. Ala points out that in her black fur and red hat and cherry lipstick she looks like the Nazi flag.

Ala still can't accustom herself to the sight of her mother wearing the ugly armband. For a woman who has always meticulously spent an hour dressing and grooming before leaving the house she knows it must be especially humiliating to wear something so sordid and vulgar. Even if her mother's armband is made of the finest linen.

Most of Ala's secrets are related to sex. Like shaving her pubic hair. Like the chemistry of excitement sometimes precipitated in her by the novels she reads. Like her furtive pulse-quickening fantasies in the darkness of her bedroom at night. Only recently has sex become a navigational chart she uses to steer herself further from the shores of her childhood. Madame once told her that her body is perfectly proportioned to be a dancer, that all her lengths are ideal, legs, neck, back, arms. It's the compliment she most cherishes. She wonders if the boy who reminds her of Kafka can see in her what Madame sees. There are times when we wish a private compliment might be made public. She notices he has a book in his pocket. A Dostoevsky novel. Ala doesn't think she could ever strike up an enduring intimacy with a boy who doesn't read novels. Her mother is proud of the fact she hasn't read a novel since she was in her early twenties. She says she has no time for fantasy.

Max has returned to his apartment. The Germans have found new barracks. He tells her they left behind a mess, but that his paintings and the most precious thing he owns are safe. She asks him what this most precious thing is, but he won't tell her. She suspects it's some kind of love token. From the girl with the green socks he talked about by the river last summer.

Madame arrives at class wearing a Star of David armband. Nobody knew she was Jewish. One or two of the Catholic students turn up their noses. Ala has already disassociated herself from these dancers. Often in the past when Madame criticised Ala she would complain rather disdainfully that she was allowing her argumentative Jewish nature to intercede between her mind and body. Ala guesses that, like Max, she is a baptised Jew. Not that the Germans make any distinction. Madame tells everyone she will no longer be able to take classes.

April 1940: Polish has always been the household language. Ala's mother speaks Yiddish to the cleaner and the janitor but otherwise insists on Polish. However, Henryk and Ala have started speaking in Yiddish at the dinner table. This annoys their mother. Ala suspects her mother secretly believes the Poles are superior to Jews, at least the high society set she frequents. She's always favoured Catholics as friends. But Ala feels a new need to identify herself more closely with her race and Henryk feels the same and so they overrule their mother. Her father remains silent. No one ever knows what he's thinking.

The family celebrates Passover this year. Even her mother is keen to do so. She makes chocolate caramel matzos, despite the difficulty of getting hold of unleavened bread. Ala likes her so much better for all the effort she makes.

July 1940: Two German officers arrive at the apartment. It's rumoured Poles tell the Germans where the wealthiest Jews live. Ala's mother spies them through the peephole. She tells Ala to feign sickness. "The Germans think all Jews carry disease so this might be the quickest way of getting rid of them," she says. Ala goes to her room and gets into bed. She can hear one of them talking loudly in broken Polish to her mother. Her mother has long since hidden all the most valuable jewellery behind two tiles in the bathroom. Just as Ala hears footsteps approaching her door she realises she has left her favourite necklace on her dressing table. She begins coughing. An amateurish performance that only serves to increase her nervousness. The German who enters her room has black hair slicked back with brilliantine. He reeks of sentimental masculinity. He carries a leather briefcase.

"Sick?" he says in German.

Ala nods and begins retching. The officer lifts his hand to his mouth. She looks at the grey eagle and swastika on his cap. Then at the twin lightning bolt runes on his collar and at his lacquered boots. His posture is stiff. His movements seem automated. He wouldn't be able to dance to save his life. He walks over to her desk and opens her diary. It's made of Florentine leather and was a gift from Max. For a moment she thinks he is going to take it. Instead he picks up her Parker pen and casually puts it into his pocket. Then he walks over to the dressing table and takes her necklace and a mother-of-pearl brooch. It occurs to her that all his authority comes from nothing more than a piece of paper in his pocket. And the uniform this piece of paper entitles him to wear. She strips him of this uniform, imagines him naked as a sexual being, and is repelled. She would like to communicate to him this repulsion she feels. She has learned inadvertently in the past how withering a female's sexual scorn can be to a man. She has hurt boys she had no desire to hurt. This man though she yearns to hurt.

When the Germans leave, her mother tells her they complained about the quality of her father's shirts but stole some anyway along with gold cufflinks, a watch of hers and some of her jewellery. "The odd thing was how polite they were."

Apparently, this is going on all over Warsaw. The Germans walk into Jewish shops – every Jewish shop has to display a Star of David - and take what they want without paying. The family jewellery store has been appropriated by a *Volksdeutsch*. The *Volksdeutsch* are Poles who claim German ancestry, often fictitiously. They receive better rations and can steal from Jews with impunity. Jews are not allowed by law to possess more than 2000 zlotys in their homes and all Jewish money in banks has been frozen. The newspapers are relentless in their attacks on the Jews. They blame Jews for the war, for stealing the jobs of native Poles, for every human disease. There's no question people are beginning to get brainwashed. The policy of the Germans seems to be to bring every base emotion to the fore – spite, covetousness, ignorance, jealousy, mindless prejudice. It's as if the Nazis are set on ripping the heart from human interaction.

Ala talks to Marcel about Dostoevsky for five minutes. Everything she says sounds naive and strained and she is relieved when he is ordered to get back to work. She reads *The Idiot* afterwards.

France, Holland and Belgium fall. Only England remains now.

Both Ala and Henryk notice some of their Catholic friends are less keen to spend time with them. The same thing has happened to their mother with her Catholic friends. This is not the case with Henryk's girlfriend, Sophie, or his best friend, Stefan. One day when they are together a group of thugs spit in Stefan's face and call him a "Jew lover". As girls Ala and Lily haven't been physically attacked, but when they wear their armbands some people look at them with disgust or amused disdain. The armband makes Ala feel like she has a contagious disease. She despairs that a thin strip of worn cloth can make her feel so different about herself, can rob her of so much of her self-esteem.

The older generation are often trying to look on the bright side. They report stories heard of German soldiers playing football with Jewish boys or German kindness shown to Jewish men and women in work details. And they find hope in the progress of the war, believing the more countries Hitler attacks the more stretched his resources will be. And they keep repeating the mantra that England never loses wars.

Ala's father is appointed a member of the Jewish Council, the *Judenrat*. He works in the Health and Social Welfare Department. Grandpa Frydman is an influential elder of the council.

Max takes Ala to the cinema, the Napoleon Theatre in Three Crosses Square. They don't wear their armbands. Afterwards they have a meal in a restaurant where Jews are forbidden. Ala steals the ashtray and Max laughs and steals the napkins.

October 1940: There are rumours the Jews are to be herded into a ghetto. Every other day the street plan of the proposed area changes. Walls are being built at many intersections and the Jewish council is made to foot the bill. Max is part of a work detail building a wall at the end of the street where he lives.

Ala misses her dancing.

One evening Ala and Lily dress up as imaginary paintings. Inspired by Klimt, Ala paints her face and arms with strange bright symbols. All of a sudden Henryk comes into the room without knocking. Lily is naked above the waist. Lily blushes crimson and Henryk looks bewitched for a moment before retreating with an apology.

November 1940: Ala and her mother are picked up in the

street by German soldiers. They are marched together with three other Jewish women to a municipal building and told to clean the lavatories. When they ask for rags they are told to use their underwear. The German soldiers watch while Ala steps out of her knickers. She thinks she is going to be raped. A glance from her mother calms her down. Mastering fear, she understands, is going to be key to her survival now. She cleans the filthy toilet bowls and urinals. One of the Germans yanks her head back by the hair. "Faster," he says. When they have finished they are told to put their filthy underwear back on. The German soldiers find this very amusing. Ala finds it hard to cleanse herself of the humiliation. It haunts her for days afterwards. Her faith in humanity has taken one crushing blow after another this year. The hope is these people get their comeuppance when the war is over.

The rumours prove to be true. All Jews are to be forcefully moved to a small section of the city. The gentiles living in the designated area have to swap homes with the incoming Jews. Ala's family is quickly inundated with offers from gentile families, most of them offering hovels in exchange for their luxury apartment. Some are aggressive and threatening but once again Ala's mother rises to the occasion and fends them off. They arrange to swap homes with Sophie's family. There is embarrassment all round. Henryk jokes he will finally get to sleep in Sophie's bed. That you can overnight swap homes seems to Ala like a children's game, not part of the ordered sophisticated logic of an adult world.

Ala has a fight with her mother over Luna. Her mother thinks it's irresponsible to take a dog into the ghetto at a time when, because of the paltry rations imposed on Jews, it's getting difficult to feed the family. "Things will only get worse," she keeps saying. Ala thinks this is truer than her father's mantra that things will only get better. But she refuses to be separated from Luna. Finally she wins, thanks to Henryk's intervention. Her mother finds it more difficult to say no to him. Ala suspects she enjoys saying no to her.

December 1940: On the night before they have to leave their home Ala feels so weightless while in bed that she begins to have the sensation of drifting out of her body. She has to snuggle up to Luna to bring herself back down to earth. She can't sleep so she lights a candle and sits on the floor in the midst of all her packed trunks. Luna looks up at her with a look of probing gentleness.

They load as many of their belongings that can be fitted onto the cart outside and bind them with cord while the neighbours stand watching. The horse pulling the cart is scrawny and underfed. Mr and Mrs Zimmerman next door have also hired a horse and cart. Jews have been forbidden to take furniture into the ghetto but word has gone around to defy this decree. Ala walks alongside the creaking cart with Luna on her leash. At every intersection they are joined by more Jewish families with wagons and handcarts. There are lots of gentiles lining the streets watching. (Ala still finds it disorientating to differentiate between Jews and gentiles, something she has rarely had cause to do in her life.) Mostly the bystanders are silent and seem sympathetic, though the odd individual shouts insults, usually ill-educated people with coarse features. Proving, Ala thinks, how vital education is in lifting people out of their base instincts. No surprise then that the Germans have all but curtailed education.

Soon there are so many Jews it has the appearance of some biblical event. Ala begins to feel more important than all the gentile onlookers. They are merely watching history; she is part of it. It is sad watching Henryk say goodbye to Stefan. Stefan is on the verge of tears. Ala likes him at that moment more than ever. Henryk and Stefan have been inseparable since they were about seven.

It becomes apparent how privileged they are to be living in Sienna Street, away from the most congested and chaotic part of the ghetto. There are trees in Sienna Street. At one point they thought they would have to share the apartment with another family but Grandpa Frydman, using his influence on the *Judenrat*, has pulled some strings.

There are notices on the wall. Typhus-Endangered Area. They pass through a gate guarded by Polish police and middle-aged German gendarmes.

There are seventy-three streets in the ghetto.

Ala's new bedroom overlooks the wall.

12

Max has finished work for the day. Said goodbye to his fellow Jewish conscripts. He finds he enjoys the manual labour. Except when it rains or snows and the smell and heaviness of his wet clothes is oppressive. He is reminded of when he was a boy and his father taught him how to drive a shovel into the earth. The pleasure to be had from working in company under an open sky. He enjoys the ploys used to make the wall susceptible to damage close to the pavement, as if he is scoring a small victory over his German overseers. He is part of a work force engaged in constructing the ghetto's walls. He and his companions can't quite decide if it's good or not that the Jews are physically quarantined. On the one hand, it means they are safe from the marauding bands of Polish thugs, a gauntlet they all had to run before the establishment of the ghetto when the obligatory Star of David armband identified them as targets; safe too from the house visits by Germans and common thieves who pilfered with impunity; on the other hand, he is building the walls of their incarceration with his own hands.

On his way home Max is propositioned by a young woman holding a baby to her breast. She offers him sex for a pittance. She is attractive despite her ragged clothes and dirty hair. For a moment his loins argue with his head and heart. It's been a long time since he has enjoyed a woman's touch on his skin. Max has always been susceptible to falling momentarily in love with any beautiful woman. Within a few moments though his loyalty to the memory of Sabina will return. As if the surge of excitement is simply a reminder of his feeling for her. He now politely declines the woman's offer but gives her enough money to buy two loaves of bread. They exchange a few words in Yiddish. More and more often nowadays he finds himself speaking both Yiddish and Hebrew. He is surprised how accessible and vibrant both languages still are within him. How poignantly they resurrect his childhood and especially memories of his father. He discovers the woman's husband has been sent away to a work camp by the Germans and that she is living in one of the refugee centres. The destitution in the ghetto is a relentless harrowing spectacle. He is often struck by the watchful faces of the children. How busily they are trying to work out exactly what it is the adults are lying about. Max feels both lucky and guilty in equal measure that Mr Kaminski's inadvertent gift has enabled him to take the immediate future for granted.

The atmosphere of the woman stays with him. Not as a source of attraction but as a charitable act he might perform. He thinks it a shame he can't move her and her child into his other room instead of the two young men he has been forced by the *Judenrat* to take in. Max's apartment is inside the ghetto. He hasn't had to move. But the two young men living with him are a constant source of irritation. Especially Zelig, a young militant Zionist to whom Max made the mistake of mentioning in jest that he had converted to Catholicism. Ever since, a barely camouflaged and enervating hostility has existed between the two of them. Zelig never cleans or washes up, he sprays urine over the bathroom floor, leaves dirty washing strewn about and holds forth brashly, loudly, as if inviting the world to admire him and his youthful swagger. He seems incapable of ever being still or silent. His strident lecturing voice and restless pacing a constant discordant presence in the apartment. In Max's experience whenever a person ceases to be a stranger reality either expands or constricts. The privacy of his home, a cherished and hard-earned extension of his inner life, has become like a rowdy public forum. He feels depleted. And he has to fight off the disdainful ideas he knows Zelig holds about him, that he is decadent, that he is ashamed of his racial origins, that he is a coward. The only thing they agree upon is that the man in the apartment across the stairs needs to be called to account. Max has decided to do this when he gets home. He hears the man shouting at his wife through his wall every night. The wife's face is often bruised. She always exonerates her husband whenever anyone speaks to her.

Max meets the Rundstein family on the stairs. The husband and wife and their two young boys and teenage daughter. They are all looking up at Max's landing where Zelig holds the wife beater by the collars of his white shirt.

"If I ever see another bruise on your wife's face I'll throw you off the roof," says Zelig.

Max has been looking forward to confronting his cowardly neighbour. His heart was racing as he approached his courtyard with the anticipation of speaking his mind. He believes the time has come to test his manhood. To make a stand for the values he believes in. When he sees Zelig has beaten him to it he can't help feeling cheated.

"Good for Zelig," says Mr Rundstein.

13

Ala has found two rainbow-striped deckchairs in the new apartment and brought them up to the flat part of the roof. There's a sprinkling of snow on the rooftops, but the sun now appears between drifting islands of whiter cloud. Up here, closer to the sky, all the places she is now denied seem closer – Saxony Gardens, the river, the cafés, the shops, the theatres, the train station. There are no parks in the ghetto; barely any trees. She misses the smell of the refreshed earth, the flickering green light beneath overhanging foliage, the flight of birds over water. She misses the distinctive individual timbre of each of Warsaw's church bells. She misses walking home at night through the fragrance of tree pollen and the laughter of lovers. Only books now enable her to experience many of the blessings of the natural world she loves but has never until now fully appreciated. She lives wholeheartedly inside every novel she reads. The escape they offer from a street that is severed by a red brick wall topped with barbed wire. Her new horizon.

Now and again there's the whistle of a freight train, the shunting of rolling stock. The clap of wings as a flock of pigeons change location. Luna is looking up at her with imploring eyes. Ala is not sure if she wants to be fed or taken for a walk. There are no open spaces in the ghetto. No grass for her to roll about in. And she attracts too much attention outside. The Germans like her. She brings out a glimmer of humanity in them. Her mother reminds her at every opportunity that Luna is a problem she created, especially when they can't feed her anything but paltry leftovers. Meat is becoming hard to find. Ala can feel her ribs when she strokes her, and her eyes are sometimes so sad she is compelled to talk aloud to her. "It's not that I'm deliberately not feeding you, if that's what you think, if dogs can think. The Germans are starving us." So much of what happens in the ghetto makes her feel mean. As if she has to share some of the blame. The Germans, she has learned, are ingenious at turning everyone against each other and even turning one against oneself.

Ala sits back in the deckchair. Snug in a fur-collared black coat. She opens *War and Peace*. Her placeholder a photograph of herself in a mock balletic pose by the fountain in Saxony Gardens.

"You look cosy," says her brother, coming out onto the roof. He speaks Yiddish. They speak Yiddish almost all the time now.

"How was your morning?"

"I had to stand in line at the post office for three hours. Ask me if it was worth it." He sits down heavily in the other deckchair beside her.

"You got a letter by the looks of it."

"From Sophie. Was it worth being jostled by people with contagious diseases for three hours? No it wasn't. The censor found nothing objectionable in her missive," he says waving the torn envelope with a look of disdain. "To be honest, I'm relieved we're only allowed to write postcards. I feel like I've got nothing more to say to her than can be fitted on a postcard."

Ala is taken aback by his confiding manner. She is accustomed to him treating her like his baby sister. "You don't mean that," she says.

"I do mean it. I've seen her in a new light," he says. He keeps tugging at his Star of David armband, as if it impedes the circulation of his blood. "I couldn't help hating her when we said goodbye. I watched her walk away and disliked the familiar proud tilt of her head, and the fact that her life would be continuous while mine has been ripped to shreds. She doesn't get it.

It's as if all this is an inconvenience to her, like a day of rain at the beach. She even writes that Warsaw is returning to normal. It doesn't seem to occur to her that she's writing to me from my home. I can't help feeling resentful towards Stefan as well."

"He was almost in tears when you said goodbye."

"I know. I'm not saying my feelings are rational. But what is rational anymore? I walked past two corpses today, including a young naked woman. Her legs were as thin as my arms. Why aren't people angrier? I'm furious all the time. I hate the Germans. Instead of fantasising about girls at night I fantasise about killing Germans. I want to spit in the face of every German I see. Instead I have to bow and lift my hat. So I've stopped wearing hats."

"I noticed."

"There should be less resignation and more outrage. Resignation is what allows poison to gain a foothold and flourish. The older generation seems to accept the Germans as some kind of scriptural prophecy we always had coming. All this talk of making the best of things. Dad is driving me crazy with his mindless optimism. If he says one more time this won't last long, that essentially the Germans are a civilised race and brings up Beethoven and Goethe I'll scream. *Let's not forget that* The Ode to Joy *is one of civilisation's crowning achievements,*" he says impersonating the voice of their father.

"He's not wrong about that. I always feel as if the world is being swept clean of all baseness when I hear it. It's a shock people can still murder and hate after something so beautiful has come into the world."

"Every German soldier I've encountered has been a block-head, an ignorant uneducated failure of a man who for the first time in his life has got some power and is bloated on it. The only experience of culture these Germans have is probably limited to crude bawling folk tunes." Henryk stands up and improvises a preposterous caricature of a folk dance, elbows and knees jerking like pistons. "Why do we allow ourselves to do what these blockheads tell us?"

"Because they've got guns?"

"Yes, and we've got prayer shawls. I hate religion too. I almost hate religion as much as I hate the Germans."

"Do you feel you never fully appreciated certain things when you had them? There's an ache in all my happy memories now. Sometimes I feel like an old woman wistfully looking back at her life."

"You don't look like an old woman. You look beautiful, sitting in your deckchair reading Tolstoy," he says. For the first time today she sees the kindness in his eyes by which she recognises the brother she knows and cherishes. The brother she remembers playing with his toys on the floor and riding his bicycle with passionate vigour, as if piloting a rocket into the future.

"You should try it," she says. "Reading Tolstoy. It does help."

"I met one of the guys on our old work detail today. Poor guy is as miserable as sin. His family are sharing a small apartment in Mila Street with another family of strangers. That area is like the end of the civilised world. It's criminal how many destitute people are crammed into such a confined space. He's had to join the Jewish police force because his family are so poor. He was directing traffic at the intersection of Chlodna and Zelazna. I've invited him to our first house committee soirée Wednesday night. Cheer him up a bit. He can play the piano so the pair of you can perform a duet. You remember Marcel?"

Ala flushes. She had been fantasising about him during the thrill of reading about Natasha and Pierre's burgeoning love in *War and Peace*. Her body is crying out for something beautiful to look forward to.

"You like him, don't you? Don't worry, I won't tell him."

"I don't know him," Ala objects.

"Look, I'm going to tell you a secret. It's over with Sophie. This," he says, waving his letter again, "proves it. Is Lily coming to our soirée?"

"I've already asked her."

He leans over and kisses Ala on the forehead.

"I feel like doing something wild." He jumps up out of the deckchair, tugs off his armband and throws it off the roof.

Ala is horrified. Only now does she realise she endows the Germans with supernatural powers. Which is why she expects Henryk's act of rebellion to be met by iron-nailed footsteps pounding up the stairs or the bullet of a sniper's rifle whistling through the air.

14

Max is walking through the crowded market between Leszno and Nowolipie Street. A fresh fall of snow, spiralling petals of white smoke, creates a hushed ghostworld overhead. He slinks down deeper into his long overcoat. He is thinking about the first house committee meeting scheduled for later this evening. The aim of these committees, as he understands it, is for each courtyard to establish a kind of social aid programme. To provide food for the poorer residents of the courtyard and raise money for those in the refugee centres. Also to organise sanitation measures and ensure the buildings are maintained in good order. Tonight, a vote will be taken to elect the janitor, now a prestigious and sought-after office because all janitors are exempt from the frequent German roundups. Max is sure and glad no one will vote for him. He has a reputation for being a loner and a dreamer, rarely offering a word unless called upon when he knows how to be charming.

He passes a woman wrapped in a long black shawl selling Star of David armbands. An old bearded man selling junk from a battered suitcase. Beggars continually solicit him, tugging at his sleeve or bowing in supplication in his path. Most talk in Yiddish, some in Hebrew, others in strange dialects which seem a mixture of three languages. At times he wishes he felt more natural fellowship with these people. That he was able to draw more sustenance from being Jewish. To accomplish which, he knows, would move him closer to a reconciliation with his father. It occurs to him he probably has more in common with German officials than he does with many of these people. And yet they are his people. And he has a responsibility now to feel an affinity with them. Then he sees a young girl struggling with a cello. He can feel the love she has for this instrument and wonders what she's doing with it. He hopes she isn't being forced to sell it for food. He hopes this with a depth of feeling that touches his heart. And he feels reprimanded for setting himself apart. All these people, he realises, carry hidden within them compelling stories of beauty and heartache.

He has a dilemma today. Every day on his way home he passes a young girl and her little brother. They always sit on the same spot of pavement on Nowolipki Street, near his home. Yesterday he bought a loaf of bread and gave it to the girl. She took the bread without saying a word or changing her facial expression. He felt a bit hurt she didn't acknowledge his desire to help. Today he is agonising over whether or not to offer them the spare room in his apartment. Three days ago Zelig and Isaac did not return home. Initially he could not believe his good fortune. It felt like the end of a war to sit alone in his kitchen without the bickering judgemental presence of Zelig. He assumed he and Isaac had moved in with their Zionist friends. When they didn't return for their few belongings he realised they had probably been pressganged into a labour detail and being poor couldn't bribe the Jewish police to replace them with someone else. The hostility he felt for them changed to sympathy. And he now feels guilty living alone in a two-bedroom apartment while so many are homeless. Despite the apprehension that these two wild children might bring lice and typhus into his home he has argued against all his misgivings. He has made up his mind.

He passes a flower shop, surprised to see inside two bunches of daffodils for sale. He imagines holding the wet luminous green stalks in his hands, brushing the radiant yellow petals against his cheek, an experience belonging to the lost world. It's when he has dismissed the idea of buying the flowers as obscenely decadent that he sees her. Never has anyone seemed to enter his vision from so far away. More radiantly magnetic than a bride in her wedding dress. He is suddenly unsteady on his feet, as if he has stepped onto a rocking boat.

"Sabina Milajkowski." He is amazed how cool and controlled his voice sounds. And there it is, the smile he hasn't seen for years. The smile that was the gift of life he most eagerly sought to earn.

"Max Silberman. I'm Sabina Lewin actually. But this is no time to split hairs."

The playful kindness in her voice pulls him into her intimate space as it always did. He doesn't tell her he too has changed his name, that he has altered it to the less Jewish sounding Blinkowski. He kisses her on either cheek, his lips so dry they gum to her cold face. Though the quality of her attention is familiar he can sense all the new experience in her and is jealous of it for a moment, of all she has achieved without him.

"Do you know you make me more nervous than the Germans. Look, my hand is trembling." He can't stop marvelling at the sight of her. Yet her presence depletes him somehow. As if taunting him with the riches of the life he hasn't lived, a life lived for someone other than just himself, the riches of the more complete person he has failed to become.

He finally pays attention to the two young girls with Sabina.

"My two daughters. This is Eugenia, and this is Ora."

Ora's hold on her mother's hand tightens as he bends down to her. Ora is the younger of the two girls.

"Hello Ora. What's your favourite thing to do?" Never has he been so anxious to be trusted and liked by a child, as if his credentials with Sabina are at stake.

For a moment the little girl in the red coat with a blue ribbon in her long black hair hesitates. She jams her fingers in her mouth, then looks up at her mother. "I like making pictures, don't I, Mama? And I like it when Mama tells us stories."

"Everyone here shares the same story. That's what binds us together," he says, immediately regretting the nervous inanity of his remark.

She considers what he says and then, wisely, decides to ignore it. "And I like singing and dancing," she says.

"Lots of things then?" He considers for a moment taking off his hat and placing it on her head.

"I like playing with my dolls as well. And I like it when Mama makes me laugh and when she cuddles me." She liberates herself from Sabina's hold, turns a full circle and swings her arms in exuberant arcs. She nearly slips on the sheets of black ice underfoot. There is a breathless quality about her, which reminds him of her mother. Sabina often appeared to be catching her breath when she spoke, as if she had run to catch him up.

"What about you, Eugenia?"

Eugenia, in a green coat, looks up at her mother and then down at her shoes. At some point she has decided not to answer which pains him.

He fingersigns to her. "It's okay if you don't want to talk," he says with his hands. He is pleased to see her interest has brightened.

"What was that you did?" asks Sabina. Snowflakes settle and melt on the shoulder of her coat.

"Sign language for the deaf. The man I worked for was deaf." He traces another pattern on the air. "You are the most beautiful thing I've seen since the last time I saw you." Then he smiles. But he doesn't translate.

Sabina returns his smile but with an undertow of uncertainty. He realises how rarely he ever had her at a disadvantage as he seems to now.

"What did you say?"

"You never taught me your sign language. I had to learn it myself. You'll have to do the same."

"What makes you think I want to?"

At that moment to tease and be teased by a beautiful woman seems to Max like the pinnacle of masculine experience.

He gets out his wallet and produces a pulped slip of paper. He shows it to Ora.

"Your mum, all her lights, helped me to find myself. And she wrote her telephone number on this piece of paper the first time we met," he says. He remembers the feeling that it was the most exciting and precious thing he had ever owned, the privacy and intimacy of her handwriting like catching a glimpse of her in the bath.

"You kept it?" He can't tell if she is flattered or scornful. He wonders if she has kept the letters he sent her and why this seems too much to ask for.

They are buffeted from every direction. Makeshift stalls line either side of the street. A woman sings. A man plays a concertina. Another man with a filthy orange eiderdown tied round his waist with rope chants passages of scripture. A woman whose stockings have collapsed over her shoes stares into a private void. There are barefooted children in rags. Exhausted beggars huddled in doorways. Slime and thin ice underfoot. A greasy rotting smell thick in his nostrils.

"I wish I could offer a walk in a park or a chocolate pastry in a café. I've been laying bricks since seven this morning. Today in Zelazna Street. I get paid ten zlotys a day. How are you off for funds?"

"For the time being I'm managing. Where are you living?"

"Nowolipki Street. I was already living there before the establishment of the ghetto so I still have all my furniture and belongings. What about you?"

"Wiezienna Street."

"Near the prison?"

"Near enough for us to hear the trucks at night. We share a small apartment with my aunt and uncle. Directly above we have a couple who scream at each other and break things and slam doors. And there are now two cases of typhus in our courtyard. Our window is boarded up against the cold so we get no light. The windows were all blown out during the bombing. Apart from that…"

He contemplates offering her the spare bedroom in his

apartment. But he finds he is afraid of her refusal; afraid of the demoralising effect it might have on him. The die is cast. She always refused him, with a playful mocking smile, as if he wasn't to be trusted at the final count.

"Your husband is a Catholic, isn't he? Where is he?"

"He left me for another woman two years ago."

"I'm sorry," he says. His voice by some trick he's not aware of performing sounds sincere.

"It was a disaster as a marriage. I no longer recognise the woman in me who chose to marry him."

"You don't strike me as having changed dramatically."

"Well, I like to think I've put all my foolishness behind me."

He waits for her to ask him if he is married. He is disappointed she isn't curious.

"You should have married me," he says, keeping his tone light and breezy.

"And deprived myself of Eugenia and Ora? Not likely! Anyway, you only wanted what you couldn't have. You'd have got bored with me after a week if I'd said yes. I think you got from me what you wanted all along."

"What was that?"

"An excuse to carry on being alone. Are you still alone?"

He nods, bowing to her insight.

He has never known if Sabina recognises her own beauty. He thinks not. That she has always been insecurely critical of every reflected image of herself. He remembers when he used to marvel that every night in her bedroom she took off her clothes as a matter of course. A ritual she gave little thought to but which as an imagined shared experience represented for him the answer to all his prayers. He realises little has changed. He might now be thirty-nine years old and she thirty-seven but she is no less attractive to him now than she was when she was a virgin. He is encouraged she barely stops smiling. He can't stop smiling either. Rarely is anyone seen to smile for long in the ghetto. Passing pedestrians stare at the pair of them as if they are flinging off their clothes or shouting at the top of their voices. Nor can his eyes accustom themselves to the beauty of her two girls. It's as if they bring a trail of bright cleansed air into the ghetto streets. Just to look at them is to feel heartened. He feels pride that everyone no doubt assumes they are his children.

Ora pulls at Sabina's sleeve while she is telling him that her parents moved to Paris before the war and tried to persuade her to join them but that she didn't want to take Eugenia out of her school and how shamefully naïve she now feels. Ora points at a young girl with a shaved head who is singing and holds out her hand. Sabina takes some coins from her purse and gives him to her daughter. Ora skips over to the singing girl and after looking around to make sure her mother is watching places the coins in a cracked saucer at the girl's feet. Then she runs back to Sabina with a shy delighted flapping of her arms as if she has overcome another of life's hurdles.

"She always insists on giving money to anyone who sings. Do you know the biggest surprise in my life is how much I adore being a mother?" she says.

He is dancing on air when he leaves her. The happiness he feels radiates a bounty of kindness and generosity through his being and brings with it a conviction that the world too is, in essence, good and kind. He has passed the two children he intended sheltering without even noticing them. Not even a corpse in a doorway, face covered with a newspaper, blackened hands curled up like pincers, can sully his high spirits.

15

"You should stand up to mother more," Ala says to her father. His limp is more pronounced today. She has to slow her pace to keep step with him, made difficult by Luna tugging at her leash. "You're more intimidated by her than you are by the Germans."

Her father turns and winks at her. She waits in vain for him to expound. One of the biggest mysteries in Ala's life is what her father thinks of her. What kind of existence she has inside his head. How he would describe her in a memoir. He never asks her questions except of the most perfunctory kind. He appears wholly unobservant. She feels she knows far more about their relationship than he does. Not the case with her mother whose critical faculties are astute and unremitting. Her father has never shown any ambition, not even to be loved. In public he is obliging, routinely affable, reluctant to ever strike a note of opposition; at home he often appears absent or quietly irritated, as if his real life is somewhere else. Ala loves him but sometimes she longs to admire him.

They are walking towards the gates at Chlodna Street. The boy who lives next door pulls up alongside on his rickshaw. Ala is surprised Luna recognises him and is pleased to see him. He leans down to stroke her.

"Do you want a lift?" He lifts his hat and wipes his brow. Zanek is very good looking. He wears his clothes as if moments before they were strewn on the floor. She likes this. It makes him seem unguarded. She was a little disappointed to discover he has a long-standing girlfriend.

"No thanks," says her father.

"No charge."

"We haven't got far to go."

Zanek waits until her father is out of hearing range. "Your mother invited me in for tea the other day. I discovered your bed is on the other side of my wall. We sleep no less than a few centimetres apart. We could tap out messages to each other at night, like people in every other prison do."

She feels uncomfortable he is flirting with her and especially that she is enjoying it. He pedals off, lifting his hat in salute.

The gates have just been closed so there isn't the usual congestion of foot traffic waiting to cross the busy street which dissects the ghetto. Mr Zimmerman, Ala's former neighbour, was struck and killed by a German truck while crossing this road. Witnesses said the truck deliberately hit him. His wife has since died of typhus. The first casualties of the war among Ala's acquaintances.

Ala is disappointed there is no sign of Zanek at the crossing. This is one of the few places in the ghetto where Jews come into contact with Germans. Her father raises his hat and bows to the two German gendarmes. It pains Ala to see her father submissive. The Germans are middle-aged men dressed in belted greatcoats with a double row of buttons. They wear steel helmets with a small red and black insignia. One is ordering an elderly Jewish couple to perform squat jumps. The other looks affectionately at Luna for a moment and then studies Ala's father with malice. He orders a short shabbily dressed Jewish man over and tells him to exchange clothes with her father. Her father smiles sheepishly for a moment, as if in appreciation of a joke. The German unslings his rifle and shouts at him. While taking off his coat, uncertain what to do with his armband, he tries to explain that he is a member of the *Judenrat*, that he has his credentials in his wallet. He takes out the wallet which the German snatches and throws to the ground. Ala picks it up. Then she has to watch her father kneel down on the pavement to untie the laces of his built-up shoe and feels a murderous surge of hatred for the German with the pink cloddish face which frightens her. When both men have stripped down to their underwear the German orders them to take off their undergarments too. Ala averts her eyes at the sight of her hollow-chested, knobbly-kneed father naked in the street. It feels like a fisted hand has hold of her heart. No daughter should ever have to stand by helpless witnessing the public humiliation and distress of her father.

The shabby clothes of the other man are much too small for her father. The two Germans find this riotously funny. Even more amusing to them is the balancing act the impoverished old Jew has to perform in the oversized built-up shoe. They point and bare their gums and throw back their heads at the hilarity of the spectacle. Then they force her father and the other man to dance and encourage the growing crowd of Jews to join in with their laughter. Ala, dizzy with stifled rage, notices the two Jewish policemen on duty are also laughing.

When the gate is finally opened and the Germans are distracted, her father backs away, towards home. Ala tries to convince him to catch up with the man wearing his clothes and retrieve them. The anger he couldn't express to the Germans he vents on her, almost reducing her to tears. He struggles to walk in the small flat shoes from which his bare heels protrude. The people they pass stare at him. Ala stares back at them, defying them to smile.

Her mother initially bursts out laughing at the sight of her husband in the filthy shrunken clothes. Then she berates him. For not asserting his authority as a member of the Jewish council, and for bringing lice into the home.

"It's not his fault, Mum. The German pig aimed his rifle at him. What was he supposed to do?"

"They recognised your father's weakness. They wouldn't dare take such liberties with Mr Kordowski. Your father loses his nerve at the drop of a hat. He's got to toughen up."

Her mother is talking about her father as if he isn't in the room. Ala can't believe how callous she is being. She walks out of the room, slamming the door behind her.

That night Ala is reading in bed. The memory of the humiliation of her father keeps distracting her from the words on the page. She has just read the same paragraph of *War and Peace* for a third time when a hollow tapping on the other side of the wall close to her head startles her. The tapping continues. She has no intention of replying. But she is flattered and excited. She sits up in bed, pulls her nightdress over her head and makes a star of her naked body on the bed. It is dangerously thrilling to realise how close the good-looking boy next door is to her naked body. And that she can act with impunity, absolved of any wrongdoing by the visual privacy of the moment. Until she remembers he has a girlfriend and puts her nightdress back on. At that moment the tapping stops as if he has heard her misgivings.

16

Darkness is falling and the snow has begun to settle again. Max makes fists of his gloved hands inside the pockets of his coat where the lining is beginning to fray and split. Every day there seem to be more people in the streets. He is jostled and shoved as he walks down Karmelicka Street. Jewish refugees from all over Poland have arrived in the ghetto. Every day he is constrained to feel fortunate, not a feeling he is comfortable with. Nevertheless, he looks forward to sitting by the fire at home where he will listen to the gramophone - Erik Satie's *Gymnopédies* perhaps, or Ravel's *Bolero* - and continue reading *Great Expectations*. It's been a long time since he has had great expectations. Sabina's reappearance in his life has changed that. He had intended reading *Bleak House* but the title put him off. As if book titles have talismanic powers. It always surprises him when he discovers how superstitious he is. Despite his contention that belief in divine providence belongs to the dark ages.

In the glaze of light from a shop window Max sees a young boy standing barefooted in the snow. He can't help recognising something of his own young self in the child and his heart goes out to him. He is about to walk over to him when a man dressed in rags grabs him by the sleeve and sprays him with spittle as he rasps out a request for alms. Max wipes his face before taking out a bread roll from the bag he carries. He is immediately surrounded by other beggars, one of whom, the barefooted boy, snatches the bag and immediately eats what he finds while running off.

He is too cold to join the long queue outside the coal merchant. He decides he will burn a small wooden table he has no need of. He buys some green vegetables from a market stall. He thanks the woman, turns and his heart lurches. Walking towards him are Sabina's two girls. He looks around wildly for Sabina. He then notices the good-looking man who is accompanying Sabina's daughters. All the life is knocked out of him. It never occurred to him she might have found a new man. Thank heavens I didn't ask her to move in with me, he thinks. Eugenia in her green coat recognises him. He smiles and offers an uncertain wave. She doesn't respond.

He feels suddenly old and defeated. All his best days behind him. The thought of Sabina got him out of bed with a spring in his step. That she reappeared in his life only to reject him again strikes him as the kind of psychological cruelty the Germans excel at.

On the corner of Zamenhofa and Gęsia, outside the café with its burnt-out neon sign, he is reminded of the two homeless children. He spoke to the girl a few days ago. Her name is Luba. He tried to persuade her and her brother to accompany him to the orphanage in Sienna Street. She told him they had to wait for their mother. That their mother was in the nearby hospital and they couldn't move so far away from her. He was on the verge of insisting she and her brother come home with him. But in his mind, he had already promised his spare room to Sabina and her girls. He has continually chastised himself for his failure of courage in not offering it to her when they met. So he bought Luba and her brother some food and two blankets, and every day the brother looked closer to death, the light of life retreating further and further back into the depths of his sunken staring eyes. Now he decides he will take them home with him. He is annoyed with Sabina, as if she gave him false hope and by so doing thwarted his instinct to look after these two children. However, they are not in their habitual spot, near the pharmacist on the corner of Nowolipki and Karmelicka. He asks a local stallholder about them.

"I think the young boy died. Combination of starvation and hyperthermia I would guess. I don't know what happened to the girl."

Max makes it his mission to find the girl.

17

"You've imposed the same taxes on the rich and poor alike and you always select the poor to form the work details for the Germans while exempting all your own friends and families. Not only are you failing to address the inequalities in the ghetto you're exacerbating them."

Zanek's girlfriend is criticising the *Judenrat* to Ala's grandfather. Mira wears a polite smile but there is a fierceness in her dark eyes. Mira is a member of Hashomer Hatzair, one of the socialist Zionist youth movements. Zanek too is a member. Mr Frydman is wearing a canary yellow cardigan. He has a full head of silky white hair. The family's wealth all comes from him. He owned a lace manufacturing factory until the Germans stole it. Ala's collection of exotic underwear was the envy of all her friends. In Warsaw people used to joke that Mr Frydman knew exactly what every well-dressed woman was wearing beneath her clothes.

"You expect us to eradicate inequality? My dear girl, not even God has ever achieved that. We're doing the best we can in virtually impossible circumstances. And the best we can do at the moment is to buy time."

Ala sees Mira does not like being called *my dear girl*.

"You can't buy time. That's something no one can do. Not even the rich."

"What would you have us do then?"

"Stand up to these beasts."

"They'd shoot us. What good would that do anyone?"

Ala catches Zanek's eye across the room. She remembers him tapping on her wall and the star shape she made of her naked body and for a moment it's as if fingers have brushed her thighs. He is radiantly handsome tonight in a white shirt with the top buttons unfastened. There's a force in him that pulls her towards his hands. Mira, she knows, has detected a connection between them. Ala has made an enemy. She has the suspicion this is why Mira is attacking her elderly grandfather.

Tonight Ala and her mother have organised a concert in their apartment, a fundraising event for the "Winter Assistance" initiative organised by the *Judenrat* throughout the ghetto to aid the poor. Marcel is going to play his own mysterious compositions on the piano. Except he still hasn't arrived. Ala is hoping Marcel will somehow sweep aside this unwanted attraction she feels for Zanek.

More than half an hour late, Marcel arrives in his navy-blue policeman's cap. He also wears a yellow armband with his service number, knee length polished black boots and a belted trench coat with a truncheon. The officious cap makes him less attractive to Ala. All uniforms provoke a loathing in her now. Ala is pretty sure Kafka wouldn't have joined the Jewish police force.

"It fills me with pride and hope to see you young men in uniform," says her mother, opposing Ala's private thoughts as if she can guess them. "You know you're the only the Jewish police force in the entire world?" A red silk blouse, two buttons undone, reveals the upper curves of her breasts.

"This is a first, you taking pride in anything Jewish," says Ala, repulsed (there's no other word for it) by her mother's flirtatious manner and flaunting of her sexuality.

"That's hardly true, Ala. How you do love to exaggerate," says her mother, deploying her light and breezy social persona. Her public façade, as if she is on official duty, annoys Ala even more than her private fussiness and easy irritability.

"It might be a source of pride were they autonomous," says Henryk. "But essentially they're just lackeys for the Germans."

"Henryk doesn't mean it the way it sounds, Marcel. I think you're doing an admirable job under the circumstances."

"Henryk's right though, Mrs Silberman," says Marcel. "We are essentially lackeys."

"I've heard you police get lots of bribes from smugglers," says Henryk.

"If you're assigned to guard duty at one of the gates you sometimes get bribes from smugglers. After a while you come to know which Germans will accept bribes to turn a blind eye. Then there are the Polish police to buy off too. That's why everything's getting so expensive in the ghetto. To get anything through, a smuggler has to grease the palm of at least three individuals. I felt guilty at first taking the bribes. But I always give half of the money to homeless people. And I have to support my parents."

"That's very admirable of you, Marcel."

"Have you arrested anyone yet?" asks Lily.

"No. But I had to escort a little boy to the prison after a pair of German gendarmes caught him smuggling two loaves of bread through a hole in the wall. I felt so protective towards him I let him go. The worst job is gathering up men for work details in labour camps. They look at you with disgust. And their wives hit you and insult you. Doesn't make you feel good about yourself when you go to bed, I can tell you that."

Later Marcel plays the piano. He plays two long pieces he has composed himself, sometimes singing along in a haunting falsetto voice.

"That was beautiful," says Ala's mother. "Were you singing in Hebrew? I couldn't make out any of the words."

"It's a language I make up while I'm playing, Mrs Silberman," he says.

"Ella. Call me Ella."

Ala and Lily go off to the bathroom together.

"Did you see the way Marcel flirted with my mother?"

"Or was he just being polite? You might be exaggerating, Ala."

"I don't like him in uniform. It makes him strut. I've made a discovery. I don't like men who strut."

"I know what you mean. I'm not sure I care for his policeman persona. All that showing off about how generous and charitable he is. It rang false, if you ask me. Did he really let that boy go the Germans arrested? Does he really give the bribes he receives to homeless people? He's wearing a very expensive watch, I noticed. I don't recall seeing that before."

"His piano compositions and singing were so beautiful though. They almost moved me to tears."

"I was beginning to think you were more interested in Zanek. His girlfriend certainly seems to have that idea."

"You noticed?"

"Hard not to. She behaves like a shrewish wife."

She tells Lily about Zanek tapping out messages on her wall.

"No wonder his girlfriend doesn't like you."

Later the younger set, Ala, Lily, Henryk, Marcel, Zanek and Mira congregate in Henryk's bedroom where they play a game of blind man's bluff. Marcel, blindfolded, walks towards Ala. His outstretched hands touch her hips. Then he lightly brushes his knuckles over her bottom.

"Ala," he says and everyone laughs.

18

When there's a knock on his door Max succumbs to the irrational hope that it might be Sabina. It surprises him his first response is to anticipate good news rather than the much more likely bad variety. He opens the door to Mr Rundstein's eight year old son.

"Hello Otto. What can I do for you?"

Otto has pulled his cap low on his forehead, almost covering his eyes. He raises two balled fists to his mouth. Max is reminded of himself as a child. The urge to hide as much of oneself from adults as possible. He remembers his childhood hiding places. The cupboard under the stair that smelled of rust and dusty calico; the scented bower beneath camouflaging shrubbery at the back of the garden. Hiding compels a heightened intimacy with oneself. But it also keeps at bay confrontation and change. Max sometimes thinks he has spent too much of his life hiding.

"Can we talk inside?"

"Of course. Come in."

Max watches Otto survey his surroundings. The boy's palpable apprehension makes everything look strange and oversized to Max's eyes for a moment. He makes an effort to put Otto at ease. He's a likeable child. Intelligent, curious, perhaps in too much of a hurry to grow up. Max wants to be liked by him. As was the case, with greater intensity, with Sabina's two girls. It's a new feeling to be put at a disadvantage by children.

"What's up, Otto?"

"I need some money."

"What for?"

"A telescope. I like astronomy."

"Someone's offered to sell you a telescope?"

Otto nods. There's something duplicitous about this request. Otto isn't the best of liars. Max understands by instinct a kindness is required of him he might live to regret.

"What makes you think I've got money?"

"Everyone says you do. That's what Zelig told everyone. That you've got hidden gold."

"Like every other Jew in the world," he says, smiling. "Does your father know you're asking me for money."

"No," says Otto sheepishly.

"So this is all your own initiative?"

"I don't know what that means."

"Where will you set up this telescope?"

"It doesn't matter if you don't want to give me the money. I'll ask someone else."

Now Max feels mean.

"How much do you need?"

"Only fifty zlotys."

"Only? Have you ever in your life had fifty zlotys?"

"No."

"I'll have to ask your father."

"He'll just say no because he's doesn't like people knowing he's got no money. He can't find a job."

Two days later Mr Rundstein comes to see Max.

"Can I ask if you gave my son money?"

Max feels like a child being reprimanded by an adult, as if he is sitting on the floor surrounded by toys. "I did," he admits.

"Did he tell you what it was for?"

"Yes. A telescope."

Mr Rundstein manages a reluctant smile.

"Well, it wasn't for a telescope."

"I noticed he's been avoiding me, as if he has a guilty conscience. What was it for?"

"A smuggling operation. He's got in with a gang. They're all kids. They leave the ghetto every day, buy food in the Aryan markets then sell it for a profit in the ghetto."

"How do they get out of the ghetto?"

"Through a hole in the wall."

Max wonders if it's the hole he helped create.

"I hit him to begin with. I was angry. I was also a bit jealous. Not being a father yourself you might not understand my emotion. I felt he was belittling me. My inability to provide for the family. The Germans are doing a good enough job of unmanning me without my son aiding and abetting. But when my stupid anger died down and I recalled how proud of himself he was when he brought home a parcel of groceries I realised this was an act of love on his part. And I shouldn't be forbidding acts of love. What do you think? Should I stop him? He says before long they'll be able to bribe the Jewish police and the Germans at the gate and the danger will be reduced."

"I think it's a decision you have to make."

"I keep telling myself that not even the Germans will shoot children. So what's the worst that could happen if he's caught? And we do need the food. He wants to get my younger son involved but I've drawn the line there. Jacob is only six."

"I think that's wise."

19

The imprint of the touch of Marcel's hand is still sometimes a hot prickling presence on the skin inside Ala's knickers. As if she now wears the touch of his fingers. But she is baffled by Marcel's gesture. Was it an invitation? Or just a casual piece of theatre? She feels an intimacy with him now, an intimacy she's not sure she wants.

Ala is walking Luna down Zelazna Street, alongside the redbrick wall topped with shards of glass, in sight of the gate that leads to the larger section of the ghetto. An icy wind steals beneath her clothes, like a breath from some uninhabitable part of the earth.

At the gate where a large crowd is waiting to cross the busy road she sees the man she loathes. The sight of her naked frightened father has imprinted itself on her heart, like a bird's claw stamped in hardening cement. She closes her eyes and concentrates on an image of her father's tormentor. She is harking back to when she and Lily played at being witches as children. She tells herself it's the theft of her autonomy by the Germans that makes her behave like a child. When she feels she has opened a portal into the gendarme's mind she silently hisses at him in her most demonic voice. *Cursed be you by day and cursed be you by night. Cursed be you when you lie down and cursed be you when you rise up.* She forms a mental picture of a pack of sharp-toothed rats and sends them scurrying into his head. *Devour him, my little beauties*, she says in her mind. She now has to touch him with crossed fingers to activate the spell. When he and his companion open the gates and the crowd surges impatiently forward she pushes her way towards him. Luna tugs at the lead and squeals in pain. Someone has trodden on her paw. A smartly dressed man in a black overcoat and a beige scarf pushes Luna away with his foot. She forgets about the German and tells the man to stop kicking her dog.

"Are you mad, bringing a dog into the ghetto?"

The man is so intent on berating her he forgets to doff his hat to the German sentries. The hated German slaps the man hard in the face and orders him to do thirty press-ups. The German then smiles at Ala and bends down to stroke Luna.

Lily has told her how awful things are in the poorest parts of the ghetto. Still, Ala is shocked. The further she ventures from home the more nightmarish the streets become. Luna attracts lots of attention. Ala sees a grey cat but never another dog. She has the suspicion some look at her dog as a wasted food source. She has always felt proud of Luna; today she is embarrassed by her. As if she is a token of some preening frivolous strain in her nature. She doesn't want to be associated with the haughty well-dressed women who make a show of their privilege. For most of her life Ala has gravitated towards the spotlight. Here there is something shabby and shameful about this aspiration to stand out in a crowd.

She squats down to apologise to Luna for feeling ashamed of her. She tells Luna she is behaving well. She tells Luna nothing is her fault. She tells Luna she loves her. Something she has never told anyone else. And when she looks up she sees Madame. Despite her creased clothes her aristocratic elegance amidst all the poverty is immediately striking. Madame's long black hair is loose today. She appears to Ala to be lit from within. That Madame is pleased to see her makes her feel immediately better about everything. Madame has no desire to talk about conditions in the ghetto. It was always rumoured she subsisted every day on only a few carrots. Probably she is better able to survive on the skimpy rations than most. She tells Ala she wants to start a company.

"Obviously we won't be able to find many classically trained dancers in the ghetto. But that offers new possibilities. We'll try to do something that breaks with tradition. I've got lots of ideas. I want you to find a space where we can hold classes. I've heard you have family connections at the *Judenrat*. I've got two male dancers and a girl. They're not very good but we'll have to work with the materials at hand. I take it Lily is here too?"

"Yes. Is this where you live?" asks Ala, concerned.

"Don't you worry about where I live. The important thing is to stay active, to stay connected to our aspiration. Do you know what dance is, Ala? It's a sequential reawakening of lost moments. What we most need is to bring back to life some of those lost moments."

After visiting Lily, she goes to see her grandfather at the *Judenrat* offices. She is excited by the prospect of dancing again.

She squeezes her way with difficulty through the scrum of people queueing at the various windows in the large ground floor concourse. Luna's leash keeps getting tangled up around people's legs. There are complaints from voices already weary with exasperation. Once again in this crush of desperate individuals pungent with rank body odours she is made to feel conscious of her privileged position. She ascends the stairs to the bureaucratic tranquillity of the first floor.

"Poor old Luna. She doesn't look like she's enjoying life much," says Grandpa Frydman.

There's an interrupted game of chess on his desk.

"She's pleased to see you."

"What can I do for you, Ala?" he says, smiling, screwing on the cap of his fountain pen.

"I need to find a rehearsal space for a small dance company."

"You're going to dance at a time like this?"

"I'm going to find work as well. Perhaps in one of the soup kitchens."

"I'd much rather you danced than worked in a soup kitchen. You know you run a much greater risk of catching tuberculosis or typhus if you're in close quarters with the destitute? I admire your desire to help but I'd advise against it, Ala."

"I've made up my mind."

"Does your mother know?"

"She'll be glad to get me out of the house. I saw a dead child on Solna Street today. A girl of about ten. I know I'll never forget her face. That's why I want to do something constructive. I want to do something to help the poor. We're closeted from all the misery where we live. It makes me ashamed."

He shakes his head with ironic exasperation.

"How frightened do you think we should be, Grandpa?"

He sits back in his chair, takes off his glasses and rubs his eyes. Her grandfather has always been a man who enjoys giving counsel, as long as he isn't interrupted. "I would say we have to see out this wretched endless winter. Afterwards, it's my firm belief things will improve significantly. As soon as we Jews are able to become more autonomous and establish trade routes with the outside world. At the moment no supplies are coming in from outside the ghetto. And that's a major problem. However, I don't believe as some pessimists argue that the Germans are deliberately starving us. I think it's more a question of bureaucratic deficiencies on their part at the moment. There's a chronic food shortage in the whole country. But once the various work forces start getting back on their feet our situation will improve considerably. The Germans will begin to appreciate our labour eventually. And who knows, perhaps the German nation will sicken and tire of their self-appointed messiah before long. I've heard reports there's a lot of opposition to the Nazis in Germany."

"I'm tired of listening to rumours. Ignorance is not bliss. The more ignorant we are, the more we're prone to base emotions. Every day there's a new fairy story rumour. One day Hitler has been assassinated and the German army is demoralised and deserting in huge numbers. The next the British have bombed Berlin to oblivion and the Russians are about to take over governorship of all Poland."

"I hope you're not going to turn into one of these radical hotheads. Who was that friend of yours who bit my head off? The young lady at the fundraising concert."

"Mira? She's not really a friend of mine."

"She belongs to one of the socialist youth movements, doesn't she?"

"Hashomer Hatzair."

"There are reports communist and Zionist youth movements are planning to stir up trouble. It's crucial we toe the line with the Germans, no matter how hard it might be. You've heard about the execution of all those innocent Jews because a Polish policeman was shot dead? Any kind of revolt here could have terrible consequences for the entire Jewish population. Perhaps you can be my eyes and ears among the young set. Report any evidence you see of subversive behaviour. I'm not asking you to spy. Just keep your ears open. If you agree to do that I'll do my bit and find you a rehearsal room. Deal?"

20

Max's pulse is always set racing when he walks in the vicinity of Wiezienna Street which he makes a habit of doing. It's been almost a month since he saw Sabina. During which time he has undergone an expulsion from his imaginative life. He began to feel dangerously sorry for himself. Like he had been damned to some conclusive defeat. Then the idea of procuring a gift for Sabina's girls revived him. *So what if she has a new man in her life? I can still enjoy some time in her company.* He went to see his brother at the *Judenrat* where he used the telephone to speak to one of his Catholic friends on the other side of the wall and asked him to get hold of some coloured crayons, watercolours, brushes, a sketch book and an illustrated children's book of Jewish folk tales. He arranged to meet his friend in the courthouse, which is accessible from both the Aryan side and the ghetto. He entered the basement door of the public building with the excuse of needing to sort out a tax problem. He climbed up to the third floor, bribed an official and met his friend in a quiet corridor. He was nervous when he had the package in his hands. As if he had committed a crime. Which, it then occurred to him, he had. He had broken at least two Nazi laws. A Polish policeman with sleepy eyelids looked him up and down as he walked back out into the ghetto and Max expected him to confiscate his gifts or at the least demand a bribe, but the man smiled at him and he smiled back. That someone's first instinct was to be kind took him by surprise, as if meanness was always what was to be expected from the world now. He was exuberant when he stepped back out into the ghetto, already picturing the joy on the faces of Sabina's two girls when they saw what he had for them. His exuberance survived the destitution he encountered in the bazaar in Leszno Street, the starving children outside the Catholic church. He gripped his parcel more firmly, fearful someone might snatch it out of his hands.

The next day he went to Sabina's address with his gifts. A makeshift wooden fence was posted around the tenement building in Wiezienna Street. Two Jewish policemen stood on guard. A large yellow notice on the front door warned of a typhus epidemic. *Keep out!*

"No one's allowed in and no one's allowed out until we've got all the occupants of the building to a delousing station," a Jewish constable wearing a signet ring told Max.

Today, the hard-packed snow with its glaze of ice is slippery underfoot. The cold is frightening. The wind blows drifts of snow up from the ground. A constant stream of improvised vehicles manoeuvres its way through the congested throng of pedestrians, pedlars and beggars. Many of the people seem foreign to Max. Refugees from rural areas and provincial towns. They look out of place in a cosmopolitan European city. Even if the ghetto bares less resemblance to a cosmopolitan European city with every passing day.

He is walking up Karmelicka Street towards Wiezienna Street. He notices a bleached and torn cinema poster of defiant love pasted to a blackened wall. Again he has to fight down the fear that Sabina has died. Yet another victim of the typhus epidemic sweeping the ghetto. He watches as a policeman moves a beggar woman on, threatening her with his wooden truncheon. The coarse-featured woman is so hungry she can barely move. He waits for a horse and cart to pass, exchanging eye contact with the driver, a man in a flat cap, a little spark of his personality kindling a reciprocal curiosity, and then crosses the street. His heart leaps, his eyes quicken when he sees Sabina. The joy that she's alive makes him want to jump off the ground. He notices she has lost weight. Her cheek bones are more pronounced. He wonders if she's been starving herself to feed her children who both appear healthy. She's delighted to see him. He sees it in her eyes. She was always happy to see him; the problem was she was also happy to take her leave of him.

"We've been to school," says Ora. He is flattered she remembers him. She looks up at him wide-eyed, as if he is some kind of exotic creature. It's a lovely feeling to be held in her gaze. "But we have to hide our books under our coats because the Germans don't want us to go to school."

"What did you learn, anything interesting?"

"I drew a map."

"We never know where we are without a map," he says, smiling at Sabina.

"It was a map of where Jews used to live hundreds and hundreds and hundreds of years ago and our teacher said one day we will all go there."

"Classes are held in someone's dingy living room," says Sabina. "Lessons are taught in Yiddish. They only speak Polish, so they're having to learn a new language." Officially it is forbidden to speak Polish in the ghetto.

He braces himself. "I saw your girls one day. With a good-looking young man."

"He's my cousin. He and his wife moved in with us when the Germans reduced the size of the ghetto again. They were evicted from their apartment which now falls outside the new boundary. So we're even more cramped now."

He feels like stretching out his arms like a bird exulting in its wingspan before taking flight.

"I was worried about you," he says. "I saw you had typhus in your courtyard."

"We were all locked in for two weeks. The Jewish police were zealous. I suppose it wasn't the best assignment, standing guard outside an infected courtyard. I had to bribe them to let me out to buy food. Luckily, the girls are fine. Ora had lice but I killed them with kerosene. Didn't I, darling?"

"I didn't want them to be killed. But they were living in my hair and wouldn't go away and they made my head sore. The stuff Mum combed through my hair stank. Yuk."

"Add to that our gas has been turned off. Someone in a neighbouring building didn't pay their bill so they cut off the gas to the whole block. He's since paid but they still haven't turned the gas back on."

"Look, why don't you move in with me. I've got a spare room that causes me all kinds of problems, not least of all, guilt. And if I've got tenants the house committee will get off my back. I can sense everyone thinks I'm decadent and insensitive living alone when there are so many homeless. It's clear my former house-mates won't be coming back. And it's probable the *Judenrat* will eventually requisition one of my rooms for refugees. Not that I have anything against refugees, but I'd prefer to live with someone I know and trust. What do you say?"

Even at such a crisis in her life he can see there's a reluctance in her to accept his proposal. She's deep in thought. It's as if she's frightened of him, of too close proximity with him. He feels hurt. He has to fight off a protective instinct to dismiss his proposal.

"Look, I know you've made a habit of saying no to me, that our relationship is even governed by this premise and that it's difficult to break with habit, but from every practical point of view it makes sense. And there are no strings attached. You'll be as independent as it's possible to be these days." He can sense how closely Eugenia is following his words, how curious she is and also confused. He's tempted to put the case to her. There's a look in her eyes, wiser than her years. Ora, meanwhile, is singing to herself and performing skips. "There's a nice big bathroom. And the room you can have gets the sun, when there is sun. Obviously, the central heating doesn't always work but there's a stove. You won't be cold. And we've got a smuggler in the building. Young Otto downstairs. He's eight and goes through a hole in the wall and comes back with all sorts of treats."

Finally she smiles.

"I'm thinking of my aunt and uncle. I don't want to offend them. They love having the girls around. It feels mean to abandon them."

"Come and see it," he says, taking her hand. "And I've got a gift for you two girls."

He is greeted warmly by the janitor. It means a lot to him that Sabina sees he is held in esteem and affection. He feels nothing but love for Mr Rundstein when he makes a fuss of the two girls.

Ora is impressed by how many books he has.

"What's mine is yours," he says. "I guess, in the main, this is what I've done since our university days. Read," he says, turning to Sabina. She smiles. She has always been able to undress him just by looking at him. It's her magic trick. His love for her sometimes makes a child of him. He knows he now has to put away childish things. That he is about to take on the most testing responsibility of his life. He experiences a moment of recoil. The cautionary counsel of the coward in him suddenly the loudest voice in his head. His ready capitulation to craven second thoughts is perhaps what he most dislikes about himself, what, he believes, has left him wanting as a human being.

Ora is delighted with his gift. Eugenia hides any emotion she might feel. Both girls seem to like his home. He knows their opinion will be key in Sabina's final decision. When they have left he struggles with the infuriating part of him that wants her to refuse his offer.

21

"Why don't we see what it's like?"

"What do you mean?"

"Why don't we kiss each other?" asks Lily.

"You want to practice on me so you know what to do if Henryk kisses you?"

"Why not? And for when Marcel kisses *you*. We both need a glaze of sophistication."

Ala laughs. "A glaze of sophistication?"

"Come on!" Lily holds open her arms and walks towards Ala. Ala runs away, laughing. Lily catches her and they struggle and collapse onto the bed. Lily, stronger, pins Ala's hands above her head, holds her captive and lowers her mouth onto Ala's face. Ala shakes her head from side to side. She is laughing and blood is rushing through her buckling body.

"Do you want me to run my hands over your bottom like Marcel?" says Lily with a demonic grin. She releases one of her hands and tickles Ala's stomach. In between gasps of laughter and struggle Ala says:

"Just because you want to expose your breasts to my brother again."

Lily intensifies the tickling and they both tumble off the bed onto the floor.

After lunch they go to a matinee at the Melody Palace on Rymarska Street. This theatre, thanks to Grandpa Frydman, is to be granted to Madame as a rehearsal space on a regular basis. Madame kissed her on the forehead when Ala told her.

Again Ala finds Marcel less attractive in his peaked cap and military belt and tin number pinned to the breast of his coat. Henryk steals his truncheon and teases Lily with it. Marcel buys some cigarettes from a street seller with a box on string slung over his shoulders and they all smoke. The auditorium is full. Ala sits next to Marcel on the wooden seats. Everyone dressed up and perfumed as if the war and the ghetto are nothing but a bad dream. Many of the women are dressed in full skirts and the fashionable colours are blood-red and grey. The armband though is a constant reminder they are all prisoners. Ala has to repeatedly convince herself it isn't a crime to enjoy herself. Nevertheless, a cold shiver runs through her when she thinks of all the starving tubercular people out in the snow while she is being entertained by a female singer and an orchestra.

On the way home Marcel hands her a folded piece of paper.

"If you like what you read kiss the paper," he says. "To show me you've understood and liked it."

She reads an eight-line poem about heaped bracken and broken windows and the prints of bare feet in dust. "Did you write this?"

He nods.

She isn't sure she does like it, but she presses her lips to the page because she doesn't want to offend him.

"You can keep it," he says. "You see those crusty yellowish stains? That's my sperm."

Ala wipes her mouth on the back of her wrist. She feels like slapping him. Instead she shoves him. He laughs all the more.

"Aren't you flattered, darling, that I think about you when I masturbate?"

It's the first time she has heard this shocking word spoken aloud. In his stupid peaked cap with his numbered tin medallion he no longer looks anything like Kafka. She knocks the cap off his head, walks over to where it sits on the cobbles and stamps on it.

Later, in bed, even while thinking about Marcel, she finds

herself anticipating the advent of a message from the other side of the wall and is disappointed when it doesn't arrive. She accidentally on purpose knocks her elbow against the wall. She wonders if Zanek too is thinking they are half naked within stretching distance of each other's hands.

It is deadly quiet outside until she hears a motorised vehicle approaching. It's the most sinister noise she has ever heard. And it's coming closer. Soon the sheen of its headlights flusters the shadows on her ceiling. She jumps out of bed and goes to the window. A crystal frost mists the glass. Three storeys below, in the smoking light of the headlights, two German soldiers and an officer and a man in plain clothes emerge from a staff car. They slam shut the doors with unnecessary force. One of the soldiers uses his rifle to knock on the door of the house opposite. One by one, floor by floor, lamps are lit in the rooms of the apartment building. A soldier stands by the car with his rifle unslung. When he looks up towards her window Ala crouches down and crawls back to bed like a cat.

22

Max is carrying two of Sabina's trunks up the stairs. Ora has become his best friend. She rarely stops chattering to him. He is still to win over Eugenia. She is guarded and shy with him. Silent unless asked a direct question. He suspects she is protective of her father. He tries not to take her diffidence personally. Inside the apartment he takes a phonograph record out of its sleeve, Billie Holiday's *What a Little Moonlight Can Do*, the last record he bought before the war began. He is stupidly proud of this record, as if it testifies to some pioneering spirit of modernity in his nature. He settles the needle down on the black disc, bracing himself for the jarring scratch. Ora is immediately excited and begins dancing. He dances with her, a little stiffly because Sabina is watching and smiling and he's far from confident in his dancing prowess. Sabina admires the paintings, especially the Modigliani portrait and he tells her its history, fingersigning the occasional sentence with a teasing grin. Later Ora sits on the rug in the living room drawing pictures with her coloured crayons. He tells her he will make up a story to join up the pictures she's drawing.

"The key to understanding every story is to find yourself in it," he tells Ora. He is showing off for Sabina. But at the same time he has always enjoyed searching out sanctity in speech, finding scripture in words. He likes to think of this as the eternal Jew in him. The primacy of the word.

Eugenia has vanished into her new bedroom. Sabina tells him she is unpacking. That she likes things to be in order.

"Don't worry. She'll eventually succumb to your charm. She misses her father. She spent more time with him than Ora did and they were happier times."

"She's so self-possessed for her age. She reminds me of you more than Ora. Even her resistance to me is like you. Ora is like everything you buttoned up set free."

She gives him a how-dare-you look but it is playful.

He makes dinner that evening by the light of a kerosene lamp. He has come to like its stink when, as often, there's no electricity. It's become the smell he associates with the return of Sabina to his life. He finds a box of matches and lights the gas. Sprinkles salt on the frying potatoes. He has to discipline himself not to appear too eager to please. Sabina has changed clothes. Every new detail about her becomes an oracle. After dinner Sabina shows him photographs. The girls too enjoy looking at the photographs. Sabina's husband becomes a rival presence in the room. Max finds it incomprehensible that this man went looking for something else when he had Sabina and the two girls. Then he is delighted that she has a photograph of him. Taken in their university days, he wears a white shirt open at the collar. He is holding a cigarette in one hand, a book in the other, a satchel slung over his shoulder.

He can't help grinning to himself later in bed. At the thought he has cheated the Germans and their determination to dishonour and disenfranchise every Jew. He has never felt richer, more honoured.

23

Zanek is sitting on the workbench beside the sink in the soup kitchen. He is idly carving a piece of wood with a knife. Ala takes pleasure in watching his fingers work, the fan of bones in his hand. She likes all his limbs, the slender supple grace of his body's vocabulary. She likes the way he expands into his smile, his whole body participating. He makes her aware of a coiled sleeping energy within still waiting to be released.

Ala is helping out in a soup kitchen run by the Zionist youth movement that Zanek and Mira belong to. She is viewed with suspicion. The young set have a conspiratorial air and all switch to Hebrew when she's within listening distance. She remembers what her grandfather said, that she could be his eyes and ears. Ala doesn't subscribe to the general hostility with which the *Judenrat* is held – both the Housing Committee and Work Allocation Bureau are seen as corrupt, offering preferential treatment to a privileged few. At the same time she would never act as a spy for them.

"I shouldn't be telling you this," says Zanek.

Ala's heated blood rushes into her toes and her fingertips. "Telling me what?"

He drops the knife and stretches up his arms, joins his hands over his head, so his shirt comes loose from the waistband of his trousers and Ala catches a glimpse of his navel. "Well, Mira is very sick. She's got some kind of tumour. She might die from one day to the next. That's the prognosis."

"I'm sorry to hear that."

"I thought it might explain why she can sometimes be a little sharp-edged."

Ala feels sympathy for Mira. But a deeper current over which she has no control produces a kind of glistening in her, as if an ocean wave has wetted a seclusion in her that has never known salt water. Guilt quickly arrives with the thought she is behaving like a jackal. Always this guilt in the ghetto. Like the pool of shadow at the root of every tree. She wants to reprimand Zanek for continually flirting with her, but she also wants to ask him why he no longer taps out messages on her wall.

Life would perhaps be easier if Marcel attracted her more. Yesterday when she returned from dancing class he was drinking tea with her mother. Whenever she sees him the sensation of his hand on her bottom returns, like a rash. He asked if she still had his poem. She does, despite her revulsion. She told Lily about it and Lily laughed and said better sperm than snot and bogeys. She wanted to see it and sniffed it when Ala gave it to her. As if it was some kind of magic elixir, which, Ala supposes, it is if you think about it. He asked her if she wanted another poem. Her mother's eyes widened and then she made a joke about the young and their poetry. He made them both laugh by making fun of the two German gendarmes he's been stationed with this week at the Elektoraina gate where the Nazis have a little wooden hut and where they strip search anyone suspected of smuggling.

"Stay clear of that gate, Ala. They always take the prettiest girls in there."

There are moments when she dislikes Marcel and others when he makes her feel like he needs her.

Luna is sick. She sleeps on Ala's bed and her laboured breathing is like a heartbreaking song she has to listen to every night. She's not had any meat for weeks. Horse is often the only kind of meat available because it's so easy to smuggle. A cart arrives in the ghetto pulled by two horses; it leaves pulled only by one.

Her father too is unwell. He still hasn't recovered from the humiliation he underwent. He's suffering with trapped wind. He frequently belches, prolonged escalating eruptions that grotesquely distort his features, and his stomach undergoes raucous convulsions at the kitchen table.

Every day the Germans bring more Jews from the provinces into the ghetto; every day there are more families camping in the streets. Stripped of all their possessions and valuables, these families stand no chance of surviving. The streets are still heaped with blackened banks of snow. The mounds of filth in courtyards crusted with ice. Spring should have arrived by now, but it's becoming difficult to believe that winter isn't now the locked and everlasting condition of the ghetto. Some streets are so choked with people selling wares that it's difficult to move. Gęsia Street and parts of Leszno Street especially. The paupers shuffle about without impetus as if on a treadmill. The better off stride purposefully around them as if late for an appointment. Few women in the ghetto now wear hats and when they do there's something a bit vulgar about the spectacle, like eating cake within sight of starving children. She is pleased her mother has stopped wearing a hat. Ala is often made to feel ashamed of the fur-lined coat she wears while so many people are shivering in rags and without shoes.

The travel agency she passes every day, a source of black humour, has finally closed. She and Lily afterwards spoke about opening a fantasy travel agency where for a few zlotys they would describe in elaborate detail wondrous holiday locations. Fortune tellers and marriage bureaus on the other hand are thriving.

Yesterday Ala saw Otto, the little boy who lives in Max's building, throw about six bundles down into the street from the Aryan tram, forbidden to stop in the ghetto, as it slowed down to take a corner. The Polish policeman on board turned a blind eye. Then three children ran out of the crowd and made off with the bundles. Many of the houses in the ghetto back onto houses on the Aryan side so smuggling isn't difficult. This is the case further up Ala's road where men are continually emerging from one particular house with huge sacks full of grain, meat and all kinds of things. Ala and Lily composed a denouncement by an imaginary upstanding Polish woman witnessing all the contraband traffic. *Dear sirs, I feel it is my duty to report to you what I witnessed today. I was walking down Zlota Street minding my own business when I saw a cart pull up outside the private residence at number 27. Three subhuman men proceeded to haul countless 100 kilogram sacks into the premises. Perhaps this information will be valuable to your Honoured Selves. It's my belief this criminal trading with the subhumans is responsible for the increased cost of living for all us hard-working, law abiding Polish people.* Ala broke some ice with her Zionist companions in the soup kitchen when she recounted the imaginary denouncement her and Lily composed. It made them laugh. Except for Mira. It didn't make Mira laugh.

Ala wishes she didn't know Mira's secret. It makes her feel grubby. It makes her feel what the Nazis call all Jews, a parasite.

24

Max watches through his window the shifting clouds cover one star, reveal another star. Then he drops his eyes to a black cat strolling regally down Nowolipki Street. The only moving shadow in the entire road. He leaves the window where it's cold and gets into bed.

Every morning he wakes up to a renewed sense of wonder and excitement. Beginning with the ritual of breakfast when the sleepy sulky faces of Ora and Eugenia, smelling of peppermint, rouse an ache of protective tenderness in him. How available to harm are their young bodies and ripening personalities has already prompted in him a consuming resolve to put all his resources of love and care at their disposal. Whether these resources are sufficient to the task is a niggling concern. But his worry that he might find living in close proximity with Sabina oppressive or disillusioning has so far proved to be unfounded. The natural ease with which they converse and how frequently they bring a smile to each other's face keeps at bay any nostalgia he might have for his old solitary life. He and Sabina talk as if they only have the moment to say everything that cries out to be said. The exchange of intelligence with trust, he realises, is the music and dance of every successful relationship. A tantrum on the part of Ora sometimes tries his patience but on the whole he is cheered by how easily he has adapted to the role of surrogate husband and father. In the company of Sabina and the girls he likes himself.

Slowly Sabina is beginning to trust him with glimpses of her private self. He has seen her barefooted in her white nightdress; he has seen her with a toothbrush in her mouth, spitting out the diluted paste. He reciprocated one time by leaving his room dressed only in his shorts. She laughed and made a playfully facetious comment. He hasn't repeated the performance. He can't help asking himself if it's true, as seems to be the consensus, that men find naked female flesh so much more exciting than women find naked male flesh. He has the suspicion that women are much more interesting to men than men are to women. And wonders why this is the case. Are men and women really so different? He realises he has no idea.

He catches a glimpse of a piece of her underwear strewn about on the floor of her room or hanging to dry, a pair of lilac knickers trimmed with black lace, another pair with a tiny red bow, and he finds himself yearning for entry into the intimacy with her they betoken. Sometimes in bed, his eyes running again and again over the same line of Hebrew typescript of the book he is reading (*The War of the Jews* by Josephus Flavius), he thinks of her vagina and realises it's the gateway to the only heaven he is capable of believing in. He imagines telling her this and laughs. He thinks of it as a binding gift of earned trust. What he has to aspire to.

His biggest fear is of course the Germans. He knows how the Germans love to humiliate Jewish men. His fear is they might humiliate him in front of Sabina and her girls. That they might knock him down while Sabina watches. He suspects you don't truly know anyone until you've seen how they cope with fear. In this respect he isn't sure he knows himself. He is frightened of a fear he might not be able to cope with. And he has the suspicion that sooner or later the Germans will bring this fear to him.

Today, like all males born in 1901, it is his turn to register for work. His job of constructing the walls of the ghetto is long since over. The walls are all up now.

Max is attentive to the mood and flow of traffic on the streets. If there's a roundup in the vicinity, the weary aimless patrolling of the paupers will be animated by a panic of momentary renewed purpose. Pedestrians ask one another if the street they are making for is safe. Max is terrified the Germans will take him away from Sabina. He has more to live for now. The only drawback of Sabina's reappearance in his life.

The length of the queue outside the building in Prosta Street is disheartening. The more impoverished men are selling their places in the line to wealthier men. Two hours later he is still a long way from the door. The Jewish policemen on duty are accepting payment to move men forward in the queue. No one complains vociferously though there are mutters. In the course of the day he meets some acquaintances, including his best friend from his university years, Edek. Edek is a typesetter and an influential member of the Bund, the Jewish socialist party.

"I told you back in our youth that, sooner or later, you'd have to become political," Edek says after they hug each other. He appears youthful in a leather jacket and white turtleneck jersey. "Or are you going to relinquish all responsibility to the *Judenrat* for what happens to us? If we do that we'll all be dead within the year."

"My only formulated plan is to take pains to avoid anyone in authority. Something I've done my whole life. Do you think they're going to force all of us unemployed men into labour camps?"

"Let's say, if I were you, I'd find some officially approved post."

Max tells him about Sabina and the girls.

"Have you become man and wife?"

"No. Oddly, I'm happy with the way things are at the moment."

"Can you never work up a sense of urgency about anything?" Edek says and grins, throwing his arm around Max's shoulder.

"Maybe not."

"But you must want to. I'd argue you haven't truly known or experienced the secret life of a woman until you're on intimate terms with her sexual being. It changes the way you experience a woman."

"Perhaps that's what worries me. I don't want the way I experience her to be changed."

Edek beats his arms for warmth. "And the memory will be something to help you with dying."

"Who said anything about dying?" Max smiles.

"I remember once upon a time only when I had a fever would I momentarily ponder death. Nowadays, it creeps into my thoughts every time I close my eyes."

Max remembers times when he had winter fevers as a child. Reading comics in bed and his mother bringing him a mug of hot milk and honey. He enjoyed illness, but the snug solitude of it, the exemption from the trials and obligations of daily life it granted rather than the fussy administrations it inspired in his otherwise distant unmoved mother.

When he finally makes it to the desk he is offered a deferral for five zlotys which he pays with a huge sense of relief. However, Edek's warning haunts him.

He goes to see his brother at the *Judenrat* building.

"I need a job."

"You're more than welcome to mine," says Samuel. Max watches as a pained contortion takes place on his brother's face. It's as if a snake is slithering up from his stomach but gets caught in his throat. A prolonged volcanic belch finally emerges which disfigures Samuel's face.

"Are you all right?"

"Dante should have created a Health and Social Welfare Department for his Inferno."

Max laughs. "Seriously. Can't you ask your father-in-law? He's a person of influence here, isn't he?"

"Oh, he's charity itself as long as his magnanimity and generosity are noted and praised. Unfortunately, I don't think him helping you will get him much publicity. Anyway, I don't like asking him for favours. Why don't you ask Ala to speak to him on your behalf? It'd be better coming from her. She can twist him around her little finger. He's not very fond of me."

"Okay, I'll do that. Are you all right, Sam? You seem exhausted."

His brother stares hard at him as if he's missing a screw.

"For most of us it comes as a shock to see how aged we've become what seems like overnight. But I suppose you always did have a talent for walking around with your eyes closed. Come to think of it, you're looking incredibly well. Am I missing something? Are we living in the same period of history?"

"Sabina's moved in with me. You remember Sabina? She's got two girls and they're the most bewitching creatures."

The miracle of this, Max sees, is little more than another of the day's peripheral details for his brother. Samuel keeps pressing his thumbprints onto the glass top of his desk. "I've tried to call Mum and Dad but their number is dead. Has been for a while now. Do you ever wonder what they are going through?"

"Of course," says Max, irritated, because he wants to talk about Sabina. But then he finds his memory is walking him from the whitewashed stone-floored kitchen of his childhood home to the dining room, always icy cold in winter, to the stairs. The stairs are the most vivid feature of his old home. He remembers the stairs as a kind of bridge, leading from day into night or vice versa. Fate has always seemed to him to be more present as a possibility on stairs. He met Sabina on stairs. He can still remember which boards on the stairway of his childhood home creaked. And there was a small dark painting of a gargoyle hanging half way up where it would almost go unnoticed. There was a year when that leering contorted face insinuated itself into every shape of shadow in his bedroom at night and seemed to spawn mirages of other monsters.

"Is that painting of a gargoyle still hanging in their home?"

"What painting of a gargoyle?"

"The little painting that hung on the stairs."

"I don't know what you're talking about. Dad wouldn't have allowed any painting in his home." The look of baffled disparagement Samuel gives him unsettles Max, as if his childhood has been founded on a story he has made up.

"I guess we grew up in different homes," says Max wondering if his brother ever knew about the pornographic photograph. "With different parents," he adds.

"What do you mean by that?"

"Your memory of our father doesn't align with mine at many points."

"You speak of him as if he's already dead."

"I don't think he's dead but I don't like to think of him in this new Nazi world."

"Well, there's something we can agree on."

25

"Are these yours?"

Marcel returns from the bathroom holding a pair of her pale blue knickers he must have taken from the laundry basket.

"I can tell by the way you're blushing they are. I'm going to confiscate them. As possible evidence," he says, stuffing them in his pocket. "You shouldn't be ashamed of your intimate excretions. They're a quintessential part of your womanhood. And fundamental to the act of creation."

Ala is again baffled, incensed and frightened by his wayward interpretation of courting ritual. Sometimes, with his mean and hurtful manipulations, his infuriating provocations and cold strategic withdrawals, she feels his overriding motive is simply to make her feel small and powerless. Like the Nazis.

"Why do you pretend to be cruel?" she says.

He smiles, ignoring her question. He kneels down beside her and picks up one of her stockinged feet and begins massaging her toes.

"Do Ella and your father still have sex? Personally, I doubt it. Ella seems sexually frustrated to me. She's a woman denied her full potential. Have you noticed the way she looks at me? It's like she's undressing me with her eyes. I must say, I find older women sexually exciting."

"Why don't you go and tell her then? She's in the kitchen," she says, making her voice sound as offhand as possible.

"I understand why you're jealous of your mother. She's a very attractive woman. I don't think your father does a very good job of making her feel attractive. What's up with him anyway? Why does he wear that built-up shoe and limp?"

"He had a skiing accident. He broke his thigh bone and it didn't heal properly."

Ala has always felt responsible for his accident. It was her who goaded him to emulate his brother and ski down the highest slope. He knocked out teeth as well as breaking his leg. He tries to cover the built-up shoe by wearing trousers long in the leg. He tries to hide his false teeth by rarely opening his mouth. As if, in private, these two changes in the way he sees himself have made him feel as ugly as the Jew in the Nazi propaganda posters. Often she wants to tell him it doesn't matter that he has false teeth and wears a built-up shoe, but he never allows any opening for declarations of the heart.

Marcel continues idly playing with her feet. "Do you ever wonder about the origins of life? For example, who was the first person on earth to ever produce a flame? Somewhere, back in time, that moment exists. It's mind-boggling to me. Or who was the first woman to ever perform fellatio on a man? Where did she get the idea from? It's somehow maddening we'll never know anything about her identity or social conditions. Don't you think?"

Ala, determined not to give him the satisfaction of seeing her shocked, shakes her head in exasperation.

"So how is life in the soup kitchen? Have you cleansed your soul?"

"It makes me feel I'm being useful."

"You know there's no helping some people? The ghetto will prove the truth of Darwin's survival of the fittest theory. You need to make sure you're one of the fittest. I'm not sure frittering away energy on the feeble and damned will help. This dog stinks," he says. He scoops up the sleeping Luna and deposits her outside the room and closes the door. "Now we're alone." He sits down on her bed. Ala is suddenly fearful he will find her diary which is under the pillow. "Your virgin sheets," he says running his hands under the eiderdown and blankets.

"What you don't know about my mum, or Ella as you call her, is that she's an accomplished actress in social situations. She could probably trick Hitler into believing she admired him. In truth, she disapproves of you. She thinks of your family as common," says Ala, incensed by his callous treatment of her ailing dog and frightened by the closed door. She regrets the cruelty of her remark when she sees how hurt he is by it. She has never seen the veins on his elegant hands so raised. It isn't even true what she said. She suspects maybe that's what her mother might think but her mother likes Marcel.

"In that case I'll return to my common home," he says and leaves with her knickers in his trouser pocket.

Later she worries he might use her knickers as some kind of trophy. As evidence he has deflowered her.

26

The Adagietto from Mahler's Fifth Symphony is playing on the gramophone. Ora is sitting beside Max in the armchair. He is showing her illustrations of the paintings on the walls of the Jewish catacombs in Rome. Eugenia is downstairs with Mr Rundstein's daughter who is teaching her to embroider. Sabina is in the bathroom, washing clothes. He turns the page. "Here we have peacocks." Max performs an imitation of a peacock's call. Ora laughs, so he carries on, more stridently. Soon Sabina appears at the door with her sleeves rolled up, the blood high in her face and a smile on her lips. "What's going on here?"

"Max is pretending to be a peacock," says Ora, still giggling.

Max feels a bit embarrassed in front of Sabina, chastened. He realises she still inhibits him. Still makes him shyly cling to restricting notions of his dignity.

"We're looking for something Ora can draw," he says. He holds up the book for Sabina to see. "The Jewish tomb tunnels in Rome. Did you ever make it to Italy?"

"Never."

"Me neither."

"Well, some of us have to work," she says, turning to leave.

"Do you want some help?" he calls out.

She returns to the doorway. "I'm not sure I want you washing my underwear," she says.

He returns her smile. Something new and exciting passes between them. As if she has playfully lifted her dress a fraction and shimmied her hips. He has to fight down an erection.

"Why don't you draw this? A flying horse," he says to Ora.

"I've never seen a horse with wings."

"All the more reason to draw it. We make things true by creating them. And we all have wings. It's just they can't be seen by the human eye."

"I don't believe you. People don't have wings."

"Let's have a look, shall we?" And he starts tickling her. She squirms and wriggles and cries out for help. "You need to find those wings of yours quickly so you can fly away."

When Sabina and the girls have gone to bed he puts Ora's explosively coloured picture of the winged horse in a frame. It's so quiet outside he can hear someone cough far down the street.

Sabina appears in the doorway. She's wearing a blue cardigan over a white nightdress.

"Am I disturbing you?"

"Not at all. I was just framing Ora's drawing. I thought we could hang it up."

"I'm surprised how good you are with children. I wouldn't have thought it somehow. Ora's taken to you. It's Max this and that Max that." She sits down next to him on the sofa.

"Just a shame how much effort Eugenia puts into not ever catching my eye," he says with a smile. He is aware of her exposed collar bone, her bared calves, her naked feet. Of how little space there is between their hips and thighs.

"Yes, but you're good with her too. You never make her feel more uncomfortable than she already feels. There's no strain or falsity in the attention you give either of them."

"When I talk to you I can always sense Eugenia's attention deepening, as if I'm a telling a story. She listens so closely to everything I say. It's almost unnerving at times."

"It's nothing personal. It's the first loyalty struggle of her life. She's not sure where to place you. Or even whether to let you in."

"I understand she doesn't want to betray her father. The irony is, she's so much like you I can't see what her father has contributed to her. She even makes me feel like the ugly toad in the fairy story like you used to."

"I never made you feel like that. At least, not on purpose."

"No. You couldn't help yourself. Which almost made it worse. As if your mistrust of me was one of your most tenaciously embedded roots."

She leans forward, holding out her hands towards the burning stove. He dismisses the idea she might want him to put his arm around her to warm her up.

"I don't think I knew myself back then," she says. "I was frightened of swimming out to places where my feet wouldn't be able to touch the ground. I didn't trust myself not to drown."

"I always marvelled at how much you opened up your mind to me," he says. "I remember the intimacy we created together made me feel like we were on a night train together, effortlessly crossing a continent, everything glimpsed out of the window acquiring an air of permanence in the memory. I still feel that holds true."

"I remember whenever I left you I told myself off for being such a chatterbox. It was a new experience for me, finding someone I could talk to without censorship. You're still a very reassuring presence. Anyway, I'm not going to defend your corner with Eugenia. I think this is something she has to work through on her own. It'll be good for her to make up her own mind. You'll have to earn her trust." She smiles. The reflection of a brightening flame in the stove runs up and down the folds of her nightdress. "Can I have a cigarette?"

He lights a cigarette for her. Their hands touch. He is made aware of how influential a part shyness plays in the scripts of his body.

"I want to thank you for what you're doing. For creating this home for us. I was struggling before. I wasn't sure I had the strength to cope. Nothing frightens me more than letting my girls down."

"I love having you all here. It's made a new man of me," he says. He looks up at Modigliani's portrait of Mr Kaminski which he has moved from his bedroom. He is thankful to his former employer every day. For providing him, if inadvertently, with the resources to take care of Sabina and her girls.

"I used to think you'd be an exhausting man to love. You had a talent for ignoring ordinary reality."

"And now?"

The door creaks open. Eugenia stands at the threshold in her pyjamas. She doesn't look at him. "Are you coming to bed?"

"Yes. I'm coming now."

It's a disconcerting revelation to discover he is capable of disliking an eight year old girl, a revelation which, in turn, makes him dislike himself. He has to remind himself Eugenia is a confused and frightened little girl. For the first time he understands the key role she now plays in his fate. She has become the custodian of the portal to the future.

27

Ala carries the dead body of Luna out into the street. The limp heavy weight of her cradled in her arms. Henryk is by her side, carrying a shovel. It feels like she is holding the death of her childhood in her arms.

Behind her tears Luna is alive again. She sees her racing in the Saxony Gardens beneath the flowering chestnut trees. The shine of mischief in her eyes when she eluded all Ala's attempts to catch her. Both of them exulting in their youthful wellbeing. And how bright-eyed and excited to see her she always was when Ala returned home. How she followed her around the house, even into the bathroom where she stretched out on the tiles while Ala soaked herself in the tub. She talked to Luna about what was on her mind, to see how her ideas sounded when spoken aloud. Luna was like the threshold guardian of her secret life. Only Luna had seen her naked in recent years, only Luna had seen her cry.

At lunchtime she goes to work in the soup kitchen. To get there she has to pass from the small ghetto into the large ghetto. She sees the helmeted German gendarme who humiliated her father. Her curse has not worked. He is always humiliating Jews while they wait to be allowed to cross the street where an endless procession of armoured cars, tanks, motorised artillery, ambulances and troop trucks stream by. Today he makes the oldest men perform squat-jumps while holding bricks and then forces one Orthodox Jew to cut the beard of another with a rusty pair of shears. He now has a new habit of firing bullets up into the air to get people's attention.

"You look upset today so I've brought you a piece of candy."

The curly-haired boy is one of the group of secretive youths who usually ignore her. Ala takes the tiny slab of caramel. Her first thought is to save it for Luna. Until she remembers Luna is now buried in a wasteland beside a bombed-out building. Vapours from the hot soup thickened with lard have steamed up the windows of the large kitchen where she sits at the scored wooden table.

"My dog died in the night."

"I remember when my dog died. The world ended for three days. But my world then wasn't bounded by barbed wire and German sentries."

Ala acknowledges his attempt at sympathy with a kindly look. "Why are you all so guiltily secretive?" she then asks him.

"Are we?"

"Yes. You don't trust me. Is it because you think I'm a frivolous rich girl?"

"Actually, I've been assigned the task of finding out if you're a *Judenrat* spy."

"Should you be telling me that?"

"No." He smiles. He is wearing an unknotted blue woollen scarf, a flat back cap. "You're the granddaughter of Chaim Frydman. The king of women's underwear."

"Why are you so suspicious of the *Judenrat*? They're doing their best to help matters under impossible conditions. My father is a member of the *Judenrat*."

"We know. I'm not saying everyone who works for them is bad. But, essentially, they're lackeys of the Germans. And lots of them are corrupt. They're making private fortunes. And why have they introduced this poll tax which is the same for everyone regardless of wealth? They should be taxing the rich and helping the poor."

"People need to focus their hostility on the Germans instead of all this infighting. We're playing into the hands of the Germans by singling out our own people for blame."

"I agree with that. But I don't want to be represented by the *Judenrat.*"

Ala splays out her hand and studies her nails. A gesture she has unconsciously copied from her mother. "Do you pray? Do you believe in the power of prayer?"

"The child in me sometimes prays. The adult in me doesn't believe my prayers will be answered. I like to think of myself as a practical person. That's why I'm a Zionist. What alternative is there anymore? We've tried to integrate ourselves into the cultures of the countries in which we've lived. We've enriched these countries financially and culturally. And still we're hated. Until we have a homeland it will always be this way; we will always be seen as immigrants, used as the scapegoats for the mistakes of politicians and the frustrations of the ill-educated and impoverished. How can you not be a Zionist?"

"I feel Polish. I feel European. Deserts and rocks and orange groves and sand storms are as alien to me as the craters on the moon. Why should we be made to uproot to a distant land simply because of the religious beliefs of our ancestors? There are people in my street who converted to Catholicism a generation ago. They don't speak a word of Yiddish. There are children whose mother and father were both born Catholics but have one Jewish grandparent."

"Serves them right. I have no sympathy for people who turn their back on their heritage. Our identity isn't decided by a piece of paper."

"Well I have little sympathy for the Orthodox Jews. Why do they wear costumes instead of clothes? Why do they have to make such a spectacle of alienating themselves? They advertise themselves as the chosen ones, which is exactly what the Germans do in their uniforms." It's something of a shock to hear her mother's words come out of her mouth.

The boy walks over to the sink. She suspects she's annoyed him, but finds she wants to annoy him more.

"And I find the endless clutter of elaborate ritual laws we're supposed to perform on given days preposterous. What kind of petty-minded and exacting god would demand we don't wear shoes some days, eat only some kind of foods other days and take a close interest in our house decorations? The daily life of Jews is so given up to religious observances it's no wonder we find it so difficult to live in the same world as everyone else. The rabbis continually tell us our Lord God won't forsake us. First of all, we were told there was definite proof in the *Book of Daniel* that 1940 was the year of the Second Coming. When that didn't happen all the sacred texts were examined for evidence that 1941 is the year the Messiah will arrive. Any far-fetched wishful reasoning is conjured up to avoid confronting the reality of what's happening. It's like the Germans were sent to evict us out of cloud cuckoo land."

He stands by the sink with folded arms. "They are informed of thee, that thou teachest all the Jews which are among the gentiles to forsake Moses, saying that they ought not to circumcise their children, neither to walk after the customs."

"I recognise that."

"St. Paul. I agree there's too much literalism in how we express our faith. But this has been our way of preserving our identity as a race without a homeland. We've had to take a more personal responsibility as individuals for continuing our traditions than other races. This would change if we had a homeland. The land itself, the nation would express the things individuals now feel they have to carry about on their person. Also, all our religious symbols are a way of showing spiritual resistance to the Germans."

"Maybe," she says.

"If you had a gun could you shoot a German?"

"Yes," she says, thinking of the German who humiliated her father, the Germans who forced her to use her knickers to clean the lavatories.

"Even if there was something pleasing about his face?"

"I'm yet to see a German with anything pleasing about his face."

Ala realises for the first time he has a nice smile.

"I thought the Germans were an intelligent, cultured race," she says. "Instead, we discover they're a bunch of sadistic automatons, incapable of thinking for themselves."

"I'm not going to argue with that." He picks up an enamelled tin mug and, turning his back on her, rinses it under the tap. "Actually, I won't be arguing with you for some while."

"Why's that."

"Tomorrow I'm leaving the ghetto to work at a kibbutz in the countryside. Fresh air, fruitful labour and seeded life." He turns around, dries his hand on his trousers and offers it to her. "My name's Wolf, by the way."

She shakes his hand.

"Take care of yourself, Ala. I'll tell everyone if you're a spy then I'm a Gestapo agent."

Ala tells Lily at dance class she now has three candidates for her love.

"And you still prefer Zanek, the one you can't have?"

"Yes. And the strange thing is, he's probably the least intelligent of the three."

"What's the attraction then?"

"He has more physical grace and would make the best dance partner," she says.

28

In an ideal world Max would like to stroll through a park, sit down on a bench and give himself up to thoughts about the situation with Sabina. However, there are no parks in the ghetto, barely any trees. He is returning from the courthouse where his friend has procured for him a basket of thirty different coloured threads and some tapestry needles. It will be his gift to Eugenia. Earlier he rifled through the stacks of books for sale in a push-cart. He found a copy of *Peter Pan*. He has something for Ora too.

He is not paying attention to the outer world until he realises there's the agitation of a disturbed ants' nest in the air. He looks up to see an open SS truck, fifty yards away, using pedestrians as skittles. A bloodied old woman prostrate in the gutter is wailing. Max stands rooted to the spot as the driver, grinning, steers the truck at a little girl who trips and disappears under the chassis. There are three officers in the back of the truck lashing out at people with riding crops and whips. Max is shoved off the kerb by the panicked crowd. The basket with the embroidery threads is knocked out of his hand into the cobbled gutter. His instinct is to leave it. He's no less frightened than everyone around him. But from somewhere deep within comes a rush of stubborn pride. He will not show fear, no matter how tightly his ribcage contracts. He bends down to pick up the basket just as the truck draws level with him. The sharp pain across the back of his neck knocks the breath out of him. The world threatens to burst into flames. He looks up to see an SS man wielding a whip. An expression of scowling drugged hatred on his face. His neck stings but he's not seriously hurt. For a while though he is shaken, with rage as much as anything. His hands are trembling when he lights a cigarette.

He sees with relief the little girl has got to her feet. She is howling and a woman, presumably her mother, is hugging her. An old woman in a black shawl touches his arm and asks him if he is all right. He is moved almost to tears by her concern. As he walks homewards he finds himself wishing for a fair fight with his German assailant. For the laws of the school playground. Not since he was a child has he felt the volcanic imperative of resolving a conflict with his fists. His hand constantly goes to the cut at the back of his neck. The faint smear of blood on his fingers pleases him. Evidence of the lash laid on his neck, his first first-hand encounter with the enemy. It's like he has become an active participant in the war instead of a helpless onlooker. He can hardly wait to show his wound to Sabina. It surprises him how boyish suddenly are all his emotions.

"Now I know why Karmelicka Street is known as the Valley of Death," he says when he enters the apartment. Sabina and the girls look up at him from the sofa. He hands his gift to Eugenia. Though she tries to conceal it, he sees she is delighted with all the coloured threads. It feels to him like cheating. As if he has bought her off. *But isn't that what parenthood often consists of? And gods too are apparently placated with offerings.* He tells Ora he has a wonderful story for her, showing her the jacket of *Peter Pan*. He takes off his coat. Then he recounts what has happened to him. Sabina asks to see his wound. He turns around and feels her fingers insert themselves gently inside his jersey. Then she takes him by the hand and leads him to the bathroom. She orders him to take off his jersey and shirt. While he strips she inspects the bathroom cabinet. He watches her study the text on a screwed-up tube of ointment. She finds a sponge and a bottle of iodine. Ora has come to watch but Sabina sends her away. Her hand rests on his bare shoulder. He can't remember ever feeling so thrillingly naked. He is embarrassed by his growing erection. As if it somehow insults her. Why does he feel this? Really, it's nothing but another manifestation of the smile he feels shining in his eyes. But how mysterious women are, he thinks. If he could see evidence that she was excited by his physical proximity he would count it as the most exhilarating of compliments. The iodine stings sharply and its stink deletes the perfume of Sabina's hair. Her body brushes his at several places. He feels their bodies are whispering to each other, independent of all mental commands. Slowly reaching a new heightened agreement. Then there is the touch of her hand at the back of his neck again. He silently thanks the Nazi for granting him this moment.

"Right, that's you patched up," she says.

"Thanks," he says, shielding his lap with clenched hands.

29

Ala is crossing Leszno Street, weaving her way through rickshaws, when Marcel appears on a bicycle, ringing his bell with gay abandon. Marcel in his policeman's cap. His brightly polished high boots in which his navy-blue breeches are tucked.

"Where have you been? I've missed you," he says.

"Are you still writing poetry?" she says, a chink of ice in her eyes.

He laughs, jumping off his bicycle and letting it fall. "You mustn't take any notice of the things I do and say," he says. "Often I don't know myself what I might do or say next. I hate formality. I hate all the formulas for social intercourse." He suddenly catches sight of something of interest and swivels on his heels. "You there!" He is addressing a distraught unwashed woman pushing a handcart with a filthy mattress strapped to it. "Smile! If you don't smile, I'll fine you. You're letting down morale." He unfastens his truncheon and waves it at her. "Come on, smile! A smile has the power to strengthen resolve. But it has to come from the heart." The woman stares back at him with alarm. "You can't please some people," he says, turning to Ala.

"I don't think she speaks Polish," she says.

"I wish we could go somewhere quiet for a romantic tête-à-tête. Except there's nowhere quiet in this whole stinking ghetto."

"You look tired."

"Shall I tell you what it's like being a policeman? It's to spend most of every day quarrelling with people. Trying to make them see sense you yourself don't see. I'm not even sure I believe in law and order. Anarchy often seems to me a much better option. Then, at some point in the day, I have to bow down to some blockhead German, show him gratitude that he doesn't strike me, a pathetic craven diseased Jew who deserves less respect than an insect. Maybe he will even grant me a smile and I can go away happy that a member of the master race has recognised my humanity for a fleeting second."

"Why not just resign?"

"My father would starve to death within a month. He drives me up the wall with his mystical mumbo jumbo but I don't want to kill him."

"What about your mother? Do you get on with her?"

"My mother's dead, Ala," he says in an offhand manner. "She crossed the great divide three weeks ago."

"Why didn't you say? I'm so sorry, Marcel."

He dismisses her sympathy with a shrug. "Every day I have to touch people infested with lice. I have to refuse all their pleas. And it's all corrupt, Ala. You have no idea. Even a percentage of the rations for everyone are held back. Some people are getting very rich. Few Jews with power are kosher. There are even Jewish police who enjoy rounding up Jews for work. See it as a sport. It's human nature to take pride in one's work even if the work is contemptible. People stop thinking about what they're doing to concentrate on how well they're doing it. How's the dancing?" He performs a mock pirouette.

"Madame is composing a choreography. We're going to perform it. But what about your mother? You must be grieving." She touches his arm. "You mustn't cut yourself off from your true emotions, Marcel."

"I wish I knew what a true emotion is. Talking of dancing, look at that," he says, pointing down to the gutter.

"What is it?"

He makes theatre of gaping wide-eyed at her naivety.

"That's a condom with sex sauce inside," he says.

Ala pulls a disgusted face. The thought of that slimed sordid thing inside her horrifies her.

"That's the life force we're looking at," he says and performs another mock pirouette.

30

In the courtyard a man is playing a waltz on his violin for Ora to dance to. She skips and twirls around him, as if blown by an exuberant wind. Max pauses to watch, leaning on his shovel. Many of the children in the ghetto have been sobered, hardened and prematurely aged by the inescapable hardships of their plight. Ora though still manages to create imaginary worlds where she is happy. Max has almost finished digging a pit. Young Jacob, Otto's brother, is helping him. Mr Rundstein is tending to the vegetables he has planted. His wife died of typhus three days ago. Max attended the funeral, walking behind the coffin in the handcart, through the ghetto gate and into the Jewish cemetery with its budding trees and leaning blackened stones. Since then lice have begun to obsess him. He checks his clothes every night before getting into bed. He has stopped giving coins to beggars. He avoids the poorest districts of the ghetto. He tells himself this new fastidiousness is out of concern for Ora and Eugenia.

The pit he's digging will be filled with sand for the children to play in. The sand stolen from a German building site near the Jewish cemetery. When the pit is finished it falls a long way short of how he imagined it.

"It looks more like an accident of nature than an adventure playground," he says to Sabina.

"As I recall, for children, accidents of nature were often the best adventure playgrounds."

"I'm off to meet my niece now."

"Make sure you come home."

Max meets Ala outside the theatre where her dance classes are held. She introduces him to her teacher. Max is struck by how much self-possession the woman radiates despite her threadbare clothes.

"You're the one who taught Ala sign language for the deaf," she says. Her voice is refined and a little hoarse. Her dark intelligent eyes unsettlingly penetrating.

Max fingersigns yes, this is indeed the case.

"I've asked her to extend her vocabulary. I have this idea of incorporating some of the gestures in a choreography. Or else perhaps you would like to attend rehearsals and contribute some ideas?"

"I could do that," says Max, noticing the clasp of her handbag is broken. "I miss not using my hands to talk."

When Madame has left, Max and Ala walk together towards Leszno Street where there is a café that offers real coffee and pastries. There are tall blackened buildings with balconies on either side. Every so often a bad odour, like the slimed water flowers have rotted in.

"Real coffee. Let's be decadent for half an hour," he says.

"Will you really attend rehearsals?"

"I don't see why not," he says, catching a glimpse of women rifling through a heap of rubbish in a courtyard.

"I'm glad you finally met Madame. I think she liked you. It's a shame you're betrothed."

"She's not married?"

"No. Do you think she's attractive?"

"Too severe for my taste. I like a woman to have a playful side."

"She's stunning when she lets her hair down. But she so rarely does. Have you and Sabina tied the knot yet?"

"We tie each other in countless knots," says Max, with a broad smile. They pass a brick stove on a corner where a woman in a black headscarf is heating a pan of water. A notice says she is offering soup for forty groszy.

"You seem very youthful. There's an inner glow about you."

"Yes. I can see in the dark these days."

"Do you remember the day when you first told me about Sabina?"

"Of course. The day war broke out."

"I never thought for one moment she'd come back to you. You made her sound like a beautiful ghost."

"I've got Hitler to thank for reuniting us. It worries me sometimes that our reunion owes its kindling to a force of evil. What about you. How are you bearing up? I'm sorry about Luna. My favourite dog in the world."

Ala begins to cry. He puts his arm around her.

"But you're dancing again. That's good."

"Sometimes it seems like the height of frivolity. With all this going on outside," she says, nodding towards a woman staggering on a broken heel who walks back and forth muttering to herself.

"You mustn't think like that. The Germans are trying to make everything we've achieved and learned and aspire to disappear. Don't let them."

"Okay. If you say so."

"You have a lovely voice, Ala."

"Thank you."

"I mean it. You really do. I was thinking earlier how well Sabina's voice suits her. There's something about a person's voice that can tell you everything you need to know about them. The notes they hit and the rhythms they use and the accompanying arrivals of breath bring up their treasures from the deep. Or their demons."

"Does Sabina have any demons?"

He doesn't have time to reply. There is a sudden panic on the street. A surge of movement towards the alleys and courtyards. Soon two German military vehicles pull up. Before Max can flee a German gendarme is prodding a rifle into his stomach. His first thought is to remember what Sabina said to him earlier. *Make sure you come home.*

Ala watches helplessly as her uncle is marched to one of the trucks. German soldiers are rounding up all the men they see. There's the echoing crack of a rifle shot. Ala turns to see a woman sprawled on the cobbles, blood bubbling out of her neck, her eyes rolling back. There's another crack. Like the snap of a whip close to her ear. This time the victim is a barefooted child with festering sores on his face and arms. There are screams and wailing. She sees it is one particular soldier with bullish thighs who is doing all the shooting. She stands transfixed, watching him scan the street for his next victim. Then Marcel appears on his bicycle. He jumps off, lets it fall and pulls her into the doorway of a pharmacy.

"That's Frankenstein doing all the killing," he says.

She has heard about Frankenstein. Everyone has. He has the reputation of being the most psychopathic of all the Germans in the ghetto.

"They've taken my uncle Max."

"They're rounding up five thousand men for work in labour camps. Does he have a work certificate?"

"I don't think so. Can you do anything?"

She watches the trucks drive off with their prey.

"I can try. He's the good-looking older man who was on our work detail, right? I liked him. He's the kind of man who would never run for a tram or get annoyed if someone shoved in front of him in a queue."

"Be serious, Marcel. It's my fault he's here. I asked him to meet me today."

"I'll do my best. Can't make any promises though. Meet me tonight at ten o'clock."

"Curfew is at nine," she says.

"So what? Let's live dangerously. Let's defy the German scum. Be a cat. You remind me of a cat sometimes. Your toes are like sweet little paws. I'll book a table. It's only a ten-minute walk from your house. 38 Sienna, on the corner with Sosinowa. You don't have to pass any checkpoints."

"Isn't that some kind of brothel?"

He laughs. "Why would I take you to a brothel? There's music and people who aren't cowering at the feet of the Germans. And I'll let you know if I succeed in getting your uncle off the hook."

After dinner, Ala carries her shoes in her hands as she creeps past the bedroom of her parents. She can hear her mother talking but not what she is saying. Her voice sounds querulous. She dares not close the apartment door for fear of the noise the latch will make when it slides back into place. She leaves it ajar.

The almost full moon looks sinister. Like a Nazi spotlight. It's the first time the moon has ever appeared to Ala as her enemy. She keeps close to the walls, seeking to dissolve her outline in shadow. She feels like a newcomer to night. It's been an age since she was outdoors in the moonlight. The night inhabits her, streaming all its mystery through her arteries, quickening her eyes. She passes the house eviscerated by a bomb during the German siege of Warsaw. Several refugee families have made it their home. Luna is buried in the backyard. She still carries her shoes, walking in her stockinged feet. The far-reaching silence is like a stage she has walked on to. She has rarely felt so illicitly conspicuous. Her fraught body is poised for some sudden explosive noise.

She finds it is like a childhood dare to press the buzzer. An enormous bald-headed man holds open the door with a conspiratorial smile. She walks into a smoky red mist. She realises with a flush of embarrassment she is still holding her shoes. The long room is crowded with people in high spirits. Every table is occupied. On a small stage, behind two brick archways, a young girl is singing an American song to the accompaniment of an accordion played by a man who shows a gold tooth every time he grins. Three couples are dancing. She sees no sign of Marcel. Two lipsticked girls in gossamer dresses look at her with disdain. One of them keeps piling up her hair and letting it fall. Ala is forced to acknowledge how far she still is from the ease and entitlement of sophisticated adulthood. At a table a group of men are playing cards with jewels as stakes. Everything is louder than is natural. The clink of glasses, the scraping of chairs, the raised theatrical voices.

The first thing she notices about the man approaching her is that he's not wearing a Star of David armband.

"Hello. Have you come for a job?" He speaks Polish with a German accent and his hair glistens with grease.

"No. I'm here to meet a friend," she says.

"And who's this friend?" he asks.

She doesn't like his ingratiating smile. "Marcel," she says.

"The policeman?"

She nods.

"I haven't seen him tonight. Are you his girlfriend?"

"No."

"I have to say you're just what I'm looking for," he says. "So pretty. Are you a baptised Jew?"

"No."

"You keep saying no." The ingratiating smile again. "Perhaps you'll change your mind about the job. Think it over. Here's my card."

The door opens. Ala has never been so relieved to see Marcel.

"Did you save Max?"

"What were you doing talking to him? He's a Gestapo agent."

"He offered me a job."

"Of course he did. He's looking for hostesses for the parties he arranges. Gestapo men do deals with rich Jews at these parties. It's not a bad job. There's no threat to your virtue. You don't have to do anything beyond serve drinks and show off what a good figure you have. Pays well and you can go shopping the next day and bring back into the ghetto whatever you want. The gendarmes are all paid to turn a blind eye."

"Are you suggesting I become a whore for the Third Reich?"

Marcel throws back his head and makes a strange noise that might be laughter. "Let me get you a drink." He summons a waitress. She is dressed in black stockings and a black apron skirt with crossover straps at the back. Her mouth is sticky with glistening red lipstick.

"Well? Did you save him?"

Marcel summons a contrite expression which is so obviously a piece of vaudeville that Ala feels sure he is going to tell her Max is safe.

"I couldn't save him, Ala. I tried but it wasn't possible. Unless I had taken his place myself. That's what my commanding officer told me."

Ala begins sobbing. He moves his chair beside hers and pulls her head down onto his shoulder. Then he makes her drink the vodka he has ordered for her. She has never tasted vodka before.

"Why don't you stay with me tonight? I don't like seeing you so upset. They have a room upstairs they'll let us use."

"He's going to die in that camp, isn't he?"

"Not necessarily. Come on, let's go upstairs, away from this racket."

"I can't, Marcel. My mother…"

"Tell her the Germans raided the place. It's happened more than once. They arrive and rob everyone. Invent a story. I can provide some details from the last raid. Wouldn't it be nice to sleep in each other's arms? I won't ask for anything more. And it'll be dangerous to go home now. I've heard there are German patrols out tonight. You don't want to end up in the prison."

Ala is always attracted to any idea of defying her mother. Even though she knows it's petty and unhealthy this competitive antagonism she feels towards her. *Why can't we be friends?* She has never asked her mother this. Yet, secretly, it's what she most longs for.

The bedroom upstairs makes Ala feel unclean. The flowered wallpaper is peeling at the joins. There's a mirror missing its glass, the framed black wood streaked with white paint. The floorboards moan underfoot and are bare except for a thread-bare rug mapped with cigarette burns by the big bed. There's a stopped marble clock on the bedside table. Marcel goes into the bathroom, telling her she can get ready for bed without him ogling her. Ala sits on the bed's stained eiderdown. She keeps thinking of returning home. It's the thought of a midnight German patrol that stops her.

"Coming," he sings out. The door opens and Marcel stands before her stark naked.

"What are you doing?"

"I can't sleep unless I'm naked. What's all the fuss?" he says, stretching his arms high above his head. Then he performs a little jig. "It's only a body. Everyone has one. You've seen enough naked corpses. At least my body is alive." He sits down close beside her.

"If you're going to behave like this I'm going home," she says.

"The Germans are turning us into peasants," he says. "What do we have left except the immediate pleasures? Why don't you be nice to me." He takes her hand and moves it down to his erection. She struggles to release her fingers from his tight grip. "Take the tip between two knuckles and press it in a rocking motion as if you're squeezing the oil from an olive."

She frees her hand. "Why do you pretend you haven't got a heart? There must be more to you than just vanity. And yet I feel like I can only please or wound your vanity. You can't be reached on any deeper level."

"I'm just mucking about," he says. He puts his hands on his head and looks down admiringly at his naked body. "I don't mean to upset you, Ala. Surely you know that's the last thing on my mind. Though sometimes I have to admit I'm not sure what's going to happen next in my mind. At the end of the day, it's just another part of my body, like this finger," he says, wagging his index finger at her. "Or haven't you ever seen an erect penis before? I suppose if that's the case it must appear a bit exotic and slightly unnerving. He likes you though, Ala. Look how much he likes you. He's saying hello."

"Stop doing that."

"Doing what?"

"Making it twitch."

"You're fascinated though, aren't you? And your blood has heated up. There's a warm prickling flush all over your body. Seeing as you don't have any demands of your own why not submit to mine? That's what most women do."

"I'm upset because of what's happened to my uncle and you're being mean and obscene."

"Well, I've got something else to say about him."

"What?" she says.

"I did manage to save him. I replaced him with some hapless man I caught passing by. If he was so stupid to walk past lines of condemned men he deserved to be condemned himself."

She punches his chest. "You're cruel."

"I thought you'd be grateful. Uncle Max wasn't very grateful either. In fact, I was tempted to shove him back into the line."

32

Max is haunted by the haggard face of the man seized to replace him. He had no idea of Marcel's intentions until he marched the man over and brusquely shoved Max from his place in the line of condemned frightened men outside the labour office at the corner of Leszno and Zelazna. The man was carrying a loaf of bread and one of his shoes was untied. Max exchanged eye contact with him and was made to feel deeply ashamed of himself. He feels sure the man is a father of young children. And now his children will wait in vain for his return home. *This man has had to forfeit his life in order to save mine.* Because everyone knows no one survives these labour camps where the inmates are systematically worked and starved to death. Max cannot reconcile himself to this bargain.

He hears distant gunshots as he walks down the deserted Ogrodowa Street. And then the motor of an approaching vehicle. He slips into an alley which eventually opens up a vista of a succession of broken stone arches leading into a courtyard. Soon he is lost. At one point he comes face to face with a naked pink mannequin. Her hands held up and a welcoming smile sewn onto her face. It takes him more than an hour to get home, by which time it is past curfew. He can't help feeling gratified by the concern on Sabina's face when he enters the apartment. She doesn't hug him though. No breach of the forbidden zone between their bodies takes place. Ora is excited to show him a new drawing she's finished. For her no thread of continuity has been broken. Eugenia, looking exceptionally pretty in a polka-dot dress, gives him a shy glance.

Max is withdrawn and silently troubled all night. Not even Ora can lighten his mood.

After Sabina has put the girls to bed she comes to join him in the living room.

"You ought to know how worried Eugenia was about you. She asked me three times if I thought you were safe when you didn't come home. It would appear her diffidence towards you is all a ploy. She's using all her female guile to reel you in."

Max smiles. This does make him feel better. But his need to punish himself is like a physical ache which won't be appeased with heartening words.

"That man taken in my place will die so I can live. I feel sick with guilt. I keep seeing his face. We exchanged glances. His eyes burnt into me."

"You don't know he will die. And who's to say you won't be shot or herded off to a camp tomorrow. I love how you make yourself responsible for the wellbeing of me and the girls. But you can't make yourself responsible for every poor soul in the ghetto. If you do that we will lose you. And I don't want to lose you. Every day on the streets I see people having full-blooded arguments. Everyone seems to forget it's the Germans that are responsible for our captivity. Why do we go on blaming each other and ourselves? If that man dies the Germans will have killed him, not you."

Max takes the last cigarette from his packet and lights it. "We can share it," he says.

"You recently told me I used to make you feel like the ugly toad in the fairy story. What you didn't understand was that I was always frightened of your private thoughts. I could sense how critical and exacting and incisive they were and I was frightened of you turning them on me. I felt like I wouldn't be able to stand up to them. I also guessed you would turn them on yourself at times. Tonight, you're letting me see that part of you. The hermit crab in you. This kind of judicial introspection is debilitating. The enemy of action. It also ends up being selfish.

We need you to be inspiring. We can't indulge pity at a time like this. I understand you're upset and it's to your credit you empathise so deeply with that man. But it's not your fault. Feel sympathy for him by all means but don't beat yourself up in the process."

"I wish wise words could rewire the circuit along which we think," he says, handing her the cigarette. "You're right of course."

"For me it's simple. I want to live to see the day when that loathsome German uniform is reduced to filth and tatters and the smug hateful expression is wiped off every German face. I want to see their noses rubbed in the inhumane cruelty of what they've done. You should want that too. Finer feelings have to play second fiddle for the time being. And with that, I'm going to bed," she says, handing him back the cigarette.

"I finally got to see Frankenstein today," he calls out. "I'd put his IQ at about twenty-five."

"That's better," she calls back.

33

A little girl with closely cropped hair has appeared in the doorway. She stands holding a toy animal, staring wide-eyed at the dancers. Madame marches over to the girl, orders her to leave and forcefully shuts the door behind her. Ala wishes Madame didn't always have to be so harsh. Didn't always repel every current of human warmth. The jealousy with which she guards her body is forbidding; Ala can't imagine her sharing its intimacies with another human being. Sometimes she wonders what Madame does when she isn't dancing. It's as if she vaporises like breath on a mirror when Ala tries to imagine her at home.

The choreography Madame has created has no musical score as yet.

"I know someone who might be able to help, Madame," says Ala. She has forgiven Marcel, even laughed with Lily about his behaviour in the squalid room. Eventually he took her home and she enjoyed the challenge of creeping back into her home without waking her parents. And to his credit he did rescue Max from the German work detail. "He's a brilliant pianist and composes his own pieces. They're beautiful."

"Send him to me," she says.

Madame now performs the most extended passage yet from her new choreography. There is nothing that excites Ala more than the marvel of watching her teacher discipline some new articulation of beauty and grace out of her body. How she fuses together into eloquent locution mesmerising quirks of movement Ala has never before seen the human body make. It's like she's mapping out some brave new glistening world of human possibility. Ala's body follows in imagination. Her muscles memorising every leap, twist, fall and recovery. The percussive slap and squeak of Madame's bare feet on the boards excites Ala like a call to adventure. Her body strains with the eagerness to get out on the dancefloor and emulate Madame's movements. She is twirling now across the stage like an accelerated flamenco dancer. This dance, Ala realises with excitement, is going to demand new things of her body, unlock new energies. A slow sinuous wave passes through Madame's body as she flops in slow motion down to the floor like a puppet whose strings have been cut and then uses her forehead to lift herself back up. Ala detects a defiant message to the Germans in this gesture. Now she is curled up on the floor, now stretched out on her back like a welcoming lover. She lifts up her hips, spine arched, head thrown back, and finishes by performing a scuttling movement on her heels and fingers, like a crab. Ala marvels at the primitive grace of this. It's her most expressive choreography to date. Ala suspects it will also be her most moving and beautiful. In every passage she feels there is something both lost and gained, something remembered and something else anticipated. It's like she's made a flowing visual narrative of the unseen poetic truths of our inner life.

Madame is short tempered with praise. No one applauds or compliments her. She sits down at the front of the auditorium with a black ledger in her lap. Her face glistens with a film of sweat.

"Now I want you all to perform a short, improvised piece and finish with the sequence I have just shown you. Remember, it's your differences, your individuality that excite me. I don't want a company of slavish automatons."

There are seven dancers now in the company. Five girls and two boys. Madame orders Lily to take the floor. Ala suspects Madame is auditioning them for the part of Cassandra, the working title of her new choreography. And she suspects she is in competition with Lily for the lead role. And therefore she can't help wanting Lily to fail. She is able to justify this meanness with the conviction that it matters more to her than it does to Lily. She wants to play the part of Cassandra more than she has ever wanted anything.

Lily technically isn't the best dancer but she possesses an emotional eloquence Ala feels she herself lacks. Lily is less inhibited. She does the crab crawl well, but there's little that's imaginatively creative about her improvised sequence. Madame puts on her spectacles and writes something down in her black book. Then she takes off her spectacles before looking up again.

The second ballerina is Hanka. Hanka dances better than Ala expected.

Now it is Ala's turn. She summons into her mind the German who pulled her hair while making her clean the lavatory with her knickers. It is to his ghost she performs, speeded up, her favourite gestures of the sign language Max has taught her. She has chosen the various hand gestures purely for their aesthetic charge but in her mind she is dramatizing defiance to the German, to all Germans. Then she dances what Madame has shown her. Her entire body is aglow as she dances. She pictures a taut yet flexible web of connected filaments along which light flickers and flows.

"Two, three, four. Open up, Ala."

A splinter has embedded itself in her bare foot. It becomes so painful she has to stop.

"I'm not impressed, Ala. You have to dance through your pain. To dance is to push through resistance," Madame says.

Ala has to fight back the tears. Nothing galls her more than to disappoint Madame.

34

They have just proposed a lunchtime toast to the Russians. The news that the Germans and the Russians are now at war has electrified the ghetto. Many are now predicting they will be liberated before the end of the year.

"It amazes me how quickly news spreads through the ghetto," says Sabina. "Who needs radios?"

"I suppose we ought to remember that not all news has any foundation in truth," says Edek's wife. "Do you remember the day word went around English agents had assassinated Hitler? For about three hours the entire ghetto was ready to organise a huge party."

"This is the best soup I've had all month," Adam tells Sabina.

"You need to compliment Max, not me," she says.

There's a look of annoyance on Adam's face that he quickly hides. Adam is an uninvited friend of Edek's. Max is troubled by Adam's dislike of him. It was evident the moment they shook hands. He has an irritating habit of whistling the same refrain from a dance tune when left out of a conversation. He reminds Max of a salesman. All his talk part of a campaign to impress Sabina. Earlier Max helped Sabina air the bedding. They laughed together in the sun at the open window. He wants nothing more than to be alone with her again. He is not happy to share her.

"And here's to the English," says Adam, recovering his good spirits and turning his attention back to Sabina. "It gives me a deep sense of satisfaction down in my solar plexus every time I hear another German city has been bombed."

"Tell everyone what you saw in our courtyard yesterday," says Edek to his wife.

"Oh, that was so macabre. The children were playing a game with a corpse. Daring each other to touch it. It was an old man with a rabbinical beard. He was stripped down to his underpants. His legs stiff and wide apart. I should have put an end to the game but I was fascinated. I couldn't believe what I was seeing. You could tell by the hurried way they touched him that some of the younger children expected him to suddenly come back to life and frighten them. Then an older boy knelt down and began tickling the dead man's feet. They all hooted with nervous laughter."

"We saw a man leading a cow down Zamenhof Street yesterday, didn't we?" says Sabina.

"Yes. I drew a picture of it," says Ora.

"And tomorrow we're going to the children's library to see if we can find a book about cows, aren't we?"

Ora nods with solemnity.

"All the children in the street were fascinated by this cow, as if it was a being from another planet. A crowd of kids followed it down the street. I was tempted to join them."

"I had a favourite cow when I was growing up. I could always recognise her in the herd. She had the kindest eyes I've ever seen. I used to talk to her," says Max.

"I've never heard that story before," says Sabina.

"One thing I've learned about people is that they tell lies about the hidden parts of their lives," says Adam. "Not that I don't believe in your cow," he adds, locking eyes with Max for a moment.

"My cow would be glad to hear that," says Max.

"Max has built a sandpit for the children in the courtyard," says Sabina.

"They need food, not sandpits," says Adam, with a disdainful smile for Max and then a cheeky one for Sabina.

Max hasn't the will or inclination to argue with this man

despite his incessant competitive provocation. He has lost count of how many times Adam has interrupted or belittled him today. There is a bite in his eyes every time he looks across at Max. He repeatedly runs a practised acquisitive gaze over Sabina's figure. Not caring if Max sees. Probably hoping he does. He tries not to mind that Sabina is evidently enjoying Adam's attention. He is conscious of how different they are as men. Adam is roguish, vigorous, tactile, attributes he himself lacks. It's hard to imagine Adam, insistent, incessant as he is, unsuccessful in love.

"Anyway, enough of this depressing talk," says Adam. "Let's embrace the moment. What do you say, Ora? No thinking about gloomy things from now until you go to bed."

"I don't go to bed at lunchtime."

"Neither shall you if I can get my way."

"That's dangerous," says Edek, "because in my experience Adam always gets his way."

Max withdraws further back into himself. The hermit crab, as Sabina called it. He begins to hear only his own thoughts. When he hasn't spoken for ten minutes he feels his silence has become like an obtrusive argument. And the longer he remains silent the harder it becomes for him to speak, as if any word from him now will have the effect of shattering glass.

After lunch they play records on the gramophone. Adam dances Sabina around the room. He grips her firmly at the waist as if at any moment he might lift up her up into the air. Max watches him stop to look at himself in the mirror and then point at the Modigliani portrait and laugh, inviting Sabina to share the wit of whatever dismissive comment he has made. Max feels an affinity with Eugenia who refuses all Adam's overtures to dance with him. Ora isn't so fussy. And when Max finds himself becoming irritated even with Ora he decides he has to get out. He tells himself that he is over-sensitive because he is still haunted by the man who replaced him in the labour detail. He invents an excuse that he has to deliver the money collected by the house committee to the two poor families who live in his courtyard. In truth he performed this task two days ago.

"I won't be long," he says, without taking his jacket.

There are four Polish policemen in the courtyard, *blues* as they are called. Max is seized by the arm. The sun is warm on the back of his neck.

"Employment certificate," the man barks at Max.

"I don't have one but…"

"No *ausweis* then it's work detail for you."

"I've got money upstairs," he says. The man, a fellow Pole, strikes him with his truncheon. It's not a venomous blow but shame at what he's doing, Max senses, has curdled into anger. The man has a partially closed right eye, as if he is squinting, as if he is unable to quite believe what he sees. He escorts Max outside to a waiting rickshaw. Max sits down on the makeshift wooden boards; the policeman sits in his lap. "So you can't escape," the man says, with a hint of humour. Max finds himself smiling, a reflex action; politeness is branded so deeply into his nature. Another policeman does the same thing with the man he has caught. The rickshaw driver struggles to pedal his vehicle into steady motion. Pedestrians pause to stare and Max feels the full force of the horror of what is happening to him in the sympathy he reads in their eyes. Then his inner turmoil blinds him to everything outside his head until they pass the quarantine centre where a long line of ragged and frightened refugees spills out onto the road. It occurs to him that Sabina, oblivious, might be dancing at this moment. The cruelty of this thought only intensifies his disbelief at what is happening.

He is taken to the detention centre at Leszno Street from where Marcel rescued him. Some of the captured men are paying the Jewish and Polish policemen fifty zlotys for their freedom. It maddens him that he left the apartment without his wallet. That this one small careless act has cost him his freedom and maybe his life. The remaining men are mostly downtrodden, impoverished, refugees from the provinces. He realises how right Sabina was to reproach him for overindulging his conscience. He knows now it was essentially posturing on his part.

If he had fifty zlotys he would pay for his release again without a second thought, even it meant condemning another man to take his place. That he is back at this place seems a kind of divine justice. He struggles to accept he won't be returning home to Sabina and the girls. He sees the blistered brown paint of his front door, the familiar lock responding to his latchkey through a mist of painful enchantment as if it already belongs to another era. He can't believe they will eat dinner tonight without him. Can't believe she will no longer be within reach, had he only been brave enough to reach out his hand and touch her.

He and his fellow prisoners are made to stand in ranks, three abreast, and counted. A Polish police official then addresses them, tells them that conditions in the camp will be better than those in the ghetto. Max is tempted to smile at the outrageous absurdity of this assurance. They are locked in a warehouse all night, without water, without food. Sabina is laughing with her girls in the dream Max remembers. He wakes aching with the discovery of how much he will miss being a witness to the love, intelligence and play that Sabina bestows on her girls. He has no will to enter this new day.

At dawn they are marched out of the ghetto. It is surreal to be back in the normal world. Every detail simultaneously insistent and remote as ordinarily detail is experienced in dreams. The envy he feels for the few people walking the streets at leisure, sitting in trams, going to work or market, as if today is merely another unexceptional day. The sight of the river with its promises of freedom pains him. It is a beautiful morning. A film of peace over the water as if it's a realm outside of time. For a moment he forgets his hunger, his thirst. He is consumed by longing. The longing to simply walk away. To return to his home. It is stupefying, maddening, to be forbidden such a simple harmless wish.

A car pulls up and two German soldiers and an SS officer jump out, yelling at everyone to run. They are made to run all the way to the Eastern Railroad station. It's strange to see

German soldiers running alongside Jews. Like the beginning of the breakdown of the barrier between the proud disdainful overlords and the minions. Anyone who falls with exhaustion is beaten. Max discovers he is fitter than he thought. Despite his thirst, his hunger, the stitch in his side, the tightening heaviness in his legs, he runs without faltering. At the station they are taken to a warehouse and each given two shovels. Someone gives voice to what they are all thinking. "You don't think they're going to make us dig our own graves?"

A passenger train arrives with two freight cars at the rear. There is no room to sit in the freight car. Everyone stands, falling into each other at every curve, every sudden screeching and hissing of the brakes. Through the slits in the boards he catches glimpses of the awakening countryside. The names of the stations they stop at are called out. With each new name he is further away from Sabina. She constantly tugs at him, as if at the other end of an invisible rope.

The door of the car is slid open. The station sign says Szymanow. He has never been here but knows it isn't too far from Warsaw. Thoughts of escape continually haunt and then taunt him with their implausibility. They are made to line up on the platform and counted again by Polish police. There are no Germans.

They walk most of the day. The Polish guards ride in two horse-driven carts commandeered from local farmers. When they reach a village, they are allowed to rest. Some of the prisoners buy bread from the villagers. Max has no money to buy bread.

The barracks are newly constructed. At the sight of the surrounding barbed wire he feels something cold and pitiless enter him. He is allocated a bunk by the man designated as group leader. A top bunk in the three-tiered shelving. A thin spray of straw serving as a mattress. In the barracks he sees the man who replaced him, who has been on his conscience. He already looks five years older than he did three days ago.

Max learns they are to dig a canal several kilometres long. The evening meal is macaroni and potatoes. He searches for a face he likes, someone with whom he might strike up a friendship. It worries him that he appears more intelligent, better educated than virtually everyone he sees. He knows the Nazis don't like intellect. He knows the kind of men assigned to guard duty are generally coarse small-minded types empowered by fascism and delighted to have the chance of humiliating their social and intellectual superiors. He tries to imagine what Sabina is thinking and feeling at this moment. To what extent she is missing and worrying about him. Less than twenty-four hours ago they had stood shoulder to shoulder airing her bedding out of the open window of her bedroom. His skin prickles from head to toe with longing. There is no consolation to be found in any of his thoughts.

"Don't be too disheartened. In my experience you tall thin nervous types fare better with this kind of life than more athletic types."

The man who says this to Max has a missing front tooth and a fresh gash on his forehead.

Book Two

1942

1

Madame has completed the choreography for Cassandra and re-hearsals have begun. She has studied the way the hungry move, the destitute, the mentally ill. She has incorporated stylised interpretations of some of these movements into the choreography. They are eerily beautiful and moving. Ala is happy she has been chosen to dance the leading role, even if Madame's manner of telling her wasn't very flattering – she said she had to make do with slim pickings. She has told Ala not to cut her hair. In one section Madame makes her speed up a sequence of conventional ballet moves and impart to them a calibration of madness.

There's another section where Ala uses the sign language Max taught her. Her uncle is still missing. This new winter is ferocious and Ala fears for his safety. One day she went to see Sabina. She was struck by her beauty - her elegant bone structure, her long legs, beautiful hands and small bust. Her mouth a little large for her face. Ala understands why her uncle found it difficult to forget her. Even though she didn't strike Ala as a very sexual woman. (Ala has lately begun evaluating the erotic charge of every female she meets, guessing the degree of inhibition to which they succumb.) During her visit a man arrived at the apartment bearing gifts – cocoa and white rolls and canned pineapples. Ala immediately felt indignant on Max's behalf and took a dislike to this man introduced to her as Adam. She didn't like the easy way he made himself at home in her uncle's apartment. It was clear he was courting Sabina; not so clear to what degree Sabina was encouraging him. Ala could tell Sabina's eldest daughter didn't like him which suggested he was a frequent visitor.

Ala and Lily, early for rehearsal, are changing into their leotards backstage. They are talking about sex. Ala tells Lily the memory of Marcel's erection is more attractive than it was at the time.

"Sometimes I wish now I had touched it," she says and flushes and then laughs at herself and her shyness. Ala sometimes sees Marcel's erection in her mind's eye at the most inopportune moments, like yesterday when she was having tea with her grandmother. It occurred to her that her grandmother had touched an erect penis. She didn't know why this should be so shocking. She is finding that more and more often a moment now suddenly becomes sexual. Sex seems to be a clandestine but ubiquitous pulse in the air that promises shelter from the persecutions of time and space, a liberation of the body and spirit to which she is denied.

"But you'd rather have Zanek's excited member in your hands," teases Lily.

"I'm curious what happens when…you know."

"It spurts out with surprising force," Lily tells her with her most mischievous smile. "One time it hit me in the eye and gummed my eyelashes together. It smells like bleach. Thankfully it doesn't taste of it."

"You've tasted it?"

"Henryk likes me to do it with my mouth."

"Stop it!" Ala pulls a face and laughs.

"And he does the same with me. It always makes me uncomfortable. I can't help feeling it must smell bad down there or taste of urine."

"Do you think the war is making us coarse?"

"What do you mean?"

"I can't imagine our mothers talking like this."

"Don't you believe it," says Lily.

"Aren't you worried about getting pregnant?"

"We try to be careful."

"How?" Ala shivers at the remembrance of the sordid slimed thing Marcel pointed out to her in the gutter.

"When he's getting close he pulls out and I finish it with my hands. You wouldn't believe how sticky that stuff is! And how hot it is for a moment on your skin and then quickly turns cold."

"Madame would be furious if you got pregnant."

"I'm not like you. I don't live to make Madame happy," says Lily and they both laugh because Lily is only teasing even if what she said is true.

"Most women make themselves too dependent on praise from men. But I can't imagine any man's praise meaning as much to me as Madame's," says Ala.

"Unless you're a lesbian," says Lily, grinning and covering her breasts protectively with her hands, "that will change. Just wait and see."

"You think you're so superior to me now just because you've done it and I haven't."

"I am superior," says Lily, kissing Ala on the forehead.

The theatre is a long low narrow building with a slightly raised stage, musty fraying velvet curtains and about a hundred greasy folding red velvet seats. It smells of neglect and rising damp. Ala is startled to see Marcel when she steps out onto the stage. His policeman's cap perched on the piano. He hands her a folded piece of paper. She opens it.

I want to put both my hands inside Madame's knickers. Do you think she would have a fit?

PS. Be nice to me today. I'm feeling shy.

It turns out Madame approves of the compositions Marcel has played for her. And of his haunting voice singing out words that have no meaning until he sings them. Madame tells him to improvise while they run through sections of the dance. It's clear Marcel has managed to charm her. When, at one point, he mischievously plays an improvised nursery rhyme at a particularly dramatic moment in the choreography Madame smiles instead of scolding him.

Ala finds she is more nervous than usual with Marcel in the room. Three times Madame gets angry with her, reducing her, in feeling, to a clumsy child. Soon though the music he plays takes her deeper into the heart of the choreography, making it more full-bodied and her participation in it more rhythmically consuming. She becomes aware of how this dance is adding new depths to her understanding of the human condition. Never before, she feels, has Madame so artfully exalted the possibilities of the female body in movement. Ala jokes afterwards with Marcel and the two male dancers that the female body has a more extensive vocabulary of grace than the male body. Everyone feels elated. There's the sense Marcel's musical accompaniment has added a vital missing dimension.

After the rehearsal Ala stands with Marcel outside the theatre. A light flurry of snow is falling. The crystals melt on the peak of his cap. Woodsmoke billows out of a basement grating by Ala's feet.

"Your armband is getting rather grubby, darling," says Marcel. "I might have to fine you."

"You were wonderful," she says. "It's amazing how well suited your compositions are to the choreography." She moves a step away from him, fearing he will get a whiff of her sweat and especially her sex which often exudes a peaty, salty odour when she dances.

"One thing's certain, every wealthy male pervert in the ghetto will come flocking to see your bare legs," he says. He stamps down on a thin plate of blackened ice. "I have to say though at times you shocked me. Who would have guessed there's a wild animal lurking behind those sweet foal eyes of yours?"

"A foal *is* a wild animal."

"Touché," he says.

"How's your father? I heard he was ill." Typhus has returned to the ghetto. The new epidemic is more widespread than before. Not surprising as they say more than 50,000 refugees have arrived in the ghetto in the past few months, with no belongings and nowhere to live. They are the first victims of starvation, hypothermia and typhus.

"The high and mighty looks after him. He's indestructible. I'll probably meet my maker before he does. One of us is in the wrong and we're back to bickering who that might be."

"I think you enjoy being in the wrong."

"I don't like sanctimonious self-satisfied people, if that's what you mean. At least when I misbehave I know I'm in the wrong." He digs his hands into his coat pocket and produces a handful of jewellery which he holds out to her in an open palm. "Take your pick, darling," he says.

"Where did you get all this?"

"Perks of the job," he says, his breath smoking in the fading light.

There's a barefooted old woman sitting on a wall on the opposite side of the street. Ala watches her try and fail to get to her feet. It's as if her shadow is about to engulf her and she is trying in vain to escape it.

"Don't you feel ashamed?" she says.

"All the time. I feel ashamed of us Jews as a race. Of our passive fatalism, of our mindless belief in the imminent intervention of a fairy story divine protector, of our elders and their policy of appeasement. No wonder the Germans hold us in such contempt. The only Jews I admire are the smugglers and criminals. At least they show some initiative. At least they disobey the Germans. To collude with them gives me a smidgen of satisfaction in this cesspit of slavish submission. And here you are, prancing about on a stage, desperately trying to incur *Madame's* favour, while Rome burns."

"We're doing our best to keep people's spirits up. Why can't you see that?"

"Why does she call herself *Madame* anyway? Her egotism gets on my nerves. She thinks she's the Führer. I'm only surprised she doesn't make us all click our heels and salute when she enters the room."

"Stop it, Marcel."

"I like your resistance to me better than your acquiescence. Perhaps this is why I'd rather slide my thing into your bottom than into your vagina."

Ala stares at him, open mouthed, wide-eyed. For the first time she thinks he really might be insane. Then she snatches the jewellery from his hand and tosses it into the kerb.

2

Black specks dance inside his eyes and his head swims. Max is climbing the stairs of his building. The dizzying vacuum inside his body is preventing him from feeling any appropriate emotion. The joy of homecoming, the excitement of seeing Sabina again both withheld from him by the anarchy of his metabolism.

Sabina opens the door as he is leaning breathless against the wall, three steps from the landing. She is like something illuminated in searing detail by a lightning flash in a world of darkness. Eugenia and Ora are standing behind her. Ora, he sees, has her fingers jammed into her mouth. For a moment they all stare down at him as if he might vanish were they to cease concentrating all their attention on him.

"Go back inside, girls," says Sabina. "And Eugenia, get a glass of water." Then she walks down to him and takes his hand. She leads him up the stairs. Eugenia appears with a glass of water. Max manages to smile as she hands it to him. He gulps it down in the blink of an eye and begins spluttering. Sabina leads him to the bathroom. Sits him down on the rim of the tub.

"First we need to get these clothes off you and burn them. And then I'm going to kill the lice in your hair. We've still got some kerosene. Hopefully the gas is working." She runs the hot tap of the bath and steam soon begins to issue from the jet of water. She kneels down before him. He stares down at her beautiful hands prising off his ruined shoes with a gentleness that seems like a miracle after all the brutality ugly hands have inflicted on him in recent months. She tells him to lift up his arms and pulls

145

the filthy shirt over his head. She unties the piece of string that holds up his trousers, pops open the buttons and makes him raise his hips so she can slide them down. He is embarrassed by his filthy shorts, but she pulls them down too with no fuss. Now he is embarrassed by the ugliness of his unmuscled boyish body, the lice bites in his armpits and on his thighs, which bleed whenever he scratches them. She gathers up his clothes and takes them out to the stove. It's bewildering he cannot appreciate the wonder of what has just happened. That she has undressed him. Never would he have been able to imagine such a longed-for event happening in this dutiful, almost impersonal manner. He is tempted to say something about the shortcomings of the human imagination.

"When are you going to say something?" she asks and smiles.

"I can't quite believe you're here," he says. "I can't quite believe I'm here." There's a ghostly whistling in his ears that makes his voice sound like it no longer belongs to him.

"Well, you are and I'm very happy you are. Now, let's kill these lice."

After he has got into the bath and while Sabina is kneading the heated kerosene through his hair Max gets an erection despite the scalding of his scalp. That his exhausted battered and brittle body can find the energy for excitement in any form is stupefying. He is mortified by it. He tries to will this inappropriate indiscretion into passive obedience, but despite the black scum on the surface of the water, he knows she has seen it and behind his exhaustion and difficulty of focus he cannot remember ever being so ashamed in his life. He wants her to know it has nothing to do with anything he's thinking. He's not sure why it should cause him such shame. It is completely mysterious to him what Sabina thinks about it. He is grateful to her for ignoring it. She is telling him she has run out of money, that she has sold her wedding ring and her two favourite evening dresses.

"I've never in my life felt so exposed and frightened as when I stood in the street selling my clothes. Genia was mortified with shame but Ora enjoyed it and keeps asking when we can do it again. Everything I wear she now suggests we sell. Did you know you're supposed to pay for a licence to sell anything on the street? A Jewish policeman wanted to fine me five zlotys. I told him if I had five zlotys I wouldn't be selling my clothes. My aunt and uncle have been helping out but they're not much better off than I am. Your friend Adam has been helping out a little with food parcels."

His erection withers. It's like it has spoken his feeling of irritation out loud. He wants to complain that Adam is no friend of his, but he knows if he shows any sign of being ready to engage in conversation she will want to know about the camp and he doesn't want to talk about that. Then everything begins to blur again.

When she starts scrubbing the back of his neck and then his armpits he is dimly conscious of the wonder of what's happening again. This is an unmapped realm of experience for him, as divorced from precedent as had been the brutality and deprivation of the life in the camp. This is like an otherworldly reward for having survived an otherworldly horror.

The next thing Max remembers is Eugenia standing shyly by his bed, holding a bowl from which steam rises. He rubs his eyes and sits up.

"How long have I been asleep?"

"Two whole days," she says. "You had a fever." She hands him the bowl of soup.

"Did you make this?"

"I helped," she says. Her eyes downcast while she grips her elbows behind her back.

"It's lovely to see you again, Genia," he says.

She shifts her weight from one foot to another. "I'll go now," she says.

"Thank you."

He realises he has no recollection of getting out of the bath. The last thing he remembers is Sabina applying cream to his blistered lips. While he eats the soup he tries to picture Sabina dressing his inert body in the pyjamas he is now wearing. He pictures her hands tying the cord around his waist, fastening all the buttons. He has a smile on his face when Sabina enters the room and sits down on his bed.

"Did you put my pyjamas on?"

"Not only that, I carried you. You weigh less than Eugenia."

"I feel like you could blow me out of the window if you took a deep breath and puffed hard," he says. With a healthy flush of embarrassment, he recalls his erection in the bath. He isn't sure how he feels about her now having knowledge of this most private part of him. He finds himself hoping she doesn't think less of him. Then he looks at her left hand. The wedding ring is absent. "I wasn't hallucinating when you told me you had sold your wedding ring. Look, I've got some savings. Under the rug over there, there's a loose floorboard. From now on, what's mine is yours." He begins getting out of bed. She puts her hand on his chest.

"You stay where you are. We can sort that out later. Thank you."

He is glad she doesn't make a fuss about accepting his money. Especially when he remembers how difficult it once was to get her to accept anything he offered. It's a sign of change in their relationship. A lifting of prohibition on her part.

"Your niece came to see us a couple of times," she says. "She's very protective of you."

"What do you mean?"

"Adam was visiting the first time she came. I think she thought I had moved him in. If looks could kill Adam and I would both now be in the Jewish cemetery."

"I don't like him much. Perhaps because his appearance coincided with my abduction."

"Was it awful, that camp?"

"Half the inmates died. I don't know how I survived. I guess I've got a tougher constitution than I thought. Someone there believed naturally thin people cope with starvation better. There was a Catholic priest in the village who gave sermons urging the congregation to provide us with as much help as possible. Which they did by slipping us food on the sly. That's what saved those of us who survived."

"How did you get out?"

"Believe it or not, a good German came to our rescue. I'm not sure who he was but he visited the camp and declared the conditions were inhumane. Within two weeks the camp was shut down. The work we did was completely useless. What's been happening in the ghetto?"

"The girls go to school. A proper school. The Germans now allow elementary schools. We all had to give the Germans our furs. The Jewish police delivered the bulletin to the janitor of every building, then it was announced over the loudspeakers. We were also expected to pay a tax for the privilege of gifting our fur to the Germans. I gave mine to Otto downstairs. He went into business selling furs on the other side of the wall."

"I'm glad Otto is thriving."

"Many have taken heart from the implication that the Germans are struggling to clothe their army in Russia. Napoleon was the most frequently cited name in the ghetto for a while. *War and Peace* the most popular novel. What else? I sometimes have a craving for wild strawberries with sweetened fresh cream. And Frankenstein has been murdering children."

"I'd forgotten about him."

"Tell me I shouldn't feel guilty taking your money."

"Just pretend you're my wife." He becomes shy as soon as the words leave his mouth. As if she can read in the air how much he wishes this was true.

"I feel calmer with you around."

"Yes, I'm a good sedative."

"No. I don't mean it like that. You quicken and clarify my thoughts. Make me feel more decisive. I often found things getting on top of me when you were away."

"The thought of getting back to you and your girls was my main incentive for surviving in that camp. I can't tell you how much strength you gave me."

3

It's like a wind is standing still for a moment. Ala is able to rejoice at the sight of all her favourite people gathered together in the enclosed courtyard. Madame is teaching a group of children, including Ora and Eugenia, dance moves to the accompaniment of a string quartet. Max is talking to her mother. Sabina is laughing with her father. Marcel is sitting on a broken wall with Henryk and Lily. Zanek is here without Mira and looks especially handsome today in an open-necked shirt. For a moment she feels like she is surveying the scene from a distance in time, as if it has acquired the lasting significance of a moment of history.

The house committee in Ala's building have pooled together many of their books and set up a lending library, all proceeds of which will go to the soup kitchen where she works. To inaugurate the library a party is being held in the courtyard. The entrance fee is ten zlotys which entitles the guests to a membership card. It was advertised in the magazine of Dr Korczak's orphanage and the famous doctor is in attendance. The biggest surprise though is that Marcel has brought his father who is a pious heavily bearded Jew in gabardine. Ala is aware of Zanek watching as Marcel walks over to her with his father. The absence of Mira dares her to hope they might have broken up. Even though she knows it's more likely her rival has turned up her nose at the prospect of fraternising with a community of people she views as privileged and spoilt.

"This is my father," says Marcel, "who is feeling better about everything because a rabbi told him that the Jews will be released from captivity on the next Rash Hashanah. The rabbi saw it in a dream, didn't he, Father?"

"Marcel likes to tease me," he says, taking Ala's proffered hand. For a while they exchange pleasantries. Ala is polite, on her guard. Everything outward about Marcel's father proclaims his Jewishness. Ala can't help feeling he views her with disapproval, as if she is another of Sienna Street's baptised Jews. He has heavy lidded eyes and a permanent squint, as if he is looking through a keyhole. Marcel hasn't inherited his good looks from his father.

Marcel's father tells a story about a friend of his who has been caught up in an extortion scheme. He doesn't tell the story very well. His point is that Jews are cheating other Jews out of large sums of money. Then he tells another story.

"I've recently heard about a Jewish carpenter who constructs elaborate well-disguised hiding places for valuables in Jewish homes. The problem is that a few days after he completes his work members of the Gestapo arrive at the house, head straight to the concealed vault and carry off all the valuables. Why does this man feel no loyalty to his own race? And why does his betrayal cause us so much pain? No doubt his argument would be he's looking after his immediate family. This is one question life in the ghetto throws up. To what degree should we extend our loyalty from our loved ones to our race as a whole?"

"This is a diplomatically edited version of what my father thinks," says Marcel. "Truth is, he gets more righteously indignant about rich Jewish women than he does about the Germans. He thinks it's a sign of moral decline that Jewish women still wear lipstick and laugh. Isn't that true, Father?"

"I do think the rich could do more for the poor, yes."

"But why is it always the women you rant about? To you it's a heinous crime that a woman wearing smart clothes can walk past a starving child without emptying her purse or walk past a corpse without breaking stride. You called them inhuman. A disgrace to the Jewish nation. What difference would it make if they didn't wear lipstick or even if they emptied their purses? Look around you. These are the women who according to you are inhuman. Ala's mother over there is wearing lipstick. Most of the refugees the Germans dumped on us were living corpses. They brought them here to humiliate and shame us. To make us feel still more helpless. And you gleefully play into their hands. Misdirecting all your anger at your own people. The people who deserve the most respect in the ghetto are the criminals, the smugglers. German law is barbaric, sadistic. Under that law we should all be criminals. So what if these smugglers get rich? They bring raw materials into the ghetto. There are workshops now, manufacturing goods. Shoes, toys, furniture, surrogate honey, candy, artificial flowers, pyjamas, windows. The list is endless. And they bring food into the ghetto."

"Food for the rich."

"Everything filters down. There's a reason some people are rich. It usually means they are possessed of more initiative."

"Or simply that they're more selfish."

"We're all selfish at heart. Every human being spends ninety-nine percent of his time thinking of himself. It's a delusion to believe otherwise. And nobody listens. Not really. You've never listened to me. And I've stopped listening to you."

"That's not fair," he says smiling apologetically for Ala. "I'm listening to you now."

"The Germans have enslaved and humiliated us, rich and poor alike. All these fine distinctions you make are so inappropriate in these times they are vulgar. They're going to kill us all sooner or later. That's the Nazi plan."

"Now you're being melodramatic," he says, smiling again at Ala. "Essentially, my view is it's now so important for all of us to unite under our faith."

"Says my father who's losing another few drops of his faith every day."

"That isn't true. Of course, it's hit me hard your mother is no longer with us…"

"I'm sorry," says Ala.

"Yes, I still find myself turning to her with something I want to say. The shock repeats itself over and over that she's no longer here."

Marcel moves a step away and ostentatiously yawns.

"I'll leave you two young people alone. Very nice to meet you, Ala."

Ala is touched by his humility.

"He's got his precious writings in that parcel he's holding. He belongs to some kind of secret society of scribes. His chosen subject this week has been the behaviour of Jewish women in the ghetto. Except almost everything he writes is warped by his own sentimentality. I loathe sentimentality. It forces one to become cynical."

"Why are you so hard on him?"

"He deserves it. He treated my mother like a slave and a social inferior. He wore her out with all his dictums and regimentation. I used to worship my father. Nothing mattered to me as much as his attention and approval. I memorised whole pages of Hebrew writings to please him. I had the Psalms of David at my beck and call for a whole year. He barely took any notice. He was always up on a higher plane than my mother and me. We were like household utensils. One day I used a Torah scroll as a plaything for our dog. I'd chuck it and the dog would fly off to retrieve it. I thought he'd beat me when he saw but he didn't. He simply looked at me, shook his head and buried his head in another of his holy books."

"He seemed fond of you to me," says Ala.

"He spouted off all that nonsense about loyalty to humiliate me in front of you."

Marcel's provocative buffeting impulse is absent today. He appears kinder, more emotionally engaged, more vulnerable. What if this is the closest to love I ever get? she thinks.

The hired fortune teller wears a lilac turban. There is sorcery in her heavily mascaraed eyes. Numerous bracelets jangle on her bony wrists. She is introduced to the crowd in the courtyard by an assistant. A middle-aged man in a tightly fitting brown suit with nicotine stained fingers. He walks out into the audience and stands beside Zanek.

"Signora Agata, I want you to tell us what colour shorts this strapping young male is wearing beneath his trousers."

"Navy blue but he could do with a new pair," says Signora Agata in a husky midnight voice. Her dark gypsy face remains inflexible and humourless.

"Would you care to show us if Signora Agata is correct, young man?"

Zanek fishes inside his trousers and tugs up a section of fabric above his waistband. Everyone applauds. Everyone turns to each other with an O-shaped mouth.

Signora Agata does the same trick with a woman and her brassiere. Identifies the colour and fabric correctly.

"What colour are you wearing underneath your clothes?" Marcel asks.

"Let's wait and see if Signora Agata can guess," says Ala.

"When will the war end?" calls out someone.

"For many of you it will end later this year," says Signora Agata. There is a widening of eyes and scattered applause. She now walks among the audience. Ala is both relieved and disappointed when she passes her and Marcel by. She has taken Sabina's left hand and is studying her palm.

"You will face a difficult decision. You will choose both the right and the wrong option."

Her next victim is Ala's father. He looks mortified with embarrassment. He hates being the centre of attention.

"I see a train journey," says the fortune teller.

"That concludes the performance. If anyone wants a private consultation with Signora Agata you can find us at Leszno 46," says the assistant.

Everyone applauds.

"What a load of mumbo jumbo," says Marcel.

"She knew the colour of Zanek's shorts."

"Who is he anyway?"

Ala looks about for Zanek but can't see him anywhere. He comes and goes, flits in and out of her life like a reminder of the flighty nature of all excitement.

4

The miracle is the change in Eugenia. She now looks him in the eye when she talks to him and smiles when he makes a joke. She has begun asking him questions. Yesterday he spent an hour teaching her to waltz and foxtrot. Today, as they climb the wooden steps of the new bridge over Chlodna Street, Eugenia, in her green coat, takes his hand. An accolade that touches him deeply.

A horse and cart clatters past when they are in Leszno Street. Max receives a pungent draught of heat from the animal's flanks. Then he notices Adam with a big grin on his flushed face. He lifts Ora high into the air and she squeals with delight. Then he lifts Sabina in a bear hug. The greeting he offers Max is as heartily insincere as he can make it. It occurs to Max that his dislike of Adam is more visceral than his dislike of the Germans. During the ensuing conversation he learns they all went to see a puppet performance of Gulliver's Travels together while he was away in the camp. He steels himself not to slip down into the cesspit of his jealousy.

He soon curses himself for comparing Adam unfavourably to the Nazis. Feels superstitiously as if his thought has summoned the two German gendarmes in a rickshaw who now appear in the street. Max recognises the boy pedalling the vehicle as one of Ala's Zionist friends. His expression, unseen by his two passengers who are grinning like imbeciles at each other with their pistols unholstered, is a complex chemistry of fear, apology and loathing. Pedestrians part in a panic on either side of them, like alarmed birds taking flight.

The first shot shatters the glass of a window. Then the screaming begins. The next shot knocks a young Hasidic Jew off his feet. The trembling of his legs revealing he is still alive. Then another bullet rips off part of the face of a beggar child. Max protects Eugenia with his body. Fear stirring the roots of his hair. In the panic Ora is tripped and begins to cry. Max watches Sabina take her by the hand and pull her to her feet. Then he sees one of the Germans is taking aim at her. The wide vista of the street narrows to the electrified sightline between the barrel of the gun and Sabina's back. Max thinks about shouting at the German to attract his attention. He hears the noise his voice will make and sees himself become the target of the gun as if these things are happening. But the German has changed his mind. He aims his gun at an old woman in rags.

"Your beauty saved your life today," he tells Sabina later when the girls have been put to bed. In truth, he has been worried all evening by what he perceives as a failure of courage on his part. He didn't act, didn't shout when Sabina's life was in danger.

"What do you mean?"

"One of those murderers took aim at you for a moment, then changed his mind and shot an old woman instead. I saw the moment he changed his mind in his eyes. But I shouldn't have told you that. Sorry," he says, mortified by the trembling that has overcome her body.

"If anything happens to me," she says when she has regained composure, "you have to promise me you will look after my girls."

She places her hand on his chest. He looks down at her fingers splayed over his blue jersey.

"I know I don't have to ask that. Sorry," she says.

The smell of fried onions from dinner lingers in the room which is lit by two candles. The flames sometimes twist and jump and then settle again. In the distance, tunnelling through the darkness, a motor can be heard, sinister in the vast stillness and silence of the night outside. Only when it expires does he realise how much tension it brought into the room. He watches Sabina smooth her skirt over her thighs.

"I've got this idea Adam is a portent of evil," he says. "Every time he shows up in my life something awful happens soon after." He braces himself, dreading the answer to the question that has pushed its way to the forefront of his mind. "You're attracted to him, aren't you?"

"A little. But against my will. He gets under my skin. I suppose there's something attractive about a man who has the magnetism to lead you astray. Life, generally, is so predictably plotted out. Or it was before the Germans arrived. Sometimes, as a woman, you can't help wanting a man to wrestle your arms to your sides."

He lights a cigarette, wondering why he can't get under her skin, why it would never occur to him to wrestle her arms to her sides, except in play. He hands her the cigarette. "I can't stand his cosy clammy way of putting his hands on everything female," he says. His smile makes her smile back. "Would he ever take the trouble to understand you?"

"Do I want to be understood?"

"I don't know. Do you?"

"Sometimes I like the way you *mis*understand me," she says and smiles. All complexity momentarily wiped from her face. "It reminds me of how exciting secrets and mischief are."

He likes this comment of hers. The jersey he wears feels suddenly warm, as if a cat has been sleeping on it.

"In our courtship days my husband liked to think he understood me, but he simply magnified what he liked and saw nothing else; then, when he had me under contract, he began magnifying everything he didn't like about me and saw nothing else."

Max suspects this is a doubt she has about him but feels it would be presumptuous to protest his innocence. He himself doesn't know how he would react if the sight of her bared breasts became a commonplace occurrence.

"I've had to change some of my ideas about you," he says, not wanting to talk about Adam or her husband anymore. "For one thing, you inhabit your body much more now. When I first knew you your mind and your body seemed like two separate entities that weren't on very intimate terms. Thought didn't seem to become feeling in you. You always seemed to me like someone who didn't quite feel real to yourself. It frustrated me that I failed to make you real to yourself. Of course that might have simply been the effect I had on you."

"It was. To some extent. I used to think of you as a house without a roof. Magical at night but wholly impractical during the day. I also felt you had made me part of your integrity. And that frightened me. But it's also true that when I became a mother I found my feet. I lived more happily in my body. It was a constant marvel how much physical wellbeing I took from mothering. How much more overwhelming my feelings became and I surprised myself by taking the force of those feelings in my stride."

His hand makes contact with her fingers as he takes back the nearly finished cigarette. Her thigh is a whisper away from brushing his own thigh. He wonders what she would do if he kissed her. The memory of his failure all those years ago to entice her into a physical union overwhelms him with shyness. He assumes someone like Adam gives little thought to imaginary consequences. He hates how much weight he himself gives to imaginary consequences.

5

Ala is avoiding the brown puddles between the cobbles. Sometimes she can't help spontaneously enacting some fragment from Madame's choreography. Even when she is out on the streets. It's like letting her body talk. A calling back of herself into her body. She exalts in the strength in her legs, the suppleness in her shoulders and spine, the poise in her hips, the grace in the soles of her feet, the circulation of the blood in her veins, the muscle flow in her body. She now makes a windmill motion of her arms. Feeling herself dissolve into the exuberance of the disciplined gesture. Then she sees Mira. Mira's features are set in a determined scowl as she approaches.

Two days ago Ala and her mother had tea with Zanek's mother. Ala was disappointed Zanek wasn't there. Bored and impatient to leave. Then he arrived with Mira. He told everyone he had just become an accessory to a crime. That two Germans had ordered him to drive them to Leszno Street and there shot people from the back of his rickshaw. Everyone sought to quell his distress. Mira didn't say a word but emitted hostility. Ala could sense her mother was taking a growing dislike to Zanek's girlfriend. And when the atmosphere in the room lightened and everyone was able to laugh again she let off her firecracker.

"Talking of the Gestapo, your son and my daughter seem to share some secret code." Her mother smiled and took another sip of her tea.

Ala's blood ran cold. The previous night Zanek had tapped out another message on her bedroom wall. This time she replied.

She had no idea what it was he was saying, but it didn't much matter to her. It's the strip-searching excitement of his intimate proximity she cherishes.

"What do you mean?" asked Zanek's mother.

"They have some kind of midnight tryst. They tap out messages on the wall that separates them. The pair of them keep my husband and me awake at night with their infernal wall tapping."

Mira got up and left the room. Ala dared a glance at Zanek before he followed her out. Irrationally, she felt she had betrayed him. Dread that Mira would return and create a scene kept her picking at her clothes, digging her nails into flesh.

"I can't believe you did that. Why did you do that?" Ala asked her mother when they left the apartment. Her anger was further fuelled by her own stupidity – why had it not occurred to her that her mother might be listening?

"Because the supercilious conceit of that girl was getting on my nerves. Who does she think she is with her superior airs? Anyway, actions have consequences. It's time you learned this."

"He started it. He'll never talk to me again now."

Ala hasn't found the courage to go to work at the soup kitchen since. She is nervous every time she leaves her house for fear of bumping into Zanek or Mira. Now, seeing Mira marching militantly towards her, she feels sick with apprehension.

"Stay away from my boyfriend," Mira says. She stares Ala in the eye for a moment and then slaps Ala's face. Then she walks away. Ala stands rooted to the spot. People stare at her. She steels herself not to cry.

"Mira doesn't like you, does she?"

Ala doesn't know where Chaya has appeared from. Chaya is Wolf's sister. She too works at the soup kitchen.

"It's not your fault Zanek likes you. And you can't really blame Mira for being jealous. I'd be jealous too."

Ala manages to return her smile.

"I think he'd leave her if she didn't have some mysterious hold over him. And I think she knows it. Do you like him?"

"I don't know."

"Which means yes. Everyone wants to fall in love, don't they? Love seems the only way of rising above all of this."

"Are you in love?"

"Maybe. But he never notices me."

Chaya is only sixteen. She has been a member of Hashomer Hatzair for a year. She has told Ala they have become more her family than her blood relatives. She sleeps in the dormitory above the soup kitchen so as to participate in the lectures and group singing and camaraderie. The last time they spoke, when they were washing up together in the kitchen, she told Ala about a lecture on astronomy she attended. "It was wonderful to escape up to the stars for two hours," she said.

"Why don't you come with me? I'm going to see two orphaned children. I've got some food for them." She holds up the grubby canvas bag she holds.

They enter the courtyard of a bleak tenement in Mila Street. The stench makes Ala gag. There is a huge mound of trash underneath one of the three-storey buildings and the frozen sewage is beginning to thaw. Many of the windows are missing glass, covered instead with rags. Ala realises how much of her time she has been living in mirrors.

"How do people manage to live like this?" she says and immediately regrets the naïve crassness of her remark.

"I know," says Chaya, without judgement.

On the staircase many of the treads are missing and there are few bannisters; those that remain wobble in their sockets when any pressure is applied to them.

The two children Chaya has come to see are huddled together in a corner. The room has no furniture. The little boy has a shaved head and slits for eyes. The girl is startlingly beautiful. She wears a knitted filthy white hat. Ala immediately feels a connection with her. As if she has always been a secret waiting at the back of her mind.

"Where are their parents?"

"Both dead. A man was looking after them, but he's now in hospital with typhus."

"I'm going to take them home with me. They can't live like this."

Chaya raises an eyebrow.

Ala kneels down in front of the girl. "Will you let me help you and your brother?"

The girl looks at her blankly.

"They don't speak Polish; only Yiddish."

Ala changes language. She feels more unknown to herself in Yiddish. As if what she says has less consequence. She finds out their names are Luba and Henryk.

"My brother is called Henryk," she says. It seems another sign she has been summoned to help these two children. She promises Luba a hot bath and hot food for her and her brother. She sees they do not have a single toy between them. Nothing to hold onto.

The girl gives a frightened nod.

"Wait here," she tells Chaya. "I'll go hire a rickshaw."

The rickshaw driver she waves down wears a white shirt with the sleeves rolled up and has a toothbrush moustache that reminds Ala of Hitler. For a moment she is struck by doubt. Suspicious of her motive even, as if she is trying to stave off the idea that she's a privileged rich girl with no connection to the harsh realities of the ghetto. And then there's the prospect of facing her mother. She realises with a start how intimidated she is by her mother's authority. It's a secret that she keeps from herself.

It is her first time in a rickshaw. She feels embarrassed to begin with, as if she is putting her privilege on display. Then she achieves a separation from her surroundings and sees them with a fresh eye. She is struck simultaneously by the squalor and the bustling enterprise. She tries to engage Luba in conversation and then spends the last part of the journey bracing herself for the opposition she expects from her mother.

"What have we here?" Her mother stands with her hands on her hips, blocking the doorway.

Ala is surprised there is no anger. She sees a flash of amusement in her mother's eyes but also warmth and compassion. She is made to feel guilty for underestimating her mother.

"I thought we could give them a bath and some hot food. Then tomorrow or maybe later in the week take them to Dr Korczak's orphanage. In the meantime, they can sleep in my bed. I'll sleep on the sofa. We got a rickshaw here, didn't we? And the man pedalling had a moustache like Hitler's. Why would any Jewish man want Adolf Hitler's moustache?"

"I'll run a bath; you go and ask Mrs Schulman if she can spare some clean clothes for them."

6

Max is woken by the feeling that something is awry in the composition of the darkness in his bedroom. A displacement in the air shifting shadows. At first, his pulse beginning to race, he has the crazy notion it is the ghost of his old flatmate, Zelig. Come to settle some mysterious old score. Then a whisper of Sabina's heated perfume reaches him.

"Where are you?" she says.

Her voice moving towards him in the darkness seems too much to ask for.

"I'm here," he says. The mattress tilts as she sits down on the bed. To his eyes she is nothing more than scented outline, a thicker swell of shadow. A current of cold air shivers down the length of him as she pulls back the sheet and blanket. Then a blast of perfumed heat as she slides in beside him. Her hand finds his navel and her fingers splay out, extending their domain. He scoops her to him by the small of her back and can feel her breath on his mouth. Her toes find his feet and his calves. The contact makes his blood sing. The world, set to a new music, is rising and falling beneath him. That's his feeling, as if he is riding ever higher on a swing.

"I've changed my mind about you," she says.

"I haven't changed my mind about you."

And finally he is kissing her. The soft sweetness of her lips. The beat of her pulse within his own body. He realises how long he has been waiting for this moment; how viscerally connected to it he has been since the moment she entered his life. He is tempted to obey the rush of blood and dramatise an urgent devouring passion, as lovestruck men make a habit of doing in the movies. Frenetically press his desire on her, as if they have only one brief moment to consummate it. But this is not his overriding desire. First, he wants to feed into her all the tenderness and thanksgiving in his fingertips. He wants to write a thank you letter to her and to life on her skin. His hands now like an animal exploring and outlining new territory. To touch her willing naked body is to feel the full force of how much happiness she is capable of bestowing on him. It's a power that might frighten him if he felt he possessed it. But he still can't quite believe this is happening.

Shadows are visible on the wall by the time they make love. When he enters her and feels her muscle tighten around him and the slippery suction of her belly and breasts and has the smell of her musk in his nostrils he feels himself in possession of the acceptance and trust he has always craved. He reminds himself to vary the angle and calibration of his thrusts. Then he is mindful of the humiliation of orgasming too quickly. He screws shut his eyes and drives his mind from the moment. Soon he has achieved the necessary act of separation, his mind as if divorced from his body, tutoring it from a distance. That he can achieve the detachment to mentor his performance is a further facet of the marvel of what is taking place tonight.

She falls asleep afterwards. He feels like the body beside him which he sees in all its exposed privacy for the first time might belong to some beautiful wild creature that doesn't usually allow itself to be touched by human hands, like a lioness, and that he has won its trust is the kind of miracle he hasn't believed in since childhood. He still fears she might change her mind. But he is relieved there has been no disappointment. No hint of recoil now that he has got what he has always wanted. A little sadness perhaps that an era is over. That he has entered a new stage of his life. The only thing that bothers him is that not once did she touch his erection. As if it was an ugly part of him she didn't want to acknowledge. He once had a brief affair with a woman who was bewitched by that part of his body, who lavished attention on it, ravished, apparently, more by the act of giving pleasure than receiving it. He remembers her as possessing a wild look in her eyes while making love, as if caught in a storm, drenched and windswept. He wonders if this signifies Sabina's feeling for him is less consuming, that there is less humility in it. This woman though had eventually become cloyingly submissive in the day to day world. He realises he can't imagine Sabina venturing so far outside of herself and neither can he imagine her ever becoming submissive. Which is a good thing, he tells himself. Most of all though he wishes she would wake up and he could seek out new hidden places in her, unknown even to her, bring them to life with his touch, experience again the gasps and tremors of her arousal.

Dawn is breaking outside the window. Morning has come too soon. Lozenges of golden light liquefying the wall opposite. His memory supplies the absence of birdsong and scent of refreshed soil. It's easy to believe at this time of day that there exists a world immune to change behind the surface of things. Easier to forget about the Nazis too.

"If life were normal I'd probably go shopping today," she says, releasing him from the press of her groin. "I might treat myself to two new pairs of silk stockings. And maybe I'd buy you a new pair of shorts."

"I've got Hitler and his racial policies to thank for this night. Should I feel grateful to him?"

"Once I dreamed I slapped him in the face. He was a pathetic little man in my dream. But let's not talk about Hitler."

Max wants to discuss with her how this moment has come about. He wants to know all the steps that led her to walk into his bedroom in the middle of the night. He wants to trace the present moment back to its origins. He wants to understand better the history of this new world. He sits up to get a cigarette. He catches sight of her naked foot outside the covers. Wonder returns to him at the realisation he can now hold her bare feet in his hands whenever he wants. That he has permission to roam the entirety of her.

"Edek once told me a man hasn't truly known or experienced the secret life of a woman until he's on intimate terms with her sexual being. He thinks this knowledge changes the way you experience a woman."

"And what do you think?"

"The closer I get to you the more attractive you become," he says. "At one point I thought how disbelieving my younger self would have been had he been told this night awaited him seventeen years down the line."

"No more disbelieving than my younger self," she says.

7

The Germans have turned off the electricity. Yet another reason, Ala thinks, for hating them. The backstage area is lit by carbide lamps and candles, as is the auditorium. Marcel still hasn't arrived. The performance should have begun fifteen minutes ago. Ala is anxious she is going to be sick, so nervous and simultaneously mad at Marcel is she. Madame is reassuring the company they can perform without the music. They've done it before. But they all know the performance will lose some of its magic without Marcel's beautiful piano compositions and his haunting voice.

Then Marcel appears, unapologetic, unflustered. She both wants to slap and hug him. Madame reprimands him.

"It's good to keep people on their toes," he says.

There is applause as Marcel walks out onto the stage. Ala hears in her head a sequence of Madame's commands as she waits for her cue. *And go. Stay on the beat. Push. Passe. Down. Turn. Like a bird with outstretched wings waiting for the wind to lift it. Round. Now lose all your strength. You are a petal falling from a rose. And diagonal. And rock. More expression in your hands. Reach out. Reach within. Feel yourself naked now. You are all the beauty in the world for this moment.*

Marcel has begun playing the piano. The music, which has become an intimate part of her being, enters her as a summons. Her body forms a line with it. The line will soar and sink, collapse and recover, bend and break. It will release in her a bounty of capacities. She is inside Madame's design now; everything else dissolves in the smoke of oblivion.

Her opponent now is fear. It's like a shadow that skips onto the stage with her. Fear of disappointing Madame, fear of resistance or amnesia in her muscles, fear of her period arriving. Within three minutes, fortified by Marcel's beautiful music, she knows she has overcome her enemy. She has distilled herself into rhythm and grace. A tidal force has risen up in her and possessed her. There is no check in the flow of her body. She experiences every sequence of movements as a songline moving through her body. She has a luminous outline on the stage. That is her feeling. And that she has summoned and has under command all her forces for one moment in time. She is rippling light. She is liquid gold. She is spinning bedewed filament into a web. She has entered another dimension.

"Oh you beauty," says Marcel when the performance is over. He kisses her on the mouth and then kneels at her feet in mock adoration. There's a shine in Madame's eyes. She puts her hand on Ala's skull and smiles.

They all walk back onto the stage to receive the applause. It lifts her up like the swell of the sea. Ala feels she is aglow in a world of love. The candles flicker and trail a wake of connected puppet shadows that reach up the walls. In lieu of a bouquet, she and Madame are presented with a lilac branch each. Ala takes a deep draught of the forbidden flowers. The perfume expresses the complexity of what she feels. The joy of having eked out the best of herself, the approaching sadness of the return to her everyday self. Drops of perspiration slide down between her small breasts. She makes out Zanek and Mira in the audience and Max and Sabina and the two girls. Her mother and father are sitting with Henryk and the two orphan children, Luba and little Henryk. Grandpa and Grandma Frydman are here too. Even Wolf and his sister. It pleases her she has given them all a memory in which she has spun out the best of herself. As if every time they think of her now she will be rising and falling and rising again barefooted in a lustrous red chiffon gown with kohl smudged around her eyes.

Ala is surrounded by people complimenting her. She finds she is not entirely comfortable being singled out for praise and tries to deflect it onto Madame. Out of the corner of her eye she watches Zanek leave with Mira. She is disappointed he doesn't compliment her.

"There were two marvels tonight," Max tells her. Sabina is standing very close to him. Something wonderful has happened between them. It's like a scent they both exude. Ala feels both happy for them and a twinge of jealousy. "I felt I was moving in unison with you in some realm just outside myself. It was a magical sensation. That's the first marvel. The second is the reappearance in my life of those two children," he says nodding towards Luba and Henryk who are watching Ora perform some dance movements of her own. "I was on the verge of adopting them when Sabina and her girls appeared in my life. And then they vanished. I feared the worst. I've felt guilty ever since. Constantly keeping an eye open for them and worrying about them."

Ala looks around for Marcel. She feels more attracted to him tonight. There is a quiet purring euphoria in her that needs an outlet. An inclination to bestow on someone a share of the superabundance of her own happiness. She imagines going back to the room above the nightclub and this time doing everything he asks. But there's no sign of him. Instead Wolf comes over to speak to her. Manliness has grown in him. His face is tanned and darkened with stubble; his body aglow with vigour.

"I'm impressed," he says.

"Thanks," she says. "The pain is beginning to make itself felt now. I feel like I've been pared down to the ache in my muscles and the soreness on the soles of my feet. Am I grimacing? I ache all over. You have to hide the pain while you're dancing. Often you're not even aware of it. Life on the farm has done you good. Have you left now?"

"I'm not sure," he says with a slightly theatrical air of mystery.

Ala has noticed Wolf's fly is undone. Her eye keeps going to the tuft of bunched white fabric between the open buttons of his trousers. Her hand as if magnetised to the oversight in his attire against her better judgement. Sometimes nowadays she thinks the time has come to rebel against her better judgement. She feels like she has grown into a more expansive idea of herself tonight, emboldened and a little wild. As if the dance and all the praise has performed a new alchemy in her bloodstream. She steps forward and with both hands deftly fastens the undone buttons on his crotch. It's like a dare her imagination goads her with.

Wolf, she sees when she steps back, is appalled. The first inkling of shame rises in her. She hadn't meant it as anything but a piece of playful mischief. But, clearly, that's not how he sees it. Her good mood is ruined. She feels humiliated. Before he can say anything, she tells him she has to go. She walks over to her father who is standing alone and hugs him. She asks him where her mother is. He shrugs his shoulders, as if he couldn't care less.

8

Earlier Ora complained that her shoes hurt. It isn't easy to find shoes in the ghetto. So many children with their quickly growing feet walk barefoot or in improvised footwear. Max asked Eugenia if her shoes hurt. She said no but he senses sometimes she simply doesn't want to create difficulties. They went to the market in Gęsia Street and bought a pair of second hand shoes for Ora from a veiled woman with feverish eyes. Max was careful not to touch her when he handed over the banknotes. He carefully checked the shoes for lice before allowing Ora to put them on. Ora is now swinging her arms high as she walks. As if she is marching through a kingdom of ceaseless wonders.

He and Ora now have four secret handshakes - entwined index fingers means Ora or Max is feeling sad; entwined middle fingers means we need to cheer mum up; entwined third fingers means I have a new secret (though there is no decree the secret should be shared); entwined little fingers means faith, hope and charity but the strongest of these is charity. Max always produces coins for some beggar when Ora grasps his little finger. He encountered problems helping Ora understand the difference between faith and hope.

Edek is sitting on the stairs outside the apartment when they arrive home. A rucksack between his feet. He tells Max he needs somewhere to stay for a few days.

"Of course. What's happened?"

"I've heard my name is on a Gestapo list. The underground press has begun to irritate them apparently. And we've got an

174

informer in our midst. Can you believe that? A Jew who is willing to help the Gestapo. It makes me want to tear out my hair in despair."

"Come in. You remember Sabina?" Max still can't get used to how proud of her he feels, how proud of himself that he has earned her trust, that he now knows by heart every contour and niche of her naked body and every day learns new secrets of her mind.

With Edek in the apartment Max and Sabina revert back to a more formal manner with each other. As a result he becomes still more appreciative of all the hidden marvels behind her social façade. He finds himself feeling sorry for Edek for having no knowledge of what is underneath her social mask and underneath her clothes.

"Congratulations," says Edek when Sabina has gone to bed with the girls.

"Is it that obvious? I try hard to hide how elated I am. It's not exactly the most appropriate state of mind to carry through the streets of the ghetto. Often the apartment is raucous with laughter and I can't help imagining what the neighbours are thinking."

"You're getting one over on Hitler. Enjoy it while you can."

"Have you heard something?"

"I attended a meeting where a young girl from one of the Zionist youth organisations gave us details of what has been happening in Vilna and Lodz. The systematic murder of tens of thousands of Jews. There we were, lots of middle aged men, listening to this impassioned young girl telling us that the time has come to resist the Germans with arms. She dismissed the voices that said the Germans would never dare do such things in Warsaw. She said our point of departure should be to consider ourselves already dead. Only then might we rouse ourselves from our fearful passive inertia. She made me feel old and useless. Much as you are with your return to the heady virile vitality of young love."

"Sorry," says Max.

"Tea was served when this girl had finished pouring out her heart. An old rabbi representing Agudat Yisreal got angry with her and accused her of being hysterical and a liar. He had no doubt God would never allow such a thing to happen to His people. He said the greatest threat facing the Jews was the increasing tendency to abandon Judaism and that the Nazis are God's warning. He asked her what she hoped to achieve by spreading panic in the ghetto. She looked at him as if he was a spoilt child. She had nothing but contempt for all the theoretical hair-splitting that followed. And I don't blame her. It's only the Zionist kids who are determined to act. I admire them. And I used to call Zionism an ideology of escapism. It's my party that's burying its head in the sand with its groundless faith in forming a united front with our Polish comrades. As soon as the Germans arrived we saw how deeply rooted and widespread antisemitism is in this country. The Poles on the whole don't like us any more than the Germans do."

"What good can a few kids with guns do though? The Germans will lose this war. The English are dropping thousands of bombs on German cities every night. The Russians still aren't beaten despite recent setbacks. And now there are the Americans. Once they've defeated the Japanese, the Americans will turn all their might on the Germans. Isn't the best option to sit tight and wait it out?"

They both freeze as the purr of an engine gains in volume. Edek follows Max to the window. Headlights sweep aside the thick tide of darkness down on Nowolipki Street. Max holds his breath as the truck comes into sight. Then lets out a sigh of relief when darkness lacquers the street again.

Max is in bed, looking up at the shadowplay on the ceiling, as if it is a coded text of prophecy, when a volley of echoing gunshots splinters the silence. Afterwards he lies awake straining to locate the origin and nature of every sound he hears out in the night. These fugitive noises, the anticipation of them coming closer, make him realise how much tension he is carrying in his body. He finds himself picturing the cemetery just outside the ghetto. The glint of moonlight on the headstones. He is on the verge of sleep when he hears more gunshots, perhaps two streets away.

9

Ala is walking with Wolf through some of the most destitute streets of the ghetto. Dun-coloured, malodorous narrow streets choked with carts and vendors and beggars and staring unwashed children inert on their haunches. Wolf has told her he has a surprise for her. She was embarrassed when she saw him again and taken aback by his invitation. She agreed to see him in the hope of ridding herself of the hot embarrassment he has made her feel. Even Lily was shocked when she told her she had buttoned up his flies. But his prudish judgemental response to her playful gesture at the theatre still irritates her. *Why couldn't he just laugh about it instead of getting on a moral high horse and making me feel so small and humiliated?*

Wolf now helps an elderly woman to her feet after she collapses while sifting through a mound of rubbish.

"That was good of you," she tells him.

"She was probably well-off once upon a time. The beggars now are a better class of people than they were a year ago. The poorest have been eliminated. Now it's the turn of the least intrepid of the formerly more affluent."

Ala is wearing a loose pearl grey dress of thin cotton with leather boots and a blue cardigan. Since the performances of Cassandra, she feels a new confidence which she wears in her hips, as if her passage through the hours is set to music. But amidst all this squalor, her nice clothes, her clean hair, her scented healthy body, make her stand out in a way that causes her discomfort.

"Nothing is gained by feeling guilty though," she says. "I'm tired of feeling guilty because then I realise how helpless I am. Perhaps it's God who ought to feel guilty."

"I didn't mean it as any kind of judgement. It's just an observation I've made having returned to the ghetto after being away. It makes you realise we might all be reduced to this kind of abject misery sooner or later."

He has told her about the farm where he works. It was begun as a training centre for the Hashomer Hatzair, as a preparation for agricultural work in Palestine. The crops they produce come to the ghetto and are distributed to the orphanages and soup kitchens. The Germans have so far allowed all the young Jews at this farm a relative degree of freedom.

"How pious are you, Wolf? Do you obey all the Sabbath laws?"

She senses he likes her saying his name. As if it's a rope ladder she has climbed to get closer to him.

"I try to."

"You don't open doors on the Sabbath?"

"No."

"And you think God cares? He might even be laughing at how gullible you are."

"I think it's important to live symbolically."

"I've heard you receive military training and sing nationalistic songs every day at your farm. Does that mean you're going to fight the Third Reich?"

"Who told you that?"

It was his sister, Chaya. But she doesn't want to betray Chaya so adopts what she feels is a mysterious knowing air.

"Why don't you join our movement? You already have one foot in the door. One thing it provides is an outlet for your anger."

"Dance does that. It provides an outlet for all my emotions."

"All of them?"

"Yes."

"Why are you always following that Jewish policeman with your eyes then?"

"Marcel?"

"Did you know he's having an affair with an older woman?"

Ala is surprised by the flush of jealousy she feels.

"How do you know?"

"I've seen them together. It was plain as day something is going on between them."

"What does she look like?"

"Attractive. Middle-aged. Privileged. She was in the audience when you danced. They left together."

If it was Madame, a crazy idea that momentarily unsettles her, Wolf would have identified her. An even more troubling idea now occurs to her. Her mother vanished the night of the premier of Cassandra and didn't return home.

"Do you know what my mother looks like?"

"No. Why do you ask?"

"I wasn't sure if I introduced you or not," she says. A divide has been driven between the outer and inner world. Outwardly she strives to appear offhand and composed, while within a distressing possibility passes under review in the privacy of her mind. What if she now told Wolf the awful suspicion she is harbouring? Sometimes you wish your thoughts might be overheard; other times it's among life's greatest blessings that they remain private.

"Here," he says and hands her a slip of paper. Only now does she notice they are walking towards a ghetto boundary gate. "Show this to the guards," he says.

"We can't leave the ghetto," she says.

The Jewish policeman is already opening the gate. She looks over at the German gendarmes on the far side, assuring herself Frankenstein isn't among them. Then she realises where they are.

"You're taking me to the Jewish cemetery?"

"You're now outside the ghetto," he says. She feels the touch of his hand on her back through her cardigan and thin dress.

She wonders if he has brought her here to show off how freely he is able to move around. Men, she knows, like to impress upon women that they are in possession of keys to a wider world. It's often a huge part of their vanity. The grotesquery of this variation of a courting ritual, as if the neglected cemetery is an exotic resort, makes her inwardly smile.

They walk between rows of gravestones. The shadows of trees in new leaf shift over the tilted inscribed grey stones. Pollen has collected in the engraved names. There are yellow and blue wildflowers in the midst of the overgrown grass, ground ivy and ferns, and there's the intermittent scent of moistened soil. Ala soon begins to feel a current of wellbeing wash through her, as if she has finally been allowed outside after an interminable illness.

"No more Cassandra then," says Wolf.

"We were only allotted three performances."

"I don't think I could channel my creativity into anything so evanescent. You paint a picture or make a sculpture or write a book and it's always there as a tangible testament."

"Dance is more like life. It happens and then it's gone."

"Isn't art supposed to transcend life?"

"Dance does transcend life." Ala skips ahead and performs a new, recently learned sequence of movements. The sun is warm on her forearms; the long grass tickles her legs. "See," she says and smiles. "Madame is composing a new choreography. This one she plans to stage outside in a crowded part of the ghetto. Make it look like an impromptu expression of protest on the part of the ghetto's inhabitants. She has this idea of forming a chorus of about thirty women into a chain and making them enact a medley of abject movements repeated over and over. She wants the Germans to see it."

"They might start shooting at you."

"I know. My legs go weak every time I picture it happening."

"What's the purpose of it?"

"I don't know. She doesn't tell us. Maybe she wants to move the Germans to compassion, make them feel ashamed."

"Fat chance of that happening. If the Germans were capable of feeling shame or compassion the ghetto walls would have come down a year ago."

"The awful thing is I feel shame and compassion every day but it doesn't fundamentally change my behaviour. Sometimes I wonder what it will take to set me on a new course of action. Do you think the Germans secretly know they're in the wrong? Or are they really as mindless as they act?"

"You don't want to know what I think."

"Maybe I do, maybe I don't. One thing I've learned about you is that you're sometimes wrong when you're certain you're right."

This makes Wolf smile. Ala wonders if he has brought her to the cemetery to kiss her. Lily keeps telling her stories about how wonderful it is to be touched. *At times it's like an immensity opens up inside and there's no longer any boundary to your body. Like a finger held over a hose pipe and the water spraying, bursting, erupting out in all directions. Or like a star inside you that bursts into thousands of glowing particles that reach every corner of your body.*

Ala wants to experience that bursting star.

Suddenly she hears a long-forgotten sound. The twittering of birds. Before long she catches sight of a pair of thrushes pecking at the seeded grass. And then a squirrel making an acrobatic leap from one branch to another.

"This is why I brought you here," he says.

Ala stands on tiptoes to kiss him on the mouth. The awkward first moment is anti-climactic. She's not sure he's kissing back. She presses her length against him. She is made to feel he doesn't like her taking the lead. That he expects her to follow his lead. She feels like he is judging her again.

Ala has always assumed sex is straightforward. Two people like each other and everything follows seamlessly from there, until the arguments begin at a later date. She is discovering how far from being true this is.

10

Max watches Ora look down at the grey-bearded old man sprawled on the pavement. A blood-stained handkerchief is laid out by his side. Her eyes are gaping with sympathetic bewilderment. She looks up at Max, as if for an explanation. He makes a sad face, strokes her head and says nothing. A few yards further on she begins to skip and swing her arms again. Then, clutching a handful of her dress and screwing it up, she asks him why the barefooted children have scraps of paper stuck to their bare feet and ankles.

"They've lost or outgrown their shoes," he says. "Like you did."

She lifts up her lower lip, her way of telling the world she's sad. Then she entwines her little finger around his little finger. Their code when she wants to give someone a coin. He hands her two zinc coins and watches as she shyly walks towards the three young boys sitting in the kerb and drops the coins in their tin mug. Sabina, Eugenia and Ala have walked on ahead in the meantime.

"Will they be able to buy some shoes now?"

He is less quick witted with Ora than with anyone else. He supposes this is because he is often simultaneously reluctant to tell her the truth or to tell her a lie.

"Or they might decide to spend your money on something else," he says.

They are about to turn into Smocza Street when three nearby gunshots panic everyone. Max takes Ora's hand, which feels on his palm like a baby bird with an urgent pulse. Further down the busy street Sabina, Eugenia and Ala are at the rear of a crowd being herded by a cordon of Jewish policeman waving their truncheons and blowing whistles. Sabina is wearing a green linen skirt and a red cashmere cardigan. She keeps looking over her shoulder at him and Ora. He struggles to work out what is happening. Why the Jewish police are behaving so aggressively. He watches a policeman shove Sabina between the shoulders. She almost trips. She turns and says something damning to the Jewish policeman. It's then Max notices the camera. A uniformed German is filming from the back of a jeep. The camera is trained on Sabina and the Jewish policeman. Max doesn't lift his hat as he walks past the Germans in the jeep. He feigns oblivion to their presence even though he always struggles to quell the contempt he feels for these minions of the Third Reich. He still finds it difficult to acclimatise himself to the anarchic presence in his nature of this murderous loathing. Every German face sets it surging through him. He has always believed himself to be a man clean of hatred.

A Jewish policeman yells at him and threatens him with his wooden truncheon. Max is aware of the camera on him as he picks Ora up and moves more quickly towards Sabina and the crowd further down the street.

11

Everyone is asking what it means that the Germans are filming in the ghetto. They have filmed corpses and the appalling sanitary conditions inside the refugee centres and they have filmed elegantly dressed Jews enjoying lavish meals inside restaurants. They have filmed Jews enjoying a concert and Jewish men and women bathing naked together. Every scene they film is staged. It's generally agreed the motive of the German film is to make the Jews appear contemptible.

Today at rehearsals Marcel improvised some music for the new choreography. Everyone amused themselves imagining Marcel playing the piano outside in Muranowski Square which is where Madame plans to perform the new dance. His new music, hypnotic repetitive refrains overlaid with swirling cascades of solo notes and his haunting high voice, is even more beautiful than his compositions for Cassandra. One piece reminds Ala of a lone track of footprints crossing a wide expanse of freshly fallen snow.

When the rehearsal ends Ala watches him joke with the two male dancers who he is always excessively scornful of to her in private. He calls them Auntie Bernhard and Auntie Marek and mimics their effeminate coquettish gestures.

She is getting ready to leave when he walks over to her. "Let's stay behind," he says. "I don't have to be on duty until five."

"Don't you want to hurry off to see your lover?"

He looks alarmed for a moment, but quickly recovers his equilibrium. Ala has questioned her mother about the night she didn't return home. She could detect no sign of duplicity in her answers. She went for tea with a friend, got talking and realised she wouldn't be able to get home before curfew. For the first time since her teenage years, she told Ala, she slept on a sofa. Ala was ashamed she ever harboured the idea she might be Marcel's secret lover.

"That's over," he says. "Anyway, from what I hear, you're keeping your options open."

"What are you talking about?"

He winks at her.

There is still an unpredictability about Marcel that flusters her. She is always a little apprehensive of what he will say or do next. And he has the power to fill her field of vision. She can't see beyond him when he is physically close. Always he sets up a yearning for a deeper connection, though not necessarily with him. She has only seen Wolf once briefly since the kiss. She could find no trace in him of the intimacy they had shared. As if he had disowned it like something dreamed. He made her feel, for the second time, that she had done something wrong.

"Ala and I are going to run through the opening sequence one more time. I've got a new idea," Marcel calls out to Madame who is packing her rucksack.

"I can't stay. I'm wanted elsewhere."

"That's fine. We'll lock up," he says.

Lily gives Ala an enquiring look. Ala lets her know with a gesture she has no explanation.

When everyone has left Ala feels a little frightened.

"Do you really want to go through the opening sequence?"

"Yes, but I think you should dance it naked. I think it'd do you good. To even things up I'll play naked, if you want."

Ala laughs. And at the same time wonders if he has a sixth sense. Several times she has danced naked in her room at night and imagined an audience.

"You think that's funny?" says Marcel, with a broad grin.

"Yes, I do."

He executes a series of melodramatic chords on the piano.

"Funnier than that?"

She nods.

He plays still more portentous chords and sings along in a tuneless funereal voice.

"The thing is, we never know how much it costs a person to say the things he says."

Is this his way of telling her he feels exposed, vulnerable? Ala is mystified. He doesn't appear vulnerable; he appears fully in command of himself. He curses a fly and begins chasing it, pretending it is a Jewish woman and he is a Nazi. He shouts German insults at it. Ala pictures herself dancing naked for him. She realises it is an important part of her self-esteem to think of herself as bold, adventurous, uninhibited. And Wolf has left her feeling unattractive, inept. And she imagines how outraged her mother would be. Another important part of her self-esteem is to believe herself more liberated than her mother.

"I'll do it on one condition," she says.

"What?"

"I blindfold you."

"Oh, even better," says Marcel and performs a virtuoso trill on the piano. "Use your stockings."

Her thighs are feverishly hot and sensitive as she unrolls her stockings. There is a lively nervous eagerness in her touch, as if she is poised on the tips of her toes, when she ties the black fabric around his eyes, making sure the knot is tight at the back of his head. She wonders if the stocking smells of her, of her skin's secretions and her scent. It's the first time he has made himself subservient to her, as if he is ill and she is taking care of him.

"Can you see?"

"I might just as well be in Paris," he says. Stretching out his hands in an idiot performance of a blind man. "*Vous* êtes *ici*? *Ou* êtes *vous*? *Je ne vois rien*."

She hears the rustle as she removes her skirt and tosses it aside as he might hear it in his heightened intimacy with darkness. She decides to take off her brassiere which she hadn't intended to do. There has never been any possibility of her removing her knickers. Not in a million years. Even if he wouldn't be able to see her shaved pubis, the red blotches on her puckered skin.

"Ready," she says. "But how are you going to play blindfolded?"

"I'll improvise and sing."

The acoustics are different in the empty theatre as if they are alone together at the edge of a world. She finds she cannot lose herself in the dance, especially when she realises they didn't make sure the door to the theatre is locked. Marcel stops singing. He gets up from the stool and blunders towards her with his hands outstretched. The idiot performance of a blind man again.

"Stay still," he says.

"What are you doing?"

"Do you think in the future people will dance naked on a stage with the same naturalness people now dance clothed?" he says.

She looks closely at his hands, moving ever closer to her. The long tapering fingers, the elegant ridges running up to his knuckles. As they are about to make contact with her bare flesh she shuffles to one side but he is too quick for her. He touches her where she has never been touched and it's like a new heart begins beating between her thighs.

"Cheat," he says, inserting his fingertips inside the waistband of her knickers. "You weren't naked." He reaches up for her small breasts and covers them with outstretched hands. She wants him to kiss her but instead he drops to his knees and draws patterns on her inner thighs.

"I can smell your musk," he says.

She doesn't want to hear this.

"You're all aquiver," he says. He slides his hand up her thigh and inside her knickers. "You've got no floss of hair," he says.

She steps back and tries to lift his head away from her navel. She feels she isn't grown up enough for what is happening, a feeling she often has in the ghetto. It occurs to her that the infectious sense of desperation in the ghetto is constantly making her do things she would never, in normal circumstances, agree to. Kissing Wolf in a cemetery, tapping out amorous messages to a man betrothed to someone else and now dancing topless in a theatre while a blindfolded Marcel accompanies her on the piano. It's like for heated moments she becomes an unpredictable stranger to herself. Ala wants to believe she has surpassed all need of a mother. Her new habit of ignoring scruples is perhaps an attempt to hurry forth the advent of a new chapter in the book of her life. The scruples she casts aside always though return and bleed out weakening venom, rendering her a young daughter again, taking her back to the chapter she wants to leave behind.

"You don't like it?" he says.

Ala looks down at his head between her thighs. She isn't sure what he is doing now. She feels estranged from her body. Neither does she feel he is enjoying what he is doing.

"You taste like the sea. I feel like I'm on holiday."

There is bitterness in his voice. She pulls away, tugs up her knickers, covers her breasts with her hands, even though he is still blindfolded.

"You see. It'll never work between you and me," he says.

"Someone horrible always takes you over whenever you try to be nice," she says, fastening her brassiere.

He removes his blindfold. "I'm not nice, Ala," he says with his derisive smile.

"You can be."

"I met your boyfriend. Wolf. We had a chat. I know I'm not good enough for you but neither is he. He's a bully with all his fixed sanctimonious ideas. That's what I told him. And that I had deflowered you. He wanted to hit me. I enjoyed his impotent anger. It epitomised the entire ghetto."

12

Max lifts Ora so she can spit into the basin after cleaning her teeth. Sabina is washing up the breakfast things. Breakfast was hot milk and toasted bread, crisscrossed with branded marks from the grill, with a last sliver of jam. Eugenia stands in the doorway, in her pyjamas, waiting her turn. Outside the summer sky is gloomily grey and the first raindrops spot the window that overlooks the courtyard.

"Where is east?" asks Ora.

Max points at random. "Over there," he says.

"I don't want to go there. I want to stay here."

"Who said anything about going east?"

"Children at school."

Yesterday, at midday, notices appeared in the ghetto. All the strength drained from his legs when Max read the black gothic typescript. He has always known his happiness wouldn't last. That it is inappropriate at a time when the world is at war.

All Jews living in Warsaw, irrespective of age or sex, will be deported to the East.

1. **The following are exempted from deportation:**

2. **everyone employed by the authorities or in German enterprises who can present appropriate evidence of this;**

   a. **all Jews who are members or employees of the Judenrat at the date of publication of this notice;**

b. all Jews employed in firms belonging to the German Reich who can present appropriate evidence of this;

c. all Jews who are fit for work, who to date have not been included in the employment process; these should be put in barracks in the Jewish District;

d. all Jews who are members of the Jewish Order Service;

e. all Jews who are part of the personnel of Jewish hospitals and who are in the Jewish disinfection columns;

f. all Jews who are close family members of the persons named in a to f. Only wives and children are counted as family members;

g. all Jews, who on the first day of the deportations, are in one of the Jewish hospitals and are not fit to be discharged. Unfitness for discharge must be certified by a doctor appointed by the Judenrat;

3. Every Jewish deportee has the right to take 15 kilograms of his property as baggage. Baggage weighing more than 15 kilograms will be confiscated. Objects of value, such as money, jewellery, gold, etc., can be taken. Food for three days should be taken.

4. The deportation will begin on 22 July at 11 a.m.

Max is sitting behind Sabina in the bath. He is lathering shampoo into her hair. A single candle burns on the windowsill. The melting wax an intermittent pleasing pungent scent. Reflections of the water ripple over the ceiling and the skittish shadows seem to possess agency, as if miming a story of their own. The deportations began today.

"Even if my brother can get me a job at the *Judenrat* you and the girls still won't be exempt from deportation. I know this isn't the most romantic way to go about it, but we need to marry."

"I'm already married."

"I don't think the Germans are going to do comprehensive background checks on everyone's personal history. We need that slip of paper that exempts us from deportation." He cups her small breasts and presses his lips to the back of her neck. "Will you marry me?"

"What choice do I have?" she says.

He tries not to mind the hesitation he detects in her voice. He continues rinsing the shampoo from her hair. Scooping up the bath water in a mug and tipping it over her head. "Tomorrow I'll find a rabbi who will marry us. If only we could celebrate by going to Italy. That's what I used to imagine. We got married and honeymooned in Venice, Florence and Rome. Can you imagine Ora's face at the sight of the Grand Canal with all the gondoliers in their striped jerseys and black hats?"

She rests a hand on his thigh. "You're not going to go fanciful on me, are you? I need a practical husband. The girls need a practical father."

"Yes, from now on we have to continually think ahead. Plan every day in detail before it begins. The girls should no longer go to school. They should never be out of our sight."

"I still can't believe it's the Jewish police and not Germans who are rounding people up.

"They targeted the refugees and the beggars today. I caught sight of the lines when I collected the girls from school. Some of the Jewish police were vile. Hitting people with their truncheons like they had become Nazis. There was little resistance and no need to hit anyone. Many of the captured Jews seemed on their last legs. It was impossible to imagine them becoming a productive work force."

"They say the Germans need farm labourers in the Ukraine and Byelorussia," he says.

"Do you believe that?"

"I don't know. My brother says they intend deporting seventy thousand of us. Our task now is take every precaution we're not among those seventy thousand. And step number one is that you become Mrs Blinkowski."

"Blinkowski? What happened to Max Silberman?"

"Long story. I converted to Catholicism. For career purposes essentially. You know how prejudiced Poles are against Jews."

The stiffening alertness he senses in her body worries him, as if she is silently making a case against him.

"I can't believe you never told me this before. What other secrets are you hiding from me?"

13

It is day three of the resettlement programme. What everyone now calls by its German name, the *Aktion*. While her mother stands over a steaming pot of lentils Ala's father tells his family six thousand Jews were loaded into freight cars today and that the same number will be removed tomorrow. "If they carry on at this rate they could clear the entire ghetto in eighty days."

Yesterday there was a rehearsal. Marcel didn't show up. It has shocked everyone that the Jewish Police are carrying out the roundups with very few Germans visible. The consensus was that Marcel should now quit the police force. "Otherwise we should stop dancing to his music," said Hanka.

No one wanted to dance but Madame insisted and threw herself into the preparations with even more purpose than usual. She frequently lost her temper. Harangued Lily with such vehemence that Lily broke down in tears and left. By the end of the rehearsal news had filtered through that the roundups were taking place in the more destitute parts of the ghetto. Ala was struck by the tension around Madame's mouth.

Usually fear in the ghetto creates tidal surges, a rising flood of people following the same line of retreat. Today there is no pattern to the anxiety electrifying the streets. Ala notices there are no longer any beggars on the streets, no longer the emaciated living corpses curled up or stretched out on the pavements. She is on her way to the soup kitchen, something she hasn't dared do since Mira slapped her. She witnesses a long line of wretched Jews being herded by cordons of Jewish policemen northward from Mila Street into Smocza Street. And then a horse-drawn cart loaded with the old and sick. The horror of what she sees overwhelms any feeling of compassion.

The soup kitchen is empty except for a few helpers when she arrives. Zanek is sitting on a workbench by a sink. Ala's heart begins pounding. Her breasts burning against the fabric of her brasserie. It's a revelation to discover again how fresh and consuming is her attraction to him. It's as if she clicks her fingers and there he is, summoned up by some deep detailed wish within.

He picks up one of the three green bottles standing by his side when he sees her.

"You shouldn't be out walking the streets," he says. His open-necked white shirt reveals a section of his collarbone.

"It's awful out there," she says. She finds she is holding a screwed-up dishrag which she has no recollection of picking up. Against the radiance of Zanek's presence she notices how grubby appear the cracked white tiles behind his head.

"You have to hand it to the Germans," he says. "They're very good at creating theatre. They've created villains of the Jewish police. To enable the machine to run smoothly they employ their victims as cogs."

She allows this comment the gravitas it deserves.

"Do you like Wolf?" He coughs out the question abruptly.

"I don't know."

"You kissed him."

"He told you?"

"It made Mira laugh. You also buttoned up his flies."

Ala blushes. The more she tries to marshal the rush of blood the more implacable it becomes. It feels all wrong that they are talking about sexual etiquette when outside families are being hounded from their homes. She wonders why he doesn't appear to think this. Through the window she watches a group of children playing outside. She once saw these same children baiting one little boy in this courtyard. They had stolen his cap and were throwing it to each other. The little boy was in tears which only seemed to goad the children to humiliate him further. Ala broke up the cruel game and told them they were behaving like Nazis. Today she sees the bullied little boy is included in the game.

Zanek licks his lips. She has learned it is something he does when he is nervous. "Personally, I don't think you and Wolf are very well suited. He's too old fashioned for you. He's attracted to you against his will. He'll try to give you lessons on how to behave."

The apparent jealousy with which he says these things troubles Ala. She thinks of Mira. And her tumour. That she might die from one day to the next. And that she and Zanek have been friends since childhood. She wants to tell Zanek this is why she kissed Wolf. Instead she asks him where Wolf is.

"He's gone back to the kibbutz. He met your friend, the Jewish policeman."

"Marcel."

"He told Wolf you and him had spent a night together. He showed Wolf a pair of your knickers. He carries them around with him evidently. He implied you were stringing Wolf on to make him jealous."

"He stole those knickers from my bathroom. And I didn't spend the night with him in that way," she says feeling she is on trial.

Zanek smiles. He taps his thigh as if summoning notes of music he might sing along to. "Your Marcel strikes me as being a bit crazy. How is he coping with this new assignment?"

"I don't know. I haven't seen him. He'll probably be disgusted with himself, but he likes feeling disgusted with himself. He didn't turn up to rehearsals yesterday. Not that we rehearsed. It obviously isn't appropriate at the moment."

"I don't agree," he says, still smiling. "The important thing is to keep up morale. What good are you doing anyone by remaining inactive?"

"Actually, I lied. We did rehearse. Madame insisted. I'm worried about her. She didn't seem herself at all. I think she lives in a poor area. The kind of area they're taking everyone from. I want her to move in with my family but I didn't ask her."

"She doesn't strike me as someone who would accept charity easily."

"No. That's what stopped me from asking her. Now I've got no way of getting hold of her. Do you think these people are really being sent to work?"

"The Germans love their euphemisms. It's another part of the theatre. What do you think?"

"My brother works at the *transferstelle*, the customs yard in Stawki Street. He says they put at least a hundred people inside each freight car. Most of the people I saw today were so sick and malnourished they wouldn't survive a long journey in those conditions."

"That's what I think. They may well put to work those who survive the journey, but they'll do their best to make sure not many do. It's like a new variation of the starvation policy they've subjected us to in the ghetto. Kill us without seeming to do so." He reaches out and takes her hand. "Don't make the mistake of feeling yourself safe, Ala. Keep your wits about you and don't act recklessly. I've heard there are some members of the Jewish police who keep their eyes open for rich Jews on the streets so they can apprehend them and then extort money for releasing them. It's likely to become dog eat dog out there while these deportations continue. You have to promise me you won't climb into one of those freight cars no matter what you're told. The time has come to resist."

Ala is unnerved by the intensity with which his eyes lock onto hers. As if he fears he might be looking at her for the last time. He is still holding her hand when Mira enters the kitchen.

14

"I don't want to take the place of your father in your heart," Max says to Eugenia. It's a lie. He does want to replace her father in her heart. Nothing he has heard about her father makes him likeable. Not least of all the fact of him abandoning his two daughters and then renouncing them when it became clear how the Germans intended treating Jews. Max and Eugenia are sitting side by side on the sofa. Outside whistles can be heard, thankfully distant whistles. "He's still your father, not me. Think of me as a pretend father."

"Okay."

"That said, nothing would make me prouder than to have you as a daughter. Every day I marvel at how well you seem to know your own mind, how composed and brave you are. And it's lovely to watch what good care you take of Ora. You're smart, you're gifted and you're very beautiful, Genia. So, from now on, what is it?"

"One for all and all for one," she says.

"One for all and all for one," he says, repeating the new household mantra.

Max and Sabina are now registered as married. He told her she is his kibbutz, his homeland; that she and her girls have transformed the parched desert of his life into blossoming fruit-yielding orchards. Only Eugenia, Ora and Ala attended the service performed clandestinely by a rabbi. Ella, Ala's mother, gave him a beautiful ring for the ceremony as a gift. The canopy was made of the rabbi's prayer shawl and two bannister rails found in a courtyard. Eugenia, on a chair, and Ala held it up. Ora was upset, so Ala passed her end to her and lifted her up. When the rabbi recited the seven blessings the shawl flopped over Max's face thanks to Ora's restlessness. Sabina made the seven circles around him. They drank the wine. After the ceremony the rabbi spoke of his belief that God would soon perform a miracle to rescue His people. Max felt he was being spoken to as if he were a child.

Max is now officially employed by the *Judenrat*, as a clerk in the housing section. The chairman of the *Judenrat* has committed suicide. He refused to sign the resettlement order when he learned children were to be among the deported. This has increased suspicion about the true nature of these deportations. Max hasn't been to the office in Krochmalna Street once since securing the job. It's too dangerous to venture out into the streets during the day. The whistles of the Jewish police provide clues as to where the blockades are taking place. Yesterday there was a blockade in Max's street, but in a tenement further down the road, towards Karmelicka Street. He has learned how the round-ups take place. The Jewish police cordon off a courtyard and then herd all the occupants of the apartments outside. Everyone with a work certificate is allowed to stay; all those without are shepherded to the trains. The other way of escaping is to offer the Jewish police a bribe.

The wooden ladder is splashed with paint. On one rung is a red handprint. Max is fascinated by it and its recording of a moment in time he can't remember, a moment that cannot be made into a story. He's not even sure the handprint is his own. He settles the ladder into place beneath the trap door. To climb up into the attic makes him nervous. Forcing him to imagine a scenario in which it might be a desperate last measure. He doesn't believe his job at the *Judenrat* makes him, Sabina and the girls safe. To ever take the Germans at their word would be the height of foolishness. He hasn't been up in the attic for many years. Sunlight through the skylight gold-sections an oblong of splintered wooden boards. The dust tickles his throat. His every move solicits a resounding groan from the floorboards. Not for one moment does this musty space convey the reassurance of a sanctuary. He picks up a balding shaving brush balled in cobwebs and dust, then the crisp paint-stained pages of an old newspaper. October 7, 1932. The year of Eugenia's birth. A year when Sabina was lost to him. He tries for the first time to picture Sabina pregnant. And realises how many of her memories he is completely absent from, as if it's only a minor role he has been granted in her life. Then he reads an advertisement in the newspaper. A woman seeking a lost cat. He shakes his head at the innocence of a world where the disappearance of a cat is a family tragedy. Cats, he thinks, are beautiful creatures. He regrets never having owned one. He pictures the delight with which Ora and Eugenia would greet the introduction of a kitten into the household. Just as he has pictured their delight were he able to lift them onto a gondola on the Grand Canal. Ora and Eugenia, he understands, might as well, as things stand, be very old women on death's doorstep for all the new opportunity granted to them.

He has to push at the skylight with sustained force to get it to budge. He hauls himself out onto the roof. The blood rushing up into his shoulders. He is pleased his body responds with vigour to the demands of nimbleness and exertion made of it. On the roof the air is cleaner, the world larger, the future as if more remote. A breeze ruffles his white shirt tucked loosely inside his trousers. King of the castle, he thinks. It's his first taste of what physical freedom feels like for a long time. Even though he knows every horizon is unreachable to him except as an experience of the eye. He realises he has been happy with Sabina and the girls without ever knowing a physical sense of freedom. Would he be even happier were he able to swim in the sea with Sabina? He sees the image from above, the incoming tide filling and eroding the footprints they leave behind as they venture into the surf. For a moment he gains an elusive whiff of the tang of brine and seaweed. He'd love to piggyback Ora into the percussive slap and spray of the waves. Another simple moment of pleasure that German law denies him and his new family.

Then he hears whistles and shouting. From his roof he can easily climb down onto the neighbouring roof. Down in the courtyard a woman is upturning a washtub, soapy water running off over the cobbles. Three children are playing hopscotch.

The blockades generally confine themselves to only a section of one particular street. Therefore, he wants to know if it's possible to escape via the rooftops to a neighbouring street. Or else if there's a secure hiding place up here on the rooftops.

15

The Germans have now offered free bread and marmalade to everyone who volunteers themselves for resettlement. The congregation point is known as the *Umschlagplatz*. In bed at night Ala sometimes sees vivid unknown faces in her mind before sleep arrives. They look at her with knowing eyes. It unnerves her that she doesn't share their recognition. There's something malevolent about the way they look at her. And it's as if they are waiting for her. Waiting, she has come to think, for her too to be taken to the *Umschlagplatz*.

Henryk returns every evening with stories of what happens at the railway siding. This evening he has a more urgent tale to tell.

"How long would you imagine it would take a train packed with miserable Jews to get to the Ukraine? At least three days? Well, one of our workers jotted down the serial numbers of some of the carriages today. And guess what? Those same carriages were back in Warsaw later the same day. Those Jews aren't being resettled in the Ukraine. They're being taken on a three-hour journey, which means they aren't even leaving Poland."

Ala hates being cooped up at home all day. She is frequently at loggerheads with her mother. Her mother, she senses, often gets angry without knowing why she is angry. Ala sometimes takes refuge on the roof. She is here, drying her hair and reading *The Trojan Women*, when she hears the singing of children. She jumps up from the deckchair, walks over to the edge of the roof and looks down at the long orderly column of children, all holding hands, all carrying bundles. They are escorted by a cordon of Jewish policemen. She knows these are the children from the orphanage where Luba and Henryk now live. Adrenalin surges into her chest and limbs. She charges down the stairs in her bare feet, her hair still wet.

She runs past Dr Korczak who is leading the singing from the rear of the processional column. Luba is frightened when Ala grabs her arm. Ala realises there must be a wild desperate look on her face.

"You and Henryk must come with me," she says, composing herself. She has pulled Luba, Henryk and a girl in a blue pinafore with pigtails who is holding Henryk's hand out of the orderly marching lines.

"What do you think you're doing?"

The Jewish policeman fingers his truncheon.

"These two children have to come with me," she says, still gripping Luba's small hand.

"Says who?"

"They are my brother's children."

"What have you got in exchange?" he says, looking her up and down.

She looks down for her eighteenth birthday present ring but realises she isn't wearing it. She took it off when she washed her hair. "I've got nothing on me, but I live over there and I can get you some money."

The rear of the singing column has now marched past them. "Too late," he says.

"Aren't you ashamed of yourself?" she says, succumbing to a blast of hatred for this man.

"Right, you can join them," he says, grabbing her wrist.

She tries to free herself from his grip. "My father works for the *Judenrat*," she tells him in desperation.

"Good for him. You can explain that to the Germans in the *Umschlagplatz*."

16

"You've got to laugh, haven't you? I've always said the very same thing myself. I like those shoes you're wearing by the way. Did you buy them at the Hersh Fashion House? I thought so. But tell me, who is that man standing behind you and why has he got a twisted face?"

"Who is she talking to?" Ora asks Max.

"I think she's in shock," he says.

Sabina's aunt is standing in front of the floor length mirror, talking to people she sees on the other side of the glass. Her hair is matted and she smells of urine. When Sabina went to see her aunt and uncle this morning the entire tenement where they lived had been cleared of occupants. Only Mrs Segal remained. Sabina was unable to get any kind of explanation from her aunt. Her uncle, it has to be assumed, was taken to the *Umschlagplatz*. Max is finding it difficult to suppress the irritation he feels. The crazed woman has brought a poisonous atmosphere into his home. She unnerves him. He knows Sabina thinks of him as calm, as someone unlikely to get flustered in a crisis. But this woman is giving the lie to this idea.

He kneels down in front of Ora and tells her to get on his shoulders. "Let's try to get her attention," he says.

Aunt Elsa is leaning very close to the glass. Her elbows are raised as she speaks, like bird's wings. She keeps succumbing to bouts of girlish giggling. Max stands behind her with Ora sitting astride his shoulders. He bends down so Ora can see herself in the glass. "Right, now wave to her or pull faces at her. Anything to get her attention," says Max.

"She frightens me," says Ora, quick to latch on to the general habit of talking about Elsa as if she isn't present.

"I'm actually a good swimmer, even if I do say so myself," says Mrs Segal.

Max improvises a dance. Ora, on his shoulders, makes hand signals.

"What are you two up to?" says Sabina, entering the room with Eugenia.

"Max told me to make faces at the strange woman," says Ora.

"Did he? And that's no way to talk about Aunt Elsa."

Max is made to feel ashamed he has acted with such unfeeling immaturity. He has disappointed Sabina. But his irritation towards her aunt increases. She has made him question how much goodness there is in his heart.

"I think that man with the twisted face should see a doctor," says Mrs Segal.

17

Ala holds Luba and Henryk by the hand as they are escorted through a gate in Dzika Street into the *Umschlagplatz*. The square, flanked by tall ugly concrete buildings and cordoned off with barbed wire fences, is crowded with bewildered frightened people of all ages. Most of them sitting on the ground with a few belongings. Women are wearing summer dresses and sandals. Soldiers in yellow uniforms Ala has never seen before stand around in pairs. She notices a man defecating while the shadow of a tree dances its leaves over the ghetto wall behind him. A woman in ruins who walks in circles, leaving in her wake footprints of blood. Ala can't see the train but she hears a whistle and iron shunting noises. Then she sees Marcel striding towards her.

"Are you insane? What are you doing here?"

Ala is taken aback by his fury. She begins to sob. She can't help herself.

Marcel sidles up to her and whispers: "I might be able to get you out. I can't get the children out though. Tell them you have to come with me for a moment."

She is struck by the strained and haunted expression on Marcel's face. His eyes are bloodshot. She has never seen him so bereft of self-possession. She looks down at Luba. The little girl is staring into space. Ala can feel her fear in the hot press of her hand. She realises to save herself she has to sacrifice these two children. She tells herself that no one knows for sure that the deported might not know a better life wherever it is they are being taken. She tells herself not even the Nazis would kill children.

"Come on!" Marcel hisses at her.

Luba loosens her grip on Ala's hand. As if she has already understood she and her brother are to be abandoned. Ala has never felt so disgusted with herself in all her life.

"Are you sure you can't get them out as well?"

He stares hard into her eyes. "How much guilt do you think one person can swallow? I've already reached my limit and now you want me to take personal responsibility for the murder of these two children. If I could get them out do you think I'd even hesitate? Do you know what I feel like doing? I feel like smashing my truncheon into the face of one of these German pigs. And if he shoots me so much the better." He draws his truncheon and marches off towards two German gendarmes.

Ala chases after him and tugs at his arm.

"Let's get out of here," he says.

She tells the children she has to go. She tells them to join Dr Korczak. She tells them he will look after them now.

"And get that frightened disgusted look off your face," says Marcel as they walk away from Luba and Henryk. "You need to appear composed. If anyone asks, you're my wife. You came to tell me I'm wanted at headquarters."

As they approach the exit gate she watches a Jewish policeman hurry to light the cigarette of a helmeted German soldier. She feels the disgusted look return to her face.

They pass the two gendarmes at the gate without a problem. Marcel shows no sign of fawning to the Germans. Ala wonders if she will ever be able to forgive herself for what she has done. They walk in silence on the narrow pavement. Further down the street, flanked on either side by four and five-storey balconied buildings, a group of Jews marshalled by Jewish policemen stand aside to make way for a grey truck with the tarpaulin cover rolled back. The truck pulls up outside the entrance gate of the *Umschlagplatz*. Ala is horrified when she catches a glimpse of Madame, her long black hair loose and dishevelled, among the many people crushed into the back of the vehicle. A German gendarme arrives at the back of the truck. He pulls down the flap and orders everyone out.

"*Alle Juden raus, schnell, schnell.*"

It is a shock to see how brutally the German pulls at Madame's thin arm. With how much disdain he treats this self-possessed proud woman who no one dares to ever oppose.

"Marcel," she pleads.

Marcel rifles through his pockets and produces a silver ring. "Stay back here," he says.

She watches him walk towards the two soldiers with a thumping heart. Both have their rifles drawn. Marcel points at Madame, then shows the soldiers the ring. One soldier has blue eyes and straw-coloured hair; the other has a red nose and heavy-lidded eyes. It's the German with the blue eyes who pockets the ring. Then he shoves Marcel hard in the chest. Marcel, unprepared, loses his balance and falls heavily to the ground. The soldier, smirking, points his rifle at him. He makes a firing noise. Then he turns his attention back to his prisoners.

"*Alle Juden raus, schnell, schnell.*" It's like an automated voice, capable of only one command.

Ala's head is a cyclone of emotions. She's embarrassed on Marcel's behalf for his humiliation at the hand of the German. At the same time she struggles to accept the helplessness and heartbreak with which she has to stand by and watch Madame disappear. Her mentor turns to look back and they exchange a last look. The intense wild appeal in Madame's eyes is like a thrown flame. For a moment Ala feels like she is standing on a heap of ashes. She watches her become smaller and smaller in the crowd, the last image of Madame's face already branding itself in her memory, leaving a black mark.

Marcel grabs hold of her elbow and hurries her away from the vicinity of the *Umschlagplatz.*

It occurs to Ala that in all probability her body is now the custodian of all Madame's creative inspiration.

18

Sabina is astride Max on the bed. Her head arched back, her eyes closed, her mouth miming a silent O. Her hand moving between his shoulder blades woke him up from a dream in which his father was telling him a story, a finger stabbing at the air in his customary manner, a story of perseverance and courage and how injustice in the world can always eventually be righted. His orgasm is now stirring into being down in the core of his body. Outside, dawn is breaking. He can see the carved angels on the legs of his desk. He concentrates on them to prolong the moment. His orgasm arrives while his attention is fixed in horror on the opening of his bedroom door. Aunt Elsa enters the room wearing a hat and carrying a bag. The confused expression on her face undergoes no change as she lays eyes on Max and Sabina's naked coupling. The final throes of his orgasm take place without his participation as he watches Sabina's aunt fiddle nervously with a small silver medallion around her neck. There's a pained expression on her face, a blankness in her eyes, as if she's trying to summon a memory to explain what she's looking at. It occurs to him that her oblivion to the reality of what is happening around her is enviable. She leaves the room without saying a word.

"I'd better make sure she's all right," he says.

In the living room Elsa groans as she lifts her legs up onto the cushions of the sofa. Max removes her hat and helps her get comfortable. He covers her prostrate body with a blanket. This act he performs naked as though she is a domestic animal to whom his nudity is irrelevant.

Sabina is wearing her nightgown when he returns to the bedroom. The roundups will begin soon. The demonic voice amplified through the German megaphones, the whistles and shouts and screams, the clamour of the cyclone raging through the ghetto. Trigger-happy Ukrainian and Lithuanian auxiliaries have joined the Jewish police in carrying out the roundups now. Max has little faith safety resides in the flimsy piece of paper given to him by the *Judenrat*.

"Let's talk about the best plan of action again," he says, snuggling up to Sabina under the covers. "Should you and the girls hide up in the attic at the first sign of danger or do we trust in my *Judenrat* work certificate to exempt us from deportation? If I'm dealing with Jews I'm confident I can talk my way out of danger but these Ukrainians and Lithuanians make me nervous."

"People say they shoot anyone they find hiding," says Sabina.

"You'd rather place all your faith in my work certificate?"

"I don't know. I won't be separated from my girls though. If they hide, I hide too.

"Perhaps they really are sending us to do agricultural work in the Ukraine. People have received postcards from relatives telling them conditions there are much better than in the ghetto."

"By all accounts the Ukrainian guards here are more bloodthirsty and sadistic than the Germans. Would you want to go to the Ukraine?"

"I'd like to go to London or New York. Isn't it extraordinary how civilised those cities now seem? As if they belong to an entirely different species of human being."

"I've shown you where you can hide on the neighbouring roof. Perhaps we should go over the drill again today."

"I'm not sure I have enough courage for this, Max."

Neither is he sure he has the necessary courage for what lays ahead. The idea he might fail her and the girls, that she might witness some shameful shortcoming in him haunts him sometimes at night when he lays awake while she sleeps.

"And what about Elsa? Supposing she starts talking while we're hiding?"

They haven't spoken about her aunt who, they both know, is a liability. Max cannot bring himself to say what he thinks. That they will have to leave her to her own devices.

"Do you think she talks to ghosts? Beings we can't see but nevertheless do exist?"

"I'm not sure I believe in ghosts."

"You were a ghost to me for a long time," he says. "You haunted me because you were a keeper of secrets. That's what ghosts are. The keepers of secrets. The custodians of the missing parts of stories."

"The Germans are ripping all our stories to shreds. To think only two weeks ago my prevailing concern was that neither the girls nor I had had any new underwear for over a year. I wanted to be prettier for you."

"I like you just the way you are. And I love the tiny holes in your knickers. They perfectly match the little holes in my shorts. Anyway, thank heavens for Eugenia. She's going to darn my pyjamas today. And who knows, she might even embroider butterflies onto them."

"Keep making me smile, Max. I feel safer when you make me smile."

19

The small ghetto is being evacuated. It's seven o'clock in the evening. Zelazna Street is crammed with people moving possessions. Many with pushcarts piled high with luggage tied with dirty string. Ala, her mother and father all carry a trunk and wear knapsacks. Henryk is carrying the Singer sewing machine. They edge slowly towards the bridge. Ala has to step over the corpse of an old woman. Blood from her bullet wounds has been stickily footprinted onto the cobbles.

Frankenstein is one of the gendarmes outside the wooden guard hut. The German who humiliated her father is his partner. They are raking through the contents of a suitcase, stealing everything that takes their fancy. Ala breathes easier when she is climbing the wooden steps of the bridge over Chlodna Street.

"I don't understand why you're so reluctant to ask Max to take us in," she tells her mother who won't stop opposing the idea.

"He's got his own family now. He won't want us there. There must be lots of empty apartments after all the deportations."

"Does it not strike you as reprehensible to move in to the apartment of a family that has been herded off on a cattle train to who knows where?"

"You need to put aside all your finer feelings, Ala. The world in which finer feelings have a place is gone, kaput."

"We'll take our things to Max's and then decide what to do," says her father, transferring the heaviest trunk from one hand to another. It pains Ala to see the effort in her father to conceal his limp while struggling with the weight of the baggage he carries.

On the far side of the bridge German gendarmes have cleared a stretch of the road. Four Jews have been separated from the crowd – a young boy, an attractive teenage girl, an elderly man and Zanek's mother. A Jewish policeman is translating the German commands.

"You four Jews have been chosen to race. The loser will be shot. But you have to hop like frogs. I will now show you how to hop like a frog."

The Jewish policeman looks questioningly at the gendarme. The German slaps his face. The Jewish policeman crouches down on the cobbles and performs three squatted jumps. The Germans guffaw like imbeciles. One of them then walks between the parted crowd and stops about twenty yards away and shouts out that he marks the finish line.

"*Achtung, fertig, los!*"

The young boy, the girl and the elderly man squat-jump frantically towards the finish line. Zanek's mother however remains standing. She looks both proud and terrified. She is wearing a pretty blue dress with black stripes. One of the Germans steps forward and shoots her at close range. There's a vacant calm about the way he shoots her. Ala doesn't understand how he can so thoughtlessly attain such detachment from his humanity and murder in cold blood a defenceless woman. Zanek's mother collapses onto her knees, her shoulders slumped. Blood oozes out of her moving mouth. Ala senses her mother is inclined to go to her aid. Then the German shoots her again, between the eyes. And then again, as if for punctuation. Ala stares down with giddy incomprehension at the now untenanted body of Zanek's mother.

The Germans begin shouting at everyone to move on and hit people with their rifles. After the shock has subsided Ala commits the murderer's face to memory. As if she will be called upon by a court of law to give evidence against him.

They pass street vendors selling bread and potatoes and then enter a road that is strewn with broken furniture, clothes and household possessions. Ala looks up at a woman in a flowered housecoat howling at an open window. She's shrieking out names and throwing down photographs one by one into the street. A picture of two children posing beside a carrot-nosed snowman lands close to Ala's feet. Then she thinks she catches sight of Zanek pedalling his rickshaw. She is relieved when she realises she has hallucinated him. She doesn't want to be the one to tell him about the fate of his mother. Meanwhile, her mother and father are quietly arguing. Her father, who doesn't like shows of emotion, is angry with her mother. Her mother raises her voice.

"I'm trying to understand if that was brave of Rachel or stupid. I had tea with her five hours ago. We shared stories of our childhoods and laughed together. Now she's dead. Because she refused the indignity of being mocked. I want to understand, Samuel."

"It was bloody stupid of her," says Ala's father. "That's all you need to understand. Disobey a German and you pay with your life. Something we all need to remember at all times now."

Ala gives her mother an I-told-you-so look when Max welcomes them with open arms. He gives her a hug and tells her how sorry he is about Madame.

Ala is still haunted by Madame's farewell glance. And her abandonment of Luba and Henryk. Sometimes she thinks she could have done more to save them. It's something she turns over and over in her head. She has tried to talk to both Lily and her brother about how dirty the events in the *Umschlagplatz* have made her feel, as if the world will never be clean again, but her guilt and heartbreak cannot be lessened by any amount of analysis. Max's words have no more power to alter her feeling than a commiserations card.

She now notices the wild woman in carpet slippers staring wide-eyed at everyone.

"That's Aunt Elsa," says Max.

"I'm sorry, Max. There was nothing I could do," says Ala's father.

The *Judenrat* has been ordered to reduce the number of employed personnel by fifty per cent. The Germans are demanding 7,000 of these employees and their families for deportation. Max is among those who have been cut from the list. Members of the *Judenrat* have also been ordered to assist the Jewish police in the roundups, something Max had no intention of doing.

"I assume you've taken steps to get another job."

"No. Not yet."

"You need to get your skates on for once in your life."

Her father's tone with his younger brother is by turns condescending, peremptory and sardonically affectionate.

"You can buy employment in one of the German workshops," her father continues. "That's your only way of getting a stamp on your registration card. Without a work certificate you'll be deported. That's why we've brought you the sewing machine. You're more likely to get employed if you donate that. You should get Ella to teach you how to use it. The Schultz workshop is nearby. It occupies an entire block in Nowolipie Street. They make and mend clothes for the German army. That might be your best bet."

"Don't you have to be quartered on the premises in barracks if you work there?"

"Yes, but you can take your family with you. Looks to me like you've been living in a kind of fool's paradise here. Those days are over, Max."

"I've been making the best of things. I don't see what's foolish about that."

"The *Judenrat* has had to move to a new building, in Zamenhofa Street. It appears they want all the Jews closer to the *Umschlagplatz* and the trains. He was murdered yesterday," says Ala's father, nodding up at the painting by Roman Kramsztyk on the wall. "Shot in a courtyard in Chlodna Street. Did you know him?"

"I met him a few times."

"I heard he flew off the handle when they manhandled him. Let that be a lesson."

"What do you mean?"

"You've got a quick temper," he tells Max.

20

Ora has become more withdrawn. This new life of hiding indoors both frightens and bores her. Often now she stands close to Sabina and holds onto her leg. She is troubled by the arrival of Ala's family. She is excited though that she is going to sleep with him and Sabina. She jumps up and down on the bed. For a moment life is as it should be, a child rejoicing in a new opportunity. Eugenia is quiet and shy. Max can tell she has formed her own ideas about the gravity of the situation. He would like to know what these ideas are but Sabina thinks the less the girls know the better. Sabina is struggling, he knows, to personify with conviction the parent's pledge of providing safety.

In bed, with the smell of the expiring wick and melted wax of the candles, Max misses the late-night intimacy he shares with Sabina when they always have their most binding talks. The sanctuary of her body too is out of bounds, though he sometimes slips his hand between her thighs and cups her mound because the wetness there is an elixir of life to him.

The dark thoughts come to him when everyone is asleep. Fear of death now like a bruise beside his heart. The building moans at night. He is noticing it more and more. Awake in the dark, the future becomes whatever he most fears. He hasn't told Sabina that he is running out of money. He hides from her his fear that he will fail her and the girls when they most need him. He now recalls the conversation with Henryk earlier when Ala's brother described the freight trains. He has pictured himself, Sabina and the two girls crushed into one of these cattle cars.

Henryk told him the cars have a small window with iron bars. Max remembers the small iron file he has somewhere in the apartment.

The rumour in the ghetto is that the destination of the trains is a place called Treblinka, in the midst of a pine forest not far outside Warsaw. And that no one taken there is ever seen again. Some say the Jews are asphyxiated there in steam baths; others that it is merely a transit stop where everyone is disinfected before the journey to the east continues. Treblinka has a pleasing sound as a word and yet has become the most sinister combination of vowels and consonants in the language. If he and Sabina and the girls are ever caught in an *aktion*, he is determined to possess some means of escape.

He slips silently out of bed, taking with him a book of matches and fumbling about in the darkness for his shoes. He gropes his way towards the door, holding his shoes and avoiding the board he knows creaks. He can't see Sabina's aunt in the living room but he can sense her watchful presence. Out in the hallway he tries the light switch but there's no electricity. He creeps past the door of the room where his brother, Ella, Henryk and Ala are all sleeping. In the kitchen he lights a candle, feeling himself suddenly more alive and vulnerable in the small arc of flame, his serrated shadow an oversized effigy on the whitewashed wall and ceiling. He opens a drawer beneath the marble table top. Here he finds the file. He also takes out an old metal door handle. The trap door into the attic is in the hallway. The ladder tucked in a corner by the coat rack. He carries his skittish light up the rungs of the ladder. His boyhood returns to him, a body memory of clandestine escapades, as if his childhood had been a benign rehearsal for the deadlier perils that awaited him as a man.

A scratching noise over in the far corner of the attic pumps adrenalin into his chest, as if he is about to have an argument. He catches sight of the rat scurrying off close to the sloping heavily shadowed wall. Then his heart quietens and he can hear the submerged distant sound of metal objects striking stone. It seems to originate from more than one direction. He guesses it is the sound of Jews opening up underground sanctuaries with picks and axes. He finds himself reproaching himself for not being more enterprising. He is not a practical man. Deep down, he feels like a frightened boy impersonating an adult. It's a new experience to envy builders and bricklayers and carpenters. All the so-called uneducated men who have never once excited any envy in him until now.

He climbs out onto the roof. There are thousands of stars above the blacked-out city. For a moment he gives himself up to the riddle of space and time they pose. Then he remembers the nocturnal boat trips with his father and how sometimes he would feel there was something up there among the stars that knew of his existence. He felt the intimacy of this connection originated deep within himself, like the secret source of a river. He never told his father or anyone else about this feeling.

He scrambles about on the tiles until he finds a comfortable place to sit. To begin with he feels what he is doing, sitting on a roof practicing how to file through metal, is a preposterously inadequate measure to take against all the imagined dangers to come. Then he begins to picture the battles taking place all over the world under these same stars. American sailors on board ships patrolling distant oceans; English tanks edging forward through sand storms in faraway deserts, RAF bombers returning home after unleashing earthquakes and firestorms in German cities. The safety of Sabina and her girls, he realises, is dependent on the efforts of all these unknown men out there beneath the same August sky.

It takes him an age to file through the door handle. The muscles in his arms ache, the joints in his fingers. His hands are smeared in blood. The bloody handprints he leaves behind when he returns to bed, like clues in a crime scene, will be noticed the next day.

21

Frequent gunshots have kept everyone in an electrified state of tension throughout the sultry day. At six in the evening Ala and her mother enter a building with a coloured fanlight above the open front door. A shiver of foreboding raises the hairs on Ala's neck and arms the moment she is inside the ghostly vacated building. In the first apartment they enter there is a jumble of children's shoes by the front door. Two mugs of half-drunk tea sit on the scored kitchen table and a wooden toy horse lies on the floor. There's burnt porridge in a saucepan. A damp tea towel thrown on the windowsill. The glasses by the sink are greased with fingerprints. Ala realises she could never sit on any of the empty chairs at the table. That it would be like sitting in the lap of a ghost. All the abandoned objects she beholds discharge something heavier and murkier than sorrow, as if, separated from their story, they have become meaningless. Ala feels she is standing in a world where narrative has stopped.

In another room the loud ticking of a clock adds to Ala's unease. It strikes her as pitiless that time goes on regardless. That the universe is without compassion. It is people that bring compassion into the world. Just as it is people that bring hate into the world. All the cabinet drawers are pulled out. There are family photographs in bevelled glass frames on every surface. Ala guesses from the photographs the occupants were sophisticated Jews from Warsaw. There are no religious artefacts. The husband is a good-looking man with a side parting and a generous smile in his dark eyes. The wife has dark hair with a fluffed-up fringe over her forehead and a rather fussy pinched mouth. She looks defiantly plain. Ala soon begins to feel all the objects in the house are watching her, with disapproval.

"I could never live among other people's possessions, especially knowing they have probably been murdered," she says, turning to face her mother who is standing in the doorway.

"We don't know they've been murdered. But you're right about this apartment. It gives me the creeps."

"Let's just stay with Max."

"Poor Max. We've barged into his love nest. We're interrupting the last happiness he might ever know."

"How can anyone be happy at a time like this? Anyway, I think he likes having us there. It's fortifying to all be together."

"To be honest, Max isn't someone who inspires confidence. And then there's that crazy woman. She's a liability if ever I saw one. That grating little girl voice of hers and all her friends in the mirror. She's driving me insane. I'd feel safer somewhere else. I'd prefer to be with you and Henryk alone."

"What about Dad?"

"He inspires even less confidence than Max. But of course I meant with your father as well."

"How can you say that about Dad?"

"Pardon me for speaking my mind."

"Anyway, Max isn't *that* happy because he's almost run out of money."

"How do you know?"

"He told me."

"I had no idea he confided in you in that way."

Ala sees her mother is flustered by this piece of information. The expression on her mother's face rarely changes quickly as it has done now. Even when she laughs she seems to think about it first and still be thinking about it even in the midst of her enjoyment.

Ala leaves the room. She walks into a bedroom full of lacquered mahogany furniture. Fluted green velvet curtains in which dust has collected. A colourful embroidered eiderdown askew on the big brass bed. She is struck by the indentation of a head visible on a pillow. While looking at the coloured glass bottles on the dressing table she has a sensation of being watched. She looks up at the mirrored doors of the towering wardrobe. In the dusty glass she sees the woman in the photograph, sprawled on the floor by the bed, staring up at her. For a moment the breath is knocked out of Ala. A bullet has blackened the area where the woman's right eye should be.

"You scavengers are a disgrace," someone shouts as Ala and her mother are leaving the building.

22

Max and Ella are folding a coverlet. Awakened dust motes fountain in the shafts of sunlight. When he joins his corners to the corners she is holding his face is close to hers. His downcast eyes focus on her hands. It is stupefying to realise that her hands have been inside his trousers. Some intimation of increased heat in her tells him she too is thinking back to that long-ago evening. It's something he has never told anyone. They had both been a little drunk. He was still a virgin. His brother was in hospital with his broken leg. He likes to believe Ella took the initiative. They kissed and Ella put her hand inside his trousers. The voice in his head was urging him to pull away. But soon she was wiping her sticky wet hands on the seat of his trousers. It felt like a service she had performed for him. He was unable to look his brother in the eye for a long time afterwards. His guilt was remorseless. Not long after, he made the decision to change his name and religion. He felt he ought to seal the dislike of himself he felt. And he wanted to distance himself from his family.

He is conscious now that nothing he is thinking can be said. It's a moment in his life that is unspeakable, an isolated outpost of shame he refuses to ever visit. He still feels sick at the thought of his brother ever finding out. For a long time, until the Germans arrived, it was the worst thing he could imagine happening.

"Well, we've made it through another day," he says, banishing the memory from his mind.

"It's good to see you happy, Max," she says, taking the coverlet and stepping away. "Even if circumstances aren't allowing you to enjoy it to the full."

"Thanks for teaching Eugenia how to use the sewing machine."

"Look, there's no easy way of going about this," she says. "I want to give you some money. Ala told me you've almost run out. Here are five thousand zlotys. To help you look after Sabina and the girls. Samuel doesn't know I'm doing this and I'd rather it stays that way. But I think he's right and you should try to find work at one of the German factories. Offer the sewing machine and some money and I suspect they'll take you on."

Max has trouble accepting the money. The values of the old world are difficult to renounce, even if the world has been turned on its head.

"Think of the money as rent. If a condition of working at one of these factories is living on the premises and you have to move, we'll stay in your apartment. It makes sense. Not that we're trying to get rid of you."

He mirrors her smile.

"To imagine leaving my home seems like the beginning of the end to me," he says. "Like ushering in catastrophe. I keep thinking, perhaps they'll overlook us. There are so many people in the ghetto." He has imagined a pair of high ranking Germans in some office studying a map of the ghetto and pencilling in the sections of streets to be blockaded the next day. Indifferent to the upheaval, misery and panic their pencil strokes cause.

Ella sits down on the mattress, smoothing her skirt over her thighs. "I felt like that when we were forced to leave our home. It's like overnight you lose half of your body's strength. Your legs feel weaker beneath you. It's astonishing how much of our resilience resides is our routines, even in our things. It affected Samuel too. He's never liked change. I sometimes think every person's chances of surviving this war will be largely how adaptable they are to change."

Max acknowledges the wisdom of her remark with a nod.

"And another thing, you've got to offload that mad aunt. I don't want to sound callous, but can't you put her in a hospital?

You've got enough on your plate without having to take care of someone who's lost her mind."

23

A horse-driven cart loaded with Jews hugging bundles and bags passes by. A woman with storm-tossed hair and floundering arms is running behind it. "Give me back my child," she cries out. A returning call of *Mama* issues from the cart. The cart picks up pace as the horses are incited to gallop. "My child. My child," screams the mother. She trips and falls and the cart disappears into Niska Street.

The voice of the little girl calling out for her mother haunts Ala for the rest of the day.

Henryk, returning from work, reports that the number of shootings has greatly escalated. Dead bodies strewn in every street. He goes to visit Lily and returns, distraught, with the news that her family's apartment is empty.

To be alone, he and Ala climb up into the attic and from there up onto the roof. The radiant moon and glittering grid of stars frighten Ala. As if they hold answers to questions she doesn't want to ask. Henryk comforts her when she begins to cry.

"We don't know for sure she's been taken," he says.

"If you take away Lily from my life it's like half of it evaporates. I share more happy memories with her than with anyone. None of those memories will be happy now. I always thought memories provided a secure foundation but it feels like all my memories are cracking like ice underfoot and pulling me down into murky depths I didn't know they had."

"If I could have a wish," says Henryk, bristling with a rage he has been trying to master, "it would be to be a Russian soldier or a British bomb-aimer. I'd give anything if my sole task every day was to kill as many Germans as possible. I want German blood on my hands," he says holding out his palms.

Ala remembers a time when he wanted a train set more than he wanted anything, and later a bicycle.

"We don't know for sure everyone on the trains is killed, do we?"

"Not for sure, no. But I want you to leave the ghetto, Ala. You can pass as a gentile. Would any of your old friends help you? You could try Sophie. I think she'd take you in."

"There's a death penalty now for gentiles helping Jews," she says.

"I know," he concedes. "But we can't just sit around waiting for our turn. A friend of mine at work is a member of Betar, the so-called fascist Zionists. They've got professional soldiers who fought the British in Palestine and are training people in armed combat. They've got weapons. They say people in the future will not want to be Jewish if we don't put up some kind of fight. And I agree. They've built a tunnel out of the ghetto. Maybe I can arrange it that you get out of the ghetto that way."

24

Ora entwines her middle finger with Max's middle finger. *We have to cheer Mum up.*

"What do you suggest?"

"We could buy her a cake?"

"Unfortunately, no one is making cakes today."

"Why not?"

"They can't get hold of the ingredients they need. We can't even find any bread."

"I know."

Max hasn't consulted Sabina about taking Ora out with him to find bread. She was downstairs with Eugenia when he left. Initially he said no. But Ora pleaded, looking up at him with beseeching eyes. He hates how often he has to watch her being denied what she wants nowadays. Kept, as she is, continually a prisoner in the apartment, denied almost everything she wants to do. So he relented. It's six o'clock in the evening and though the roundups should be over for the day he has an uneasy feeling. His instinct is to return home but his pride baulks at the idea of reappearing empty-handed. One last bakery further down Nowolipki Street, he thinks. They pass a woman sobbing and talking to herself.

"Can she see people we can't see, like Aunt Elsa?" asks Ora.

"When you get older you begin talking to people who have disappeared from your life," he says.

"Mum doesn't. And you don't."

"I used to talk to your mum all the time when we didn't see each other."

"What did you say?"

"I rewrote the stories we told each other. I never liked your mum's endings."

Every day Max is forced to acknowledge how frayed his nerves are when irritation with some petty root overwhelms him. To protect his own sanity he has to find ways of pretending the normal, the habitual still exist. Ora is better than anyone at helping him achieve this. She takes little interest in the future. She gives less importance to the Germans. To some extent she acts as a bulwark. But now she suddenly surprises him. "Why don't the Germans like us?" she asks.

Max squeezes her hand. "Every day of our lives," he says after thinking for a moment, "we learn new things and these things make our minds become a more exciting and larger place to play in. If you are lazy or happy to remain ignorant or jealous of other people this doesn't happen. Your mind remains small and you become easily bored and angry. You want to go out into a playground because you only feel important and strong and excited when you are part of a crowd. And in the crowd you do what you're told by the person who shouts the loudest. Shouting nearly always brings hate into the heart. And hate stops you seeing with your own eyes. Hate eventually makes you blind. The Germans don't like us because they can't see us and things you can't see are always a bit frightening."

"I hate it when mum cuts my fingernails and I hate it when Genia laughs at me. Will that make me blind?"

"It won't make you blind but it might make you a bit short-sighted for a while."

"It's Hitler who shouts the loudest, isn't it?"

"I didn't know you knew about Hitler."

"I'm not stupid."

"I've never for one moment thought you are."

"I don't like Hitler."

"Well, that's yet another thing we have in common. Me and you are soulmates. Do you know what a soulmate is?"

"No."

"A soulmate is someone who can make beautiful things come true."

"Like in stories?"

"Exactly."

A horse-driven cart clip-clops towards him and Ora from the corner of Nowolipki and Karmelicka. A Jewish police officer is sitting beside the driver. The horse is labouring under the weight of all the dazed Jewish captives in the cart. Two German motor-cyclists escort the vehicle on either side. While Max catches the eye of an old man with a kindly face in the cart a pair of Jewish policemen emerge from a building nearby. Before Max can react, one of them has snatched hold of Ora and is shouting at the driver to stop the cart. Max grabs hold of him from behind, knocks off his peaked cap and wrestles him to the ground. He is spitting out invective at the hateful man. In his rage he loses sight of Ora. He gets in a good punch to the man's jaw. It's the first time he's hit anyone since schooldays and the constant fights with his brother. As a boy he always ended up with tears in his eyes every time he hit someone. They always caused him shame in front of his peers. He never understood their source or purpose. There are no tears now. A blow to the back of his head throws him off his adversary. Then he is kicked in the face. He is kicked several times. Through a fog of vertigo he is aware of women shouting. Three Jewish policemen haul him into the cart. His nose is dripping blood down his white shirt front. His temples are pounding and there is a growing pain in his eyeballs. The old man he had minutes earlier sympathised with touches his arm. Max's only relief is that Ora isn't in the cart. The closer they get to the *Umschlagplatz* the more signs there are of Nazi barbarity. Corpses sprawled in the gutters while women wail on the pavement, opening their arms out to the sky.

25

Ala is doing her best to console Sabina who is beside herself with grief and rage. She tries to show her the breathing exercises Madame taught her to relax all the muscles in the body. Sabina takes no notice of anything she says.

"What was the stupid man thinking of? How dare he do that? How dare he take my daughter out without asking me."

She and Sabina are scouting the streets which are busy now as everyone emerges from their homes to seek food. While the crazy aunt spoke to people in the mirror Ala's mother and father argued when it first became known Max had taken Ora with him to search for bread. Her mother defended Max but her father accused him of being a peacock and flirting with every female on the planet.

"He's always flirted with you and he only does it to get back at me. It gets on my nerves."

Her mother laughed. Ala realised how close to hysteria everyone was. Sabina spoke of Max as if she harbours nothing but contempt for him. Ala felt hurt on his behalf. She wanted to remind Sabina that he had taken her and her girls in and looked after them for a year. Now every cell in her body yearns for Max and Ora to suddenly appear with a white loaf of bread tucked under their arms.

There are many people no less desperate and distraught than Sabina on the street. No one takes any notice of Sabina's wild-eyed panic. It's the accepted state of mind. When Sabina again hurls vicious insults at her uncle, Ala suggests they split up. But she might be invisible for all the notice Sabina takes of her. Ala leaves her and crosses the street.

With every passing moment the likelihood that Max and Ora have been taken to the *Umschlagplatz* occupies more space in Ala's thoughts. One by one, everyone she knows is ending up there.

Instead of Max, she sees Marcel. He is surrounded by people shouting at him. A woman slaps his face. He doesn't appear to register anything. He doesn't even appear to recognise her when she is standing in front of him.

"Marcel? It's me. Ala."

He is holding his cap in his hand. His dark hair flattened by sweat.

A bearded man shoves her aside. "God will punish you for the disgraceful things you've done against your own people," he says, stabbing his index finger close to Marcel's face.

Ala takes Marcel by the hand and pulls him into an alleyway, away from the crowd. Marcel slides down the wall and sits hugging himself. Ala crouches down beside him. She takes his cap and tosses it aside like a piece of burnt toast she is throwing to the birds. She tells him the Germans have taken Lily. He doesn't say anything so she hugs him. For a while Marcel allows himself to be cradled in her arms. Then, abruptly, he stands up, collects his cap and walks off without saying a word.

26

The cart bumps and jolts over the cobbles. Now only a few hundred yards from the *Umschlagplatz*. Max's attention is caught by a young man on the sidewalk. A rage emanates from him that electrifies the intervening space. He watches as he hurls something at one of the German motorcyclists with all the force of which his emaciated body is capable. It's a piece of broken glass and it strikes the German. The young man stands on the pavement shouting abuse at the Germans in Yiddish. Max takes advantage of the panic caused by the gunshots to jump out of the cart and dash into a doorway.

When he enters his apartment, Sabina marches up to him and slaps his face. He sees only a wild unrecognisable woman full of loathing and fury when he looks at her.

"They didn't get Ora," he says. "I made sure they didn't get Ora." How puny his bravado sounds, as if he is making a plea at the foot of an erupting volcano. "I didn't see what happened to her because I was being beaten. It was a Jew who snatched Ora. A Jew."

"Who do you think you are? You had no right to take my daughter out without asking me. You're not her father." He's never seen her angry before. It's a shock to realise he doesn't like her at the moment. He even wonders if he'll ever be able to like her again.

"Let him tell us what happened," says Ella to Sabina.

Max recounts what happened. He mentions the angry Jewish boy who saved his life by distracting the Germans. "He sacrificed his life and by so doing unknowingly saved mine." No one appreciates the debt he owes this unknown young man. Sabina glares at him with no lessening of contempt, as if she would prefer it had he not been saved.

"You're like an adolescent boy, Max. Don't you think that if ever there was a time to grow up it's now?" says his brother.

Max glares at his brother. He wants to punch him in the face. At the moment it seems the only thing that might make him feel better.

Ella takes his arm and escorts him into the bathroom. The sight of his swollen and bruised face in the mirror is a like a reflection of how his heart feels.

"Let's just hope and pray Ora is safe and she comes home," says Ella, opening the cabinet above the sink and sorting through its contents.

"If this is what life is going to be like from now on…"

"We may as well let the Nazis murder us? Is that what you're thinking?"

Max looks at Ella in the mirror.

"And take no notice of your brother. He's pent up. Everyone needs to calm down."

"What if they have taken Ora? She's never going to forgive me. It was idiotic of me. My brother's right, I can never say no to females."

Ella smiles. "Stop beating yourself up. Now let's put some of this cream on your face."

Max recalls the day he returned from the camp and it was Sabina attending to his wounds. Then he recalls the conversation by the river with Ala the day the war began when she asked him why he had never married and he spoke of his fear of ever arousing disdain in someone he loved. His worst fear, it seems, has been realised.

A rapping on the front door freezes Ella's ministrations. Max hurries out into the hallway. Sabina is already flinging open the door. And there, like a breathtaking magician's trick, stands Ora with a woman wearing a headscarf and a long black skirt. While Sabina sobs on her knees, the woman apologises for taking so long to bring Ora home. "She couldn't remember the address or the way here," she explains. Ora, frightened, complains that Sabina is hurting her.

At midnight Max is still wearing his blood-stained shirt. He is alone in the living room with Aunt Elsa. Sabina hasn't talked to him all evening. She retreated early into his bedroom with the girls. It is a shock to him how quickly his morale has collapsed. How flimsy is the façade of his equanimity. All his immaturity is now making itself felt. His instinct is to hurt Sabina back. Get himself deported tomorrow so that she misses him, so that all her tender feelings for him might be in the ascendancy again.

A single candle lights the living room. Elsa's shadow gesticulates over the wall. She is standing stooped close to the mirror. "He's leaving now," she says. "I said I would see him off but I'm not going to. I've got too much to be busy with."

Max grows unnerved by the pauses she leaves, as if only he can't hear the answering voice.

27

"This is what I heard. In the *Umschlagplatz* a Ukrainian snatched a little girl from her father and swung her by the legs so her skull smashed against a wall. The father made no attempt to intervene, which my friend said seemed the point the Ukrainian wanted to make. For a moment there was an air of suspense in the *Umschlagplatz*. My friend who saw it said he thought for a second all the Jews were going to revolt. But they didn't. No one did a thing. After about five minutes, as if he had thought carefully about what he was going to do, Marcel walked over to the dead girl and smeared her blood and brain matter over his face. Then he walked over to the Ukrainian murderer who was laughing with a companion, spat in his face and hit him with his truncheon. He was able to hit him twice before his companion struck Marcel with the butt of his rifle. The pair of them beat Marcel to a pulp with their rifles. They killed him."

Ala hears this story from Henryk in the *Judenrat* offices where the family are now sleeping. An order was posted the day after Max's escapade with Ora that all residents had to leave the section of Nowolipki Street where Max's apartment is situated. Ala's father decided to move his family to the *Judenrat* building for the time being, until a better solution can be found. Max, Sabina and the girls have moved into barracks in the Schultz workshop.

Ala has little difficulty imagining Marcel carrying out this act. She sees it as him finally emerging from a hiding place. She remembers the night they spent together and how he flaunted his erection at her. *Take the tip between two knuckles and press it in a rocking motion as if you're squeezing the oil from an olive.* She wishes now she had done what he asked. That she had given him this small moment of pleasure. Why all this prudery about physical contact, about the naked body?

There is some respite from the unrelenting exhausting terror when most of the Nazis leave the ghetto. It's rumoured they are carrying out deportations in Otwock and Falenica. Everyone dares to hope that the deportations in Warsaw are over, that they have survived, that they are valuable to the Germans as a workforce. The prophet Zechariah is quoted – *And it shall come to pass that in all the land, said the Lord, two parts therein shall be cut off and die, but the third shall be left therein. I will bring the third part through the fire, and refine them as silver is refined, and will try them as gold is tried.*

Then news that the commander of the Jewish police has been assassinated sweeps through what remains of the ghetto. Leaflets circulate in which responsibility is claimed by the Jewish Fighting Organisation. No one has ever heard of any Jewish fighting organisation. More executions are promised to any Jew collaborating with the Germans. There is also a rumour that a Jew attacked an SS officer with a pair of plyers, ripped open his throat before being shot. There are arguments in the *Judenrat* building. Much talk about the accountability of God. Many of the older generation vent anger at all attempts to fight the Germans. There are still some who believe the Germans need a legitimate excuse to kill them. Ala loses her temper with an overweight elderly man who denounces all resistance as irresponsible egotism and suicidal bravado and feels guilty afterwards for ridiculing him in public. But she has come to realise people take solace in the lies they tell themselves. That, as a general rule, the human mind prefers comforting lies to abrasive truths. Probably she is no different.

The following night there is an escalating growl up in the night sky. Sirens scream out their warning dirge from beyond the ghetto walls. Ala takes Henryk by the hand and leads him out into the street. They look up at the sky where the swinging smoky beams of searchlights light up the undersides of the clouds. The planes appear as silvery black silhouettes. Spurts of blood-red tracer curve up towards the bright moon. Coloured smoke blooms over the rooftops. A great flock of silhouetted birds whirl in panicked formation. Henryk decides it's the British and the Americans, that they have heard what is happening in the ghetto and have come to rescue the Jews of Warsaw. He cheers every explosion. In the wash of ghost light provided by the searchlights Ala dances an entire section of Madame's unperformed choreography on the cobbles of Zamenhofa Street.

28

Max now has a *meldekarte*, the six-page booklet containing his photograph, details of his employment and an official Nazi stamp. He has been put to work sweeping floors and doing odd jobs, hardly, he assures himself, an invaluable service for the German war effort. Adam, his nemesis, works in the same building. He seems to have influence with the Jewish foreman. Max is taken aback to discover how forceful their mutual antipathy remains. Eugenia and Sabina both sit at sewing machines all day. Eugenia volunteered because she so much enjoys sewing, even if it's mending Third Reich uniforms. Ora plays with other children in an office, supervised by the mother of one of the children. He, Sabina, the girls and Aunt Elsa share a bedroom with six other people. Aunt Elsa talks to herself during the night and irritates everyone. There is one man who wants to suffocate her. This same man Max has seen fending off phantoms in his sleep.

The compound, a block of buildings in Nowolipki Street, is closed off with a wooden fence and guarded by gendarmes. No one is allowed out. All buildings not part of a German factory are now out of bounds. The ghetto has been straightened into a much smaller area, a network of enclosed labour camps.

In the mornings all the workers are given a piece of bread and ersatz coffee; in the evenings watery soup and another piece of bread.

Sabina is icy and distant with him. Her heart now a foreign place. It's like both the sun and moon have disappeared from their relationship. There is never an opportunity to be alone with her. It's as if she has decided she will be safer without him. Sometimes he catches Eugenia's eye and knows she at least still feels some affection for him.

Max barely ever possesses enough private space to stretch out his arms. Yet he has never felt so alone. This new communal life takes too much of his air, as if he is trapped in an elevator stalled between floors. He knows lots of Jews are still in hiding outside the small proscribed areas. To be a renegade, a hunted outcast, despite all the dangers, seems the more attractive option. He finds himself wishing he was back at home, perhaps hiding out in the attic and on the rooftops where he can at least see the horizons denied to him. One day, while he is idly sweeping and a woman is singing a lullaby on the other side of a wall, he meets Edek.

"You're working here too?"

"No. I needed to speak to someone here. You wouldn't believe some of the places I've been hiding. One day I had to stand stock-still for hours behind a loose board in a fence. At one point there were gunshots and wailing no more than six feet away. I stumbled over corpses when I emerged at night. What happened to you?"

"What do you mean?"

"The cuts and bruises on your face."

"Three Jewish policemen."

Edek shakes his head in exasperation. "At least some of them will be getting their just desserts before long."

"Can you get me out of here? If only for twenty-four hours."

"What do you intend doing?"

Max tells him what has happened with Sabina. It feels good to finally have an outlet for the whirlpool of self-recrimination and self-exoneration that has been draining him of resilience.

"This is no time to indulge in debilitating emotion. You need to keep your wits about you, Max. You need to shake yourself out of this overly emotional state. Sabina's probably not in her right mind at the moment. No one is. Just let her be for a while."

"That's why I want to get out of here."

"Okay. I'll arrange it that you leave with me this evening. Meet me at the gate at seven."

Outside the compound at sunset the pink and gold flushes on windows remind him of the high expectations he has always had of the future. As if the best days were always still to come. Now, he is forced to concede, they are all almost certainly behind him. The street is littered with household objects. Overnight, treasured belongings have become trash. What he sees is like an eloquent depiction of the destructive power of time. With no sign anywhere of the redeeming power of love. He steps around a mattress with rust marks left by the bedsprings. Now and again a solitary furtive figure appears and quickly disappears. Otherwise, there's a pervasive stillness as if the world has stopped turning. On the stairs of his building he listens carefully for sounds of activity. He can't decide if he feels like a ghost of himself or if it is his home that has withdrawn into the spirit world. When he enters his apartment it's like all the familiar fixtures are denying memory of him. There's a moment of unease during which he feels like he's being made to prove his identity. He is relieved to find his home hasn't yet been ransacked. He picks up from the floor a map he drew for Ora. He began with their home represented by a drawing of Ora herself who he depicted as a kind of mermaid with a silvery tail and to which she took exception. Then he traced out routes to London, Paris, Venice, New York, Cairo and Jerusalem, drawing images of the landmarks of these cities in coloured crayons.

He knows it was careless of him to put Ora at risk, but he can't help feeling Sabina's hostility has deeper roots, as if she has been surreptitiously collecting evidence against him from day one. He realises he has always been unsure of her feeling. As if she has kept a part of herself secret and apart, as if she has continually conducted an argument with herself about him. He feels he has to accept their bond isn't as exalted as he believed. Just another ordinary relationship with niggling unspoken grudges, mistimed or inappropriate interventions, insensitive failures of understanding, secret yearnings for escape, a growing historical archive of small but significant acts of treason. Adam's presence is a constant taunt. He knows Sabina flirted with him when he was away in the camp. Suspects they would now be a couple had he not returned. Ora would have accepted the transference of roles within days. Oddly, it's Eugenia with whom he now feels a fateful connection, with whom he feels he shares a bond deeply layered with consequential mystery.

He goes into his bedroom. Picks up all the items of clothing Sabina has left behind, and one by one lifts them up to his face, searching out her scents. He wonders why she has left behind the silvery grey dress with the red and blue and yellow flower motifs she wore with a belt the day she moved into his apartment. It's like another compliment she paid him that she has retracted. He finds a pair of her stockings, a lace bra and the pair of panties with the tiny red bow in a drawer. He can't decide if he ought to take these articles of clothing to her, if he any longer has the right to handle her intimate things.

29

Ala stands with her mother and father outside the *Judenrat* building where a selection is taking place. No one, it seems, is any longer safe. All those selected for deportation have been made to kneel in ranks. Latvian guards are robbing and beating them. Young men with a dull glint of cruelty in their eyes. Their contempt of kindness like a collective consensus, a binding pact among themselves, as if kindness is a deplorable weakness. Some of the women around Ala are busy with their compacts and lipsticks, urgently trying to make themselves look younger and healthier. One or two of the older women, anticipating this moment, have recently dyed their hair. There's an atmosphere of this being some kind of macabre beauty contest. Ala knows she is an attractive young woman. Even though she has rarely been able to own the confidence such a gift ought to impart. She studies the German officer who will be her judge. The most striking thing about him is that he is wearing pristine white gloves.

Ala steps forward to expose herself to the German's appraising gaze. Like her father, she is dismissed with a cursory glance to the left. She can't help wondering bitterly what the German found so unattractive about her. Her father lays a consoling hand on her shoulder. He so rarely touches her that she has to stop herself from crying. She is close to tears every moment of every day at the moment. Her mother has not been selected for the transport. Grandfather Frydman too has somehow survived the selection. There's an ingenious horrifying cruelty about these selections. A woman is separated from her child;

a husband from his wife. Then the lucky one is subjected to a harrowing trial of conscience. Ala's mother, without hesitation, walks across to join her and her father in the condemned group. Grandfather Frydman does not follow her and stands refusing eye contact with his family.

They are made to kneel on the cobbles while the selection continues. A Latvian guard with blonde hair and blue eyes, probably no more than nineteen years old, steals Ella's wedding ring and then shouts at Ala. Grandma Frydman, exhausted, collapses forward on her hands. The Latvian turns his attention away from Ala. He strikes at the back of her grandmother's head with the butt of his rife. Then again with more force. And a third time. Blood spurts out and splatters Ala. Its wet warmth quickly turns sticky on her arm. A fly circles her head, lands on her arm. Ala begins to shake, as if she has a fever. She has to summon all her strength not to scream.

Two hours later, escorted by the Latvian guards, they are marched through the devastated streets towards the *Umschlagplatz*. Ala's knees are sore and bleeding. More than once, like a recurring motif in a nightmare, she sees a black hand-held funeral cart, dripping blood behind it. The Latvians shoot up at windows for sport and sometimes at people walking out of step in the column. Ala notices a faded billboard advertising shampoo. The innocent world the poster evokes as remote now as her childhood. At the *Umschlagplatz* Ala, her mother and father are shoved through the gate into the heaving sea of people inside. For a moment the hope rises in her that Marcel will appear and rescue them. She has forgotten he is dead. Then she is picturing him in his final moments, with the child's blood smeared on his face.

They are shoved on as gunshots behind make the crowd surge forward. At times, in the tight crush of bodies, Ala's feet find no purchase of ground beneath her. Soon she has lost her canvas shoulder bag. What feels like the whole sum of her identity is inside. Her journal, her favourite photographs, all her identification papers and a birthday card from Madame among the things she has lost. In the hot sun the stench of sour breath, excrement, urine and sweat is nauseating. A man with punched staring eyes asks her mother if she has any poison for sale. Many are reciting *Shema Yisrael*. There are Jewish policemen amidst the crowd who use their truncheons to hurry the terrified crowd onwards towards the train.

Ala has heard that the system at the *Umschlagplatz* is unpredictable. Some days the Nazis gather too many Jews and when the trains are full set the remaining captives free; other days they hold the excess captives overnight in the large ugly municipal building that now acts as a hospital for contagious diseases. So when her mother tugs and steers her towards that building Ala knows what she is thinking. *Get as far away as possible from the train.* Then she realises her father is no longer holding her hand. She sees him a few feet away, his grey jacket crumpled, his shoulders drawn in. He is no longer wearing his hat and his hair is dishevelled. A Jewish policeman is striking him with his truncheon. He is being driven further away, towards the narrow alley that leads to the trains. He looks round and his eyes are wide with terror. Ala fears her mother will dislocate her shoulder so hard is she tugging at her arm. There are more gunshots. She loses sight of her father. She resists the relentless tug of her mother. "We've lost Dad," she says. Her mother pulls at her with more force.

30

It pains Max to say farewell to his gramophone records and paintings. He knows there's little chance he will ever see them again. He tries to believe it is their inevitable demise he is mourning rather than his own. He is on his way back to the Schultz compound having spent a night in his own bed. The temptation to remain hiding in his apartment overridden by the urgency he feels not to allow Sabina out of his sight. He has to hope she will find it in her to forgive him. She is all he has in the way of motivation and courage. When, during the night while he listened to the relentless muffled underground clinking of hammers and chisels, he imagined not returning to the German workshop, banishing Sabina from his sightline, it was like his mind was lit by only the dying flame of a match, bounded on all sides by a swelling tide of darkness.

He sees only a few solitary people on the early evening streets. He exchanges eye contact with a young girl wearing tangerine lipstick. She is furtive and frightened and emaciated. Broken glass crunches underfoot. Dirtied white feathers lay everywhere and have collected in piles in the gutters. Many who chose to believe the Germans and volunteered for resettlement emptied their quilts and pillows of feathers before the train journey so as to make them easier to carry.

A street urchin with matted hair and a blistered sore on his top lip approaches him. He is wearing a man's grey jacket which is too big for him.

"What will you offer for a white loaf of bread?"

"Otto? It's me, Max."

"I know."

"Where's your father?"

Otto mimes a knife slitting a throat.

"And your brother and sister?"

He shrugs.

Max offers him fifty zlotys for the loaf of bread. Otto dismisses this proposal with wily condescension, as if he is the adult and Max is the child. Without permission, he takes Max's canvas bag and rifles around inside. He takes a shine to Sabina's underwear.

"You'd rather have a woman's used underwear than money?"

"For my girlfriend, yeah."

Max can't help smiling. He decides Sabina will be happier with a loaf of bread than her underwear.

"For 5,000 zlotys I can offer you a place in a bunker," he tells Max after the deal is done. "It's got a water supply, good ventilation and three exits."

"How many of you are there down there?"

Otto shrugs his shoulders. "Think about it," he says. He pulls out the navy-blue flat cap tucked inside his waistband, places it jauntily on his head and walks away with an air of self-possession few adults now possess.

Max is standing by a faded red poster pasted on the wall of a tenement building. It lists the names of Jews executed for leaving the ghetto back in January. He has never seen this before. One of the names is the daughter of a former client of Mr Kaminski. She was only twelve.

When he returns to the Schultz compound he can't find Sabina or the girls. He asks several people if they have seen her. He asks if there has been an *aktion* in the factory today. It becomes more difficult for him to keep his voice steady. He crosses the courtyard. Children are playing *Selection*, a new game they've devised in which some play the Nazis, others the Jews. The children playing the Nazis have learned all the familiar German commands and insults and the haughty contempt with which they are barked.

No one is interested in his growing panic.

After a while he realises he hasn't seen Adam either.

Eventually, deflated, his steps shortening, his shoulders slumping, he decides to wait in the room where they sleep. Someone else has taken the stretch of floor where previously Sabina, Eugenia and Ora's bedding lay. There's no sign of Aunt Elsa either. Punishing himself, as if he deserves no better, he begins to wonder if Sabina and the girls might not be better off with the more practical and vigorously wilful Adam. He sits against the wall, summoning strains of Mahler's *Ich bin der Welt abhanden gekommen* into his head. While listening to it last night in his apartment he had stopped himself from recalling favourite moments with Sabina, as if worried he might wear these memories out before he most needs them.

It's dark when the first explosion sends a shockwave through the building, rattles all the windows and shakes dust down from the ceiling. There are both cheers and screams from those around him. More explosions follow. For a moment the floor seems to buckle beneath his feet. The concussion of the latest explosion makes his teeth ache and tightens his chest. He gets to his feet and stumbles over bodies in the dark. People collide with him in the darkness on the stairs. It becomes apparent bombs are falling in the ghetto. The reflection of a searchlight lights up the room he enters. Skeletal shadows fidget over the walls. He looks from one ghostlit face to another. Expressionless eyes in bloodless faces stare back at him. Sabina isn't among them. He hurries into another room. Two young men stand at the window cheering. The sky outside is lit by sparkles and flares. The older people are sitting up with uncertain smiles on their faces.

He stumbles and gropes his way down to the ground floor and enters the large room full of desks and sewing machines. In the spluttering anarchy of the warlight he finds Sabina's face and their eyes meet.

31

Ala and her mother have bought themselves another night of life. The trains were full. They are being held overnight in the echoing chaos of the unlit hospital building in the *Umschlagplatz*. They sit slumped against a wall in a cavernous room full of muttering and coughing shadow figures. The stench of excrement and vomit is suffocating.

"Do you have a feeling about Dad?" asks Ala. Her voice sounds strange in her ears, slurred and childish. She can smell how foul her breath is.

"What do you mean?"

"Would you sense if he was no longer alive?"

"Is that what you feel?"

"I don't have a good feeling about anything."

"My tongue feels swollen as if it's about to choke me."

The Germans have turned off the water in the building.

"Suck your fingers."

"It was callous of me not to help when we had more than we needed. I turned a blind eye, Ala. Do you know I once made excuses for not donating any money to the children's hospital in Leszno Street? Only now am I ashamed of myself. Now that we too have joined the legions of the living dead."

"I've never heard you talk like this before," says Ala. "It's not you and I don't like it. Anyway, you ought to know by now that the Germans are clever at getting us to ask the wrong questions."

There's a prolonged silence, broken by the sound of a man coughing a few feet away and somebody else moaning and praying.

"Can I ask you something? Did you become the person you hoped you'd become when you were my age?"

"Why are you asking me this now?"

"Because I think we should talk. Tomorrow we'll be on that train. We're not animals. The least we can do is hold on to our humanity. We never talk. I suppose I regret not taking more interest in you. Do you know my most constant emotion the past few years has been the irritation I felt towards you? I always became a different person when you were watching me. A person I didn't like."

"And you think that's unusual? Children never share the blame. It's always the parent who faces all the charges. My mother was my greatest enemy. My first experience of war."

Ala sees again the back of Grandma Frydman's mutilated head and the fat flies feasting on the seep of her brain tissue. It occurs to her that in normal times they would be grieving now. Yet she has barely given a thought to the murder of her grandmother. It's the image of the handsome Ukrainian soldier shooting a little girl after the train had left that she can't get out of her head. At sunset he was joking with a pretty Jewish nurse in a white coat when he noticed the distraught abandoned child. He raised his rifle, shot her and then continued chatting to the nurse. The grotesque smile the nurse felt constrained to keep on her face as he continued joking with her was for Ala emblematic of the collective insanity that has overtaken the world.

"Do you know your father never once let me see him without his false teeth? He never took them out. I think those teeth and his built-up shoe made him feel deformed. But it was not something he would talk about. After the accident he disappeared into himself. He thought twice about laughing, about talking even. He developed a close-lipped smile. And of course our physical relationship suffered as a result. More than suffered. But he was a very kind man. And I wish I had been more understanding. I realise now how much there still is I want to say him. I keep seeing an image of him in his built-up shoe being goaded by some German pig."

"You're talking about him in the past tense," says Ala, realising she is thinking about him in the past tense too. She has remembered the one or two times she brought a boy home and how she would make a point of disassociating herself from the boy initially on encountering her father. As if to reassure her father that he was still her favourite.

"They're putting us on those trains to kill us. It's stupid to believe any different. What use are all these children and old and sick people to the Germans? Which means the Germans have murdered hundreds of thousands of Jews in little more than a month. And yet no one seems to care. Where are the English and the Americans? Where are the decent people? Do they not know what the Nazis are doing? Poor Henryk. He must think he's lost us all."

"Do you remember that fortune teller? She said she saw a train when she looked at Dad."

"I was unfaithful to your father once. I hope he never suspected. I hope the memory of me provides him with some strength wherever he is now."

"In the ghetto?"

"What do you mean?"

"You were unfaithful to him here?"

"No. Of course not. Forget I ever said that. It was years ago and it was a moment of madness. It didn't mean anything."

"Did you know Marcel was attracted to you?"

Ala senses her mother's unseen face relax into a brief smile. "I don't think Marcel was attracted to women. I think he might have been the other way inclined. I think most of the time he was spinning yarns."

Ala wonders if this observation of her mother's might explain the often unfathomable behaviour of Marcel, the disgust that so often overcame him at moments when he and she might have kissed. "I'm still quite naïve, aren't I?" she says.

Her mother puts her arm around Ala's shoulder. "Nothing wrong with that, darling. You're still very young after all."

The sound of someone squirting out a prolonged stream of diarrhoea is amplified in the high-ceilinged room. Ala shivers at this reminder of the organic nature of human life. Her brain struggles with the likelihood that by this time tomorrow she will no longer exist.

Then she hears an escalating growl up in the sky. Initially she thinks hunger and thirst are making her hallucinate.

"Bombers," says her mother. She gets to her feet and pulls Ala up. A loud explosion jars the foundations of the building. The entire world seems to rock on its axis, as if a new reality is pushing up from the depths of the planet's core. It ought to be terrifying, but Ala finds she wants to shout with exhilarating relief. She walks with her mother towards the exit of the building as more bombs fall. In the reflected sheen of a searchlight and a nearby fire she sees panicking SS guards running towards the gate of the *Umschlagplatz*. It is wildly gratifying to witness that they are cowardly men at heart. She wants to yell disparaging insults at their backs. Many of the captive Jews are staring up at the sky and cheering, as if God has finally appeared there.

Whistling high-explosive incendiaries rain down on the city. Ala stands with her mother watching the white flashes and red fire balls. The night is lit up like day. Several bombs explode nearby with incandescent thunder and howls of rushing hot wind. The ground does not stop shuddering. Ala looks up at the undersides of clouds lit by the searchlights. Then she and her mother join the crowd of Jews walking to the gate. There are no guards there. Everyone begins running through the firelight brightening the midnight streets of the ghetto.

32

The bombs frightened Ora. Now they have stopped falling she and Eugenia are asleep. Sabina sits down beside Max against a workbench. The glow of a nearby fire on the large mullioned window provides enough light for him to see her in some detail. She is wearing one of his white shirts. Her legs bare. He is overjoyed she chose to wear an item of his clothing in his absence.

"Don't ever do that again. I thought they had taken you," she says.

"I'm sorry. You were right. It was irresponsible of me to take Ora out."

"I lost my mind for a few days. Take no notice of the things I said. I didn't mean them."

"I sold your underwear to Otto for a loaf of bread. He wanted it for his girlfriend."

"Where did you go?"

"Home. Do you think it's a good idea staying here? Might we not be better off hiding in my attic? Or Otto spoke of an underground bunker. I feel trapped here."

"Let's not think about these things for a while. I think they have the right idea," she says, referring to the gasps and groans and slapping of moist flesh of a mating couple nearby. She puts her hands in his lap. Unfastens the buttons of his trousers while looking him in the eye.

He feels ashamed of himself for doubting her.

She pulls down his shorts. Her face is almost touching his erection. It's the first time she has ever run her eyes so intently over his naked body.

"I want to see what happens," she whispers.

He gives her a puzzled look.

"I've never seen what happens. And I've never even had the stuff on my hands. And I want to say sorry. I could never look at my husband's erection. And I rarely touched it. I suppose that should have been a warning. I just thought I had an aversion to that part of the male anatomy in general."

"And that's not the case?"

"No. I think you look quite princely down here."

He watches her brush his erection with her hands, with her lips, her nose, her cheeks, her eyelids. He is moved by how diligently eager she is to give him pleasure, by how much kindling communion there is in her touch. Every time he gasps her eyes widen and her mouth forms an O, as if his pleasure is a current crackling through her body too. He is hypnotised by the serpent squirm of her hips and her raised feet caressing each other as she touches him. It helps him hold back that he imagines someone might be watching in the brightening room. She smiles as she touches him. Sometimes she smiles up at him, sometimes she smiles to herself. She constantly looks up at his face, as if to gauge the level of his engagement.

33

Ala holds up her face to the late afternoon sun. The solar warmth draws up all the life in her to the surface of her skin. For a moment she experiences the memory of warm grass beneath her bare feet, her toes separating individual tickling blades and the press of the living earth against her naked heels. For a moment she is able to discontinue time.

The blockades are over for the day. She is out on the streets to hunt for bread. Hunger weakening all the muscles in which the memories of Madame's choreographies are stored. She walks past Max's building. She realises he probably doesn't know his brother has been taken to Treblinka. She realises she doesn't even know if her uncle is still alive. She is tempted to go up to his apartment when she sees Henryk. He is walking towards her, on the other side of the street. His eyes are downcast, rooted to the ground. She is struck by how ill and broken he looks. His skin dry and powdery. His trousers held up by string. She calls out to him. He stares at her disbelievingly as if expecting her to dissolve before his eyes. Ala runs over to him. The exertion sets her heart pounding. She is breathing hard, her ribcage flexing, as if she's been dancing. She throws her arms around his neck.

"You're real," he says. "I thought I was hallucinating."

But the joy has left Ala's eyes. Her heart is still racing. A symptom of her hunger rather than excitement. She has to tell Henryk about their father.

"Look!" He plunges his hand inside the waistband of his trousers and produces Ala's journal.

Now it is Ala's turn to look in disbelief.

"Can you imagine what I felt when I saw your dance bag in the sorting warehouse? Of all the tens of thousands of things in that room it seemed to glow as if attracting my eye to it. It was like looking at your dead body. I can't believe you're alive. I couldn't save the other things. Your photographs are inside though. Often they search us when we're leaving work."

His apologetic air brings tears to her eyes.

"Mum and Dad have been taken, haven't they?" he says.

"Not Mum. We escaped during the air raid. We lost Dad. A Jewish policeman began beating him in the *Umschlagplatz*. I can still feel on my fingers the loosening clamp of his hand when we were separated." She holds out her hand to Henryk, as if inviting him to see what she can feel there.

She watches her brother fight down his emotion. She remembers them both as children and how she always took her lead from him. He could bestow a compelling sorcery to any old piece of junk he held in his hands.

"There's a chance he was taken to a work camp," he says. "Some days there's a selection at the entrance to the railway siding. Able-bodied men are put on a different train."

Ala knows he too can see an image of their father in his built-up shoe, limping on the broken leg that failed to heal properly.

34

Max is jumpstarted awake by shrill whistles and gunshots. He is naked beside Sabina on the floor underneath a work bench. He hears the percussion of nailed boots on stone. Three Latvian guards storm into the room where he and Sabina are hurriedly getting into their underwear. The Latvian near him adds a whiff of alcohol to the musty mushroomy stink of the crowded room. While he is pulling on his trousers he watches Sabina hurry off towards Eugenia and Ora. Fear is moving over the surface of his skin, leaving no part of his body untouched. The Latvians are shouting. Fingers and thumbs hair-triggered on their rifles. Max pushes down the idea that this might be the last day of his life. There is a crust of dried semen on his navel. Sabina's musk a presence on his fingers and in his hair. He slips the small iron file into his shoes. Another gunshot increases the panic. Sabina is forbidden to put on her shoes by a snarling guard who shoves her towards the door. Max struggles with a moment of rage and shame that he can't defend her.

The Ukrainian and Latvian mercenaries are all young men but the members of the German police battalion standing guard outside are mostly middle-aged men. All the Jews are made to line up in ranks and wait their turn to walk up to the desk where a German SS officer sits, sending people to the left or right. *Links. Rechts.* Everyone is clutching their work certificate, their life card as it is called. Max sees the SS man is taking no notice of credentials. This selection is all about physiognomies, aesthetics. The few children are clutching favourite toys and dolls. Ora has her woollen cat with the big blue button eyes. More and more often nowadays she holds long conversations with her woollen cat. Max tries to concentrate on keeping both the fear and loathing he feels for this German officer off his face. He knows he will be sentenced to death if he provokes dislike in the man.

An old woman touches Max's arm. "I'm alone," she says. "I want you to have this. To look after your little girl." She hands him a wad of banknotes. Then she bends down in front of Eugenia. "You are young and beautiful and one day I hope you will see Jerusalem," she says.

A father is separated from his little boy. He is ordered to the right; his son to the left. Two Jewish policemen escort the boy to the middle of the street. The father hesitates. Max can't even begin to imagine the thoughts rushing into his head, the instincts surging through his thin body. When the father crosses over to join his son among the condemned, the German officer draws his pistol, releases the safety catch and shoots him in the back. He places the smoking pistol on the table and motions to the next in line to step forward.

The old woman who gave Max the money is sent to the left.

The German looks up at Max. There is no trace whatsoever on his face that barely three minutes ago he murdered a harmless man who only wanted to comfort his son. Max is unsettled by the yoking incandescence of intimacy that occurs between him and the German, as if they are discovered alone together outside of time for a moment. He looks down at the SS insignia on his grey-green neatly pressed uniform. The German orders him to the right. For an instant he is stupidly flattered that this authority figure has seen something in him worth saving. He knows the same gratitude he always felt at school when a captain of a football team chose him for his side above others, spared him the humiliation of being the last boy picked. As the German is about to ordain Eugenia's fate there's a scuffle, shouting and then a gunshot. Everyone looks over to the group of Ukrainian mercenaries. In the momentary confusion Max pulls Eugenia with him and hides her behind him on the pavement among the reprieved. His heart races with the anticipation of the German noticing Eugenia's absence at his desk. A hollow-cheeked woman in a purple shawl helps him shield Eugenia from the eyes of the Nazis. He thanks her with a movement of his head.

Now it is Sabina and Ora's turn. Ora, he knows, stands no chance of a reprieve. No child does. Max has his first doubt. Perhaps he shouldn't have taken Eugenia with him. He knows Sabina will join Ora. His heart begins racing again. He feels like he is hanging from one hand to a slowly loosening gutter. The Nazi smiles down at Ora before sending her to the left. He stops Sabina when she begins to lead her daughter away. Max sees the Nazi is going to play some kind of sadistic game with her. A Jewish policeman obeys the German's order to pick Ora up and carry her over to the group of Jews destined for the *Umschlagplatz* and Treblinka. The woollen cat with the blue button eyes falls from her hands. He sees Ora is too distressed to notice. Max is debating whether or not to join Ora in the ranks of the condemned. He tells himself he would but he doesn't trust the Nazi not to shoot him and Eugenia in the back as they make their way over. The German is talking to Sabina as if she's someone he would like to know better, as if this is a pleasing casual encounter on a street corner. Sabina keeps looking over at Ora. Ora, he sees, isn't crying. She is staring at Sabina with bewilderment. Just as Max is thinking Sabina will not be able to withstand much longer the pleading terrified appeal in Ora's eyes she turns her back on the German officer and walks over towards her youngest daughter with her arms open. The scream that rises in Max's throat when he sees the German pick up his pistol never emerges. The grasp of Eugenia's hand in his tightens and tugs. Sabina is barefoot in a thin summer dress. The crack of the pistol has a muffled quality in his ears, as if he has moved away from what is happening. Sabina performs a little skip, both her feet leaving the ground for a fleeting instant, and a red spray of mist momentarily blows out her dress. Then she falls facedown on the ground in a pose he has never seen her body assume before. It all seems to happen at a different speed from the rest of life, as if in a different realm. He stares at the widening red stain on the back of her dress which has rucked up to reveal the backs of her thighs. She twitches for a while, then is still. Max stares at her hands, willing them to move. Even now it seems like some mistake has occurred in his vision. As if he only needs to blink to make Sabina rise to her feet, brush herself down and continue with her life.

Max stands stricken in the glare of the inconceivable. It taxes all his resources to hold everything familiar about himself in place. It's like he's now waiting for the next enormity to happen. For the world as he knows it to rip apart like a painted backdrop and reveal a different reality behind. When he finally begins to understand that Sabina has now left the world, that he will never again hear her voice or behold the mysteries in her eyes or know the warmth of her body on his hands, he glares at the German officer. A thinning cloud of gun smoke still hovering over his head. He looks over at the pistol on the table. He has never held a gun before. His heart begins racing as the idea of marching back to the table suggests itself with compelling force. The pull of Eugenia's hand as she tries to free herself from his grasp brings him back to the moment. He wasn't aware of how tightly he's been gripping hold of her. He sees Ora is staring with pleading wide eyes at her sister.

"There's nothing you can do," he says quietly. "If you go over to Ora he will kill you." His voice sounds to him tritely, callously unaltered. He is bewildered to discover that he is still able to act in character. He dislikes himself for it.

Eugenia doesn't answer or even look at him. He has become her enemy again.

"I can't let them kill you, Eugenia."

He knows she hates him for holding her back. And he feels ashamed of himself. As if, as a grown man, he should have possessed the resources to prevent what has just happened.

The selection continues. Sabina's blood is pooling beside her body on the cobbles. Max cannot see her face. He keeps seeing her the split second before she was shot. Barefoot in her summer dress. An intimately known gesture in her limbs and the tilt of her head. The stubborn idea still surfaces in him that a mistake has been made. That his eyes are deceiving him. At the same time he has to steel himself to keep Eugenia hidden while she continues to intermittently struggle to free herself from his grip. And he has to offer faked reassurance to Ora who looks over at him and Eugenia with a beseeching silent appeal on her face that is sucking all the blood from his heart and is becoming more and more like a criminal act to ignore.

Trucks arrive, bringing a stink of petrol fumes. Max loses sight of Ora in the confusion as all those selected for deportation are forced to board the vehicles. Ukrainian mercenaries with rifles at the ready oversee the operation. When the trucks have left, the Ukrainians rummage through the bundles and suitcases left behind on the cobbles.

Sabina's black lace bra is laying on the floor where she and he slept together. He clutches it as he saw the children earlier clutching their favourite toys. Then he looks helplessly at Eugenia. He sees in her eyes that her loss is even more sundering than his.

"I'm sorry, Eugenia," he says, recognising more of Sabina in her face than ever before.

35

Ala sits watching her mother cradle Max's head in her arms. He has bribed the guards at the gate of the compound where he works and come to see them at the *Judenrat* building. His tears have made Ala cry too. Her tears begin to frighten her, as if they will never stop.

He has told them how every day he feels he has Sabina's scent on him.

"It's like a hallucination. I'm wearing her every day."

He has told them Eugenia refuses to talk to him.

"She won't even look at me. She does what I tell her but she won't lift her eyes to mine."

He has told them he feels deeply ashamed that he abandoned Ora, that he didn't die with her. That only his determination to save Eugenia now stops him from walking voluntarily to the *Umschlagplatz*.

"Eugenia should go over to the other side instead of me," says Ala when she can talk again. "I wouldn't be able to leave you anyway," she says to her mother. It surprises her to give voice to a thought she has never consciously formed.

"You should both go," says her mother. "We've made enquiries about getting Ala out of the ghetto," she tells Max. His eyes are empty, unresponsive. "Max. Listen to me. Do you know someone who would take in Eugenia?"

Max isn't listening.

"What about Eugenia's father? Where's he? Max? Talk to me."

"He left Sabina for another woman. He isn't interested in his children."

"What about his parents?"

"I've got an address in Warsaw."

"Why not try them? Surely they'd take in their own grand-daughter? You'd have to pay for documents. And you'd have to pay a bribe to get the two of you out. And you have to be on your guard against blackmailers. Especially close to the ghetto. I heard of a woman who was robbed of everything almost the moment she was beyond the wall. She had to return to the ghetto. You don't look particularly Jewish but that's not enough. You've got to learn to not act Jewish. You've got to learn to pretend to be carefree, even happy. You've got to saunter through the streets of Warsaw."

Looking at her crumpled and destitute uncle with his puffy bloodshot dead eyes the idea of him sauntering with a carefree air through the streets of Warsaw is so preposterously far-fetched that it might be funny under different circumstances.

"And another important thing to remember, don't trust anyone. Apparently, there are Jewish informers who work for the Gestapo outside the wall."

"I want to find out the name of the German who shot Sabina," says Max of a sudden.

"Then you have to survive. You have to survive so you can make sure he's brought to justice," says Ala. She knows it is probably folly to expect much of justice in the world but she feels she has to say something of encouragement.

"My first priority is to do everything in my power to ensure Eugenia escapes the insane bloodlust of the German nation. And my second priority is to kill this man, even if I have to do it with my bare hands."

It frightens Ala a bit, the venomous hatred with which Max says this. Her mother too, she sees, is embarrassed on his behalf. Max is anything but a warrior. The fraught silence lasts longer than is comfortable.

It strikes Ala that her uncle has barely registered the news that his brother was taken to the death camp. She supposes he has no room for any more grieving. Death, once a monumental and sundering event, as if arriving from a remote rarefied plane of reality, is now no more remarkable than the slam of a door. It's difficult for her too to grieve for her father, without a body, without a funeral. It's not even certain he's dead, just as it's not certain Ora or Madame or Lily are dead. Henryk has told her of a man at work who claims his young wife writes to him every day from Treblinka.

"He gets furious if anyone questions this claim. But he refuses to show us the letters."

36

On the orders of the Plenipotentiary for Deportation Matters, the *Judenrat* in Warsaw announces the following:

1. By Sunday, 6 September 1942, by 10 o'clock in the morning, all Jews without exception who are in the ghetto must gather in order to register in the area bounded by the following streets: Smocza, Gęsia, Zamenhof, Szczęśliwa, and Parysowski Square.

2. Movement of Jews during the night of 5-6 September is also permitted.

3. Food for two days should be taken and drinking vessels.

4. It is forbidden to lock flats.

5. Whoever fails to comply with this order and remains in the ghetto until Sunday, 6 September 1942, after ten o'clock in the morning (apart from the above-mentioned area) will be shot.

Max has no intention of subjecting Eugenia to another selection. As soon as he reads the notice he bribes the guards at the gate of the Schultz compound and takes Eugenia with him to his apartment. It's the only idea he can come up with that might restore to him some small sense of control over circumstances.

He prepares the attic for a siege. He is up and down the ladder until the small hours. Two mattresses, a carbide lamp, a kitchen knife, pails of water, books, candles, a few potatoes, three tins of sardines, several slices of toasted bread. He tells Eugenia to bring anything she wants. She brings a toy animal belonging to Ora.

"Nothing else? What about your embroidery kit? Or a book?"

She shakes her head, as if she has lost the person she used to be and all the things that defined her.

He puts Henry Purcell's *Dido's Lament* on the gramophone but it is too painful so he replaces it with Debussy's *Clair de Lune*. It's a wonder to hear beautiful music again. He tries to catch Eugenia's eye. Wanting her to share his wonder. Then he finds a hair from Sabina's head on a pillow. As a part of her once living body it brings her close with a cruel and maddening kind of trickery. He also finds a necklace of tiny silver shells and puts it around Eugenia's neck.

"This was your mum's."

He is oblivious to the history of many of Sabina's things, jealous almost of their intimate relationship with her at times when she was unknown to him except as a memory. Now she is a memory again. As if this had been the destiny she was to play in his life all along.

He discovers he has lost the button he tore from her dress as a young man. It bothers him far more than is rational.

Before returning to the attic he does his best to make his apartment appear long since abandoned. To the accompaniment of Puccini's *O Soave Fanciulla* at full volume he throws everything from the drawers and closets onto the floor. He topples a wardrobe. He strews kitchenware over the floor, breaks plates and glasses. He begins to revel in the wanton destruction. It becomes an outlet for all his anger.

Later he sits on the rooftop with a pile of Sabina's clothes in his lap. As he runs his hands over the fabrics his fingers recall the knobs of her spine and the wings of her shoulder blades, the quivering pulse inside her thighs and the slender bones in her feet. He wants to memorise every detail of her naked body and keep it forever imprinted as a presence on his hands. He remembers the guessing game he always set himself of where and how she wanted to be touched whenever she undressed for him. He remembers meeting her eyes over distances and the emblazoning of all the intervening space that took place. He remembers how every little thing observed or experienced became important as soon as he contemplated telling it to her.

He tears off a strip of the dress of Sabina's he most liked, the silvery grey dress with flower motifs and four buttons down the back which his fingers remember unfastening and puts it in his pocket.

While Eugenia sleeps he makes a map of the neighbouring rooftops. He gropes and slides and clambers his way over rain-slicked tiles. The slopes and walkways on the edge of abysses. He notes without much interest that he has become more fearless. Anger has filled all the spaces where previously fear thrived. The high isolated world he inhabits is crowded with swollen unrecognisable shadows. Once he loses his bearings and passes the same abandoned bird nest behind a chimney-stack twice. He enters every skylight and slips down into other attics, other apartments. Making a mental note of every possible escape route. Always imagining himself inside Eugenia's body, assuring himself she will be able to emulate his acrobatics. He knows it won't take the murderers long to spot the hatch to his attic. He has racked his brains for a way of disguising it. Once again leaving him rueing the fact he isn't much of a handyman. But they won't have a ladder. He has that advantage. Neither is there another ladder in the building. He has entered and rifled through the abandoned homes of all his former neighbours. He wondered what has happened to the man who bullies his wife. He was moved by the flourishing secret life shared by him and his wife evoked by the photographs in their apartment. There had been happiness. There is always happiness.

Tomorrow morning the selection will take place. Up here

on the rooftops under the moon he enjoys the illusion of being master of his fate. But the inevitability of the new day, like a fin out there in the wastes of black ocean, makes his legs go weak.

Just before sunrise he climbs back down into his attic and wakes Eugenia.

"Genia, what has happened cannot be made sense of with words," he says. "I understand your need of silence. I don't feel like talking either. I know you wanted to go with Ora. And I know you feel bad because you didn't go with her. It was a beautiful and brave and noble feeling you had. And I know nothing I can say will make you feel any better. But it's up to you now to keep Ora and your mum alive inside you. Both of us are discovering that it can be more difficult to survive than it is to die. In life, the narrative must go on. We're prisoners of our storylines. No one quite knows how or why they develop. And we have to cope with them as best we can, even when they push us over a new frontier. But the best way to punish these people who killed your mother and your sister is to survive. Your mum and Ora would want you to survive. I'm sorry I held you back when everything in you was straining to go and comfort Ora. But I'm not sorry your heart is still beating, that I can still see all the wonderful qualities you possess when I look into your eyes. When we're older something called common sense argues with our deepest wishes and often wins these arguments. I held you back because common sense told me to. Common sense can be like a telescope. It gives us a wider and bigger perspective. In the short term you might have offered Ora some comfort; in the long term nothing you could have done would have changed what happened to her. I know you blame yourself and you don't like me much at the moment because I'm trying to stop you blaming yourself. I blame myself too. We're both blaming ourselves for things that were completely out of our control. Your mum would have blamed herself if she hadn't gone to Ora. Probably she wouldn't have been able to live with herself. You have to conclude she did the right thing. You wanted to do the right thing too and I stopped you. But I wish I had stopped her too. I wish that more than anything. It was all my doing, not yours, that you didn't go with Ora. But I had a reason. And I hope with time you'll understand this. In the meantime, let's fight these people who killed your mother and Ora. Let's fight them by disobeying them, by keeping them as far away as possible. If today we hear anyone down below we're going to climb out onto the roof. You have to be brave and trust me. Okay?"

She gives him the faintest nod of her head. This little sign of engagement on her part moves him so deeply that he has to turn away to hide the tears that come to his eyes. For a moment he escapes the degradations the Germans have inflicted on him, the consuming hatred they have made him feel.

37

Ala and her mother are huddled together inside an underground bunker outside the legal area. The entrance is concealed beneath rubble in a bombed-out courtyard. She and her mother had to crawl on their hands and knees through a narrow sloping tunnel under the ground and climb down two rope ladders to get here. Inside the bunker with its claustrophobically low ceiling and earthen floor there are two rooms lit by carbide lamps. In the larger room there are three tiers of wooden bunks made of floorboards. Ala and her mother though have to sleep on the floor. Whenever Ala opens her eyes after sleep it's like waking up inside a tomb. The least effective feature of the bunker is the ventilation shaft. Ala never quite feels she has enough air. Several times she has to adopt Madame's breathing exercises to push back the panic in her body. There are probably two hundred people in the overheated underground hideout. Ala, like most women, including her mother, has stripped down to her chemise. The men are mostly stripped down to shorts and vests. The older men sweat through their vests. Colour consists almost exclusively of flesh tones. There are times when Ala feels she is shedding her humanity, losing her memory of herself and becoming more feral. Smell is often the most consuming of her senses. With every draught of the musty organic air she feels her nose twitch and imagines her nails sharpening into claws, the dirt and dust on her skin crawling over her like fur. Sometimes she feels pared down to her sweat glands. Beads of moisture like tears sliding down between her small breasts and quickly evaporating in the sweltering heat. Hunger clawing out a vacuum in her belly. For the spirit to survive it must be replenished daily. Ala is starved of replenishment.

Someone announces the selections above ground have now begun. "It's ten o'clock," he says, pointing to the watch on his wrist.

38

Earlier, in the attic, Max drew for Eugenia a wild olive orchard in Palestine so that she might try her hand at embroidering the image on a pillow case he has given her for the purpose. He feels it's important she is engaged in a task over whose outcome she has control. She is forever toying with the necklace with her dirty hands. While she works he talks to her about his memories of her mother when they attended university together.

"Your mum in those days was very shy. Full of evasions. She continually dropped her eyes. It was always a moment of triumph for me whenever I got her to hold my gaze. What I chiefly remember about her eyes are the depths of kindness they contained. There was mischief there, too. But mostly kindness. Kindness is probably the most underrated human quality. We tend to dismiss it when we come across it and seek out more exciting character traits. But kindness is often a refined form of courage. It brings light and warmth into the world. You should always value kindness when you find it. I suspect girls appreciate kindness long before boys do.

"Your mother and I used to go for long walks together and sit in cafés. I remember she had a green bicycle. She rode it to the university every day. It suited her, riding a bicycle. She was the only person I knew who had a padlock for her bicycle. I can still see her crouching down to lock up her bicycle. I used to tease her about it. I told her she needed to trust life more. I remember once I asked her to show me everything she had in her bag. The only thing I now remember is a seashell. I wonder what happened to that seashell. It's infuriating how difficult it is to recall more than one detail in every picture. Memory is like a geometry of holes woven together with slender thread, like a web.

"I always felt proud to be seen with your mum because she was so beautiful. I felt I was seen by everyone when I was with her. Some people, when you're with them, make you see yourself from outside. Often, it's because they embarrass you. More rarely, it's because they light up something inside you and make it glow.

"Your mother never liked being with lots of people. I suppose I'm the same. She prized intimacy. That's why she liked candles and moonlight so much. That's why there was often a whisper in her voice. We were very good at talking to each other in secluded corners. We made lots of energy with our talking. But she always felt compelled to put obstacles in my path, like in a cartoon when the character being chased knocks everything over in the path of the pursuer. It was all in good humour. Like she enjoyed being chased. As long as she was never caught. I think no one ever caught her until you and Ora came into the world. She was happy to be caught then.

"I've just remembered I once told your mother ghosts are the custodians of the missing part of stories. At the moment it feels like your mother has ended the story by becoming a ghost. But now you have to find within yourself as many threads of that story as possible and pick them up to resume the story about you and her. That story will continue and there will be times when she makes you happy and helps you understand who you are. You will still discover things about your mum you didn't know.

"In life we never know the full story of anyone. Only God knows that. Even if your mother had lived to be a hundred she would remain a mystery to you, just as she remains a mystery to me. We all have pivotal unspoken moments known only to ourselves. Moments of joy, of fear, of excitement, of shame, of intimate connection. To fully know anyone we would need to experience these moments ourselves. We would need to see everything unseen." He looks up to see the puzzled look on her child's face. "Sorry," he says. "I got carried away."

"It's all right. I like you talking about mum. I like knowing she had a green bicycle and a seashell in her bag."

The shrieking of nearby whistles arrives later. He and Eugenia look up at each other. Before long there is the crack of a fired bullet. The noise of the gunshot summons an image of Sabina's last moment of life to his mind. He sees in a searing flash the face of the SS officer who shot her. He sees this face at night before he goes to sleep, too. The venomous hatred the memory of this face rouses in him takes him off guard every time. The surging consuming power of it.

Perhaps two hours pass before he hears voices in the building. There is the sporadic rattle of riflefire down in the streets. Then the sound of heavy furniture being dragged about and crockery being smashed and laughter. Soon he hears voices. He doesn't recognise the language they speak which can only mean they are trigger-happy Ukrainian or Latvian mercenaries. He helps Eugenia through the skylight and follows her onto the roof. The sun is warm on the back of his neck. Down below there are two Germans in the courtyard, walking past the sandpit he dug for Ora. He puts his finger to his lips and takes Eugenia's hand.

39

Darkness has thickened around Ala. She examines the early autumn air with her nose like a woodland creature. She is on her way back to the bunker. She has a loaf of black bread in her rucksack. Purchased from a male child who whistled to her from a shadowy doorway and haggled like a seasoned market stall holder. She also has news. That nearly all the Jewish police have been deported. Jewish policemen have been obeying a German order to personally select five Jews for deportation and take them to the *Umschlagplatz*. There were rumours of sons delivering up their own mothers and fathers and sisters to the Nazis. Most people, she knows, will greet the news that the Jewish police have finally got their comeuppance with pleasure. It's a good, almost forgotten feeling to be the carrier of news that will bring pleasure.

The ghetto is deserted, a realm of dead echoes. Here and there she catches sight of the orange sparks of a smouldering bonfire. She keeps very close to the walls. It occurs to her that her training as a ballerina helps her navigate through the perilous situations she finds herself in every day. Her body is accustomed to acting on cue. She has intimate knowledge of what to expect from every muscle. At times her whole being seems primed in the timing of every step. And this intense body awareness gives her an intuitive connection with the choreography of the world around her. She is aware now of some alteration in this choreography. Some disturbing new pulse in the air around her in the darkness. She had a premonition earlier when she left the underground burrow that she would not return. The uneasy feeling compelled her to give her mother a lingering look when they parted.

She hears footfalls and low conspiratorial voices. She calculates that she doesn't have time to enter the bunker without running the risk of being seen. She crouches down behind a heap of rubble. The beam of a torch jitters close to her hiding place then sweeps away. In the ghostlight between a chink in the fallen masonry she can make out the uniforms of Ukrainian mercenaries, an SS officer and a man in civilian clothes. When the SS officer shines the torch in this man's face she recognises him as Adam, the man who was courting Sabina. He is pointing out the entrance to the bunker to the SS officer. Ala saw him in the underground hideout earlier today where he refused to meet her eye. She mentioned to her mother how shiftily he was behaving. She thought then he might be searching for something to steal. In the bunker she has noticed how humble, how tentative and resigned everyone's hands appear. Not his. His hands fidgeted with impatience, as if he was expected elsewhere.

Her indignation turns to terror at the sound of approaching boots crunching glass and grit underfoot. Heavy decisive footsteps resonant with entitlement. Ala holds her breath. She hears the exuberant spray and splash of a full bladder being emptied about ten feet away. By reflex and before she can hold it back her own bladder empties itself. The warm tangy sting of her urine runs down her thighs and pools between her grazed knees. It smells more pungent than usual. She clenches her teeth praying its sharp odour will not travel on the air.

Ala is still crouched in the same position hours later when the first glimmers of dawn appear in the sky. The blackened façade of the building to her right brightens. She has to constantly bite her lip to distract her attention from the cramps in her legs and feet. She can't swallow. Her lips gummed together with a white paste. She remembers a time before the war when Madame made the entire class adopt individual poses and then called upon them to stand perfectly still for twenty minutes as if they were modelling for an invisible artist. Mind over muscle, Madame called the exercise.

The Jews are now beginning to emerge from the bunker. This is confirmed when a hateful barking command almost make her jump up in alarm. A stone falls as she changes position. The noise it makes seems to go on echoing. Then there is a commotion. Someone is yelling and running. There are several gunshots in quick succession. Ala dares to lift her head to the chink and catches a glimpse of her mother's blackened face. She is holding up her hands in surrender. Ala is startled by how easily loveable her mother now appears in her vulnerability. If only she had been granted this vision years ago there need not have been any war between them. The heart in Ala clamours to join her mother. To hold her hand and let her know how sorry she is for all the discord she caused.

40

Max, weak with hunger, is struggling to keep his balance. Even though he is walking on solid ground. The darkness at times is so complete it is without depth or dimension. It disorientates him. He has to keep touching himself to fight the sensation of being distilled weightlessly out into the black night, to call himself back to his body. As instructed by Otto, he and Eugenia walk in their socks. When Max steps on a piece of glass and lets out an involuntary cry Otto hisses at him to shut up. Max can't help smiling at the topsy-turvy gyrations of this new reality where he takes orders from a child.

He has long since lost his bearings. He realises how deep is the reluctance in the male psyche to ever admit to being lost. Like an admission of insufficient manhood. Otto in his flat cap and torn breeches leads the way through the darkness with the self-possessed aplomb of a cat. The detailed mental map of the ghetto Otto possesses reminds Max of when he was the same age and likewise knew by heart the area around his home in every detail. How, month by month, he extended the boundaries of his map and added topographical detail. He sees it now, the familiar fields, pathways, trees, flowers, the river, the short cuts, the haunts of older boys who he both feared and admired, the bewitched homes of pretty girls, the bridge, the hiding places. It is, he realises, the most vividly illustrated map he owns. He wonders if his mother and father are still living in their home. He dreams often of his father. Standing at the stern of the flat-bottomed boat with his single oar, telling him how he is carrying the entire history of his people in his blood. In one dream they stripped down to their shorts and jumped laughing into the river. They swam side by side and he had never liked his father so much before. It pained him when he awoke that he had never experienced his father so playful and unguarded in real life.

It would appear the deportations are over, at least for the time being. Max and Eugenia have survived the frequent roundups in the attic of his apartment. Twice they have fled over the rooftops when the hunters could be heard in his apartment. Otto, who leaves the ghetto every day through a concealed hole in the wall, has supplied them with food. Otto and Eugenia often talk in secret. Otto has revived her spirits to some small necessary extent.

He can hear Otto, a busy shadow at his feet, remove bricks at the foot of the wall. The only doubt Otto expressed when he outlined the plan was that Max might not be able to squeeze through the small hole in the wall. He repeats the same doubt now. There is no judgement in the boy's remark but the implication that as an adult he is a liability is felt by Max. In another time and place he would be the hindering grownup in a child's game.

"All clear," whispers Otto.

He can't see Eugenia but is aware of her disappearing as nimbly as a reptile through the hole in the wall.

Max tests the width of the hole with his hands. He crawls into the opening head first, dust tickling his nose. He can't bring his hands up to quieten the arriving sneeze and the echoing explosive noise it makes seems to single him out in the silence for miles around. He remains stock-still for a moment listening with his entire body.

"We're going to hide in case a guard patrol arrives," whispers Otto. "I'll come and get you when you make it out."

If I make it out, thinks Max.

Max is looking up at a harvest moon. His head at least is outside the ghetto. His shoulders are wedged between the bricks.

His arms locked at the elbows. He twists and pushes and kicks to no avail. He has sand and grit between his teeth. He wriggles and squirms, contracts and pushes. He wonders if he himself laid these bricks that are impeding his passage. Several times he has to pause and take deep breaths to calm his mounting anxiety. He can neither move forward or backward now. He grows angry and grazes and hurts himself trying to force his body through. It occurs to him that it's like he's trying to give birth to himself. For the first time in his life he realises we all enter the world with the smell of our mother's sex on us. In our nostrils. He feels like he is close to a revelation. About to glimpse some secret of the origins of creation. Then he has to calm himself again because he knows a tide of madness has entered his mind and is wrestling for ascendancy.

He expresses his relief at finally pushing himself free by summoning into his mind the refrain from Debussy's *Clair de Lune*. It puzzles him for a moment that it's possible to silently summon music.

"Take off your armband," says Otto.

Max does as he's told. Otto leads him to the ruins of a building struck by a bomb. Here they wait for sunrise and the lifting of curfew. Otto leaves them then. He has his own agenda. Max sees he and Eugenia are sad to be parted.

It isn't easy to conceal his wonder that outside the ghetto walls life carries on as normal. Women in clean bright clothes heading to market; men in pressed suits reading newspapers on the passing trams; children skipping along the pavements to school. The shining bright colours of the fruit, vegetables and flowers in the market are explosive after the demoralising uniform grey backdrop of the ghetto. As the streets fill with people he becomes more jittery about his illegality as a Jew. More conscious of his threadbare clothes torn by the bricks in the wall. He feels everyone is surreptitiously staring at him. As if his skin is a different colour. He hates his Jewishness. Wants to take it from himself and trample it to dust underfoot. He wonders how much of himself would remain. His hand keeps going to the spot where his armband usually sits. As if to assure himself again and again it is not there on display. He feels light and giddy on his feet. Stupid of him to believe anger had replaced fear in him.

He has to steel himself to buy cigarettes at a kiosk. His heart thumping, as if he is a little boy again committing a transgression. When he strikes a match, watched by Eugenia, his hand is trembling. He notices a gang of youths loitering on the other side of the square. He feels sure they are blackmailers. He sees only fear, bewilderment and sorrow in Eugenia's eyes. She might as well be wearing a Jewish armband. No doubt he looks the same. He crouches down and invites her up onto his shoulders.

"We've got to look like a father and a daughter enjoying a day out in the city," he tells her. He rises up unsteadily with her sitting astride his shoulders. "Now I'm going to talk a constant stream of whatever comes into my head, like Aunt Elsa."

Max invents a story about a squirrel who steals hats.

"And every time he steals a hat he makes the owner a proposal in squirrel language as a joke. He steals a pink veiled hat from a woman. Wriggle your bottom, he says. He steals the hat of a soldier. Take me to the moon, he says. He steals the hat of a schoolboy. Teach me a new language, he says. Most squirrels bury nuts so they have food for the winter. Our squirrel buries hats. Let's call him Silas. He steals hats to impress a girl squirrel whose friend he wants to be. He hasn't yet worked out how the hats might further his cause. It never occurs to Silas that it might be a stupid idea because he's young and when we're young we do all sorts of things that will embarrass us in later life. But we also do things that are brave and fearless which will never be bettered. One day though Silas steals the hat of a man with hair the colour of straw and that's when everything in his life takes a turn for the worse."

Max talks such gibberish that eventually he manages to engage Eugenia and make her giggle. He too calms himself down with his madcap monologue. In the Saxony Gardens he lets her down. There are many German soldiers strolling in pairs. Max feels naked without identification papers.

He can't resist sitting down on the grass. The smell of it is a miracle, the warm tickling press of it on his palms and fingertips. His eyes drawn to the fountain with its arcs of glittering water and the white stone goddesses lining the gravel path strewn with fallen crisping leaves. Even Eugenia's eyes are animated by the sight of a squirrel swinging off a branch of a chestnut tree.

"I'm pretty sure that's Silas come to steal my hat," he says. Her smile and the momentary brightness in her eyes is a gift whose fugitive nature quickly pains him.

They have tea and a bun in a café. It seems to Max the bravest thing he has ever done in his life. He suspects though that Eugenia is no more able to enjoy the cake than he is.

It's when they are approaching the burnt-out ruins of the Grand Theatre where he has seen Ala dance several times as a member of the corps of the Ballet Polonaise and he is remembering the wonderland enchantment of the spotlit snow in *The Nutcracker* that he realises they are being followed.

An amused male voice, nasal and harsh, makes a meowing noise behind them. The Poles, he knows, refer to Jews as cats. I wish I *was* a cat, he thinks.

His pulse begins to race and he increases his pace without realising. He pretends to take no notice of the taunts. An elderly woman walks towards him. He is too frightened to look her in the eyes for fear of seeing disgust there, disgust that she has recognised him as a Jew.

The money he intends using for Eugenia's upkeep is hidden in his socks. He can feel it wadded under his heel. Otto warned him about blackmailers. How they operate in gangs. How usually they can be bought off. But not always. How clever they are at identifying Jews. "They look for fear, the exaggerated ways Jews use to hide it." He has kept a hundred zlotys in his trouser pockets to pay off blackmailers.

The gang swarm around him and Eugenia. One man grabs at

the waistband of his trousers and yanks at them. A button pings off. There is a fleck of spittle between the youth's thin lips. His ears stick out beneath his cap.

"We don't need proof. He stinks like a Jew."

"What do you want?"

"We'll take this for starters," says another, tearing Sabina's necklace of tiny silver shells from Eugenia's neck.

"Look, I'll give you money but don't take that. It belonged to her mother who was killed by the Germans," pleads Max.

"Who gives a shit? You're nothing but filthy Jews. You got what was coming to you. You're lucky we're not handing the pair of you over to the Germans."

They take the hundred zlotys and then order him to hand over his jacket and shoes. He takes out the strip of Sabina's dress from his jacket pocket before handing it over.

"I'm sorry about your necklace," he says to Eugenia, standing in his socks in the ruins of the Grand Theatre forecourt. He hates it that she has had to witness his humiliation at the hands of these youths. He feels like giving up. All proprietary space around him has collapsed. Anyone is free to abuse him in any manner they choose. He has the social rights of a spider or an ant. And the world seems a place overrun with vile people.

Then he sees Adam walking towards them.

41

Ala wakes from a dream in which her mother came to see her. In the dream Ala was wearing soft silver slippers and a long dress that trailed over the ground. Her mother was like a shape-shifting silhouette of herself. She knew her mother was dead. But felt a chill of fear that she too might be dead. She stood under a tree and asked her mother what it was like to be dead. But her mother refused to look at her. A cry of distress from one of the men sleeping in the room ended the dream. She now has the familiar gnaw of hunger in her stomach. She thought she might be more resistant to the challenges of hunger because of her dietary discipline as a ballerina but her feet have swollen up. She has difficulty getting her shoes on.

Also sleeping in this room is a man who was a stagehand at the Grand Theatre. Neither of them remembered or recognised the other but he shares a few of her own memories. He remembers the problems caused by the artificial snow during *The Nutcracker* in which she danced in the corps and a drunken violinist in the orchestra another night who began playing a raucous Polish folk tune during one of the quiet sections of *Swan Lake*. Sharing this memory was the first time Ala has laughed since she was separated from her mother. They hummed together the *Waltz of the Flowers*. He showed Ala a creased photograph of his two daughters who were taken from him. There are no longer any illusions about what happens to the Jews in the trains. A man escaped from Treblinka and told of the shower rooms from which no one emerges alive. News of his report spread through what remains of the ghetto within hours.

Ala now spends every day sitting at a sewing machine, fingering squares of grey-green cloth. Growing ever more delirious with hunger and exhaustion. Feeling herself pared down to this one function, like an automaton. Sometimes she thinks of the German soldier who one day will feel against his bare skin the piece of cloth she guides under the clattering needle. She puts a witch curse on every square of fabric she touches.

She, like her fellow inmates, works from first thing in the morning until late in the evening. The only reward a bowl of watery liquid with a few scraps of rotting vegetable at the end of the day. A barbed wire fence encloses the area where she works and is billeted. No one is allowed to leave. She has no way of knowing if Henryk or Max are still alive. She doesn't allow herself to think of her mother and father. But she misses her mother more than she would ever have thought possible. It's as if, without her mother, she has become a little girl again and has been left all alone in the world. One day when she saw her face in a black windowpane she didn't recognise herself. The ethereal being she was trained to be now a grubby frightened emaciated swamp creature with greasy skin.

Sometimes she thinks of Adam, the man responsible for the capture of her mother. Then she wants to see Henryk, Zanek or even Mira. To warn them about Adam. The Jewish Fighting Organisation, a ghostly, perhaps mythical, presence in the ghetto, is rumoured to assassinate informers.

Later she is woken up again by a volley of shots and the shattering of the glass in the window. Shards pelt the room, some landing on the blanket under which she sleeps on the floor. There is laughter outside. Raucous drunken German voices. And then more shots and more glass shattering nearby.

42

"Polish blackmailers got me too and gave me a pummelling," says Adam. There are cuts and bruises beneath his eyes and his lip is split and swollen. "I heard about Sabina. I'm sorry."

Max nods. Her name spoken aloud conjures her up for an instant. She is sitting on the kitchen windowsill gently swinging her legs.

"Listen, I'm trying to find someone who can put me in touch with the underground network that assists Jews in hiding. At the moment I'm staying with a Polish couple but I don't trust them. It's costing me a fortune and I'm nearly out of money. I need to find somewhere safer. Quickly. Do you know someone who might be able to help me?"

Edek has told Max about a café in Miodowa Street that the Jewish underground uses as a meeting place but also warned him the Gestapo might now know about it. Max intends using it as a last resort. He considers for a moment sharing this information with Adam who in these new circumstances has ceased to arouse animosity in him. But he remembers Edek's injunction not to pass on the information. *Not to anyone.*

"No, I don't know anyone," he says.

"Where are you staying?"

"We're not staying anywhere. We've only just left the ghetto."

"You must have somewhere to go."

Max looks around, suddenly nervous, when he hears a dog barking. Eugenia, by his side, is kicking at the ochre and reddened leaves that strew the pavement. He becomes impatient to be rid of this new magnanimous and wheedling Adam. "Good luck to you," he says, registering the new bitterness in his voice that he is always careful to hide from Eugenia. Taking her hand, he walks away. He tells her to look back and tell him what Adam is doing.

"He's just standing there, looking at us."

"Did you think there was something fishy about him?"

"I don't know."

A woman and a little boy are walking towards them. The little boy notices Max is not wearing shoes. He looks up at Max, as if trying to work out why he isn't wearing shoes, as if the clue might be on his face.

Max now turns around. The woman is looking back at him but there is no sign of Adam.

His knotted stomach never stops reminding him that this homeless walk through the streets of Warsaw is a death-defying undertaking. He is overly conscious of his every step, as if walking on a frozen lake. He can never quite accustom himself to the hostility with which his home city now seems to disown him. He is nervous of meeting anyone who knows him. As if he has lately disgraced himself. The red Nazi banners and flags with the black spider are ubiquitous. One falls down over three storeys of a building he doesn't recognise. Now and again some familiar landmark evokes a vivid memory. A café where he and Sabina talked for hours. A department store where he once bought bed linen. The box office of a theatre outside which he, Ala and Henryk stood sharing their favourite moments of Charlie Chaplin's *Modern Times* amidst the wet coloured lights on the sidewalk. The memory of those wet coloured lights, red, green and gold, makes his heart ache. He feels like a ghost, visiting his old life but no longer able to participate in it.

As they are nearing the address of Eugenia's grandparents he asks her if she liked them.

"Tell me honestly," he says.

"I never liked going there," she says.

"Are they nice people?"

"I don't know."

The address is a typical three-storey block of apartment buildings. Max has to talk at length to the concierge before he lets them into the building. The man keeps looking down at Max's shoeless feet. A squat bald man with powerful shoulders opens the door of the apartment. He takes one look at Eugenia and flushes with anger.

"Her mother is dead," Max says.

"Are you insane? Get out of here before I call the police."

"This is your granddaughter. Eugenia."

"I've never seen her before in my life. Now get lost and don't come back."

Max looks down at the bristling man's slippered feet. They are much smaller than his own feet. Any shoes he might have provided wouldn't have fitted him anyway.

Max sits down on a step and removes the money from his torn socks. He sets aside enough for some food and slips the rest inside his shorts. "Don't take it personally. He was frightened," he tells Eugenia, finding a justification for her grandfather's behaviour he doesn't feel.

"What are we going to do now?"

"I've got an old friend who lives quite close. I'll ask him and his wife if we can stay there for a while. He plays the piano and she's got three cats."

However, no one answers the doorbell. People are hurrying home before curfew. The only option is to spend the night in the ruins of a roofless skeletal building hit by a bomb.

43

"You're back," says Ala. There is no emotion in her voice. She is sitting on the floor, leaning against the wall. Green mould grows beneath the cornice above her head. She has a blanket pulled up to her chin. The broken window is not boarded up by day and rain as cold as grey stone is swept into the room. Her nose is leaking a continuous stream of mucus which she wipes away with her sleeve.

"Yes. We heard what was happening here," says Wolf, kneeling by her side. He is wearing an old sheepskin coat. "We've come back to fight."

"Fight with what?"

"Anything we can get our hands on."

Ala makes sure her swollen feet are hidden under the blanket. She can smell the sour stink of her armpits and her breath. Her hair is matted and unwashed. Her fingernails broken and dirt encrusted. She has mouth ulcers and her top lip is blistered. Wolf's proximity makes her self-conscious about her appearance and hygiene for the first time since her mother disappeared.

"Are you alone now?" he asks.

She nods.

"My parents were shot in a ditch. And my grandparents. And my brother and his two young children. We have to survive the war to bring these murderers to justice, Ala."

"We won't survive the war."

When he takes her hand she flinches and pulls away. She doesn't want him entering into the circle of her stench.

"I don't like to see you like this, Ala."

"You were right to be a Zionist."

"Come and live with us. Work for us instead of for these German monsters. You'll be better fed. Zanek and Mira and my sister are with us. You'll be with friends. In fact, I'm not asking. It's an order. In the name of the ZOB. The Jewish Fighting Organisation. Gather what you need. Your first mission will be to accompany me on a visit to your grandfather. We ordered him to pay a tariff towards the purchase of arms and he refused so we need to twist his arm."

Ala remembers her grandfather's betrayal of his wife at the selection. She shouldn't judge him for wanting to save himself but she can't help it. Just as she judges herself harshly for not going to her mother. Of all the members of her family he and she herself strike her as the least deserving to survive.

"Come on!"

44

It's seven in the morning. A gusting flurry of cold rain wets Max's face as he pays a pair of smugglers for the use of their stepladder. He is weak and nauseous with hunger. He feels like he has been punched in the groin when he climbs the wooden rungs in his stockinged feet.

"Hurry up!"

On top of the ghetto wall he struggles to clamber through the barbed wire and nearly loses his balance on the jagged shards of glass cemented to the uppermost bricks. He lowers himself down the other side, hanging from the wall by his hands, the entire weight of his body straining at the muscles of his arms, his feet scrabbling for a foothold, fidgeting in thin air like those of a hanged man. He slides down, only momentarily finding a slippery support for his foot, and curses as a searing pain shoots through his left knee on contact with the ground. He stands listening for a moment in the deserted street. He is in the wild part of the ghetto, the forbidden area. And he has lost his armband. It was in his stolen jacket pocket. He hobbles into a building opposite. Sits on a stair and massages his knee. He feels a moment's contempt for his ageing body. Then he begins rummaging about in the downstairs apartments for food. Nothing. He gulps down water from the tap and splashes it over his face. There's a tape measure on the sideboard. Commonplace objects now have the power to evoke a surging hopeless love for the past. He thought once he secured Eugenia outside the ghetto he would no longer care much if he lived or died but he finds while running the tape measure through his hands that his will to live is still strong.

He limps up to a ransacked apartment on the second floor. He tries to dismiss the pain in his knee as a temporary handicap, like his hunger. He opens all the brown terra-cotta jars on the shelves, all of which are empty. Then he sits down at the table and opens a recipe book sitting there, recalling times when he ate the dishes described. He remembers the distinctive flavour of Sabina's soup, how it differed from his own and the playful arguments they had over whose soup was the best. He remembers her making pancakes, the taste of sour cream a fleeting taunt on his tongue. Then he jumps to his feet as he hears voices down in the street. The pain in his knee no longer of importance. He enters a bedroom, carpeted with white feathers. The only place to hide is under the bed. He lets out a muffled cry of alarm when he realises somebody else is hiding there, pressed against the wall. There are footsteps downstairs in the building. Arrogant carefree voices. Max edges closer to his mysterious companion under the bed. She gives off a static of terror. His fingers make contact with her hand. Her heart is pounding with such force it conveys its distressed charge into his fingertips. He whispers what he hopes is a comforting sound.

The voices are in the apartment now. They are speaking an unknown language. One of them seems to speak through his teeth. Max doesn't like the sound of this man. He listens to the noises of cupboards and drawers being opened, the clatter of shifting cutlery. Then footsteps grow in volume. He sees a pair of lacquered black boots enter the room, the hem of a black trench coat. The body next to him stiffens and shakes with a new charge of fear. His own pulse is loud in his ears. He watches the black boots trample over the feathers. The iron bedstead rattles against the wall. The bedsprings flex and tighten. The owner of the boots has sat down on the bed. Max can see a tiny spot of what looks like dried blood on the leather heel. He struggles to believe the intruder can't hear the fist-punching pounding of his heart. He grips his mysterious companion's hand more tightly. He expects her to begin choking for breath at any moment, so frantic is the heaving of her ribs. Then another man enters the room and begins talking. His voice is unnaturally loud, as if shouting over noise in a packed nightclub. The man sitting on the bed grunts with impatience. The springs of the bedstead relax. The inverted hump in the mattress above flattens out. The man stands up and leaves the room with his companion.

His fellow fugitive is a teenage girl wearing a man's large suit jacket and a filthy headscarf knotted under her chin. She is sobbing and shaking when he helps her out from beneath the bed. Her face blanched and convulsed. She barely seems to register his presence. Her hands are clawed inside the sleeves of the oversize jacket. Eventually he finds out her name is Clara. He sits her down at the kitchen table, the recipe book still open on a drawing of fried cherry jam doughnuts. The grubby netting at the window is flustered by an icy draught.

"Is this your home?"

She shakes her head. She keeps bringing her hands up to her mouth as if to protect herself from something only she can see. Eventually she tells him her story. Her unfocussed eyes beginning to show a muted spark of life. She feels guilty because she failed to save her little brother. She keeps returning to this guilt she feels.

"Everyone feels guilty," he says. Talk nowadays rarely strikes him as anything more consequential than confetti, tatters of colour flung out to mask the black finality of defeat every Jew feels. It's like everyone in the ghetto only now has need of the elementary vocabulary of birds. We ought to squawk at each other, he thinks. A new crazy current in his mind urges him to begin squawking at Clara. "This guilt is crazy from every rational perspective," he says instead. He looks across at her. She is chewing the skin of her blackened thumb. "We feel guilty because we've been singled out to survive and we don't feel worthy of this dubious gift. It's even more crazy when you stop to think of how slim our chances of surviving for much longer are. I've just spent two weeks on the other side of the wall. If anything, it's even more terrifying there than it is here. You can't trust anyone, not even Jews."

His former acquaintances greeted his appearance at their front door with concealed fear and horror. He was something they didn't want to be reminded of. His presence made them all feel angrily ashamed. It was a former girlfriend who took in Eugenia. A woman he had treated badly because she became too slavishly demanding, because she wasn't Sabina. She agreed to shelter Eugenia as long as she never left the building and hid in a dark mildewed crawl space littered with old bottles, rags and yellow crusted newspapers whenever anyone came to the door. He misses Eugenia now. She was his last connection to the man he used to be.

"I like to remember my brother surrounded by dogs," says Clara. "That's when he was happiest. We had to leave all our dogs when we moved to the ghetto. If you're a Jew, why aren't you wearing an armband?"

It's the first time he feels seen by her. "I lost it. But what's the point anymore? They shoot us on sight anyway."

She takes off her armband and throws it down on the kitchen floor.

Book Three

1943

1

Ala is wearing a balaclava. She holds a toy gun in her coat pocket. Wolf has a loaded pistol in his coat pocket. The cell of ZOB fighters to which she and Wolf belong only possesses one real gun. Wolf has taught Ala how to use it, how to take it apart, clean it and reassemble it. They can't afford to waste ammunition so the bullets she fires at a cardboard caricature of Adolf Hitler are imaginary. After each empty click of the trigger Wolf points to the spot where he thinks her bullet has struck the target.

"Probably hit him in the upper thigh that time."

"Good. Let him suffer before he dies. Pathetic little man."

When Ala first arrived at the communal apartment Zanek threw his arms around her, pressing his groin to hers. It was like he was telling her something no one had ever told her before. The wonder was, Mira wasn't jealous. She too hugged Ala. More than anything it was Mira's unexpected effusion of affection that revived Ala's fighting spirit. They have become friends. Ala admires Mira, her courage, intelligence and determination. And it is fortifying to have a female confidant again. She pretends to Mira to be more interested in Wolf than she is. Even though she cannot help stealing covert looks at Zanek. In the ugly threadbare world in which she is confined he is just about the only thing she takes pleasure in looking at. In the kitchen Ala, Mira and Chaya prepare the meals. Ala likes to make sure every boy always receives the same bowl. This ploy of creating continuity, of pretending insignificant rituals have fateful import reminds her in feeling of when she superstitiously avoided cracks in the pavements when skipping through streets as a child. Her membership of ZOB has provided her with a new sense of purpose. Even though it will almost inevitably lead her and all its members to death. But a death with honour, as is often stressed. Ala, however, takes exception to the implication that everyone herded onto the trains died without honour. And has found herself arguing with several of the boys on this score. She refuses the idea that her mother and father, Madame and Lily all died without honour. She admires the fighting spirit of these boys but is also conscious sometimes of a vein of vanity in their bravado.

She and Wolf keep close to the walls in the dark streets. If they are challenged by a German patrol Wolf has told her to submit initially.

"I'll shoot them when they're relaxed and don't have their weapons trained on us."

It feels both empowering and frightening to walk the ghetto streets in possession of a violent answer to the Nazis.

They are on their way to see Grandpa Frydman. Wolf has tried to extort money from him by pretending ZOB holds Ala hostage. It hurt Ala that her grandfather still refused to pay up. She always believed she was his favourite.

There is a disarming clarity to every sound. An iron gate creaking on its hinges. A piece of litter scuttling over the cobbles. Water moving through a drain. A shard of glass crunching underfoot. She walks behind Wolf and several times knocks into him in the darkness when he cautiously slows his pace. Then there's a catatonic noise. Wolf has inadvertently kicked what sounds like a saucepan which skips clattering along the kerb with alarming thunder. They both remain still for a moment. It feels like they have alerted every German sentry to their presence. When they are assured it is safe to continue Ala tells Wolf this heightened state of anxiety reminds her of waiting in the wings before dancing out onto the floodlit stage of the Grand Theatre.

"We'll soon be stepping out onto the stage of history," says Wolf.

Ala thinks back to the performance of Cassandra when her greatest fear was of getting her period on stage. That had struck her then as some kind of ultimate catastrophe.

Grandpa Frydman refuses to open his door. Ala has to plead with him.

"What are you doing out at this time of night?"

"Open the door. Quickly. I need to speak to you."

Grandpa Frydman, holding a candle, edges open the door a crack. Wolf, now wearing a linen bag over his head with slits for his eyes, shoves it and her grandfather is knocked to the ground. Ala follows Wolf into the apartment. Light edges the closed door of another room. Ala takes the toy gun from her pocket. In the bedroom, lit by a candle and the skittish flames of the stove, a young woman wearing only a slip and a string of blue beads is sitting on the bed. Ala looks at her dishevelled hair, her damp cleavage, her glowing red knees and her painted toes.

"Who are you?"

"My name is Roza," says the girl, staring with alarm at Ala's gun.

Ala puts the gun back in her pocket. "Come with me," she says.

Ala brings the candle into the hallway. She has to fight down an impulse to laugh at the sight of Wolf wearing the ridiculous linen bag over his head with holes cut out for his eyes. She is reminded of the games she and Henryk played as children underneath the kitchen table. Her grandfather is wearing a flamboyant dressing gown and slippers, as if he has stepped out of another time. His cheeks and chin are blueish with shaved stubble.

"We represent The Jewish Fighting Organisation and we order you to donate 20,000 zlotys towards out struggle against the Nazi oppressors. If you refuse I have instructions to shoot you," says Wolf, flaunting his pistol. Ala helps her grandfather to his feet.

"I haven't got that kind of money."

"We know as a member of the *Judenrat* you made a lot of money taking bribes for work certificates."

"That's not true. I've never taken a single bribe, ever. Ala, are you going to rob your own grandfather? Is this what we've come to?"

"We're not robbing you. You're donating to the only worthy cause we have left. The restoration of honour to our people. Enough of this passive submission to Nazi barbarity. The time has come to fight back." Her voice and the rehearsed words it speaks doesn't seem to belong to her, as if she has stepped out of character in a game.

"I know where the money is," says Roza. "It's underneath a floorboard in the bathroom."

"You go with her and get the money, Ala."

In the bathroom Roza turns to face Ala.

"Chaim is your grandfather?"

"Yes."

"He told me about you. The ballerina. You should know he feels ashamed of himself for what he did. For not joining his wife. He told me he couldn't bear the thought of you thinking ill of him. He and your brother have been trying to find you."

"Henryk's alive?"

"Yes. We saw him two days ago. He's working in a laundry, washing clothes for German soldiers. He wouldn't say where he's living. I think he's joined a fighting organisation and it's all top secret."

Ala walks over to her and hugs her. "Thank you," she says.

"Your grandfather has helped me. He's not a bad man."

"I know."

Roza removes the floorboard while Ala holds the candle.

Ala counts the banknotes.

"58,000 zlotys," she tells Wolf.

"Take 50,000 and leave him the rest."

"That's not right. We said 20,000."

"Do you know how much one pistol costs? At least 15,000 zlotys."

"We'll take 40,000 then." She finds it difficult to look at Wolf so preposterous does he look with the bag over his head.

"Okay, boss," he says.

"Sorry, Grandpa."

"I know what you think of me, Ala. We've all discovered unpleasant things about ourselves in these times. Just make sure you kill some of these monsters with my money," he says.

2

Clara has been hiding out with Max in his attic. She sleeps over in a far corner. There is little intimacy between them despite their close proximity. It is a practical arrangement. Max rarely has a desire to talk. He feels like few words remain to him. Today Clara has persuaded him to accompany her to her old home. She tells him there are some tins of sardines hidden in the kitchen. They set out early in the morning. There's a dusting of fresh snow on the ground. The incriminating prints they leave behind worry him. The streets are empty. As if they are the last people left alive in the world.

In the ransacked apartment Clara keeps picking up her little brother's clothes and toys. Max opens the Warsaw telephone directory he has found and marvels that his name, address and number are still printed there. He remembers the first time he saw his name in this book. It gave him a discomforting shock, as if he was being watched. Then he recalls the wonder of finding Sabina's address for the first time. It all seems now like a life lived in the midst of sleep.

Clara admits to Max that she lied. "There are no sardines," she says. He expects her to begin crying but she doesn't.

"Never mind," he says.

"I keep dreaming of my home. I wanted to see it again. And I wanted these," she says, showing him the two photographs she has been staring at, as if willing them to divulge some hidden detail, some elusive and restorative secret of her history. She caresses the top one with her thumb before handing it to him.

"Your parents look like lovely people," he says. He means this. There's a shine of laughter in their eyes. It comes as a surprise to Max to discover Clara has a prior life. He has grown used to viewing everyone as bereft of everything except the instinct to survive.

Clara stuffs some clothes and underwear in a bag. They are caught by two German gendarmes as they leave the building. The older of the pair, a middle-aged man with oversized hands, shouts in German, asking where their armbands are. Max pretends not to understand. The German walks up to Clara and puts his hand between her legs and calls her a Jewish slut. Max feels like squawking at him.

"Why don't you shoot her, Willi? Sooner or later, you've got to lose your virginity."

Max doesn't understand what Willi, the younger German, says in reply. He speaks some kind of rural German dialect. He keeps blinking, as if trying to free his retinas of a troubling image. A straggling column of Jews, three abreast, hunchbacked with fear, are being marshalled down the road towards them. The Nazi with the giant hands prods Max with the butt of his rifle. He and Clara join the solemn procession.

A young man wearing a flat cap changes place with Clara. The stitched pattern of his jacket barely showing through the encrusted grime on the cloth. Then he does the same thing with Max, moving himself to the outside of the column. Max looks at him for an explanation. The boy is too preoccupied with things in his own mind to register Max except as an obstacle. Max suspects he plans to make a dash for it at some point. The German gendarme with the huge hands is three paces away in front. He keeps prodding an old woman with his rifle. In all, Max counts eight German guards. He decides he will wait until the boy makes his move. Maybe in the confusion he can escape too. If not, he has the iron file in his shoes. Despite the cold his hands sweat as once again he pictures himself on the cattle train. The *Umschlagplatz* is no more than ten minutes away. He looks at his feathery breath evaporating on the chill air and feels like he has a noose tied around his neck.

An old man in front, carrying a shabbily tied bundle, recites a psalm and prays aloud. Further up the line Max spies Otto. Even the resourceful Otto has been caught. Here and there the winds have raised mounds of frozen blackened snow at the side of the road.

At the intersection of Mila and Zamenhofa, when half of the column has disappeared around the corner, the boy beside Max pulls out a pistol and shoots the German gendarme with the oversized hands in the back. The mad rush of pleasure Max feels at the sight of this vile German writhing in agony on the ground is soon replaced by panic as shots ring out from all sides. The boy who shot the German falls to the ground. His pistol falls at Max's feet. He picks it up without thinking. It is a little heavier than he expected. The Jews are all now running off in every direction. A young man makes off with the rifle of the blinking German gendarme who is coughing up blood in the gutter. The crack and suck of air of a bullet is so close to Max's ear he thinks for a moment he has been hit. Despite everything he's been through it is still a shock to be shot at. He follows Clara down an unpaved alley and then inside a building. They climb stairs littered with wreckage, hearing the gunfight down below. Max realises he saw at least three Jews with guns, one of whom was a girl.

They enter a kitchen. He takes the pistol from his pocket. "Two bullets," he tells Clara, after checking the chamber.

3

Wolf believes in celibacy. He was shy when Ala broached the subject. It's part of his Zionist education. Twice now they have awkwardly kissed but he won't put his hands underneath her clothes. Modesty prevents her from telling him what she feels, that given the circumstances it is the height of absurdity to posit anything in the future. The persistence of this old-world modesty is puzzling to her, as ingrained apparently as flavour in foodstuffs. She tries to let him know with her body that he has permission to touch her anywhere he wants, but he appears oblivious to all her mimed encouragement. In these times when every surge of blood is precipitated by fear she wants to experience a surge of blood from a different source.

Only a narrow strip of floor divides her pallet from Wolf's. She and Wolf sleep in a room with several other members of their fighting group, including Zanek and Mira. No one is older than twenty-three. In the night she listens to the rise and fall and rise again of the moans of pleasure of one of the other girls, the stifled grunts of her lover. She wonders if Zanek too is celibate. She can't help looking for signs of jealousy in him that she and Wolf are now viewed as a couple. She is attentive to the corner of the room where he sleeps close to Mira. Not once has she detected any hint that they couple during the night.

There was a celebration the night the Jews killed their first Germans. Even though all but one of the Jewish fighters perished in the gun battle. The Germans have halted the deportations. They no longer enter the ghetto. There were more celebrations when ZOB burnt down a German warehouse.

Ala spends a good deal of time in the large brick-walled basement where ZOB have set up their headquarters. Here there is a printing press and a weapons factory. Young boys and girls making homemade grenades and petrol bombs. Bottles filled with kerosene, gasoline, sugar and potassium cyanide. Grenades made with drainpipes and filled with nails and bolts. The sense of camaraderie and purpose she feels is not unlike the rehearsals for the performance of a choreography.

Tonight she and Wolf enter another building in the nocturnal hunt for bottles. They have already found several and they clink in the sack Wolf carries.

In the top floor apartment Ala shines her flashlight around the kitchen. The cracked wall tiles and filthy net curtain. There's a blackened pot on the stove. An unstamped envelope on the table with a New York address. Ala picks it up and feels like she is holding a world of sorrow. In a cupboard under the sink she finds a bottle of vodka. She removes the cap and sniffs. She takes a swig, taken aback by the hot punch it delivers. She offers the bottle to Wolf. Her shadow, she sees, is much larger than she is.

"No thanks," he says. He has a set expression on his face. She feels reprimanded and her blood heats up with defiance. She takes the bottle with her into an attic bedroom with sloping wooden beams. The room hasn't been ransacked. There's a fine dust over everything. Life here has stood still. It's like a memory of itself in a ghost world.

"Let's stay here for a while," she says. She sits down on a rug, leaning her head back against the wall. The flashlight is on the floor by her side, sending a smoking beam across the room. Wolf sits down on a chair opposite her. Ala takes another swig from the bottle. She is unused to alcohol and already feels light-headed.

"You disapprove of Ariel and Liliana, don't you?" she says, referring to the couple who make love every night.

"It's not my way, that's all. But I don't like to judge people."

Ala picks up the flashlight and shines it at his face. "Yes, you do," she says. "You judge people all the time. It's like you stand on some touchline with a red flag."

She sees she has hurt him. In the silence that follows she can hear a distant underground hammering.

"I used to be like you," she says. "Always imagining life in terms of ideal moments. Probably my ballet training led me to be so exacting of the next moment. I used ideal moments as a map to discover who I am and what I want from life. But this new world has changed all that. Tomorrow the deportations could start again. We have three guns in our group. It seems ridiculous to cling to lofty principles or expectations now. We live in a world of basic emotions. Fear, sadness, guilt, anger, desire, shame."

"I can't accept all of what you're saying."

"For example, does it not strike you as ridiculous that the various Jewish political parties still won't unite as one fighting force because of nuances of ideology?"

"They're hardly nuances."

Wolf, not for the first time, enumerates the irreconcilable differences of position between Betar, the Bund, the Communists and Hashomer Hatzair.

"Betar or the Revisionists or whatever they call themselves have lots more weapons than we do. They have contacts with the Polish underground. My brother told me. It's absurd not to join forces with them because you don't agree with their pre-war politics."

"Anyone can join Betar. They have no security apparatus. There are Jewish informers working for the Gestapo. Mark my words, soon the Germans will infiltrate them and discover their weapons cache. If we allowed them to join us our weapons too would be lost."

Ala loses interest in the logistics of the argument. It's not, she knows, political differences that have any bearing on her and Wolf's instinct to attack each other. They are arguing on a more visceral level. She feels guilty that her sexual feeling for him lacks integrity at root; he is perhaps angry for the same reason. She harbours the hope that the act of love itself might sweep aside all her misgivings about him.

Ala takes a more prolonged swig of vodka. Wolf is still holding forth on Zionist politics. She feels a need to activate this expanding vacuum between them. She views it as a performance space. She remembers a rehearsal session when Madame told her to dramatise desire with a single part of her body. *You might press your lips to the back of your wrist or flex your toes.* Together she and Madame formulated seven different gestures of surreptitious desire which Ala repeated over and over in sequence. *Map this path of desire through your body, station by station.* The sequence was eventually incorporated into the choreography of Cassandra. For a moment she considers performing it now. But then a bolder idea occurs to her.

Ala unbuttons her coat, opens her legs wide, lifts her skirt and begins fanning her lap with it. She lets Wolf see the insides of her thighs above her black woollen stockings and the soft black purse of her knickers, all the time looking him in the eye. Wolf has stopped explaining to her the ideological positions which prevent the various Jewish political factions from agreeing on a united strategy. He is looking across at her with a look she can't read. She notices the sickle moon is visible in the skylight.

Wolf stands up, his shadow towering over her. "I think you've had enough," he says. He takes the bottle of vodka from her hand. She wonders why he is so frightened of her sexuality. The implication is, unleashed, it will bring forth wild devastating weather. Ala pictures a storm-tossed ocean, mighty heaves of swell and devouring crashing waves. His felt fear of her power makes her afraid of it herself. Then the awkward silence in the room is broken by a sound she hasn't heard for a long time. A plaintive meow. The scrawny bright-eyed kitten is looking at her from the attic room door. She jumps to her feet, pushes Wolf aside and takes the animal to her breast. It offers no resistance, as if this encounter has been ordained.

"You poor thing," she says. The lean kitten purrs against her heart. "I'm going to look after you."

"You can't keep that," says Wolf.

"Take no notice of him," she tells the kitten brushing her face against its fur. "You are now a member of the Jewish Fighting Organisation. And I'm going to call you Churchill."

4

"Mr Kurzawa?"

The elderly, emaciated and hunched man looks at Max in bewilderment. His face is a patchwork of abrasions and bruises.

"I'm Max Silberman. Emanuel's son."

"Max?" The man's eyes show a moment of wonder but quickly cloud over.

"Let's get off the street," says Max, taking his father's best friend by the arm.

They enter an abandoned and looted apartment. There is only one chair in the shuttered kitchen. Max holds it out for Mr Kurzawa. He himself sits on the table. There are shards of broken blue and white china on the floor.

"What are you doing in the ghetto? You're not Jewish."

Mr Kurzawa tugs at his tie and adjusts the spectacles on the bridge of his nose. "To be truthful I don't know what I'm doing anymore. I was hoping to find you and your brother."

"My brother was taken to Treblinka. Which means he's probably dead now."

"What's happened to the world, Max? It's gone insane. I don't want to live in this world anymore. My wife was killed last month."

"I'm sorry. She was a lovely woman," says Max, but he struggles to recall her face. He sometimes thinks all the physical hardships he undergoes are slowly eroding his memory.

"There's no easy way to say this. Your mother and father are both dead, Max."

Max looks down at the ground and his eyes stay fixed there. He is looking deeply into the past. A riot of images passes before his eyes, all now infused with the sorrowing guilt that is his prevailing emotion.

"For a while I hid them in a bunker under my barn. But everyone knew how close your father and I were. They were suspicious."

Max is deeply upset by the image he sees of his mother and father hiding underground. He forgets for a moment they are dead.

"Your father was the best friend I had in the world. We grew up together. We discovered ourselves together. I did my best to save him. People I've known all my life came in a large group and dragged them out."

"They took them to the Germans?"

"I'm not sure you want to hear this, Max."

Max has heard many horror stories about German atrocities in other towns and villages. Children made to climb trees in a Jewish cemetery and then shot down from the branches. Mothers made to stand on their children before being shot; children burnt alive in front of their parents. "I don't want to hear anything I'm told these days," he says. "But it's better to know. And the more hate I feel the less afraid I am."

"Your mother and father were beaten to death by this mob in front of my house. There were women as well as men. And there were people there who had known your mother and father their entire lives. They began beating my wife and me as well, but my son stepped in and saved us. They called us Jew lovers. They broke our windows and tried to set our house alight. The Germans have little idea who's Jewish and who's not. It's we Poles who point out the Jews for them. Every Jew in the entire district has been betrayed by a fellow Pole. They didn't stand a chance. They're nearly all dead, Max. I'm ashamed of my nationality. I was beaten a second time for burying your mother and father. I was made a pariah in the town. Our windows were smashed and one night they tried again to set our house alight. My wife had a heart attack and died. The worst of them was Chrupek and his son. You remember them?"

Max nods. He finds he has a lone memory of Mr Chrupek. He is mixing cement while he stood by watching. He was about ten. He can detect nothing hateful or violent about the man in this memory.

"The priest was inciting hostility towards the Jews too. Really the whole damn place ought to burn in hell." The broken old man tugs at the knot in his tie again. "Your father wanted you to have something. It's a bill of purchase. For a boat. Here. We did it up together just before the Germans came. It's a beautiful little boat. Of course it's of absolutely no use in times like these. But it's proof he loved you. He talked about you often. I know you two fell out."

"I converted to Catholicism."

"He told me. I'm sure you had your reasons. I'm not here to pass judgement. One thing I will say is, he never stopped loving you. I think you should know this. This piece of paper is the proof."

Max looks at the crumpled chit of paper with the official stamp. He can't help inwardly smiling at the eccentricity of the gesture on his father's part. He realises it was his father's way of inviting him to spend time at home. Winter enters his heart at the thought of his own mean-spirited feuding. He thinks of the boat and how he would have loved to take Sabina and the girls on a river trip. For a moment he has the night river smell in his nostrils again and the sense of the boat forging through the black night like a clear line of argument.

He pockets the useless chit of paper. It sits against his thigh together with the strip he tore from Sabina's dress.

5

"I noticed you and Wolf aren't talking."

Ala can tell it has cost Symcha an effort to say this. He is a shy boy with red hair and freckles who wears large spectacles and has a chipped front tooth. His greasy trousers are held up by red braces. He stands by her side touching one of the empty rusted hooks over the sink while she scrubs a large saucepan. At her feet, rubbing against her ankles, is Churchill, the kitten. Churchill sleeps with Ala every night and Ala talks to him whenever they are alone. She never tells the kitten lies, or even half-truths. Only what's in her heart. Sometimes she wishes herself inside the kitten's fur. She imagines she would be safer and happier there. She has become close to Symcha because of the efforts he always makes to find Churchill milk.

"Stupid, isn't it? At a time like this," says Ala.

"You mean that personal differences still count?"

"I still like some people more than others. Don't you?"

Symcha's face reddens. "You like Zanek, don't you?"

"Is it that obvious?"

"He likes you too except there's Mira."

It makes Ala happy to hear this. She puts down the saucepan. "Shall I show you the five basic ballet positions?"

Ala has to imagine a barre. She is wearing a black pair of trousers and a plum-coloured cardigan. Mira gave her the trousers. She performs the five gestures.

"Why don't you try? Position number one. Stand tall, heels together, toes turned outwards."

"It's much more difficult than it looks, isn't it?"

Ala takes hold of the base of his spine with one hand and his navel with her other hand. "Stand taller," she says. "No slouching." She can sense his blood heat up and removes her hands. She doesn't want him to feel she is flirting with him. She is too fond of him to cause him any anguish.

"I don't think I would have made it as a ballet dancer."

"What did you want to do?"

"I wanted to make films. Documentary films. I dreamt of making a film about Jews in various parts of the world. Palestine, America, England, Italy, France. Compare their lives and document how well they've assimilated or not. Not much chance of that happening now, is there?"

Ala squeezes out the dishrag and rubs away the stains in the sink.

"You never know. Stalingrad, North Africa. The Germans aren't looking so invincible anymore."

"Don't you think the worst moment of the day is when you first wake up in the morning? Especially when you've had a good dream. And then you remember all over again where you are and how little of life you probably have left. I haven't even fully grown up yet. That's what I resent. Sometimes I feel like the negative of a photograph. Like I'm yet to be developed."

Ala has picked up Churchill and is stroking him.

"Symcha, I need you to run a message over to Mordecai."

Ala doesn't turn around at the sound of Wolf's voice. Her blood heats up at the thought that he might have been eavesdropping. She thinks he might be sending away Symcha so he can talk to her. But this isn't the case. She is left alone with Churchill.

Later news arrives that Mira has been murdered by the Gestapo on the other side of the wall where she was acting as a courier in the purchase of weapons.

"The awful thing is, she managed to escape the Gestapo raid on the house. She climbed out of a window. She was kneeling behind a tree and the Germans were about to leave, but a street sweeper had seen her and pointed her out. They shot her on the spot."

Ala remembers when Mira gave her the trousers she's now wearing. How Mira complimented her on her legs when Ala stood in her underwear, wishing her own legs were so long and willowy, and how pleased Mira was when she saw the trousers fitted. She realises Mira might have otherwise worn these trousers when she was murdered. That they might now be buried on her dead body. For a moment she feels like she is wearing a death shroud.

"Where's Zanek?"

"He's delivering a pep talk to the workers at the brushmakers' factory. Trying to convince them not to believe these latest German promises that they'll be safe if they voluntarily transfer to a labour camp."

"Who's going to tell him?"

"I think you should tell him, Ala," says Wolf.

Ala still hasn't found the courage to tell Zanek she witnessed the murder of his mother.

"I wonder how that street sweeper will be able to live with himself now," says Symcha.

"We're just vermin for most Poles. They don't even possess a basic human compassion for us," says Wolf.

6

Towards sunset Max is darting from doorway to doorway, led by Otto, when he sees the corpse of Mr Kurzawa, stripped down to his underwear, sprawled in the middle of the road. His eyes turned back in his head.

"Machine gunned," says Otto. "Eight bullet holes. Did you know him?"

"He gave me piggy back rides when I was your age. He remembered me before I can remember myself."

"It makes you weak and careless to remember. That's probably why he's dead."

"Why don't you leave the ghetto, Otto? You could probably survive on the other side of the wall. The Germans will come to get the rest of us soon."

"The kids there all know I'm a Jew. They start shouting it and following me. I have to give them something to shut them up. Unless I sell stuff here I wouldn't have anything to pay them off with. And where would I sleep? Why don't you? You've got good looks. Better looks than me."

By this Otto means Max looks less Jewish. Every Jew, even the children, now has detailed knowledge of what a give-away Jewish face looks like and has been compelled to evaluate their own facial features against this prototype. When Max was outside the wall he felt his face was twice the size of anyone else's, as if under a microscope. And the German propaganda poster equating Jews with lice and criminality and depicting a hook-nosed, malevolent, eagle-eyed Jew followed him around Warsaw's streets like a tracker dog.

"Anyway, I want to see the fighting. I want to see some Germans die," says Otto.

When they reach the hole in the wall Otto scrambles through to the other side. Max, gripping the pistol in his coat pocket, overhears a conversation in hushed tones. He averts his eyes from his reflection in the brown puddle at his feet. He lives now at a furtive distance from his mirror image. His face frightens him whenever he catches a glimpse of it. It bears so little resemblance to how he likes to see himself. Even his hands when he looks at them nowadays seem to belong to a stranger. He reads a few of the classified advertisements in the sodden page of a newspaper in the gutter. A preponderance of people offering German lessons. Then a sack is pushed through the hole. And another one. The weight of them as he hoists them up onto his shoulders shocks him into acknowledging how physically weakened he has become. A beautiful sunset is developing in the sky. Max allows himself to drift off with its once-upon-a-time associations for a moment.

Then he hears an approaching motor and, struggling with the sacks, begins to run towards the nearest door. Otto follows in his wake. Max doesn't turn when an arrogant German voice shouts out a command. It feels better now that the immediate response is to disobey every German order. He and Otto climb up the stairs to a first-floor apartment strewn with debris and shut the door behind them. Max then draws the gun and listens. A clock ticks loudly behind him.

"Where did you get that?" Otto's eyes are wide with desire.

Max's hand is trembling.

Together they listen to the car continue on its way down the street.

"Do you want to sell it?"

"No. Buy your own gun," he says.

Max, Otto and Clara are now living together in his apartment. For a while Max and Clara took refuge in an underground bunker with about sixty other people. Max couldn't stand the claustrophobia of it. Children crying, people bickering, the sick coughing and groaning, the stink and squalor and the absence of natural light. He couldn't accustom himself to the boredom of watching himself do nothing all day. It was as if there was no longer any purpose for his mind or body. He decided he would prefer the risk of being shot above ground.

The first night back at his apartment Clara came into his bedroom in her bare feet and got into bed with him. He felt mean and churlish rejecting her childish advances. The last thing he wanted was to make her feel unattractive. He tried to explain, he spoke of his love for Sabina and everything he said sounded like a preposterous fairy story. He suspects she and Otto are now experimenting, playing games with each other's private parts. He hears Otto giving what sound like commands through the wall. And Otto is definitely more pleased with himself of late. Clara now treats Max with studied indifference. And she has begun to wear Sabina's clothes.

7

They are sitting side by side on the floor, backs against the wall, knees raised. There is a smell of sawdust and wet plaster from the camouflaging of the attic underway above them. Zanek doesn't cry or hold his head in his hands when Ala tells him what has happened to Mira. He sits staring at his shoes. His hair falling over his eyes. Ala is holding Churchill to her breast for moral support. After a long silence he lifts his head, as if from beneath deep water, and clears his throat.

"At least I know exactly what she would want me to do," he says, absently smoothing his hair with the flat of his hand. "Kill as many Germans and their Ukrainian and Lithuanian lackeys as possible. At the moment I've got five rounds for my pistol. She once told me she was never able to hate the Germans because they terrified her too much. She said hating them for her was as difficult as hating a shark. That there's only room for terror."

"I hate them. I hate the entire German race. I hate the Lithuanian and Ukrainian races as well."

"The other night I felt quite calm about the thought of dying. I was pleased with myself that I was able to face death without fear. The trouble is, I haven't been able to find that feeling again. Last night in bed I was frightened. Really frightened. I kept picturing my body without me in it. At our young age how can we be expected to accept our lives are already over? I hope I can overcome my fear. Even if it means becoming numb which is how I feel now."

There's a small rip on the thigh of Zanek's breeches. Ala has an urge to insert her index finger into that tiny hole. Instead, she releases Churchill and takes his hand. She is surprised by its swarm of warmth. The contact makes her skin come alive all over her body. When he shifts his weight and his knee rests against her knee she discovers again how much her body likes his body. Then, remembering Mira, she withdraws herself from the moment. It occurs to her that she is probably feeling more guilt than the street sweeper who betrayed Mira or the German who shot her. She is sick and tired of the guilt the Germans keep managing to induce in her. She wants to go into this battle with some active love in her heart. At the moment all her love is elegiac and sapping.

"Do you think it matters anymore what Mira might think?" she asks Churchill later when they are alone. Churchill is playing with a reel of red cotton. Ala loves to watch the kitten play. It's a reminder of what life should be like.

8

"Before you looked like a mild-mannered man who wouldn't hurt a fly; now you look like my worst nightmare."

Max has just shaved and dressed in the full uniform of an SS officer. He toys with the cap with its death skull insignia. His shadow is faint on the wall opposite the window. He wishes there was a mirror in the room. It's the first time since Sabina died that he has had any curiosity to see himself. His two companions are both smiling uncertainly at him. Each has a pistol and a grenade tucked in his belt.

"What rank am I?"

"Just act haughty."

Max looks down doubtfully at his battered shoes, his clown shoes with the flapping soles. He has been chosen for this task because he is older, taller than most. "And you could pass as a German." He was ashamed that he was flattered by this remark.

Max sits with his two companions by a greasy window waiting for any sign of members of the Third Reich. Eventually, a hundred yards away, two German gendarmes appear escorting a pair of Jews pushing a handcart piled with suitcases. Max's heart is pounding when he steps outside the building dressed as an entitled enforcer of Nazi racial policy. The two Germans stop when they see him. It's not difficult for Max to act agitated. He ushers them towards him. He points at the building he has just left and urges silence by putting his finger to his lips. As they approach he senses the two Germans are suspicious of him. As if there's something remiss about his uniform or they have noticed his shoes or simply registered his fear. He points at the building again. He puts his finger to his lips again. Just as he is about to enter the building a car enters the street. Everyone stops to look round. In the passenger seat is the SS officer who murdered Sabina. He shouts something Max doesn't understand. The car pulls up alongside the two German gendarmes. Max ignores the raucous shout of the SS officer and enters the building.

"Are they coming?" hisses Abram, the young man who told him he could pass as a German. He is holding a piece of chicken wire. His companion is standing by the window, discretely peering out. He holds a hammer. They don't want to waste valuable bullets.

"We need to throw a grenade at that jeep," says Max, unable to stand still. "That's the bastard who killed my wife."

"Calm down. Our objective is to get weapons as quietly as possible. Get back into the hallway and lure them in."

Max walks back to the doorstep. The two gendarmes are approaching cautiously, watched closely by the SS officer in the jeep. Max catches his eye for a moment. The German, he sees, is troubled by the charge of hatred directed at him from a man in an SS uniform. Max goes through the pantomime of beckoning the gendarmes on again. He is convinced they know he is an imposter but still they walk forward, rifles cocked and at the ready. Max makes sure they see which apartment he enters.

"They're coming," he whispers. His two companions stand on either side of the doorway. The door has been taken off its hinges and removed. The first German is struck by the hammer. He collapses without a sound. The second German, shouting, tries to flee but Abram gets the chicken wire around his neck.

Max derives none of the anticipated pleasure from the death of the two Germans. Alive, they looked like ordinary men with wives and children and petty concerns. Now both faces are contorted and gory in death.

The barking voice of the SS officer freezes everyone.

"Come on, you bastard," whispers Abram. "In you come."

The voice barks again but with less assurance this time.

Max picks up the rifle dropped by one of the gendarmes. He walks outside and his eyes blazing with loathing meet those of Sabina's murderer. He takes aim and fires. It's the first time he has ever fired a weapon and he is not braced for the violent retort which sends a shooting pain along his arm. The bullet pings off the jeep. He can't get the rifle to fire a second time. He yells out abuse as the jeep accelerates away. The two Jews with the handcart look at him as if he is an unsolvable riddle. Only now does he realise his nemesis shot at him. A bullet from the same gun that ended Sabina's life is lodged in the doorframe by his side.

9

"I'd like to swim naked in the sea under the moon," says Ala.

"I'd like to own a motor car and drive with the roof down through France and Italy," says Symcha.

It's two-thirty in the morning. Ala and Symcha are on sentry duty on a rooftop. They have to continually beat themselves against the cold. To keep themselves occupied and alert they have been instructed to take apart, clean and reassemble the one pistol they share. Instead they play a wishing game. Ala can't help wishing it was Zanek beside her. But it seems mean to wish Symcha somewhere else. Below, in the room overlooking Mila Street, makeshift weapons are stockpiled – petrol bombs, grenades, roof tiles, stones, metal objects. Ala can't quite believe there might come a time when she is called upon to hurl these missiles at uniformed Nazis.

"I'd like to ride in a husky-driven sleigh through the steppes of Russia," she says. "I'd be dressed in fur from head to foot."

"I'd like to meet an elephant in its natural habitat."

"I'd like one of the awful omelettes my father made when my mother was out for the evening."

"No food allowed."

"If only time would stand still now," says Ala, blocking out an array of stars with her hand and then splaying her fingers to make them reappear.

"And when it started up again the war was over."

They are silent for a while. Then Symcha says: "I keep wondering if this gun has ever killed anyone. I'm not sure it'll be of much use from up here. The grenades will be more effective."

"Says the military expert."

"I know. We're just a bunch of kids, aren't we? I'd like to have a bash at using the rifle though."

Wolf has the only rifle their group of fighters possess.

"How long do you think we'll be able to hold out when the Germans come?"

"I don't know. A couple of hours?"

"That's what I think," she says. "Which means from the moment the Germans enter the ghetto we've got two hours of life left."

"Is there something you wished you'd said to your father or mother before they were taken off?"

"We're not supposed to be talking about sad things."

"You just talked about only having two more hours to live. What's sadder than that?"

"Point taken," says Ala, rubbing herself to keep warm.

"So much of what we say has nothing to do with what we feel. Is that what you think? It's like the inner life and the outer life are two different worlds which only rarely convene. Sometimes I used to despise the sound of my voice. All the irrelevance it came out with. Talk, more often than not, is like a game of hide-and-seek, isn't it? I wish I had said what I really felt. Instead of worrying all the time how it would make me look."

Ala is no longer listening. She has noticed a pair of probing lights down in the vicinity of the ghetto gate. "Look," she says. She takes up the field glasses. In the sheen of the headlights the men in black uniform climbing out of the truck look alarmingly close and menacing. It occurs to her that these men have no idea they are being watched. The thought makes them seem a bit pathetic in their disciplined stealth. "Soldiers are getting out. I think they're Ukrainians. I'll go and raise the alarm."

Ala climbs down into the building and strikes a match. Her enormous jittery shadow on the wall seems to take possession of her for a moment, infects her with its volatility and insubstantiality. Holes have been knocked through the walls of every apartment, so it's possible to pass from one building to another all along the street without going outside. It's like being inside a honeycomb. The sense of self-importance of being the carrier of momentous news makes her breathless.

Not long after she raises the alarm a courier arrives from the brushworks. A twelve year old boy. He says there's also German activity by the ghetto gate at the corner of Leszno and Zelazna. Ala is holding the kitten.

"We should have guessed they'd choose Passover to launch the final assault."

"And it's Hitler's birthday tomorrow," says a boy buttoning up his breeches.

"Let's give him a gift he won't forget. Remember, we may not physically survive this day but if we face the enemy with courage and honour we will live forever in the pages of Jewish history," says Wolf.

Orders are relayed. Everyone knows what to do, where to go, what the protocol is. All twenty-two of ZOB's fighting units are mobilised. Zanek arrives in the basement, sleepy-eyed, hair dishevelled. Ala hugs him. His warmth floods all through her body. He looks deep into her eyes and tells her they will talk later. She isn't sure she believes this. She lets her fingers touch the skin behind his ear. She tells herself to keep the feel of him on her hands. Then she tries to catch Wolf's eye. She wants to tell him she is sorry. Even though she isn't clear what it is she has done she is apologising for. However, Wolf is too engaged in preparations to notice her. She kisses Churchill. It is hard for her to part with the kitten.

10

The imagined horror of Treblinka and its gas chambers, the tidal force of its likelihood for him as a fate gets Max out of bed. All his mind's talismans fail to defuse its terrifying charge. Memories of Sabina, the hope that Eugenia is safe, the knowledge that Ala is still alive. Nothing he owns has the heat to ward off the stark chill of his fear.

He climbs up onto the roof and smokes a cigarette sitting on the tiles. His trouser pockets weighted with the gun, his keys and some useless loose change. The multitude of stars look like fugitive musical notes. He feels the pinprick presence of something within himself made of the same substance as those stars. There is a song of Sabina up there. The stars press upon him the fact of her death. But they also start up the song by which he knows her. A song that only the soul can sing. A song that opens into silence. Everything of significance in life, he realises, is a movement towards this silence. For a while he is able to give himself up to the singing into silence of the stars and escape the crushing press of his predicament in time and space.

Dawn is approaching when he hears distant sounds of activity. He clambers from rooftop to rooftop until he can see across into Nalewki Street. The SS troops are lined up in formation. There's a tank behind them. Never has Max seen a tank in the ghetto. He watches spellbound, until an order is barked out and the columns of Nazi soldiers, six abreast, begin marching and singing.

11

"They've set up a command HQ with tables and chairs," says Symcha, handing Ala the field glasses. They are both standing at the open window of a third-storey room, a makeshift bunker of pillows on the sill. Ala sees a host of SS officers milling about close to a desk with a telephone.

Soon the Germans, preceded by two single files of Jewish policemen, are marching in closed formation down the middle of the street. They are singing with arrogant bluster. Marching in a robotic theatrical rhythm. They look brainwashed to Ala. Behind them are armoured cars and a tank. They are heading directly for the triangular ambush set up by the ZOB leadership. Ala feels pale with excitement. Her heart is thumping in every part of her body. She looks at Symcha. She can't believe she might outwardly possess the same look of composure, the same look of being prepared for what is about to happen.

"If only we had even one heavy machine gun we could wipe out the whole lot of them in thirty seconds," he says.

Half of the marching column has passed beneath the window when the first grenade is thrown. The singing stops. The choreography falls apart. The Germans disperse into small scattering groups. Eyes wide with disbelief and fear. The street below is a field of fire as dozens of petrol bombs are hurled down from the buildings on either side. Bullets are cracking through the air. A shifting canopy of smoke hangs over ths street. Most of the Germans are too panicked to think about returning fire. Now and again there's a louder explosion and the stink of geysers of black smoke. Ala lights the fuse of her first petrol bomb. The Germans are seeking cover in doorways but caught in crossfire. She throws down her lighted green bottle at three SS soldiers huddled together by the wall below. She can't resist the temptation to watch its descent and remains standing, leaning over the windowsill. The petrol splashes at the feet of the Germans and flames swarm over the cobbles, feasting on their boots and trousers. She watches Zanek in the apartment opposite launch a petrol bomb at an armoured car. The anger with which he throws it makes Ala shout out abuse at the Germans in affinity. The German manning the machine gun scrambles out of the car, his uniform aflame. Another German is running back towards the command centre without his rifle, his uniform too in flames. She thinks how much satisfaction it gives her to see the hated SS uniform on fire. She lights her second petrol bottle, counts to five and hurls it down at the cowering Nazis.

A torrent of invective rains down from the rooftops and high windows on the retreating Germans. How good it feels to finally be able to shout out loud, to express openly the disgust and hatred the Germans arouse instead of bowing one's head and biting one's lip. Ala is surprised by the coarseness that comes from her mouth. She watches a German soldier limp back towards the ghetto gate, using his rifle as a crutch.

"These Nazis aren't exactly courageous, are they?" says Symcha. "We don't possess any lethal weapons. We've driven them back with fire and abuse. Where now is the bluster and sadistic scorn with which they herded children onto cattle trains?"

It's true. Ala expected the Germans to storm all the buildings. Expected their brute force and superior weaponry to quickly overcome all resistance. Not once has she imagined the Nazis running for their lives. The sight of their fear gives her a euphoric sense of power. A feeling of good finally triumphing in the world. She is only sad that her mother and father, Madame, Marcel and Lily aren't here to witness the fearful retreat of the Germans.

The tank is sent back in. And the armoured cars. A building further down the street has the face of it blown out. But soon the tank has been struck by petrol bombs and is on fire. Ala sees a frantic German climbing out of a damaged armoured car who is then hit by a bullet. She doesn't see what happens next as another bullet cracks close to her ear, a noise like the crackling hiss of melting ice, and she ducks down behind the bank of pillows. Symcha is polishing his glasses on his sleeve. She exchanges a smile with him. Then she stands again and throws a roof tile down at a German who is taking shelter by the wall below. He looks up at her and their eyes meet. He starts backtracking close to the wall, back towards the ghetto gate. Ala is pleased he will remember the open hatred in her eyes.

"I'm going down to get any weapons the Germans have dropped."

Downstairs, Ala stands in the doorway. The abandoned tank is still burning. The armoured cars have retreated. Small fires are burning all down the street. She counts eight German soldiers prostrate on the cobbles, some of whom are moving and groaning. There are splashes of new blood among the carnage. She looks up at the window where Zanek is stationed. She is exhilarated by the agitated concern for her safety he exhibits. She runs out into the street. She makes for a German soldier who isn't moving. Blood is oozing through his grey-green uniform. A naked pulped leg with exposed white bone is visible through his torn breeches. As she picks up his abandoned rifle by the strap he opens his eyes and looks up at her. He's about the same age as her brother. It annoys her that she can't find it within herself to hate him, to spit in his face. She is looking around for any other weapons when she realises she is being shot at. She runs back to the doorway with the rifle.

She agrees with Symcha to swap the unwieldly rifle for the pistol.

"Have you got any ammunition left?"

"I only fired two shots," says Symcha. "There wasn't much

point firing this thing from up here. I thought it best to save the bullets for when I can see the eyes of the Germans."

A German ambulance arrives down below. The wounded Germans, including the boy whose rifle she stole, are lifted inside amidst taunts and pistol shots from the Jews in the neighbouring buildings. There are more wounded Germans further up Mila Street where a more intense battle has been fought. Then a small unit of Germans, no longer singing, no longer marching in formation, return for the tank which they succeed in starting up again and reverse out of the ghetto. Symcha fires off two shots from the rifle. Ala sees he is sheepish that he missed his target both times. As if they are on a date and he has failed to impress her at some kind of fairground challenge of his manhood.

The second attack arrives later in the afternoon. Now the Germans are blasting buildings with artillery fire. The building opposite takes a direct hit. Ala fears for Zanek. She hasn't seen him for a while. When the smoke clears there is no sign of him in the exposed flaming innards of the building. Symcha points his rifle down at the street but no target offers itself. The Germans have retreated beyond the ghetto gate. Through the field glasses Ala sees the officers are agitated and indecisive. The SS soldiers stand around in disorganised groups. Many in ruined uniforms. Like pieces of an upset jigsaw. Ala hands the glasses to Symcha so he too can take pleasure at the sight of the humiliation of the men who murdered their families.

"They haven't got a contingency plan, have they?" says Symcha. "I think we might have ruined Hitler's birthday."

The Germans make no further attempt to advance into the ghetto. A child courier eventually arrives and tells Ala and Symcha to return to the group command base. Ala becomes suddenly nervous. She says a silent prayer for Zanek's safety. And then adds her brother and uncle's names to her skybound plea.

12

Towards ten in the evening Max joins the large throng of Jews out on the streets. There is an air of bewildered celebration. In the fidgeting light spawned by the fires inside buildings caused by the German artillery attack, faces, many smeared with dirt and soot, possess a feverish excitement. Everyone is talking at once and hugging each other. A Jewish flag has been mounted on top of a building in Muranowski Square. The Jews have control of the ghetto, at least for one night.

He walks past a woman sitting in a doorway. She is talking to herself, reminding him of Sabina's aunt. It occurs to him that he never knew what happened to Elsa. She vanished the day Sabina was shot and Ora was deported. He remembers the one and only moment he felt seen by Elsa. Sabina emerges from the bathroom, wrapped in a wet towel and he takes her in his arms and waltzes her into the living room where Elsa eventually tears herself away from the looking glass and smiles at him.

For a moment there is nothing much for Max to celebrate out on these burning streets.

Then he sees Ala skipping towards him. She throws her arms around him. She is holding a pistol. The cold metal touches his neck.

"Isn't it amazing? We stood up to them. Don't you feel proud?"

"I was hoping you'd be outside the ghetto," he says. He is heartened he still recognises the young girl in Ala; that she hasn't been too brutalised by the apocalyptic world in which they live.

"I'm a member of ZOB now," she says, holding up her gun.

"I'm with ZZW. The fascists," he says, smiling. "And I've got one of those too," he says, producing his pistol. "Who would ever have thought that one day we'd be comparing guns."

"Yours is filthy," says Ala, smiling. "You need to clean it. Otherwise it won't go off. Do you want me to show you how? I know as much about guns now as toe shoes."

Max has this obsessive notion that the two bullets in his pistol are for the SS officer who murdered Sabina. He has a premonition they will cross paths again. And he is saving the two bullets for this moment.

"They say more than a hundred Germans were killed today."

"More than five hundred," laughs Ala. "The exaggerations going round will mean the entire German army is dead before the night is over. Every Jewish boy claims to have killed at least five. But it doesn't matter how many Germans we kill. There will always be more. It's the fact of fighting back that matters."

"I wish you'd get out of the ghetto, Ala. They'll be back tomorrow and with better tactics."

"Maybe the Polish Home Army will help us now. Maybe what happened today will give them courage to stage a revolt of their own. If the whole of Warsaw rose up now…"

They are standing beside a building hollowed out by a shell and lit from within by a simmering fire. Sparks gust through the smoky air and rise to dance among the stars. It strikes Max that the blackened skeletal landscape is the perfect evocation of a world of unanswered prayers.

Later Henryk appears. He too is carrying a gun. Max watches him and Ala hug. He finds himself remembering once squirting the pair of them as children with a hose-pipe in a garden. Their joy appearing almost too big for their small half naked bodies.

"I killed at least three of the bastards," says Henryk.

Ala exchanges an amused look with Max.

"One for Mum, one for Dad and one for Lily. We mowed down the bastards with our two machine guns. And it was our fighters who raised the flag. Two children. They both died doing it. But listen, we've got a tunnel through to the Aryan side. Unlike your lot, we've got an exit strategy. Why don't you go over to the Aryan side? I'm sure Sophie would take you in. Tell her, Max."

Before Max can say anything, Clara is hugging and kissing him. He's embarrassed by the implied proprietorship of her greeting. Of his awareness of the crush and warmth of her breasts against his chest. It pains him that Ala and Henryk might think he has already replaced Sabina. And with a girl young enough to be his daughter. And then baffles him that concerns of propriety still exist in his world.

13

"Have the Germans succeeded in giving you a sense of inferiority? With all their propaganda and bile, I mean," says Ala. She has just finished chewing a stale but edible piece of bread. She and Symcha are positioned at the window overlooking Mila Street again.

"The Poles didn't do a bad job either. I suspect the Germans have got most of us believing there might be some truth in what they say. Don't you think that's why so many Jews began imitating the Germans, wearing high boots and shouting orders."

"A good friend of mine was in the Jewish police."

"I'm not saying they were *all* bad."

"Most were. What gets to me is our lives have so little in them now of our own doing. We're like history's puppets." Ala smiles. How often, she realises, she smiles or laughs when she is much closer to tears. She picks up the field glasses. "Those flags have really infuriated the subhumans. They're obsessed with the building in Muranowski Square. My brother and uncle are in there."

Yesterday, the second day of the fighting, the Germans didn't once appear under Ala and Symcha's window. Ala watched through field glasses the Germans attack the buildings in Muranowski Square. Their tactics were different. No longer did they offer themselves as easy targets. They worked in small stealthy units, keeping close to the walls in snakelike formations, using flamethrowers and incendiary devices. They attacked one Jewish stronghold at a time. Many buildings were set on fire.

Often Ala couldn't see what was happening through the thick smoke. Once again the tank was set on fire by petrol bombs. There's now a Polish flag alongside the Jewish flag on the roof. Both have been torn and charred but are still fastened and flying, visible all over Warsaw.

"Do you believe Michal's bomb killed a hundred Germans at the brushworkers?" says Ala.

"More likely about ten," says Symcha. "But it keeps up morale if we believe we're gradually wiping out the entire German army."

Today Ala feels death is stalking her at much closer quarters. The exuberance of the past two nights has gone. Adrenaline has exhausted itself inside her. Hunger and exhaustion are taking their toll. Her heart beats as if to a war drum. Thoughts rise to the surface unbidden. Memories of happiness have lost their restorative charge. They taunt her now with their impotence.

A reconnaissance plane is circling overhead, directing the German artillery fire. Symcha makes an obscene gesture at it. It's the last thing he ever does. There is a searing flash, as if some new apparition is about to appear in the world. Then a hailstorm of fiery debris and a howling rush of hot air that burns into Ala's throat, sucks the breath from her and lifts her up off the ground.

When she returns to the moment she has to struggle to regain herself, to bring back into purpose all that she is. A large ragged hole has been punched through the floor. She lies at its edge, looking down at a constellation of small growing fires twelve feet below. She gets unsteadily to her feet. There is a ghost whistling in her head. Otherwise she can hear nothing at all. Her clothes, she sees, are ripped and blood-stained. Symcha is sprawled out on the floor, a sarcophagus of snow, except for a bright smudge of red in his singed hair where a kitchen fork is embedded in the back of his skull. Ala refuses to believe he has been killed by a kitchen utensil. She pulls at his arm. The sudden insignificance of his lifeless form is bewildering. The same repellent yet mesmerising air of both vacancy and accomplishment on his face that she has grown accustomed to seeing on corpses in the ghetto. Then Zanek appears, covered in plaster dust. He looks like an angel in the midst of all the hell fires around him. She sees the urgent look in his eyes and the busy industry of his lips, but no sound reaches her. Liquefied pieces of broken glass gum her shoes to the ground as she stumbles towards him. She sees his clothes are smouldering and falls dizzily into his arms when she begins beating him.

They have to skirt around the gaping hole in the floor. Sparks flit about her head in gusts. The exploding glass and burning collapsing timber happen with the sound turned down. Outside the apartment rampant rainbow flames surge up the stairway. There is no way down. The sticky molten ground burns through her summer shoes. The thick smoke begins to choke her.

On the roof both she and Zanek have to slap at their smouldering clothes and hair. Zanek finds a wooden plank and stamps out the flames licking at its edges. He uses it to bridge the gap between one rooftop and another. Motions for her to cross. A look of concern on his face. The windows of the building opposite are orange squares. Ala sees a woman holding a child on a third-floor balcony. Gusting flames reaching out for her. Zanek, a captured German rifle slung over his shoulder, urges her again to walk across the plank. Out of the corner of her eye she sees the woman jump to her death with her child. For a moment she too feels an urge to jump. To have done with all this exhausting terror. Instead, she puts her fingers in her ears and roots around. Trying to bring sound back into her world. Then, taking off her charred shoes and summoning all her ballerina poise, she hears Madame's voice admonishing her to stay on the beat. She walks unsteadily along the wooden board which jumps and wobbles beneath her bare feet.

14

Max has spent the past few days with the fighters of ZZW in Muranowski Square, close to the building where the two flags have been raised. The Germans have made a concerted effort every day to bring down the flags. Employing long range artillery and then working in small stealthy assault units. Yesterday there were gun fights and hand to hand fighting inside buildings. Many of the ZZW fighters died in the battle, including Henryk, Ala's brother. Max spent much of the day running, escaping through the elaborate network of tunnels connecting all the buildings in the square. They are now short of ammunition and an order has been given to avoid all open fighting with the Germans. Today, an important visitor from the other side of the wall is holding a meeting with the ZZW leaders.

Max and his companion are on sentry duty, concealed at a second-floor window overlooking the square. Jan beside him with a rifle has the reputation of being one of the most expert snipers in the group.

Everything is quiet outside until two covered trucks arrive in the square. Two Germans jump out and take position with guns at the ready. Another SS soldier open the flaps at the back of the trucks. A group of wretched Jews clamber down from both vehicles. They are made to stand in a line. Max, watching, has a sick feeling in his stomach. Then a car arrives and Max sees again the SS officer who murdered Sabina. He feels an electric crackle of fate in the air. As if a higher power is granting him a second opportunity of retribution. His nemesis is close enough for Jan to pick him off with his rifle.

"That's the bastard who killed my wife," he says.

"I know what you're thinking. But I can't do it. Orders are orders."

The SS officer is ordering the Jews to lie down on the cobbles. When they hesitate a short burst of machine gun fire over their heads convinces them to obey. There are three women in the group, two adolescent boys and a girl of about twelve along with the grown men. Two of the Jewish men are told to stand up and handed either end of a long piece of hemp rope. They are ordered to stretch out the length of rope at the feet of the line of prostrate Jews.

"What are they doing?"

"They're proving to us they can still do whatever they want, that they still have absolute control over the ghetto. And they're trying to provoke us into revealing our position. My bet is there's a large formation of German troops hidden nearby."

Max realises his nemesis has some courage, offering himself as he is as an easy target. It bothers him that he has to acknowledge this.

The SS officer walks along the line of prostrate bodies, checking their feet are aligned with the rope. Then he orders the two Jewish men to take their places at either end of the line. The sick feeling in Max's stomach intensifies.

The SS officer climbs back into his car. He unwraps a piece of grease paper.

"He's eating a sandwich. It's like he wants someone to shoot him."

The SS officer motions to the driver of one of the trucks. The driver manoeuvres the truck, aligning the front right wheel parallel with the knees of all the Jews. Even from fifty yards away Max can see the violent struggle of the prostrate bodies to master fear.

Max begins shaking Jan. "Shoot him. For fuck's sake shoot him. Who cares if we all die. We're going to die anyway. What does it matter if it's today or tomorrow?"

"You know I can't, Max." There's a gargoyle grimace on Jan's face.

They both watch the truck slowly roll forward over the knees of the victims, one by one. The screams of the Jews as their legs are crushed incite in Max an overwhelming urge to scream himself. Two men jump up and try to run but they are shot down. An image of fingers clawing at the air stamps itself on his retina before he averts his eyes as the wheels of the truck reach the women and children. Meanwhile, the SS officer sits in his car. Finishing his sandwich.

Max rests his hands on his knees and vomits.

The screams fade to moans. The SS officer remains in his car. Drinking from a flask and sometimes laughing with his driver. Max fiddles with his pistol. He thinks he might run out into the square with the pistol raised. He can see himself doing it as he thinks it.

"Don't even think about it, Max. I'd have to stop you. You know that."

"What's the point of a resistance movement if we stand by and watch that monster murder women and children? They're all bleeding to death out there and he's eating a sandwich and making jokes."

"I know how you feel. I feel the same."

"Beaten. That's how I feel. Is that how you feel? I've come up against something I'm not equal to. That's how I feel."

"What about the guy driving the truck?"

"What do you mean?"

"Did you see him hesitate? Did you see the faintest sign of any misgiving about what he was ordered to do? What's he going to tell his grandchildren when they ask him what he did in the war? Look at him. He isn't SS. He's just a normal German bloke. A citizen of the civilised country of Germany."

"Are you trying to make me feel better or worse? I don't understand."

"We're witnesses, Max. And witnesses have to stay alive until the trials begin."

15

Ala wakes up with a start. For a moment she has no recollection of where she is or what has happened. Everything smells alien. The absence of any sense of familiarity eviscerates her, makes her feel a frightening stranger to herself. She is lying on a mattress in a room she doesn't recognise. Zanek is standing over her. The sole source of light the candle he holds. Shadows shift about in the corners of the unknown room.

"Sorry to wake you but I've got a surprise for you," he says. "Can you hear me?"

"Has someone found Churchill?" she asks with an eager gust of hope. Then she realises the world is audible again. There is a ringing clarity to every sound. For a moment, marvelling at her body's surreptitious powers of recovery, she is aglow with thanksgiving as if life has returned to normal.

"Sorry," says Zanek. "I wish that was the surprise."

Ala, even in her shellshocked state, wasn't prepared for the pain the missing kitten caused her. The cat was her most tender and tactile attachment to life. The building they called home now a blackened shell.

"You've stopped shouting," he says, smiling. "That's a good sign."

Zanek tells her he is happy he no longer has to make extravagant hand gestures to make himself understood. "Not that you ever understood me." It's the first time Ala has seen anyone behave at apparent leisure for what seems like weeks. As if there's no longer any reason to feel frightened.

"I thought the fact that I learned a little of the sign language for the deaf had become a prophecy. What's happening outside?"

He tells her not to worry about that for a while. He tells her to come with him and hands her a gun.

"Keep that with you. It's possible the Germans are entering buildings at night disguised as Jews. Two Jewish boys were discovered last night with their throats slit in an attic. Not that I want to frighten you," he says and smiles.

Ala lifts the blanket to see what she is wearing. Just her slip and panties. She wonders with a prickling rash of discomfort who undressed her. When she sits up the candlelight fetches her shadow up onto the wall where it towers over her but is unrecognisable as herself.

"Don't worry, I've already seen you in your slip. And I've got some clothes waiting for you. Come on!" She watches him, haloed by the candle flame, duck through the hole punched in the wall. Ala follows him through into the apartment next door, holding the gun by the handle. He leads the way up some stairs and into a bathroom she has never seen before. He holds the candle flame over a tub, full to the brim with steaming water.

"Bath time," he says. He points to a towel and some clothes on a chair.

She looks at him with puzzlement. Does he mean they are going to have a bath together?

"The gas was on for a short time. I thought you'd like a bath," he says. "I'll be upstairs with Wolf. We're on sentry duty until three. Leave the water in the tub when you're done. I'll use it and you can take my place while I have my bath."

The water quickly turns black with a film of scurf on the surface. She feels embarrassed at the thought of Zanek sitting naked in her dirty water. She remembers telling Churchill that she wasn't interested in love or romance. That it would be delusional to think along such long term lines. But it pains her to accept the long term no longer exists. Why shouldn't she want love and romance? Surely it's important to make other things matter beside the Nazis? *Otherwise, we're just their slaves.*

She is drawn to Zanek because, unlike Wolf, she feels he wouldn't treat her naked body as some kind of sacred event. The sexual act as some kind of religious ritual which needs a consecrated date and time. Ala wants to perform the act without reverential embroidery. She wants to be kindled with a foreign energy, to be hypnotised, to not know what will emerge in her body next. She has been trained to make everything speak through her body. This is like the most exciting secret of her body she is yet to unwrap. Why shouldn't she still try to believe in a reality in which this might happen? Otherwise, she might as well be already dead. Like poor Symcha.

As she is about to lift herself out of the water she hears a creak on the stairs of the otherwise silent building. And then a whispering voice on the landing. *It's possible the Germans are entering buildings at night disguised as Jews.* She picks up the candle and blows it out. Darkness gradually smothers the faint glow of the expiring flame. Then she hears another creak outside, a few yards from the door. *Two Jewish boys were discovered last night with their throats slit in an attic.* She reaches down and fumbles around in the darkness for the pistol. The water in the tub makes a swishing noise. The release of the safety catch makes an echoing click. Every noise she makes increases the tension. Her body now is primed for the sound of the door handle turning. She sits in the bath, in the dark, pointing her gun towards the unseen door.

What if it's Zanek?

It isn't Zanek. There are at least two people out there. And they're creeping about like criminals. Why would Zanek creep about like a criminal?

Then there's the faintest click. Fear prickles her skin from head to toe. The creak of a hinge. Her heartbeat surges up into her throat. The scratch of wood resisting tile and a colder draught of air brushing her wet naked shoulders. She isn't conscious of making the decision to pull the trigger. But the gun explodes in her hand. The retort makes the muscles in her upper arm spasm. In the flash of the gunshot she catches sight of a pair of malevolent eyes looking at her from the doorway. She ducks down, careful to keep the hot gun above the surface of the water. Then all hell breaks loose. She hears Zanek calling out her name. And the unmistakable sound of a German voice and a gunshot. The bullet cracks and sucks at the air close to her head. She pulls the trigger again. A splintering explosion in the midst of which she thinks she hears the sound of a body thud to the ground. And running footsteps on the stairs. She steps out of the bath with her gun aimed at the doorway. She fumbles about in the darkness for the towel but can't find it. Then Zanek and Wolf are standing in the doorway. Wolf shines a flashlight at her naked dripping body.

"What's going on?" she asks. "Were they Germans?"

"I thought you might be able to tell us," says Wolf. "Whoever they were they fled like rabbits when you fired off your gun. And there's a dead body down here." He shines the flashlight on a slumped male body with a blackened face. Pooling blood by his side blanched by the bright light. His feet are wrapped in pieces of cloth. There's a knife in his belt and a fallen pistol close to his body.

"Did I shoot him?" Ala asks, still standing rooted to the spot.

"Through the heart by the look of it," says Wolf.

Ala looks at the gun in her hand, then back at the blackened face of the dead man. "Is he a Jew?"

"One way to find out." Zanek kneels down and unfastens the dead man's trousers. He yanks them down together with his shorts. "Not circumcised," he says, directing the beam of the torch in Wolf's hand onto the man's penis. "Looks like you killed your first German, Ala."

Ala, her heart still racing, is recalled to her nakedness by a critical look in Wolf's eyes. She reaches out for the towel and wraps herself up in it, looking down at her wet footprints on the tiled floor.

16

Stripped down to his shorts, Max sits against a wall in the bunker. The taste in his mouth as if all his teeth have decayed. Clara, wearing only a filthy slip, is sitting beside him. The slip belonged to Sabina. He remembers lifting it up over her head while she held her arms aloft. Sometimes he says her name. He says her name to himself and waits to see what happens next. Usually he gets a glimpse of her again. But when he thinks of Sabina nowadays he invariably feels less than he hoped.

About seventy other people are crushed into the underground burrow. The smoke that filtered down from a raging fire above ground earlier and threatened to asphyxiate everyone is thinning out. There's an electric light but it nightmarishly flickers on and off. The blackened faces around him continually reclaimed by darkness after apparitional demonic visitations in the stuttering light.

Earlier, when there was the regular sound of gunshots and explosions and they could hear German voices above them, a baby began crying, choking itself with outrage. A man snatched it from its mother's arms and suffocated it with a pillow. Max found he was relieved. That he approved of the man's desperate measure. *Why should we all die because one baby is hungry?* When the woman began sobbing he began wishing someone would suffocate her too. Max is now appalled at the barbarity of his emotion.

No one shares what little food they have. There's little, if any, sense of camaraderie. Max finds little to admire in the human spirit down here in this underground prison. The water in the well has been exhausted. A husband and wife are continually arguing under their breath. The woman sneers at her husband. It's something to be grateful for that no woman has ever looked at him with such shrivelling comprehensive contempt. Then he remembers the day he lost Ora and Sabina *had* looked at him like that. But that, he assures himself, was because of something he had once done, not because of the person he is.

Someone lights a candle. Every hungry and ashen face is divested of all decorum. Every mouth hangs open, hungry for air. He doesn't have the energy to move or even speak. He sits listening to the beating of his own blood. Clara is prising dirt from the wall by his side with her long fingernails. She has pretty feet. He stares at them because they are perhaps the most beautiful thing in the bunker. Clara, he realises, is someone who compels him to act out of character. They can never find the right thing to say to each other. And with every wrong thing she induces him to say his loneliness becomes more acute. He suspects this is what marriage is like for some couples. He wonders how true to herself he allowed Sabina to be in his company. Sometimes now, in his lowest moments, he thinks he might have been an expedient compromise for her. There was always a humility in the love he felt for her. He was at her mercy in a way she was never at his mercy. It's important to him that he believes they were united by a fully reciprocated love. Only then can he make her live again inside him. And without her alive inside him he barely feels real to himself anymore.

There's a commotion later which wakes the dozing Max. A young woman has dragged Otto into the bunker. Feathers are clinging to his dishevelled hair. He looks frightened.

"He's been showing the Germans where bunkers are. I saw him," she tells everyone.

There are members of ZOB in the bunker. They give all the orders. They are boys and girls almost half Max's age. There's a feeling that if these young people had been in charge from the oft things might have happened differently. He feels a little ashamed in their company and tells no one he is a baptised Jew. He sometimes now finds relics of himself, prayers and rituals of his childhood that move him with fondness and pride. He has berated himself for not silently mouthing Kaddish over Sabina's dead body. Even though he was too stunned to think of such a thing at the time.

"Then he will have to be executed," says a young man Max previously liked.

"I didn't have any choice," says Otto. Events have restored him to what he is, a frightened nine year old orphan. He gives Max a pleading look. Max notices Clara is ignoring Otto.

Max summons the energy to speak. "He's just a kid and his parents were both murdered," he says.

"Are you sure he helped the Germans?"

"He led them to a bunker further down the street. About twelve people came out. They were all shot. Including two children. He ran away in the confusion. He came into the building where I was watching it all."

"We can't waste one of our bullets on him. Are there any Germans nearby?"

"No. I think they've left for the night."

"Then someone will have to take him upstairs and throw him from a window. We'll draw lots."

Max doesn't have the energy to argue Otto's case. He has had enough. He no longer has any idea what his face is doing. He has lost all control of his features. He might be smiling for all he knows. He stands up, knocking his head against the low ceiling. He puts on his trousers. He is so dizzy with thirst and hunger that he finds it hard to keep his balance. The gun in his pocket feels heavier than the weight of his body. Clara tries to pull him back. He doesn't understand why. Otto looks imploringly at him. He wants to yell out his disgust. Disgust at himself, disgust at the world he is constrained to live in. Instead he crawls out through the tunnel into the night.

Outside there are fires burning all around him, as if the planet's burning core has broken through the surface of the world. He feels the heat reddening his face, burning up through his ruined shoes. He leaves his footprints in the fall of soot and ash filming the streets. He had been primed for deep draughts of fresh air. Instead there's the stink of burning. He thinks he detects a whiff of barbecued flesh. There is a line of naked dead bodies across the street. Their faces bloodied and disfigured. Fiery sparks spinning around in the air like demonic fireflies. Many buildings have been reduced to charred rubble. What he sees looks like the end of time. He finds it hard to get his bearings. He doesn't like this new trick, this annihilation of landmarks. As if he has suddenly become a very old man with a failing memory. He walks towards where he believes his home ought to be. The street is unrecognisable. Barely a single building standing. His rooftop kingdom gone. It takes him a while to establish which heap of smoking rubble is the remains of his home. It shocks him that his entire building has been compressed into a mound not much taller than he is. He sees no trace of anything belonging to him or Sabina. He thinks of the Modigliani portrait of Mr Kaminski. Lost to the world now like everything else he owned. His entire life seems now little more than a disappearing dream. Then he hears a scream. A child's scream. Otto's scream. Followed by a distant sickening thud. He sits down on the step of a freestanding stairway to nowhere and puts his head in his hands.

17

"No," says Ala.

Wolf has just suggested they commit suicide. She can feel the heat of the fierce look she gives him in her cheeks. They have been hiding in the underground bunker for twenty-four hours, driven here by all the fires the Germans have set raging throughout the ghetto.

"I'm not committing suicide," she says. "I want my death to be on the conscience of one of these German monsters. I want it to cause guilt and suffering."

"You believe they have a conscience? They kill us for sport, Ala. More often than not they torture us to relieve boredom."

"Exactly and that's what we should be remembering now. Let's recall some of the stories. How about the story of the little girl who was made to sing her favourite song, rewarded with a piece of candy and then shot in the head in front of her father? Can you imagine what it was like to be that father? You've still got bullets in your rifle. You've still got a grenade. Perhaps one of the bullets in your rifle is meant for the German pig who shot that little girl. But you want to use it on me."

"I mean if the worst comes to the worst. Of course I'll fight while there's still the opportunity to fight. But they've driven us underground with the rats. We can't fight from here."

Later, after Zanek leaves the bunker to search for food and water, everyone sits listening to a voice. The voice comes from above ground. The voice, speaking in Yiddish, punctured with fear, tells them to come out. The voice assures them they won't be shot, that they will be sent to a labour camp to work.

"The first person I'm going to kill is that Jewish son of a bitch," says Wolf.

They have planned for this eventuality. Everyone conceals their weapons. Ala slips her pistol inside her knickers.

Wolf's sister, Chaya, is sent out first. She is deemed by general consensus the prettiest. The logic is the Germans or Ukrainians won't shoot a beautiful young woman. Ala feels a bite of wounded vanity. It occurs to her that the last discovery she might ever make about herself is that she is less attractive than Chaya. Then she marvels at the human mind. That it can focus on something so petty even when faced with imminent extinction.

Ala follows Chaya out. Her shoulder blades are visible through her damp chemise. She draws a little strength from the cleaner air and the big sky. The weight of her gun cold against her pelvic bone. She sees there's another group of Jewish captives who are all naked and blackened with soot. A German SS officer wearing gloves is yanking a Jewish man by the testicles for sport. Ala's fingers burn as she imagines producing the pistol from her knickers. But she has to wait for the signal. Mordecai will whistle.

They are told to strip. There are mounds of brick and roof tiles all around. Electrical wires, drainage pipes, window frames, scraps of fabric, charred pieces of broken furniture, lengths of twisted iron. A film of ash over everything. Ala lingers over the act of removing her shoes. There's a pulsing star of anticipated satisfaction underlying her anxiety. The secret knowledge that the smug expression will soon be wiped off all these Nazi faces. She can tell they take pleasure from their studied indifference to the plight of their captives. That they are somehow proud of this indifference, as if it's a testament to their manliness and superiority. There are eight guards. She is intensely aware of each and every one. The Jewish man who has become the plaything of the SS officer lets out another scream. Everyone's attention turns to the spectacle. Mordecai whistles. A fusillade of shots resounds among the smoking ruins. Ala shoots at the SS officer. She instinctively ducks as she fires. His shiny braided cap flies up into the air. The retort of the gun sends blood jumping up her arm. The imperious German falls to the ground, jerking like a puppet, an expression of startled indignation on his face. He's sprawled on the ground and behaving like someone who has something lodged in his throat. He breathes through clenched bloodied teeth. Ala turns her fascinated gaze from him with difficulty, sensing danger elsewhere. All the Nazis though have been dealt with. One is running away, chased by a Jewish boy who is screaming abuse and firing shot after shot at him. The German falls.

The Jew tormented by the SS officer has picked up a brick. He sits astride his choking tormentor and pounds his weapon down into the German's face. "Treblinka," he says each time he smashes the brick down into the man's face. He is still breaking bone, gouging flesh and nerve long after the final lustre has left the SS officer's eyes. His naked body splashed with the German's blood.

The Jewish informer, a wiry man with thinning hair, a hollowed face and a pitted nose, is made to kneel and executed by Wolf. A single bullet in the back of the neck. Copying the German's favourite method of execution. She is shocked by how indifferently he performs the task. And that he seems proud of his indifference, like the German guards.

Three Germans are wounded but still alive. Their rifles are now in the hands of Jewish boys. She finds the fear on the faces of these Germans is less heartening now than she imagined. She turns away before pity can find a hold in her. Wishing she was still deaf when the screams of the German guards begin as they are beaten to death with their own rifles.

"Are you all right?"

She turns to see Zanek. He has his hand on her arm. She feels a change in her face.

"Where have you been?"

"I've found us all a luxury bunker," he says.

18

Max has a permanent headache. He thinks it might be daytime but in the underground burrow it always seems like the dark night of the soul. The fatigue in his limbs is another form of darkness. So little light flows through him now. Death awaits up above in the world of natural light and yet often down here it is the monotony of life he finds himself cursing. He listens to the sounds of a couple making love. The animal noises. There's no hint of beauty in the sounds. Max thinks back to his lovers. There were five. He tries to recall a moment which most defined each of them. But he is soon concentrating wholly on Sabina. He remembers the radiance in the air whenever she moved her hands towards him. The wonder of her bones beneath his hands. The shock of pleasure he often derived from the sight of her face. She gave him goodness in all the close attention she bestowed on him and this goodness is the glow inside him that is faltering now. Happiness, he would like to tell someone, only comes once in life. He has had his share, shortlived as it was. Then he sees her dead body down near his feet. And it's as if all his memories of her are being carried away like pollen on an autumnal wind. The face of the Nazi who shot her is soon leering at him. Larger than life. He won't get out of the way, won't let him see Sabina again. There was a discussion in the bunker earlier about what punishment should be meted out to the German population after the war. One woman thought a swastika should be tattooed on every German's forehead, even the children. "They've murdered *our* children." Max stayed silent. The end of the war seeming as remote to him as any other judgement day.

He listens to the couple making love and is tempted to touch Clara who is pressed beside him. Her body heat a foreign agent in his blood. Maddening suddenly how much he wants to cup her breasts, slip his hands inside her panties, lose himself in the musk of her arousal. He hates himself for this betrayal of Sabina. Every return of desire makes him wretched. Then he hears a voice up above. The couple stop making love. A man is telling them to surrender. He's speaking in Yiddish. He is telling them that they will not be shot if they come out. But there's terror in his voice, cracking it and pitching it on a strained octave.

There's a rumour that Jewish informers have their own dormitories in the German barracks and have access to prostitutes and lavish meals.

A woman begins sobbing. Someone lights a match. When the flame settles and illuminates a huddle of faces they look ghoulish, like the living dead. Max imagines it must be easier to kill people who no longer look human, who already look half dead. Clara takes his hand. He finds it hard to believe she derives any strength from the agitated pumping of his blood. The last hand he held was Eugenia's when, firstly, he stopped her from going to her death with Ora and then later when he escorted her through Warsaw's streets to what he hopes is safety. It moves him briefly to realise how intimately and memorably you can take a life into your custody by holding a hand.

Max crawls out of the burrow. His eyes, bleary with sleeplessness, stream with tears in the dazzle of the light of day. He has to remove his hand from the gun in his pocket to shield them. The ground seems to rise and fall beneath him, as if he is standing on a moored boat. German voices, skittish with rage, are shouting. A woman who can't stop coughing is shot. He looks through the tears in his eyes at the barren broken landscape, dune upon dune of collapsed masonry. They are ordered to place their hands on their heads. He tries to catch the eye of the Jew who has betrayed them. He doesn't understand the logic of this man. The Germans will surely kill him anyway. And yet he has sentenced twenty Jews to death in order to stay alive for another half hour. Not a good half hour either. A nightmare half hour of anxiety and dread and shame. To feel the need of preserving his life at the expense of a dozen others he must either be very vain about his importance or a frightful coward. Once again Max feels the Jewish youth were right to hold the adult population in contempt.

The SS officer isn't Sabina's murderer. He's a short stout man with swollen lips. Perhaps his best friend, perhaps they go out whoring together in Warsaw? He shows no sign of anger or hatred. He is a bureaucrat doing his job. No doubt they will all become a number he writes down at a desk later while sipping cognac. Max remembers his father once telling him that you shouldn't fight if your opponent is stronger than you are. Another piece of bad advice from his well-meaning father.

When all the occupants of the bunker have emerged they are told to strip. An SS soldier rips the watch from the wrist of a Jewish man and then spits in his face. Max is hair-triggered with tension, as if about to be launched from a crossbow. The pistol as if discharging electricity in his trouser pocket. He has to make a decision. His thoughts refuse to remain intact for very long. As if a gale blasts through his head. Clara, by his side, crouches down as if to take off her shoes but she has picked up a twisted piece of iron. He can sense some wild impulse bristling through her. Then she is charging at the nearest German guard and attacks him with her weapon. Another German drags her off, throws her to the ground. He is about to shoot her when the SS officer stops him. Max finds he has taken his pistol from his pocket. He doesn't remember performing the act. He aims it at the nearest German guard. The German sees it and there is panic in his eyes. When Max pulls the trigger, the German looks shocked for a moment. He looks down at his uniform. There is no sign of a wound. Max pulls the trigger again. There's something wrong. It feels like a toy gun he is firing. He remembers Ala's advice to clean it, which he never did. Then he is struck from behind and falls to the ground. The SS officer stops the guard from shooting him too. Max is pulled to his feet, blood dripping down into his eyes, and then marched with the others towards the *Umschlagplatz* and the cattle train.

19

Ala hears the distant barking of a dog. She thinks of Luna. It occurs to her that Luna is the only member of her family who has a grave. That there has been no funeral for her mother or father, for Madame, Marcel or Lily makes it difficult for her to fully appreciate the meaning and beauty their lives possessed for her, the ways in which they changed her life for the better. She understands why the proper burial of the dead is considered one of the most important commandments, one of the greatest acts of kindness. To mourn is to honour.

Her thoughts are curtailed by a thunderous explosion directly above. Plaster and sand rain down from the roof of the bunker. The lights flicker off for a moment and then return. Alarm has distorted every soot-streaked and hollowed face. A baby begins crying. The mother avoids eye contact with anyone as she tries to calm the child. The bespectacled man in a vest mapped with sweat marks sitting opposite Ala looks up from his book. *Ethics* by Spinoza.

One of the ZOB fighters returns to the room after a scouting mission. Ala doesn't hear what he whispers to Mordecai but she can tell it isn't good news. Yesterday a Ukrainian guard was shot while trying to crawl into the bunker. The Germans afterwards threw grenades in and blocked that exit. Then they found another exit and blocked that too. She suspects there's now no way out of the bunker. That they are trapped underground. Her neck and shoulders stiffen with tension. Panic fermenting inside.

Ala is sitting beside Wolf on the dirt floor. He has barely left her alone since they arrived in this bunker. He has been kind, solicitous. He makes no attempt to touch her when they sleep side by side. Now and again she exchanges a look with Zanek. It's as if he has respected Wolf's prior claim on her company and has withdrawn. Mostly though she is too hungry, weak and frightened to think beyond the perils of the moment. The wall between herself and the outside has become so permeable that often she has a feeling of standing outside of herself.

Sometimes she thinks of the two Germans she has shot. Last night she told Wolf about the struggles of her conscience. "Why is it a matter of indifference to them that they kill us and yet so difficult for us to kill them?"

"It's not difficult for me. They've brutalised me."

"I keep replaying over and over the moment I shot that SS officer. I want to see in greater detail the understanding in his eyes that he was being shot by a Jewish woman. And I want it clarified that he was a monster deserving of death. But I keep thinking of his humanity. That once upon a time he was a ten year old boy who climbed trees and splashed in water." Wolf had not comforted her. Perhaps he didn't notice her tears.

Now there is the sound of motorised pounding above. The Germans are using drills again. They have listening devices and sniffer dogs. This is how they root out all the underground burrows. Yesterday they heard Stukas dropping bombs on the ghetto.

Ala initially marvelled at the resourcefulness of the underground realm. She dared believe she might survive the war down here. The several entrances were ingeniously camouflaged. The bunker was built by one of the ghetto's most notorious smugglers deep beneath the ruins of a house destroyed during the German siege of Warsaw in 1939. There are four large rooms, numerous corridors, kitchens, a flushing toilet, a gas range, beds with mattresses, armchairs, tables, a radio set around which people listen to the BBC. There is electricity, running water and a ventilation system. And, once upon a time, there was a huge stockpile of food. Now Ala has begun to long for a sharper taste in her mouth than bread and grain.

When the fires swept through the ghetto Ala and her group took refuge in a number of different bunkers. Most were sophisticated. She felt pride in the industry of the Jews. There's virtually an underground city beneath the ghetto.

Smoke is now funnelling down into the bunker accompanied by a hissing noise. No one any longer remains silent and still. There is widespread panic. Some are saying prayers. The bunker has been transformed into an oven. Many have stripped down to their underwear, faces handprinted with charcoal marks. Ala is aware now of a sweetish disinfectant smell which catches in her throat.

"Gas!" someone shouts.

Ala copies what others are doing. Wraps a piece of cloth around her mouth and nose and keeps her head below the tide of poisonous smoke. She is wearing nothing but a slip, her rucksack and soft shoes. The next thing she knows Zanek has grasped her hand and is tugging. He is shouting to people to follow him. The corridor is congested. Everyone coughing and choking and sobbing. Ala hears a gunshot from the room she has just left. She guesses someone has committed suicide. She can see all the way through to her own death, as if it's only a few footsteps away.

Soon she has lost her bearings in the vast underground labyrinth. The smoke is thickening. The only light now is the flashlight Zanek holds. He grips her so tightly he is leaving a small bruise on her arm.

She follows Zanek up a metal ladder and then crawls on her hands and knees through a narrow rising tunnel padded with blankets.

"Quick," he urges her from the ground above. She lifts her head out of the opening. She feels like a burrowing animal just regaining new life after hibernation. The light brings tears to her tired eyes. When she can see again she is shocked by the devastation. Barely a building is standing. Every vista is like a stopped frame, petrified and lifeless.

There are only seven of them who have escaped. One of the young men, Natan, is wearing a torn and filthy SS uniform. He was always a joker in the bunker. Pretending often to bark out Nazi orders.

"I know of another bunker quite close to here," he says. "I think it's this way."

Natan walks alongside them with his pistol drawn as if they are his captives. They are like furtive animals. Often stopping in their tracks and listening like startled deer in a forest. They can hear the sounds of German activity all around. There are charred corpses amongst the rubble. They startle crows feasting on barbecued remains. Then Ala catches her breath when she walks out from behind a broken crazy-shaped wall and is face to face with three German soldiers sitting on the rubble eating sandwiches.

Natan, adopting an officious air, shouts something at them. It sounds to Ala like a non-existent word that only vaguely resembles German. The three Germans jump to their feet, suspicious but instinctively obsequious when faced with higher ranked insignia. Natan shoots one and then another. He insults them both. The third is shot by Zanek. They take their weapons and the remains of their sandwiches. The mouthful of white bread and cheese Ala eats as she walks is a sensory celebration inside her mouth. Every noise they make sends a charge of apprehension through the entire group. Sometimes Ala doesn't understand how her heart can accommodate so much tension without combusting.

They can't find the entrance to the bunker. They decide to take refuge in the rubble until night falls. The stink of burned bodies and the heat of fires is carried on the breeze. Only now does she think about Wolf. She remembers the gunshot she heard inside the bunker. And his determination not to allow any Nazi to kill him. As if this was the only form of salvation left to him. She begins to shiver. She is still wearing nothing but a chemise. She opens her rucksack and pulls out a man's jersey that falls loose and long from her slight shoulders.

They are still crouched down in the rubble when searchlights begin sweeping over the ruins. For a moment Ala can see the detail of her hands. A lone figure appears, silhouetted by flames. It is a woman in a cotton dress and headscarf. She is holding her arms up to the stars and berating God. A sustained blast of machine gun fire soon silences her.

20

The train hisses and shudders into motion. Max has been hit repeatedly with a rifle. Blood is crusting on his face and on his body beneath his clothes. Filth is matted into his hair. Clara too has been badly beaten. She sits beside him, hugging her drawn up knees. Listless. Silent. There is a stink of chemicals which irritates his throat. And gusts of human stench. There are about thirty people in the boxcar. The Germans waited hours for more captured Jews to be brought to the railway siding. But only a few arrived. The stout SS officer with the swollen lips was noticeably irritated by the poor turn-out.

Through the gaps in the wooden slats Max watches the red glow of the burning ghetto recede into a memory.

The train switches from track to track, the grinding reverberations heightening his headache. He imagines someone in their Warsaw home idly pausing to listen to the passing train, quickly to become an irrelevance. Then they cross the Vistula river. The iron on iron noise increasing in density and pitch. The train is heading east. Towards the pit behind the precipice on which he has been perched hiding for so long.

A committee of young men are voicing the imperative to escape. They still have a spark of rebellion in their eyes. For Max all their spirited explosive words are like fireworks that fail to ignite. There are guards on the roof of the car. Max can hear them laughing. Two of the young men begin tearing the wire from the small opening high on the bolted door. Max recognises the young man who ordered Otto's execution. He refuses to catch Max's eye. Max turns his attention to a woman examining the seams of her dress. Watches her squash all the lice and eggs her thumb runs over.

The train keeps screeching and hissing to a halt. The screech and hiss like the sound of death inside his head. It occurs to him that death is the last secret his body now holds. The young men have to stop their work of ripping free the barbed wire every time the train stops.

When darkness arrives, it's calculated they haven't travelled more than twenty miles. Max tries to keep the moon in sight through the slats. He is no longer hungry or thirsty. He is empty of feeling. It's like everything he knows has dissolved into the dark at the back of his mind from where it can no longer be summoned. Only the struggle against imminent panic at the forefront. As if every night shadow that has ever frightened him has convened there and is jostling for attention. The busy endeavour of the young men puts him further on edge. The train starts up again. Still heading east. The wire is finally removed. Otto's executioner gives everyone instructions on how to jump from the moving train. Max finds it hard to concentrate on what the young man is saying. As if he is talking about something that does not concern him. Something about the necessity of turning your body in the direction the train is going once you've found a foothold on the other side of the door. Nevertheless, he supposes he will jump. Though he hasn't thought about it.

Four or five people clamber up out of the small window and then disappear into the night before the shots arrive from automatic weapons up on the roof. The train doesn't stop. A spray of bullets rips down through the roof. People begin wailing and saying prayers. It's too dark for Max to see who has been hit. There are agonised groans all around him. A warm body has collapsed into his lap. What he knows is blood seeps into his trousers. He suspects it is the woman who was killing lice. He pushes her away.

Soon the evacuation through the window continues. Otto's

executioner helps a young woman onto his shoulders and through the small opening.

"What about you? You owe it to all the people you've lost to make the attempt." The young man touches Max on the arm. They are shadows to each other with burning eyes.

When Max gets to his feet his legs are trembling so violently he has to sit down again. He realises he no longer has any strength left to resist. His legs won't stop shaking. The shaking comes from deep inside, from a place within over which he has no jurisdiction. He waves the young man away. Clara is unresponsive to the young man's exhortations too.

"The Germans put us to sleep. First, they put us to sleep and then they kill us," the young man says.

21

"Climb through feet first," says Zanek, directing the torchlight on a small punched hole in the wall. The coldness of the water as Ala jumps down sends a shock to her heart. The stench of the sewage, slopping around her knees, immediately nauseates her. There are rats jumping and scrambling over the curved brick walls like circus gymnasts. Their eyes like pinpricks of malevolence in the torchlight. Ala is followed through the hole by others. The polluted water and slime slops up and spatters her face as they splash down into the sewer. The constant dripping and sloshing of water is echoed and heightened to a lucid pitch. A water rat scrambles over her head, squealing and clawing her neck. Her echoing scream opens up a terrifying void inside and around her.

They walk in single file. The incessant echoing drip of water is hypnotic. In the torchlight, reflections of the agitated water shimmer over the curved brick walls. The tunnel narrows, the stink intensifies, and she has to crouch and the bricks chaff against her hips. The water rises. Slopping around her bare thighs. Excrement clinging to her skin, slinking its way inside her underwear. She feels like some primal creature in a nightmare. As alienated as she's ever felt from the memory of herself dancing the Mazurka from Chopin's *Les Sylphides* in a white tulle tutu in the spotlight of the Grand Theatre stage.

They are making their way through the complex network of sewers to a designated manhole where an escape committee will be waiting for them. Or so they have been told.

A woman ahead screams.

"It's a dead body," someone else explains. Ala soon feels the stiffened corpse bump against her. She is thankful she can't see it.

The line comes to a halt. Word reaches her that barbed wire is blocking the way and has to be cut away. The water level rises. Soon Ala is trembling with the cold. She can no longer feel her feet. Madame once told her her lack of stamina for hardship was her greatest flaw as a dancer. *Every choreography demands different levels of effort.*

Every so often thin spokes of light lance through manhole covers overhead. It seems ever less plausible to her that a humdrum world of daylight and daily chores exists no more than ten feet above her head. It's like she has entered a different dimension of time, a different dimension of reality and the connecting portal has been lost.

A light suddenly appears up ahead. It grows in circumference. Everyone freezes. The same thought goes through every mind. *Germans.* There's little point in retreating back to the ghetto. Only death awaits them there. The intensifying glare fills Ala's vision. She can't see through it.

"Jan," someone tentatively calls out. The password.

"Warsaw." The whispered word echoes back to them through the tunnel.

It's a band of lost Jews. The jubilation of lots of people smeared in excrement reuniting is surreal. Ala is disappointed neither her brother nor her uncle is among the group.

The surging tide of sludged water slops up into her mouth. She retches. She is numb and drowsy. Pulses of coloured light flicker on and off behind her eyes. There is no heat in her body. Zanek repeatedly squeezes her fingers, utters words of encouragement and tugs at her hand and she wades on. He gives her a sugar cube to chew on. She runs her tongue over its granular surface and the dizzying sweetness of it is a miracle in her mouth.

They arrive exhausted at the designated manhole. There is a

shelf they can climb up onto and escape the freezing filthy water. Ala sees there are three children among them. These children want to break her heart. That's how it feels. From above she can hear fragments of casual conversation, pedestrians crossing the road, cars passing.

Hours pass and then the manhole cover is opened from the street and a starburst of daylight blazes into the black underworld stink. Word is passed around that there is no truck to take them to the forest. That they will have to wait until tomorrow. Ala's encrusted clothes have become a kind of skin.

There's an argument during the night. A man who can't bear it anymore wants to go up into the street. He is stopped at gunpoint. Then he starts sobbing. The group to which he belongs have been forced to stand in the icy slopping sewage. They decide to wander off to another manhole cover where they will able to pass the night on a shelf above the sewage. A young woman in a blue headscarf promises them she will come to fetch them when help arrives.

Ala sits on the concrete shelf with her head resting on Zanek's shoulder. She manages to sleep intermittently. She dreams of Madame. In the dream the air is like silver gauze and Madame performs movements that Ala knows are impossible for a human being. She suspends herself in the air and flutters like a piece of chiffon caught in a wind. Then she stands with her back to Ala. Ala is terrified that Madame will turn around and she will see her face. She knows there is something monstrously changed about Madame's face. Some grotesque alteration that her sanity will not be able to withstand. As if only scraps and remnants of desiccated flesh now cleave to her skull. When she wakes up she is shaking and then she screams because there is a rat by her side. Zanek cradles her in his arms and makes reassuring noises. Thirst has crusted her lips together. It's as if all the fear she has swallowed has lodged and dried in her throat.

Hours later, which seem to pass without her participating in them, Ala climbs up the metal rungs of the ladder. Caked grime stiff at the back of her knees. A roaring sea noise in her head. The dazzling sunlight is like an ethereal explosion of silent noise. It is another obstacle she has to fight her way through. She doesn't recognise the Warsaw street she climbs up into but its appearance of once-upon-a-time brings a disbelieving sob to her throat. She is ushered dazed through the opened flaps at the back of the tarpaulin-covered lorry. Followed quickly by Zanek who still has his rifle. His face blackened. He takes her hand. The rank odour of his clothes so at odds with the beautiful bone structure of his face. Ala's blood is wild with the impatience for the lorry to drive away. At every moment she expects to hear the hateful bark of German voices, the crack of gunshots. Outside, in the middle of the road, the young woman in the blue head-scarf is arguing with Natan. She wants the truck to wait while she goes back down into the sewers to round up the group that moved to another manhole cover. "I promised them," she says. Natan, his SS uniform smeared in excrement, tells her what she is proposing is suicide. A sizeable crowd of Polish pedestrians has gathered to watch the spectacle of phantoms climbing out of the sewers. Ala wants to tell the young woman she shouldn't have made promises. That they don't live in a world where promises can be kept. That she has to stop remembering, as they have all been forced to stop remembering. It's insane of her to believe she can orchestrate events to her choosing, as if life in the ghetto has taught her nothing. Everyone in the back of the truck is growing angry with the young woman in the blue head-scarf. Someone says to leave her behind. Surely at any moment German gendarmes will appear around the corner at the end of the street. The young girl draws her pistol. She threatens to shoot Natan if he doesn't wait. He tells her she can shoot him later. Finally, she climbs into the back of the truck and begins sobbing and they drive off.

22

The train has been stationary for more than an hour. The tinnitus in his ears recedes for a moment behind birdsong. The rising sun has revealed the carnage inside the boxcar. The woman who was killing lice now a corpse herself. Drying blood is sticky on the splintered wooden boards. Only twelve remain in the boxcar, three of whom have bullets wounds. There is no trace of personality in Clara's eyes when he looks across at her. As if she is now outside of time and space. Through the slats, he sees a thinning mist over the land. There is the scent of pines and refreshed earth. His spirit, he realises, is now already removed from the blessings of the natural world, he and the natural world now inhabit different realities.

The door is opened with incensed shouting from the guards outside. Max is struck by a rifle butt as he jumps down. The guards make it clear they know about the uprising in the ghetto. They are enraged that Jews had the audacity to fight back. Not for the first time he realises the hatred of the Nazis is harder and colder than anything he himself or perhaps any Jew can muster in opposition. He already senses this is a place possessed of its own pitiless obscene laws.

The clouds overhead look like the imprint of horse hooves. It's a regret of his that he never got to ride a horse. For a moment he daydreams about galloping away from this place on a white horse. No bullet can hit him in his fleeting fantasy.

There is a picturesque station further down the long platform. He sees a red cross painted on one door. And a ticket window, flanked by flowerbeds, with a closed sign. Further along the line grass grows between the tracks and then the tracks abruptly end. For a moment his eyes are rooted to that place where the tracks abruptly end. Eloquent as it is of the discontinuation of time that awaits him. His life is barely more than a fugitive dream now. And soon to become an irrelevance. He finds himself praying Ala and Eugenia will survive, that there will at least be one person in the future who remembers him. The thought of being conclusively erased from the world's memory brings another surge of darkness into his mind. The shaking in his legs begins again, the shaking from deep inside.

Only now does he remember the strip he tore from one of Sabina's dresses. He searches his pockets for it. The only thing that matters for the moment is that he still has it. He has the pulped chit for the boat his father bought him but not the strip from Sabina's dress. Then he remembers that he slipped it into his shoe in the underground bunker. He is hit again when he crouches down to retrieve it. But he now holds it bunched up in his palm.

The men are separated from the women. The women led into a wooden barracks. The men are ordered to line up in formation and undress. Max puts the strip of Sabina's dress in his mouth.

A man, only half undressed, is dragged out of the line and beaten to death by two Ukrainian guards. Max is struck by the irrelevance the identity of this man has for the two guards who kill him, even for everyone, including himself, who watches him die. His streaming blood attracts a scrum of fat flies.

The presence of so many exposed genitals reminds Max of the photograph his father found in his pocket when he was a young boy. The image of that vulgar man with his gargantuan erection seems now like a prophecy. Evidence of the cruel sadistic tyranny that can be unleashed in men when they accrue power at the expense of someone else's vulnerability and fear. Only now as the image vividly returns does he realise how disdainful was the expression on the man's face. How brutal was the grip of his hands on the young girl's head while she knelt down between his fat thighs. That photograph alienated him from his home. It made him the innocent keeper of a guilty secret. It led to him being accused by his father of a crime he never committed. It still pains him that his father automatically thought the worst of him. Just as everyone, it seems, is inclined to think the worst of every Jew.

He catches sight of Clara as the women are whipped into leaving the hut. She is naked and all her hair has been cut off. Her shorn scalp is bleeding in several places. He sees she has bigger breasts than Sabina but her nipples are smaller. Suddenly he has the feel of Sabina's breasts as if imprinted on his palms. For a bittersweet moment it's as if she is physically with him. He can feel the essence of what she meant to him. His brain then finds this interesting. How the body can sometimes restore the intimate detail of a moment that the mind has seemingly forgotten. He struggles to accept that soon he will be denied this simple pleasure of puzzling out theoretical questions in his head.

Then he is looking at his naked feet again. He caresses one foot with the other, the last chance he might get to treat his body with some kindness. He is moved by the vulnerable innocence of his bare feet. Then he remembers the vulnerable innocence of Ora. He has the warm weight of her sleeping body in his arms for a moment, a vivid muscle memory of carrying her to bed one evening. It seems to him now a terrible waste that he didn't stop to savour every one of his most poignant memories when he had the time. He tries to bring forth other memories that merit being experienced one last time, but he can't help picturing Ora arriving here at Treblinka alone. Made to strip naked, shorn of her hair. He wants to tell his father he was wrong about God. That there is no loving god and we live in an unfeeling universe. He imagines telling his father this in Mr Kaminski's sign language. Then he receives an image of how lovingly his father always touched the mezuzah by the front door of their home. He sees the stack of firewood under the porch and the path worn through the grass of his childhood home. He remembers the feeling of homecoming. For the briefest instant he is full of love for his father. He realises he hasn't thought about his father with affection as much as he should have.

The sun has begun to rise. It has almost climbed over the treeline on the horizon. It would be good to feel its heat on his skin one last time. He doesn't much grieve that all the traits of his personality will soon be brought to an end. There's nothing unique about him as a person. Except for his memories. His memories tell a story that is unique in its details. But perhaps, overall, it's a story like many others. What he finds most difficult to contemplate is that soon the window on the world life provides will be taken from him, the gift of being a witness to the daily narrative of life on the planet's surface.

Max is struck by a Ukrainian guard. He is forced to run down a narrow path flanked on either side by a high fence of branches and strewn with bloodstained white sand. Towards an ominous concrete building with a blue Star of David painted on its façade. Everything outside and inside him ebbs away into blackness, everything except the terror of a panicked creature inside him that he doesn't recognise as part of himself.

23

Ala and Zanek are walking through the forest. She can feel the pulse of the natural world beneath her feet. The sun burns through the edge of a cloud and prickles her shoulders and the back of her neck. They are on their way to meet a contact who, it is hoped, will supply the group in the forest with food. Ala takes deep draughts of nature's bounty. She is overwhelmed by the beauty of the world. The golden lichen embroidering the stones. The flight of birds. Sunlight striking transparency in leaves overhead. Every wildflower among the moss is sustenance to the damaged wings of her spirit. She wants to know the name of every flower and plant and tree she sees.

Zanek begins softly singing a lullaby. "My mother used to sing that to me," he says. "I keep dreaming about her. She is standing at a gate, waving to me. She used to do that every morning as I went off to school." He fingers his braces that are hanging loose. There is a stray shred of tobacco on his lower lip.

Ala still hasn't told Zanek she witnessed the murder of his mother. She is wearing someone else's clothes today. Given to her by a woman in the forest. She no longer has any idea what she looks like to other people. Every time Zanek smiles she is reassured. His smile is nourishment for her. She knows she should tell him how his mother died, with dignity, with a spirit of rebellion, but she can't bring herself to wipe that smile from his face.

She gently removes the piece of tobacco from his lip with her wedding finger.

"To be among trees, Ala," he says, spinning around on his heels.

"Will you lift me up? I want to sit among the branches."

Zanek takes the rifle from his shoulder and lays it down on the ground. He lifts her up by the waist and for a while there is a struggle that makes them both laugh. "I'm not as strong as I used to be," he says. Finally she manages to haul herself up into the crook of two branches and sits there swinging her legs. She tells herself not to care if she is showing her knickers. Zanek stands with his hands in his pockets, looking up at her. Last night they bathed together in a pond. She washed his hair. They had not been alone so the beauty of his naked body in the moonlight has remained a gift she hopes to open another night. Later, to keep warm, they slept in each other's arms on the forest floor under the stars. He didn't kiss her but she could feel his erection pressed against her bottom throughout the night, as if the urgency of his desire wouldn't let him sleep. She too was unable to sleep. Several times she was on the verge of putting her hands on his body. She now imagines telling Lily why she likes him so much. I like the way he holds himself, the way he transfers the weight of his body in movement, and the way his hair sits on his head. I feel we have a kind of feral understanding. Time spent with him speeds by but also has a lingering quality, as if moments outlast themselves.

"In another life you could have been a dancer," she tells him.

"Why do you say that?"

"Madame always used to say she could tell who would make a good dancer simply by how they manage their hands. Anyone who doesn't know what to do with their hands will never make a dancer. You've got very elegant expressive hands. They never look awkward."

"I like that compliment," he says. He sits down on the grass. "We've survived, Ala. Can you believe it?"

Ala dares not believe it. Last night superstition stopped her from imagining performing Madame's choreography in a peacetime theatre and later made her impatient with herself that she hadn't told Zanek to make love to her there and then.

They are about to leave when she sees three men approaching. They are moving stealthily through the trees with rifles at the ready.

"We've got company," she says. "Partisans, I think."

Zanek picks up his rifle and gets to his feet. Ala, still up in the tree, crosses her legs. The three men appear in the open. One of them looks up at her with an expression in his eyes she doesn't like. He has a flattened reddish face and a bulbous nose widening at the nostrils. Ala trusts her immediate feeling about people. Some people quickly make her feel safe. This man frightens her.

"Comrades," says Zanek. "We're ghetto fighters."

Ala has the feeling it is a mistake to announce themselves as Jews. Zanek lowers his rifle. She has the feeling this is another mistake. She holds onto the branch with a tighter grip.

"Is that so?"

All three young men have their rifles trained at Zanek.

"Do you know who we are? We are members of the NSZ."

The NSZ is an anti-Semitic partisan organisation. More committed, they say, to killing Jews than Nazis.

"We have a common enemy," says Zanek. He has squared his shoulders but Ala can see the surges of tension they hold.

"Well, we have a rule. No filthy Jews allowed in our forest." The man with the flattened face says this and pulls the trigger of his rifle. The bullet strikes and shatters bone. Ala screams. Zanek falls and a pool of his blood filters through his shirt onto the moss and wildflowers. Ala stares at an expression on his face that doesn't belong to him. He has already left his body.

The man with the flattened face reaches up for her ankles. Ala draws up her feet. Sits in the crook of the branches with her knees raised. Dizzy with fear and loathing and grief.

"If you don't come down I'll shoot you." The man turns to his companions and begins unbuttoning his trousers with a smirk on his face. A blonde youth with a fidgety mouth has a kinder look about him. Ala has already registered this. It's him who walks over and offers to help her down. Ala wishes the tree would somehow gather her up, protect her from what will happen next.

She stares up at the sunlight playing in the leaves of the tree while the man with the flattened face takes her virginity. He has a pistol tucked in the waistband of his trousers which grinds against her pelvic bone. She tells herself she no longer wants to live in this world populated with monsters. But the light dancing among the leaves overhead is a beautiful spectacle. Like a living emblem of the aspiration deep at the heart of her being. She tries to leave her body, the horror and humiliation of what it is being subjected to, to join the lights dancing up there among the leaves.

"I thought all Jewish women were whores but she was a virgin," says the rapist, buttoning up his trousers. He takes the pistol from his waistband.

His muck mixed in with her blood begins to ooze down her thighs.

"Come on, Janek. You've had your fun. Let's get out of here."

"He's right. There are probably more of them close by and they're armed."

"Yep. She's only a girl, Janek. You don't have to shoot her."

Janek though shoots Ala. He shoots her three times with a look of disgust on his face.

Postscript

It is Yom HaShoah. Holocaust Memorial Day. I stop my car and get out as the siren wails. All around me are frozen figures standing by their cars with bowed heads. Most of them are too young to have ever seen a Nazi uniform except in films. Instead of thinking my own thoughts I try to imagine theirs. I've become expert over the years in taking evasive measures.

Soon afterwards, in East Jerusalem, I drive within sight of a stretch of the wall. We've had many arguments in our family about this wall. I'm secretly pleased both my children feel a good deal of sympathy for the Palestinians. But still I argue with them. I remind them the Nazis didn't conjure up antisemitism out of thin air. That it was a poison in the collective mind of almost every nation and had been for centuries. It's a convenient fallacy to now attribute the violent hatred of Jews to a few sinister extremist organisations as if everyone in 1940 who wasn't a member of the SS was kindly disposed to the Jews. It's true, as my daughter says, that we tend as a nation to get a little carried away with the same nationalistic fervour that throughout history has been our and every other ethnic minority's nemesis but let's not forget, I tell her, what we have been through, for how many centuries we remained homeless and persecuted. Is it any wonder that sometimes we can hardly believe our eyes when we stand on our own land? Is it any wonder that we feel forever threatened and obliged to wave flags and arm ourselves with weapons inside this new precarious home we have created? Is it any wonder we eventually chose to build a wall around ourselves when we finally acquired a home?

I'm on my way to see a propaganda film the Germans made of the Warsaw ghetto that has been recently unearthed in some vault. As a rule, I refuse all invitations to participate in anything related to the Holocaust. It's a personal choice I have made. My daughter thinks it isn't good for my emotional wellbeing that I keep everything bottled up. She often complains that she has never seen me cry.

I never wanted to dwell on the fact of my survival. For one thing, it always made me feel unworthy. For many years I can't say I thanked Max for saving my life. In fact, I blamed him for preventing me from accompanying my sister to Treblinka. I still cannot bear to think of her, a tiny child, alone on that train. I've tried to imagine dozens of times what Ora's last few hours of life were like. Was there a woman who, in the final moments, took her hand? Then I think about those uniformed grown men who didn't think twice about murdering children, about the complete absence of what we call humanity in them. But those men were not freaks of nature. They were ordinary men. What they did was human nature. A dark facet of human nature we like to believe has now been civilised out of existence. But in every volatile political climate I detect that same insane blood lust rearing its ugly head. Personally, I don't believe building walls is the answer. I'd rather see them come down. But, at the end of the day, there's no place like home and the rudiment of every home is its walls.

I think sometimes of the life Ora was meant to have had but which was taken from her. I spent long years listening out for her forgiveness. I was consumed by loneliness. A craving for her company. I felt I had been granted one moment to act with courage and I had failed. I even began to believe Max holding me back was a fiction I had invented to appease my sense of guilt. It was only when my son and then my daughter were born that I fully acknowledged Max's role in my survival and I was able to warm to his memory. I stopped feeling I was one of the reprieved dead. Max and Ala's family are now extinct, as they say elephants and tigers and all manner of flora and fauna soon will be. But my daughter became a veterinarian surgeon and my son a teacher. (My grandson wrote this book, which I still haven't been able to bring myself to read.)

I have an order of nuns to thank for my survival. The Sisters of the Family of Mary. For a while they ushered in the idea that the Catholic god was more powerful, more benevolent than the Jewish god. And they gave me a second history. I was told I was no longer allowed to remember my past. An iron rule that came to govern me my entire life. What I chiefly remember about the convent is the constant clamp of icy terror in my body that any day the Germans would come to take me away. It took me a long time before I ceased to feel like I was a trespasser in life. Perhaps I have never stopped feeling that.

A young woman meets me outside the cinema. She is a little bit in awe of me. Overly respectful. This is another reason I prefer to keep my memories to myself. I don't enjoy the unwarranted respect with which strangers treat me. I've learned that often our fate is decided not by our spiritual qualities or failings but by the toss of a coin. And then by the toss of another coin. There's no self-worth to be commanded from the happy outcome of a toss of a coin. I remember reading about Emanuel Ringelblum, the man who organised the Jewish archive in the Warsaw ghetto. He had a choice of two hiding places when he escaped the ghetto with his family. His choice was overruled by his wife. The people who hid in his chosen refuge all survived the war. Ringelblum, his wife and child were all caught and executed. In times of extreme peril there's no question you learn a lot about the quality of the luck you have been born with.

The young woman asks if she can call me Eugenia and explains to me that they will film me watching the film. That I'm free to comment whenever I choose. I suddenly realise just how apprehensive I am. I don't like admitting weakness to others. For me it's always a private moment. The theatre is empty except for the young woman and the camera crew. When the lights dim the knot of apprehension tightens at the back of my neck. I'm not even sure I would be able to recognise my mother. I do not own a single photograph or keepsake of my childhood. Perhaps if I was able to see an image of my mother and Ora the cleansing tears my daughter speaks of might arrive. Who knows?

The silent film shows street scenes. Some streets I immediately recognise and the images wash through me like pounding waves, as if to tumble me back into their midst. The boundary between me and the screen begins to dissolve and it becomes a struggle for me to remain anchored in the present moment. Time is looping back on itself. All my attempts at self-mastery are quickly reduced to a sham. Now and again I catch myself leaning forward in my seat, conscious that my eyes are bulging or refusing to look. I no longer have any idea what my face is doing. Probably grimacing and collapsing into its most ugly lines.

It's May 1942, two months before the cattle trains arrived to herd the inhabitants of the ghetto to their deaths. Most of the faces I'm looking at suggest their owners can already taste death in their mouths, smell it on their fingertips. It's distressing to allow any face to vanish without affording it a measure of sympathy but there's no getting away from the fact that some faces make a much deeper emotional appeal than others. I think about this for a while. I know we can't have all looked the same to the Nazis despite all the supernatural rubbish they believed about us as a race. I find it hard to believe Ora's beautiful face wouldn't have made some Nazi guard question his footing as he watched her enter the gas chamber. That he didn't learn something damning about himself at that moment.

Then I think I might have seen Ala's dancing teacher in a brief street scene. She returns to memory as vividly as if I had seen her yesterday. I remember she was kind to me and Ora in a courtyard where a scary woman told people's fortunes.

The young woman seems to sense I have seen something of intimate significance and tells me it's fine if I want to make any comments or observations. I know my reticence is disappointing her. I tell her it is especially painful to look at the faces of the children. I don't tell her it's a little shocking to realise even children inspire different degrees of sympathy. I can't stop marvelling at the fact that the ghost of myself as a young girl is never physically far away from the location shown on the screen. The ghetto, after all, wasn't very large. My mother, Ora and Max are at every moment somewhere just beyond the frame. As if only a door needs to be opened to reveal us as we were, all perhaps sitting at the kitchen table, dunking pieces of black bread into the soup my mother made. For a moment I know an overpowering wish that the cameraman would hear my plea across the decades and make his way to our home on Nowolipki Street. As if his filming of the ghetto and my watching it fifty years later are consecutive connected moments.

I recognise the wooden bridge over Chlodna Street. The black and white image acquires splashes of colour in my memory. I crossed it several times with my mother, Ora and Max. It was here Frankenstein was often posted. I tell the young woman this. I tell her I read he was caught and sentenced to death in East Germany long after the war ended. And that I remember the fear his name aroused. "Hitler, I remember as a figure of fun, a sort of cartoon baddie but Frankenstein was the stuff of children's nightmares." I feel ashamed at my absurd determination to keep my tone light as soon as the words leave my mouth.

Then I glimpse something that sets my pulse racing. A crowd scene. The moment is over before I can register it. I ask for the film to be rewound. This time I know where to fix my eyes. And there is my mother. I can't explain to myself how I recognise her. A gesture in her limbs perhaps that is engraved in my memory like a handprint in cement. A Jewish policeman shoves her between her shoulders from behind. She turns and gives him a piece of her mind. I see her face, detailed and animated as it never is in my memories. The moment is over in the blink of an eye. I ask for the film to be rewound and shown again. Of all the moments in my mother's life it's bewildering only this one has been preserved.

This time I see myself and Ala. The briefest glimpse of us both in profile. Then several yards behind, Max and Ora. Ora is holding her toy cat with the button eyes. I had forgotten about this toy cat until now.

"Have you seen someone you recognise?" says the young woman. "A memory you might like to share with us?"

CPSIA information can be obtained
at www.ICGtesting.com
Printed in the USA
BVHW071355180819
556130BV00002B/247/P